SMELLS LIKE FINN SPIRIT

ALSO FROM RANDY HENDERSON AND TITAN BOOKS

Finn Fancy Necromancy
Bigfootloose and Finn Fancy Free

SMELLS LIKE FINN SPIRIT

RANDY HENDERSON

TITAN BOOKS

Smells Like Finn Spirit
Print edition ISBN: 9781783297290
E-book edition ISBN: 9781783297436

Published by Titan Books
A division of Titan Publishing Group Ltd
144 Southwark Street, London SE1 0UP

First Titan edition: February 2017
10 9 8 7 6 5 4 3 2 1

Names, places and incidents are either products of the author's imagination or used fictitiously. Any resemblance to actual persons, living or dead (except for satirical purposes), is entirely coincidental.

Randy Henderson asserts the moral right to be identified as the author of this work.

Copyright © 2017 Randy Henderson.

No part of this publication may be reproduced, stored in a retrieval system, or transmitted, in any form or by any means without the prior written permission of the publisher, nor be otherwise circulated in any form of binding or cover other than that in which it is published and without a similar condition being imposed on the subsequent purchaser.

A CIP catalogue record for this title is available from the British Library.

Printed and bound in Great Britain by CPI Group (UK) Ltd

What did you think of this book? We love to hear from our readers. Please email us at: readerfeedback@titanemail.com, or write to us at the above address.

To receive advance information, news, competitions, and exclusive offers online, please sign up for the Titan newsletter on our website:
www.titanbooks.com

To Christy,
for all the obvious reasons, and three secret ones

CONTENTS

PART I

PART II

PART III

PART I

1

CONSTANT CRAVING

September 4, 2011

I felt twitchy as the Bumbershoot festival crowd flowed past me in the shadow of the Space Needle. The collective hum of their spiritual energy pulled at me like the seductive whispers of a thousand sirens, strong as the compulsion to take just one more turn on Civilization before going to bed—compelling, but nothing that couldn't be defeated with a great act of will, or perhaps an urgent need to use the bathroom.

I leaned on a concrete ledge outside the food court, along with my girlfriend, Dawn, my sister Sammy, and her girlfriend Fatima as we took a break from browsing booths and watching concerts. The light breeze offered a bit of relief from summer's stubborn September heat, though it also brought the occasional whiff of the upwind garbage cans or the body odor of an unwashed teenager. I fluffed my Space Invaders T-shirt as the throbbing beat of a distant rock-rap band provided the background for a hundred passing conversations, a dozen laughing children, and one jet flying overhead.

I took Dawn's hand and focused on it, running my thumb gently over the guitar calluses on her pointer finger, the brown curve of her palm's edge forming a kind of yin yang with the tan of mine, the warm and solid reality of her presence helping me to ground myself and shut out the call of all that energy.

I looked up to find her smiling at me. Gods, she was beautiful. And between that impish smile and the lavender cloud of finger coils framing her face, she could easily have been an animated goddess of chaos. Even the simple gray T-shirt and brown jeans didn't mask her blazing energy, her—

"You've got shiny eyes again," Dawn said. "Those for me? Or are you just hungry?"

"I'm hungry for you," I replied, and my stomach growled loudly as if to argue.

"Well, for that you'll have to wait 'til we get home, but here's something to hold you over." She leaned in and drew me into the warm haven of a kiss.

Someone knocked against my foot as they passed—and my foot kicked out, my red Converse connecting with the folds of a yellow dress.

"Hey—" the woman said, tugging at her dress. "Jerk."

"Sorry!" I said. "I didn't mean to—"

She rolled her eyes and re-entered the flow of bodies.

Damn it, Alynon, I thought at the Fey spirit trapped in my head.

Alynon Infedriel, knight of the Silver Court and a huge pain in my spiritual butt, harrumphed, then replied in a weak voice that only I could hear, *'Tis not my fault she had no consideration.*

What did I tell you about taking control? I thought back.

She interrupted a perfectly good kiss! And there hasn't been nearly enough good kissing going on lately, let alone—

Drop it, or I'll be staying up tonight watching Cop Rock

instead of going to Dawn's. Never mind that he was right.

"Alynon being a pain again?" Dawn asked.

"Yep."

You would not so starve your own happiness to spite mine, Alynon said.

Yes, well, unlike you, I have control over my lizard brain.

Indeed, you have more Mothra than Godzilla in your nature.

I'll take that as a compliment, given that Mothra was protector of the Earth.

Indeed? Protector of the Earth now, are you?

I did not reply. I hadn't felt like any kind of hero since Elwha. I turned my focus back outward, but that let the energy of the crowd draw my attention again.

Three months since the battle at Elwha River, when I consumed Dunngo the dwarf's spiritual energy—a desperate act of dark necromancy used to stop a crazy shapeshifting jorōgumo. An act that had utterly destroyed Dunngo's spirit, forever. I'd been extra sensitive to the spiritual energy around me ever since, feeling something like lust at the thought of touching it, using it. The strength of the feeling had faded slowly, diminishing with lots of "me time" and some serious meditation work. But being around so many people at once made the accumulated weight of their spiritual energy hard to ignore. All of that power—

"There are just too many damned people in the world," I said.

"Oh, people aren't so bad," Dawn replied. "It's all the Stupid, that's the problem."

I shrugged in non-committal agreement. Maybe I was simply used to small-town life, or still adjusting to our world after twenty-five years of exile in the Fey Other Realm, but as I looked around I just saw streets clogged with cars, walkways stuffed with bodies. A great river of people in their summer clothes, buying and talking and walking and—I could feel them, their spirits, like glowing apples waiting to be plucked. All that spiritual energy, being wasted on watching reality television and eating fried nuggets of chicken sawdust. I could do so much more with—

I knocked my thoughts onto another path with the force of Bowser in a bumper car, took the irritability which desire had sparked in me and turned it toward my other source of irritation and worry: Mattie, my niece. I checked my phone, but still no messages from her.

I didn't know what could be keeping her. The Seattle Center's amusement park had been torn down and removed while I was in exile. Who gets rid of awesome rides and instead offers a museum of glass sculptures? I just didn't understand this world I'd returned to, sometimes.

I leaned forward, looking past Dawn to Sammy and Fatima. Sammy typed something into her phone, her default state when not actually interacting with the world around her. Her red jeans, green Converse, and black sleeveless T-shirt with silver wings on the back made Sammy look more the rock star than Dawn. Fatima sat cross-legged, her green and gold dress spilling over the concrete ledge, and her black curtain of hair falling forward to shade her eyes as she sketched with rapid strokes in her ever-present sketch pad.

"Sis, any word from Mattie yet?" I asked.

Sammy didn't look up from her phone. "Yes, she texted me that she's eloping with a fire juggler and I totally forgot to mention it."

"So, no then?"

"Can't fool you, can I?" Sammy's typing didn't even slow. "Chillax, brother o' mine. She's a teenager at a music fest. She's just off somewhere having fun."

Dawn squeezed my hand. "It'll be okay. You both needed to get out of that house. It's September and you look pale as an Irishman's arse in winter."

"I've been busy," I said.

"Uh huh. You've been sitting around your room playing video games," she replied. "If I'd known you were going to go full-on basement dweller over that Genesis, I would never have bought it for you."

Hear hear, Alynon said.

Sit and spin, Alf, I thought back. "You want me to be able to talk with your friends without sounding like an idiot, right?" I replied. "I have a lot to catch up on."

I had twenty-five years of games, movies, music, and life to experience; in fact, everything that had been created or happened since my spiritual exile to the Other Realm in 1986. With Dawn's help, I was immersing myself in one year each month, so that I could really absorb it all and build up my knowledge and experience in a natural progression. This month I'd reached 1992, and was loving the music. But what had blown my mind, not to mention my free time and a good deal of my regular sleeping hours these past months, were the video games.

I mean, the RPGs alone! Curse of the Azure Bonds, Bard's Tale, Ultima, Wasteland—it was like I'd woken into a fantasy world myself.

But then throw in games like Monkey Island, King's Quest, Sonic the Hedgehog, Flashback, Mortal Kombat,

Dune, Mario Kart, Super Star Wars, and—well, I needed three of me just to play them all as much as I wanted. And there remained nearly twenty more years of games for me to catch up on.

"Besides," I added, "I'm technically working, if you count it as research toward me learning to design my own games again."

Fatima looked over. "I thought you were running a dating service for magicals."

"I am," I said. "But it hasn't exactly been bringing in the dollars." Since helping Sal the sasquatch to find his perfect soul mate, customers had finally begun to trickle in for the magical matchmaking service I'd started. Unfortunately, most couldn't afford to pay much, or preferred barter. And despite Mort's promptings and my need for income, I never felt able to turn someone away who came searching for love. "Besides, gaming has always been my true love."

"Gee, thanks," Dawn said. "Does this mean I should dress up like a video game hottie to grab your heart?"

"You say that like you don't love the idea," I replied.

"Damn. You know me too well." Dawn grinned, and gave me a kiss. "You know I support your dreams, baby, but I just don't want you to be disappointed."

I leaned in close and said for her ears only, "I've seen you in several costumes, and haven't been disappointed yet."

"Damn straight," she said. "Though I still can't believe you look better in that Catwoman outfit than me."

I blushed, and glanced to make sure Sammy hadn't heard, but she gave no sign as she continued tapping at her phone. "Ha ha," I said, just in case.

"Seriously though," Dawn continued, "I'm not sure making games works the way you think anymore. They've become like big budget movies these days, all corporate product and profit, right, Sammy?"

"Not necessarily true," Sammy said without looking up from her phone, clearly able to hear us. Great. "You could probably code a mobile game by yourself. In fact, retro gaming's in right now, so you might even do well."

I blinked. Had Sammy just said something encouraging rather than sarcastic? That was only slightly less rare than Alynon being helpful. It must be Fatima's influence. That, and the number of bands that Dawn had helped Sammy meet in person this weekend.

"Well then," Dawn said, and gave me another squeeze, "we should look into some programming classes."

I didn't mention that I'd already looked into classes and been confused by all the different types of programming options—long gone were the simple days of BASIC. Dawn liked to take charge and lead the way anyway, and I'd found it easiest just to let her.

Of course, her general distrust of the Internet meant she preferred to do things by talking to real people, so we'd probably be spending a few days visiting local colleges rather than a few hours using the magic of the Google. But Dawn had her own kind of magic. Somehow she would make an adventure of it, and probably make friends with the admissions folks, and next thing I knew I'd be enrolled in an already full class for free through some kind of archaic loophole. For the same reason I'd learned not to get in her way once she had a goal in mind, I'd also learned not to question the power of Dawn, but just to sit back and appreciate it.

So all I said was, "That would be great."

The sound of a band doing sound checks echoed from the mural amphitheater stage across the way.

"Ooo, I think Starfucker's coming on," Dawn said.

I wasn't sure if that was a good thing or not. I didn't recognize most of the bands playing this music and arts fest. In fact, none of the artists I'd grown to enjoy over the past couple of months were performing. Nirvana. Boyz II Men. Sleater-Kinney. Blur. MC Hammer. Milli Vanilli. But I'd enjoyed some of the bands that did play.

A cloud of marijuana smoke drifted over us from a passing knot of teenagers.

"If Mattie doesn't show up soon," I said, "maybe we should skip taking her backstage to meet the Presidents tonight."

"Nice try," Dawn said. "I know you're not excited about PotUS, but that's just cause you haven't heard them yet. Besides, Mattie is going to Hall and Oates with you Monday, the least you can do is see the Presidents with her."

Damn. "You know how to cut right to my heart," I said. "Like a real Maneater."

"Maneater, huh?" Dawn said, the corner of her mouth dimpling up. "I can go for that."

A shout went up from a group of hackysackers on the grass in front of the mural stage, drawing my attention back to the flows of energy.

"I just want to know Mattie's okay, is all," I said, tearing my eyes off of the crowd and their spiritual pull again. "There's all kinds of negative energy here."

"Mattie's danger is yet to come," Fatima said as she sketched, and with the noise of the crowd and sound checks it took a second after hearing the words for their meaning to register.

"What?" I stood up, and strode quickly to Fatima.

"Mattie's danger?" I looked down at her sketch. It appeared to be Dawn dancing in front of Stonehenge.

Fatima looked up at me, and blinked, her eyes taking a second to focus on mine. "What?"

"You said Mattie's danger is yet to come. Did you see something happening to her?" Fatima was an arcana like me and Sammy, a human magic user; but where our family gift was necromancy, hers was sorcery, and more specifically the gift of prophecy. Though if you asked me, her true gift was in making Sammy smile, a miraculous power whose strength must truly rival the gods to break through the shield of my sister's determined cynicism.

Fatima frowned, and looked back down at her sketch pad. "I—maybe?" She lifted the page, and flipped through a series of images. I caught what looked like Donkey Kong, and Dawn playing her guitar with an expression of fury, and Mattie reaching out through a narrow window in stone, a terrified look on her face. "I don't think her danger is immediate. Though everything feels . . . unclear, distant for some reason, like the near future is encased in amber." She shook her head.

Dawn moved to stand beside me. "Something wrong?"

"I don't know," I said.

Sammy put a hand on Fatima's arm. "You okay, Fates?"

A smile quirked up the corner of Fatima's mouth. "I'm fine. Probably just tired. Two hours sleep does not a bright Fatima make."

Sammy gave Fatima a light poke in the side. "And whose fault is that?"

"Yours," Fatima replied, and finger-combed her hair back. "You know what red wine does to me."

"Uh," I said, "about Mattie—?"

Sammy sighed. "I told you, I'm sure she's fine."

"She's *not* fine," I said. "Fatima's visions aside, Mattie's definitely hurting. She just hides it well."

In fact, we'd come to Bumbershoot today largely for Mattie's sake. It had been a rough few months for all of us, but she was barely sixteen years old. Beyond the normal teenage challenges and changes, she'd been taken hostage by her undead grandfather, found out her mother was possessed during her conception in order to grant her the Talker gift, and then her father had almost died to keep bumping spiritual uglies with the ghost who did the possessing. Add on top of that several major shakeups in the family, with my return, and Pete largely disappearing into his new life as a waerwolf, and her teacher and family friend Heather betraying us then becoming a waerbear—we were one crazy messed up family.

So when Dawn got the chance at some cheap festival passes through her new record label, it was decided to bring Mattie out for some normal, healthy family time at an event she might actually enjoy.

"Thanks, Captain Obvious," Sammy said. "But here's a news flash—our family has always been messed up, and we each got through it. Mattie's not a fragile egg, she's a smart young woman who's twice as together as you were at her age."

"I'm just worried . . ." I trailed off.

"What?" Sammy asked. "That she's going to go up in the Space Needle with a sniper rifle just because she's having a rough patch? Trust me, if you meet a teenager who never has an emotional crisis, that's when you should be worried, 'cause they're an alien or robot or something and your butt is toast."

Indeed, Alynon chimed in. *I would be more concerned

about the enemies your family has made than what harm your niece may bring upon herself.*

Great, thanks, I thought. *Like I needed to be reminded of that right now.* "Don't forget we saw Barry here," I said.

Dawn rolled her eyes. "Barry's harmless."

Easy for her to say. Barry did nothing but flirt with her. But Barry, mister life of the party with his easy charm and perfect smile, also happened to be a waerdog pledged to the Forest of Shadows, the darkest of the Fey Demesnes. I still couldn't believe he was running around free after the battle at Elwha, but technically he hadn't participated in the battle, he'd only been there as a duly appointed representative in an official duel. And now, he was playing in a drum circle on yon grassy hill with a bunch of hippy-looking kids I suspected were a pack of his fellow waer-folk.

"Hey guys!" Mattie called, appearing out of the stream of people. She wore one of Sammy's old Bikini Kill T-shirts, and had dyed her hair bright green with blue ends.

"Where were you?" I snapped, my nerves still on edge from all the spiritual temptation. "We were supposed to meet here a half hour ago."

"Sorry, Uncle Finn. I was on my way and got distracted by a breakdancing troupe. You would have loved them."

"You freaked me out," I said, but my irritation quickly faded at the sad look on her face. I sighed. "I'm glad you had fun. Just, text us or something. We were worried."

"I know," Mattie said. "Sorry. I lost track of time."

"Dawn!" another voice called, and a woman marched toward us from the direction of the mural stage, waving. A silver persona ring flashed on her hand, the ID ring of an arcana.

"Kaitlin!" Dawn waved back. Kaitlin cut across the crowd

to join us. She stood a head taller than Dawn, with bleach-blond hair and wearing all white.

Kaitlin and her partner, Wesley, formed the band BOAT, and had known Dawn for several years.

They were also arcana, a fact Dawn had been unaware of until recently. But for that reason I actually looked forward to talking to them. Of all the bands I'd met since Dawn signed to Volvur Records, they were the first I might be able to say something intelligent to instead of just feeling like a dork.

Dawn and Kaitlin embraced. A bright blue azurite gem flashed in Kaitlin's Persona ID ring, identifying her as a sorceress, an illusionist.

"Grab lunch?" I asked, looking at the Casio calculator watch I'd inherited from Zeke. Sadly, my Pac-Man watch had died a watery death in the Elwha.

Just past noon.

Sammy stood, and lifted her laptop satchel. "I don't know about food, but I'd kill a damn Yeti for some air-conditioning right now," she said.

Fatima gave a sad look up at the sun, but didn't protest. We all gathered our things and shuffled inside the food court. As we filed through the door, Mattie moved up beside Dawn and said, "How come *you're* not playing this weekend?"

"I only signed with Volvur a couple months ago," Dawn replied. "It was way too late to book me here."

"You'll play here next year though, for sure," Mattie said.

"We'll see," Dawn replied, but her tone was practically giddy. "They're planning to send me on tour, for sure."

Kaitlin looked over her shoulder at Dawn. "We should totally talk about doing some shows together. I think our messages mix really well."

"Shit yeah!" Dawn replied.

I wasn't sure how excited I was at the thought of Dawn getting mixed up in BOAT's brand of messaging.

BOAT had been approved by the Arcana Ruling Council to help popularize and spread disinformation about magic by creating a cultish sort of "philosophy" and mythos to go with their band. The truly weird thing was, they seemed entirely earnest about it all, and it was hard for me to tell where the line existed between them doing this as some kind of giant promotional art project, and them actually believing what they were saying, whereas Dawn's lyrics all came right from her heart. Still, sincere or not, BOAT's messages seemed positive.

It seemed the ARC had finally learned its lesson about leaving the creativity to the artists, at least. Past attempts at disinformation and creating excuses for plausible deniability had not gone over so well, and even the ones that had been somewhat successful—LSD, Orson Welles's *War of the Worlds* broadcast, Gwar—had caused some problems of their own.

A wave of cool air and food smells washed over us as we entered the Armory, Seattle Center's food court. The space looked like a gentrified warehouse, all pleasant greens and blues and grays with a high roof held up by pillars spaced widely throughout. Along the outer walls ran a series of restaurants, and there were food stands spaced throughout as well. Scaffolding for lights and speakers dangled from wires above, with a stage opposite the entrance that often held some kind of cultural performance. And in the center of the floor you could look down into a section of the Children's Museum that filled the level below, a section made to look like a mountain and bit of Pacific Northwest forest complete with running waterfall.

The spaces between were packed with people at small plastic tables.

Sammy scored seats at a table far back in one corner by an emergency exit, as isolated as we could hope to get in the crowded space, and the rest of us dispersed to get the food of our choice.

As I stood waiting for my order at the MOD Pizza counter, a laugh cut through the noise of the crowd, a snorting staccato beat that I would have recognized anywhere. I looked over to see Dawn laughing at something Kaitlin said a couple of counters down, and then smiling in my direction.

Damn I loved her. Granted, I didn't have the years of experience that I should have at love, but then I supposed there were plenty of people my age who hadn't had more than one true love in their life. My brother Pete and his fiancée Vee were getting married in a few days, and more than once as I'd listened to them talk about the traditions of a brightblood bonding ceremony, I had thought of Dawn, and—

"Whip cream?" the young lady behind the counter asked.

"What? Oh, uh, yeah! Of course."

I collected my food and shake, and turned around to find an unfamiliar older man watching me intently, with a brute lurking beside him who looked like Dolph Lundgren with a buzz cut and neck tattoo.

"Hello, Phinaeus," the older man said. "I have some rather urgent business to discuss with you."

The faint purple birthmark like an upside-down heart on his right cheek sparked recognition.

"Justin?" Justinius Gramaraye was a second cousin. I could see the Gramaraye nose now above Justin's weak chin and too-thin lips. It was definitely him. When I last saw him and his twin brother, Jared, they were barely twelve years old, a full two years younger than me at the time. But the man staring at me appeared at least sixty-five years old. And not a distinguished Sean Connery sixty-five, or a charming Beatles "will you still love me" sixty-five, but more like someone who'd spent those years earning money as a subject of medical experiments, and then blown every dime of that money at the local dive bar.

The rare "gift" of actually Talking to spirits drained the necromancer's life when used, aging the necromancer. My mother had been a Talker, which had contributed to her death. And I was a Talker, but had no desire to use the gift if I could avoid it. If Justin had manifested the gift after I went into exile, that might explain his aging, but not his otherwise sad state. Vegan albinos had more flesh and color to them. "Jesus, Justin, you okay?"

"Show respect!" Justin snapped.

My skin tightened with goosebumps as I realized my mistake.

This wasn't Justin. This was—

"Grandfather."

2

WE DIDN'T START THE FIRE

Grandfather's reaper grin confirmed my guess.

He had taken possession of Justin's body through dark necromancy, aided by the resonance that family blood and the shared gift of necromancy created between them. Just as he had done to Grayson, his onetime apprentice and bastard son, despite the fact that he had destroyed Grayson's spirit to fuel the possession.

Much as I had destroyed Dunngo's spirit to fuel my own magic.

The tray suddenly felt heavy, and my stomach in no state for food.

"Come," Grandfather said. "Let us go someplace less public and speak."

"How about we don't," I replied, "and you just send me a nice Solstice card from, say, Hades?"

Grandfather motioned to the brute at his side. "I could have my friend involve your mundy girlfriend in our discussion, if you prefer."

I looked over at Dawn, but she and Kaitlin were faced away from me now, unaware of my situation.

Shazbot.

"Fine. Let's chat, just me, you, and Deputy Dolph."

Deputy Dolph didn't look too thrilled at his new title—in fact, he looked like the kind of person always just waiting for an excuse to be angry—but Grandfather merely nodded to him, and he led the way back to a utility hall clearly meant for employees only. We stopped in the hallway with its plain white walls and concrete floor, the fluorescent lighting especially bleak and pale after a day in the summer sun.

I swallowed against a suddenly dry mouth as Grandfather turned to face me. I waved at him. "I take it Grayson's body finally gave out?"

"Indeed," Grandfather said. "When you turned against your family duty, I no longer had the magic to sustain it."

I ignored the bait on the whole "duty" thing. We'd just have to agree to disagree on whether being used to fuel his immortality was a family duty or not.

"So you just took another body?" I asked. "You said Grayson volunteered to be sacrificed for your use, that he was a soldier for the cause. Are you going to tell me Justin was another True Believer? Gods, don't tell me he was actually your kid, too?"

"Not exactly," Grandfather said with a slight smile. "But as a Gramaraye, he too had a duty. And trust me, he was doing nothing special with this body, nothing nearly as important as saving our world from the Fey. The sacrifice of his spirit will be honored one day."

I did my best to hide a sudden shiver—and to convince myself it was one of fear rather than desire at the memory of how such dark power felt, or the uncomfortable echo I heard in his words to my own earlier thoughts about all the wasted lives in the world. I straightened my shoulders. "Well, I have to say, I'm not sure this whole Mumm-Ra thing is working for you. You look like the Crypt Keeper on a bad scare day."

Grandfather's reaper smile faded into a decidedly unamused look. "The . . . entropy is an unfortunate side effect I have yet to eliminate. Especially as I no longer have your help in acquiring the power required to maintain possession."

"I never helped you," I said. "I was used by you." It was the reason Grandfather had framed me and gotten me exiled to the Other Realm for twenty-five years—due to our unique spiritual connection, he'd found a way to draw raw magical energy from the Other Realm through me despite the barriers between worlds. It was a variation on the trick that Katherine Verona had used to make her daughter the spiritual equivalent of an atomic bomb in the Other Realm.

"You say potato, I say stop whining," Grandfather replied, waving the distinction away.

"I'm surprised you have enough mana left to freejack anyone after all these months," I said. "You must have quite the stockpile."

"Who said I'm using mana?" Grandfather replied, and looked down at his hands. "Sadly, the levels of raw spiritual energy required to maintain control is not kind to flesh."

My goosebumps turned into pterodactyl-bumps.

Grandfather must be summoning spirits—or killing folks and capturing their spirits—and consuming their energy to fuel his immortality. He had gone full-on Lich King evil.

"You're insane," I said, taking an involuntary step back. "You may have found a way to stick around past your expiration date, but you only have so many relatives to use up."

"Indeed," Grandfather replied, with the tone of someone

who had just been asked if they'd like to order the daily special.

"So let me guess. You're here to tell me I should return to exile so you can stop using up bodies like disposable underwear?"

"Actually, Phinaeus, I only need to possess one more body."

The look he gave me made it pretty damn clear which body that might be.

"Um, what?" I said.

"If I am right, I no longer need to place you in exile, because once I have control of your body I will have an existing link to the Other Realm."

I blinked. "You mean Alynon?"

Grandfather's smile widened. "Yes. And what could be a more fitting solution to my immortality, and to the success of our war against the Fey, than to use one of their own to fuel that victory."

"Well," I said. "Aren't *you* just the leader of the club that's made from you and me. But I'd rather not join."

"You say that as if you have a choice," Grandfather replied. "Trust me, what my . . . allies have planned for you and your loved ones is sure to be far worse. You have upset our plans more than once, and we are all too close to our endgame to risk you doing so once more." He glanced around us as if expecting those allies to back up his statement.

"I still don't understand why your merry little band of Illuminati wannabes can't see—"

"I don't mean we Arcanites, dear boy. I mean the Fey."

Damn.

We'd suspected that Grandfather's Arcanite cult had allied with some group of equally extremist Fey. There just had been no way to explain how either one or the other group could have performed all the acts of sabotage and manipulation and destruction. But it had not made sense. The primary goal of the Arcanites was to wipe out the Fey and establish arcana supremacy—for our world's own good, of course. What Fey Demesne or group would be willing to work with them?

"Who—"

"Please, dear boy, do not ask me who my allies are. That really is insulting to think I would share my plans like a bad movie villain."

"Well, to be fair, you did have a secret underwater lair and are planning to rule the world, so, you know, if the straitjacket fits—"

"You still refuse to see the true threat the Fey pose," Grandfather said. "But had they found you before me, you would not be so glib. Even now I'm certain their agents seek you out."

"Funny," I said. "They've had months to seek me out since the whole Elwha thing. Why do I have a feeling that your plans to use me as your personal Lazarus Pit was the final straw?"

Grandfather gave a "what can I say" shrug, then motioned toward the exit door at the end of the hall. "Why don't we go someplace safer to complete our . . . discussion. Unless you wish to involve your—"

Deputy Dolph suddenly spasmed, slamming back against the wall. His eyes went severely bloodshot, his jaw clenched, and his neck muscles stood out enough to make a Cardassian jealous.

"Fury!" Grandfather said.

"He's berserking?" I asked, backing away as Grandfather did the same. "Why?"

"No, fool. A Fury has possessed him. He is fighting it, but he will not win. You must escape."

"Me? Escape?"

Grandfather made a disgusted sound. "Truly, that habit of repeating what I say has always annoyed me, Phinaeus. The Fey have sent Furies against you, and me. I can handle myself. You—"

I didn't wait for him to finish. I dropped my tray, mourning the lost pizza as I turned, and ran.

A Fury. Holy frak.

Furies were unpredictable and volatile creatures, Elder Fey spirits drawn to powerful anger and hatred, possessing their victim and projecting the dark emotions outward like a destructive emotional plague. Furies had responded often to calls for vengeance in olden times, before arcana had managed to contain enough of them that the remaining few fled and remained mostly hidden.

When they did attack, they were relentless and devastating. Creatures of chaos and single-minded focus, they might be willing to cause death and mayhem among mundies, careless of the visibility. More than one sporting event had devolved into riots thanks to the Furies being drawn to such concentrated passion and rivalry.

But a Fury with purpose, controlled? Only the Fey could have managed it.

Grandfather hadn't been lying about that, at least.

I dodged and wove my way between the people with their trays and tables, checking behind me. Deputy Dolph had not followed. Which meant either he was busy ripping Grandfather's arms off, or Grandfather had managed to somehow bind or banish the creature. I wasn't sure which I preferred.

I reached our table where thankfully everyone now sat with their food. "We have to get out of here, get somewhere safe. Now."

"What's going on?" Sammy asked.

"Both Grandfather and a Fury are in the building—"

All color drained from Sammy's face, but her eyes practically flamed red as she stood and said, "That bastard better not come anywhere near me again." Fatima put a hand on her arm to reassure or steady her. Grandfather had kidnapped and tortured Sammy six months ago, at the same time he'd taken Mattie. Though Sammy hid it as well as she hid most of her emotions, Fatima had confided that it still caused my sister nightmares.

"Furies?" Kaitlin asked in a shocked tone, and looked around the crowded space. "What did you do to attract *them*?"

"That story's enough to fill two books at least," I said. "And right now, we need to get someplace safe."

"The EMP?" Mattie said as we all moved toward the emergency exit.

I thought about the shining, undulating bulk of the EMP museum building just a quick sprint away. There were arcana wardens inside, tasked with guarding the ARC Sanctum hidden beneath the Science Fiction museum area.

They would not be happy to see me given that I'd broken into the Sanctum with Zeke six months ago, and left a number of the wardens injured in the process. But keeping those around me safe was more important than fear of a possible beat down just then.

"The EMP," I agreed. We sprinted in that direction as quickly as the crowds allowed.

"You know," Dawn said, striding beside me. "After being

away from your family the past month, I almost forgot about all the, you know." She waved at our situation, her many silver rings glinting. One of those rings held a ladybug suspended in amber and charged with a bit of my energy, marking her as an Acolyte, a mundane allowed knowledge of the magical world.

"I'm sorry, I know—"

My phone buzzed in my pocket. I slowed to a fast walk and fumbled the phone out of my jeans, half expecting a call from Grandfather with an all clear and a claim that I now owed him. But the image of a bald black man with a faded scar across his forehead glared out from the screen. Reggie had been less than thrilled when I took the picture, catching his expression as Mort offered him a cheap boxed red wine with dinner.

I had a reflexive urge to ignore the call. Reggie was an enforcer, a policeman of the magical world, representing the area's Arcana Ruling Council. As it did every time Reggie called me, fear surged up in me that the ARC had learned about my use of dark necromancy. But Reggie was also a friend of sorts, working to root out the Arcanites. Somehow, I didn't think his call was a coincidence.

I hit the answer icon, and held the phone pressed hard to one ear while covering the other to hear over the music and crowd. "Hello?"

"Finn?"

"Yeah, Reggie, I was actually going to call *you*. My—"

"Just listen! The Arcanites are deeper in the ARC than we thought. I discovered something about their plans, and—gods, I still can't believe it."

"What?" I asked. Reggie sounded freaked out, which

freaked me out, as if I weren't freaked out enough already.

"They—shit, they found me! Damn it. Check your e-mail!"

Then the phone squealed feedback in my ear, and the call ended.

I came to a stop, and everyone else in our group halted with me.

"You okay, Uncle Finn?" Mattie asked.

If the Arcanites still infested the Arcana Ruling Council and its branches, if they were bold enough to go after Reggie, then we could be walking right into their trap if we fled to the museum.

"Change of plans. We go for the car, and home."

Sammy gave an enormous sneeze. I turned to ask if she was okay, and she let out another sneeze. If a butterfly flapping its wings can cause a hurricane on the other side of the world, Sammy's sneezes probably caused hurricanes on distant planets.

They also served as a warning of magic being directed at her, since Sammy was allergic to active magic and magical creatures.

I spun around. Deputy Dolph plowed through the crowd in a beeline for us like a linebacker charging for a sponsorship deal.

It was probably too much to hope that he'd dispatched Grandfather. More likely that his orders were to target me specifically, in which case he would ignore anyone else unless they posed a threat.

"You guys go on," I said. "He's after me." I pulled a collapsible steel baton out of my pocket, but did not extend it as I looked from Sammy to Mattie and back.

"Fuck," Sammy said, but only hesitated a second before saying, "Be careful." She nudged Mattie back into motion toward the car, Fatima joining them.

"Nice try," Dawn said, not moving, and Kaitlin still at her side. "We stick together."

"Dawn, I have a plan, but it won't work if you're with me. And we don't have time to argue."

"I can give Finn a head start," Kaitlin said, "create the illusion he ran a different direction. But I won't be able to maintain it for long."

Dawn's eyes narrowed, and she said to me, "You'd better get your tight little butt back to me in one piece, or I'll come after you in the afterlife."

"Aw, that's, like, a quote from *Last of the Mohicans*, isn't it?" I asked.

She just rolled her eyes and said, "Toe pick!" Then she sprinted after the others.

"Toe Pick" had become a phrase we shared after watching *The Cutting Edge.* When I said it to Dawn, it usually meant "Good luck, go get them," like when she was about to perform. When she said it to me, she claimed it meant "Focus!" but what I suspected it really meant was "Don't do something stupid!"

Why is everyone telling me not to be stupid? I asked Alynon.

No response. He must still be out of it from exerting control over my leg earlier. There's no way he would have passed up an opening like that willingly. Which was a shame, since a little advice wouldn't have been unwelcome just then.

Kaitlin moved a little away from me. "On my go, run for it." She looked from me to the Fury for a minute, squinting as if trying to see through it, then said, "Okay. Go!"

I pushed my way through the flow of people on the concrete walkway to reach the grass beyond, then sprinted a short ways before looking back.

Dolph Fury wasn't moving toward Sammy and the others, or me, but remained focused on the place I'd stood when Kaitlin placed the illusion in his mind. The magic took its toll on Kaitlin though. She wavered as though she wanted to pass out, her reserve of magical energy, or her strength of will, rapidly drained under the weight of the Fury's focus and emotion.

I put a little more distance between myself and the Fury before a howl of anger could be heard over the thrumming rock music. The illusion had ended.

A fight erupted around the Fury, shoves and punches and shouts rippling outward along the line of people as if someone had started a game of telephone with the world's meanest Yo Mamma joke.

"Hey!" I shouted. "Blind Fury! Come get some!"

The Fury's bloodshot eyes locked on mine, and I waited until I was certain he was coming for me, then took off running across the grass, ragey Deputy Dolph in furious pursuit.

3

LOVE SHACK

I was in pretty good shape physically, thanks in part to Alynon's efforts in the years he possessed my body, and in part to the fact Dawn and I had begun taking Wing Chun classes together. But the Fury had taken possession of a clearly athletic enforcer, and Furies were able to push their host bodies to extremes, pumping adrenaline and blocking pain. I would not be able to stay ahead for long.

In Dolph's path, a little girl in butterfly face paint giggled an adorable laugh. The Fury recoiled, staggering in an arc away from the girl, gaining me a little ground.

I ran toward Barry's drum circle on the nearby hilltop.

Most of the young men and women in the circle had dreadlocks, and the men had their shirts tied around their waists, exposing too-pale skin to the Northwest sun. A cloud of body odor and patchouli smell surrounded them. Barry especially loved patchouli to help hide his waerdog scent from other brightbloods with a strong sense of smell.

"Barry!" I said as I ran up. Barry looked up, surprised, and the mind-numbing rhythm they'd been playing faltered.

"Woah brah!" he said. "You totally harshed our groove

there. We were so in the zone."

"Uh, sorry. Look, I just wanted to say hello, no hard feelings and all that." I held out my hand.

"Oh! Right on, man. We're all good." He took my hand.

I summoned up my magic, and prepared to transfer a bit of my spiritual energy to Barry. If I could mask his spiritual resonance with mine, the Fury just might go after him. Surely a pack of waerdogs could handle a Fury better than I could. For all I knew, the Forest of Shadows Fey sent the damn thing.

But I hesitated, looking at the curious young faces of the drummers, and released the summoning. I just couldn't do it.

Gods I hated Barry. But that didn't mean I had the right to sic a Fury on him, and especially not on these other kids, who for all I knew were just a bunch of stoners drawn to Barry's puppy charm. Besides, Dawn might think I did it out of jealousy or anger. She liked Barry. Everyone liked Barry. The bastard.

"Barry, do you have any tips on dealing with a Fury?"

"Furies?" Barry looked surprised, then gave his damn charming smile. "Only love can truly conquer fury, my friend. Why?" He looked past me. "Oh. Bummer, dude."

Dolph Fury was close enough I could hear him breathing harshly as he began running up the hill we stood upon. Then he stopped several feet away, and grinned at me with a gap-toothed smile, a bit of saliva running down his chin.

The red of his eyes seemed to fill my vision, setting the world aflame.

I turned back and punched Barry in the face. "Thanks for nothing!" I shouted as rage flared up within me like a grease fire of anger—anger that Barry had tried to steal Dawn from me, anger that I ever worried he might succeed, anger that he reminded me how close my choices had brought my family and the Elwha brightbloods to disaster. Anger that—

Barry sprang to his feet, and licked my face.

"What the—" I felt a sudden urge to giggle. Barry had just used his waerdog powers on me, infecting me with his simple joy. I smiled.

Then anger surged back in like water into a sinking car.

"Run, brah!" Barry said, and shoved me away from Dolph Fury. Some part of my brain understood, and I began to run again.

The Fury screamed, and chased after me, ignoring Barry and his group. The anger faded as I gained some distance and the Fury had to focus again on controlling Dolph's body in a flat-out run.

Barry had just helped save me. I owed him one.

There was simply no justice in the universe.

But knowing that Barry wasn't aligned with the Fury made me reconsider the merits of his advice. Love was the answer? How the hell did that help me? I wasn't taking this thing anywhere near Dawn.

I glanced back. Dolph gained on me with every step. I could feel my muscles already beginning to strain. Soon, energy would be replaced by lactate and acid buildup, and I would reach my limit far sooner than the Fury, who would simply push Dolph to the point of true collapse.

I looked to the Pacific Science Center ahead.

Maybe I could speed up the process of collapse—for Dolph Fury, not me of course.

I pushed myself to my limit.

I entered the courtyard of the Pacific Science Center,

running along a narrow concrete path that wound through reflecting pools, spanned by tall white arches that looked like elven towers from Rivendell. I nearly knocked several visitors into the water in my haste. Shouting apologies behind me without slowing down, I reached the nearest side entrance. Locked. Thank the gods. I tugged the skeleton key on its cord from under my shirt. A thief's finger bone covered in runes, the artifact was rare and an example of combined thaumaturgy and necromancy from darker times. I held it against the door, and the lock released. I ducked inside and closed the door behind me, making sure it locked again.

Dolph Fury would have to find another way in, buying me some time.

Children packed the hall, lined up to see an exhibit of Harry Potter movie props and settings. Dawn adored Harry Potter, and had made an exception to our one-year-per-month pop-cultural immersion plan, saying a geek like me couldn't walk around ignorant of Harry Potter and not raise a lot of questions. I'd loved the books and movies both, but had needed serious convincing it wasn't another part of the ARC's disinformation campaign to create plausible deniability about the magical world.

I turned and ran away from the exhibit. The last thing I wanted was to lead a Fury into a pack of children. At least, not until I was prepared to stop him.

I made my way to the insect displays, a room with a black widow, a scorpion, bees, and more small and deadly critters, most dead and preserved.

What are you doing? Alynon asked drowsily as I slowed next to the scorpions. *Keep running!*

Welcome back! I thought back at him. *I'm making my*

stand. I should be able to animate and control as many as a dozen of these creepy crawlies and use them to poison the Fury.

*La, I hesitate to point this out, yet given how prone you are to fits of self-flagellation and annoying bouts of melancholy . . . *

I sighed. *Yes?*

Are you truly ready to kill a possessed man to rid yourself of the Fury?

Frak. He was right. Deputy Dolph wasn't exactly an innocent bystander if he worked for my grandfather. But he hadn't actually ever attacked me or anything. He was being used against his will. And even if he weren't, killing him shouldn't be my first choice. Even as accustomed to death as I was being from a family of necromancers, life remained sacred.

And what worried me most was that Alynon had to point it out to me.

Well, what choice do I have? I asked defensively. *You know more about Fey spirits than me. What* should *I do?*

I do not know. I only know that a Fury's bane is not anger but that which is opposite of anger.

"Meaning?" I muttered.

Peace. Love. Joy.

Great. Don't suppose there's a Care Bear around with a belly full of magic?

I looked around. And realized that there was, in fact, a possibility.

"Stop!" A voice called out. "Sir, if you do not leave peaceably we will have to use force."

I turned, startled, and saw two security guards who closely resembled Jon and Ponch from CHiPs backpedaling, as Dolph Fury stomped toward me like He-Man in a 'roid rage. Jon-guard held up his hand, and the Fury touched it.

Jon shuddered, and said, "It's not fair. It's not fair!"

Ponch took a step back and put his hand on his nightstick. "Hey, you okay?"

Jon turned, his face contorted and red, and launched himself at his partner.

The Fury continued marching at me as the two guards fell to the floor, Ponch desperately trying to fend off the wild attack of his partner.

Crap.

I turned, and ran into the butterfly house. I had to push past several people in line, but they were distracted watching the two guards rolling on the floor like high school brawlers.

The butterfly house was basically a clear-sided hothouse the size of a large room, filled with bright and beautiful flowers and hundreds of even more beautiful butterflies.

I ran around the island at the room's center with its fountain and tropical trees, placing it between me and the entrance.

Dolph Fury pushed his way into the butterfly house, driven by whatever compulsion had been placed on him to pursue me into hell itself. He spotted me, and began marching purposefully toward me.

A cloud of butterflies descended on him like a pack of wild children on a herd of injured piñatas.

It is really hard to stay angry when you're in a room full of butterflies under normal circumstances. It's like trying to be angry with your girlfriend as you watch *Ghost* together. It just doesn't work. At least, I found it impossible. I mean, when Patrick first talks to Demi through Whoopi, I completely forgot how I was kind of upset at Dawn for writing a comedic song about our own romance. I just took her hand, grateful to have her in my life, alive and beautiful and amazing, challenges be damned and—

Well, you watch that movie and tell me you aren't moved even a little.

But when butterflies focus their energy on you, it transforms you. That is their power after all, their very nature—transformation. And it was the exact opposite of the Fury's nature.

Dolph Fury gave a terrible, deep scream, and then collapsed.

The butterflies, having depleted the bright but tiny spark of magic that animated them, fluttered down out of the air like leaves in autumn.

I stared for a minute at the unconscious man surrounded and covered in a blanket of butterfly wings, something bothering me. And then I realized what it was.

Furies normally traveled in packs of three.

I fled the scene before someone figured I was responsible for it all, and ran to rejoin Dawn, Sammy, Mattie, and Fatima, hoping desperately that I wasn't too late.

4

EVERYBODY HURTS

I reached Sixth Avenue, several blocks from the Seattle Center, and found everyone standing unharmed in the shade of the Travelodge near Dawn's old wood-paneled green station wagon, which she called Rattley Wood. I breathed a sigh of relief. Actually, I breathed a harsh phlegmy cough of relief after running through the heat to reach them, but let's pretend I arrived looking all awesome and heroic and not all sweaty and spitting out mucus.

"What happened?" Sammy asked, checking behind me.

Dawn threw her arms around me, and squeezed. "Well, I guess I don't need to kill you for dying."

"No," I said, still catching my breath, and swallowed what moisture I could as Dawn stepped back. "But I thought—"

"Guys!" Mattie shouted. I turned to follow her gaze. A red-haired woman charged at us from across the street, her eyes bloodshot, her face a mask of anger.

A second Fury. It must have followed Sammy and the others, and then waited for me to show. Which meant the Furies were definitely after me, and not our group in general.

"Into the car!" I shouted, and pulled out the baton. I

extended it fully with a whipping motion, and charged at the Fury.

This was total suicide I knew. Or at least, close enough. A couple months taking Wing Chun lessons together with Dawn hardly made me Bruce Lee, or the Last Dragon. Hell, it didn't even make me *3 Ninjas* good. But maybe I had a one percent shot at this *not* being total suicide.

Two darts shot past me trailing fine wires and punched into the chest of the woman Fury just below her collarbone. Her run turned into a tumble as she spasmed, electricity coursing through her muscles, and the Fury within her issued a horrible screech.

I turned to find Dawn holding her red plastic Taser. "I think she was *shocked* to see me," she said in a terrible Arnold Schwarzenegger voice, and yanked the wires out of the phaser-shaped weapon.

"Oh my gods, I so love you right now," I said.

"I know," Dawn replied, and grinned.

Mattie climbed back out of the car, and shouted back inside, "You're not my mother! My mother left me, and I thought it was *my* fault my whole life! But it's not, it's this messed up family and our messed up gift! I hate you all!"

Sammy leaped out the other side and shouted over the top of the car at Mattie, "You ungrateful brat! You're not the only one who lost their mother young! But I've been as much a parent to you as your asshole father!"

"What in the hell do you think you're doing?" I demanded, irritation surging. "Now is not the—"

You're all being manipulated! Alynon shouted in my head. *The third Fury! Snap out of it!*

Mattie and Sammy both turned their angry glares on me.

"Nobody asked you!" Mattie snapped.

"In fact," Sammy added, "nobody asked you to swoop in and ruin all of our lives!"

Stop this before—

I pounded at my own head. "Shut the hell up!"

Sammy's face went red with rage, and she began stomping around the car toward me.

Dawn stalked up to me, waving her Taser in my face. "Don't shout at them like that!" she said. "We've all put up with a lot while you've been trying to figure your crap out, you should be kissing our butts!"

Oh for Bright's sake, Alynon said, and my hand jerked up to my chest to press against the amulet Dawn had gifted me a few months ago, an amulet to protect against chemical influences on my body, magical or otherwise. *Activate it!* Alynon demanded, though his voice sounded faded, distant. *Or are you too stupid?*

Rage swirled up in me, and I shouted the activation phrase.

The rage evaporated like the dreams of youth, and I could think clearly again. The third Fury must be nearby, close enough to be manipulating us. And apparently, the Fury's powers stimulated changes in our body and brain chemistry to incite the rage that—

Sammy's fist caught me squarely on the jaw, sending me tumbling to the ground.

I blinked away tears as Dawn leaped on Sammy. Fatima climbed quickly out of the car and went after Dawn. Mattie screamed at them all to stop ruining everything.

I rubbed at my jaw. I had to end this quickly before someone got seriously injured, or ended up on *COPS*, or worse. I looked around us carefully, searching with my arcana sight for the shimmer of a glamour, but saw nothing. Which meant the creature was truly masked somehow, fully invisible. I focused, and reached out instead with my necromantic gift, sensing for nearby spiritual energy. I quickly identified and tuned out the spirits of the brawling women. That left a flickering and damaged presence... directly behind me.

"Stop it!" I shouted at the women, and rose to my feet as if I were going to launch myself at them. But instead, I turned and swung the baton at the air behind me.

My forearm hit something solid, causing the baton to fly out of my hand. But I heard an exclamation of pained surprise.

I gave my best front kick at the air. My foot connected with an invisible shin bone before rising too far, sending a spike of pain through my foot, but I pressed on, throwing several punches. They all missed.

I paused to sense again for the spiritual energy of the Fury's host, formed the calm focus required, and exerted my will. It was—

Guilt washed over me, a crushing, suffocating wave of guilt, a mental assault rather than a physical reaction as images floated across my mind.

Felicity, a brightblood witch and our family's au pair, staring with an expression of frozen horror at the ceiling, murdered to frame me, to send me into exile just so Grandfather could draw raw magical energy from the Other Realm through our bond.

Zeke, the massive berserker with his blond Mr. T mohawk, his skin blistered and blackened, wisps of smoke rising from his eyes as he died to save his sister, Vee, from my Grandfather's minions. Died because I couldn't stop

Grandfather myself, and because he'd exhausted himself fighting my battles.

Father, spouting nonsense rhymes and staring at me as though I were a stranger, his mind fractured when Grandfather used my mother's ghost to possess and control him as part of some insane Arcanite plot. Driven mad to frame me, and now beyond my ability to help with my gifts so untrained.

My older brother Mort, who resented the favoritism I'd received from Mother and Grandfather before my exile, who took extreme measures to secure his control over the family business, and as a result became addicted to a succubus—a succubus I accidentally sent to the Other Realm and almost certainly destroyed. The damage my grandfather had wrought on Mort—the damage I had done little to heal and much to deepen—had helped to deprive Mattie of a true father, a true family, for years.

The images and memories came faster now, cascading over me like a waterfall of suckiness.

Heather, my high school crush and a brilliant alchemist, whose need and danger I had been too blind and too slow to see.

Sal the sasquatch's sister, who had died because I sent blood witches against her, and because of the mana drug that my grandfather used on her and many other brightbloods.

Alynon, desperate to remain in his own body in the Other Realm, but I had forced him back into the prison of my mind so that I could be in *my* body, in *my* world.

Dunngo, the dwarf who died in a heroic act to help me. Dunngo, the dwarf whose spirit I destroyed in order to stop a jorõgumo, to save my younger brother Pete, and to prevent a brightblood war that our hidden Fey enemy had tried to start.

Dunngo, whose spirit I consumed to fuel my magic, an act of dark necromancy that haunted me every single day.

And Dawn.

Dawn, the woman I loved. Dawn, the woman who loved me despite everything. And because of that love, I had all memory of our youth together stolen, and had nearly gotten her killed several times. Even now, she still couldn't play the guitar for long stretches due to the injury a jorõgumo had given her while with me. Dawn was not an arcana able to use magic. She was not a brightblood, one of the "magical" beings in our world. She was mundy, mundane, without magic. As long as we were together and I kept getting pulled into these conflicts within the magical world, Dawn would be in danger.

But I couldn't find the strength to leave her, or to let the Arcana Ruling Council's enforcers wipe her memory of all magic.

Self-loathing bubbled up like boiling tar, black and acrid. I could feel it heating up, the fires of anger ready to erupt again.

But throughout the assault of images and memories, part of my mind remained sheltered within the focus I had created to sense for spiritual energy, protected behind a wall of mental and spiritual defenses formed out of habit from years of necromancer training. That part recognized that the Fury had switched from the more direct manipulation of my body's chemistry to a psychological attack, and that I remained in serious danger. Before my mental shelter could collapse, I reached out with my senses and found the human spirit of the Fury's host to my left. My hand shot out, my fingers jammed against invisible clothes and flesh.

I focused my will and with my necromantic gift I summoned that human spirit, bracing myself for the pain of spiritual feedback that would hopefully cripple the Fury worse than me.

The pain did not come. My magic did not rise up, did not respond.

The Fury knocked my hand away, and a wave of guilt crashed over me again. I nearly fell to my knees under the blow.

Instead, I turned my rising anger back against the Fury before that anger turned inward and consumed me. I lashed out in a wild backhand swing, and felt my fist connect. I gave a low side kick, and something crunched beneath my heel. An invisible punch hit me in the stomach, but cocooned in the armor of wild emotion I barely felt it. I faced the direction of my invisible enemy and gave another front kick. I connected again, and something slammed back against the car.

I sprinted to my baton, picked it up, and ran back to the car, swinging wildly in the area the Fury must have fallen. On the second swing, a loud *clunk!* announced solid contact, and the baton flared bright blue.

The emotional assault ended, and I stumbled mentally for a second as if my mind leaned against a strong wind that suddenly died.

The women all slowed then stopped in their struggle, and looked dazed as well. Dawn had Fatima in a headlock. Sammy had Mattie by the hair. They let go with shocked, embarrassed expressions, like someone who shoots an intruder and then discovers it was Grandma come to visit. We all stared at each other for a minute.

Fatima burst into tears.

"Shit," Dawn simply said.

Then Mattie threw back her arms and her head, arching and rising to her tip toes, shuddering. When she fell back to her heels, she lowered her head, and looked at me, her eyes going bloodshot.

5

POISON

Oh no. Oh gods. The last Fury hadn't been destroyed by butterflies or incapacitated by the power of a Taser. I had merely damaged its host, and it had moved to a new one.

But it had to have a weak hold at best on Mattie after expending so much of its magical energy already.

"Mattie!" Sammy said.

"I can tase her," Dawn said uncertainly, raising her Taser.

Mattie's eyes snapped to Sammy, and Sammy fell back a step, shuddering.

Then Sammy launched herself at Dawn, as Fatima moved to grab her, begging for her to stop.

Mattie turned her red gaze back to me, and I felt the emotional assault begin again.

I squeezed the baton in my hand.

"Mattie. Please. Fight it!"

Gods, how much anger must Mattie have packed down within her that a weakened Fury had been able to take control so easily?

I thought of all the reasons we had brought her here today, and knew the answer was, unfortunately, a lot. And this would only add to her pain, I realized, this day that was supposed to have been one of joy for her, one of escape from all of the insanity of the past months, turned into yet another damn disaster thanks to Grandfather and the Fey.

Thanks to me, to my actions that had made me an enemy to be destroyed. And once again, that chaos and danger spilled over onto the ones I loved.

The Fury's assault seemed to find purchase in that thought, like a wriggling root that finds its way into a crack in the sidewalk and begins to grow, breaking and shifting the concrete around it. Tiny fissures began to form in my mental and spiritual barriers.

I stepped forward, and spread my arms wide, dropping the baton.

"Mattie, I love you. I am sorry," I said.

Fury Mattie appeared startled by my action, a hint of alarm flickering across her expression, and she took a step back from me.

"I love you," I said again. "We all love you. I know it has been hard, learning about your father's choices, and with everything you've lost, but you still have us all, I promise. We haven't left you. You still have your family."

Fury Mattie made a hissing noise, recoiling from my advance, her back coming up against the car. I came within striking range, and she began to beat and kick and claw at me. Her fist connected with my jaw, nails raked along my arms, she got in a kick that left me worried about a cracked shin bone. But I pushed through the blows and pulled her into my arms.

I held her in a tight hug, trying to project all of my love and caring for her through my squeeze.

She kneed me in the groin.

I began to slide toward the ground, my hold slipping, but I grit my teeth against the pain and waves of nausea, and said, "We love you, Mattie."

Sammy had stopped chasing after Dawn and Fatima, and blinked now, the three standing in the street a second. Then they all rushed over to me, and soon Mattie was wrapped in a cocoon of hugs. She squirmed and fought as we held her tight and spoke over her screams.

"I love you, Mat-cat," Sammy said. "You're the daughter I would have wanted, and I don't even like kids."

Mattie's struggle grew even more frantic.

Dawn squeezed. "And I may not be your aunt, but I always felt like one, and I hope you know I will always be your family."

Fatima said, "We all love you, our little queen."

Mattie was practically convulsing now.

"We all love you," I repeated.

With a final, horrendous screech, the Fury fled Mattie's body, the tattered, weak remains of the Elder Fey spirit speeding away into the blue summer sky.

Mattie collapsed into our hugs, sobbing.

We held her for a long while, none of us speaking except through our hugs for Mattie, and for each other, agreeing by silent consent not to discuss the blows given, or the hurtful truths spoken, but to focus only on our love for each other.

"Let's get out of here," Sammy said at last.

We slowly stepped apart. Mattie rubbed at her eyes, and gave a weak smile, then pushed her blue and green hair back from her face.

I held on to Dawn's hand. "We should all go to the house, and stay behind wards until we figure out what in Hoth is going on."

Fatima took a step back. "I should go home and make sure Kitty Pryde is taken care of. I'll Zipcar it and meet you guys there." Her right hand casually crossed to her left shoulder to hold up the torn corner of her shirt.

Sammy shook her head. "I'll call Gwenda—"

"No," Fatima said. "Kitty will be a nervous wreck for weeks if someone else just picks her up. I can take her to Gwenda. Besides, I need to make sure my carrots are watered."

"You and your carrots," Sammy said, and sighed. "I think your life is more important than carrots."

I located by feel the invisible body of the Fey host I'd knocked out, grabbed it by what felt like a jacket, and dragged it away from the car. "Fatima should be safe," I said. "The Furies were after me."

Sammy rolled her eyes. "Well, there's a shocker."

"It's not his fault—" Dawn began.

Mattie winced. That brought us all up short, then Dawn and Sammy both said "Sorry" at the same time.

Sammy sighed at Fatima. "Fine. I'll see you at the house. Bring my gear?"

"Of course," Fatima said. She and Sammy held each other for a long, silent moment, then Fatima touched Sammy's cheek, pulled out her phone and walked briskly in the direction of Capitol Hill.

The rest of us piled into the car, and headed for the Seattle-Bainbridge ferry.

We had to wait a bit for the 3:45 P.M. boat, but thankfully nobody tried to attack us in the ferry holding lines. Once on board the ferry, we headed up to the top deck to get some fresh air, and walk off the uneasiness we all felt. The breeze off of the Puget Sound was cool in the summer afternoon heat. The lowering sun glinted off of the windows of restaurants that lined the pier, and the buildings old and new that rose in pop-up book layers behind it.

"So," Sammy said, facing me once the ferry pulled out and Seattle fell away behind us. "What did you do this time? Steal some ruby slippers? Read from the Necronomicon? Piss off the Olympians?"

"Wait," Dawn said. "Are there really gods on Mount Olympus?" She looked toward the Olympic Peninsula, and our own Mount Olympus at its center.

"Yeah," Sammy said. "And it is never a good idea to get mixed up with them, trust me."

"I didn't do anything," I replied. "I swear. The Arcanites are finally making their big move, whatever it is, at least that's Reggie's guess."

Dawn took my hand. "And their big move is to attack you? I mean, don't get me wrong sweetie, I think you're pretty awesome, but if their goal is world domination or whatever, why send ghostly rage-monkeys after *you*?"

"Grandfather said because I've managed to mess up their plans before."

Sammy snorted. "I've been telling you since I was old enough to talk, your ability to annoy was going to get you killed one day."

"Gee, thanks, sis," I replied. "Grandfather also thinks if he steals my body he'll have a direct line to the Other Realm, which I'm guessing the Fey wouldn't like. But what worries me most is that the enforcers should have stormed in by the end to stop them."

"Plus," Sammy added, "that one Fury was invisible, not just glamoured. It had the help of arcana magic, or an artifact."

"Exactly," I said. "So at least one arcana with power and influence helped them. And someone is keeping the whole thing secret so people don't start pulling on threads that lead to the Arcanites. Which means the Arcanites really do still have power within the ARC."

"Can't gnomes get you anything you want?" Dawn asked. "So maybe they stole these Furies an invisibility cloak or whatever?"

"Gnomes wouldn't do that," I said. "They may operate a black market of sorts, but the ARC allows it because it's useful to arcana. If the gnomes ever did anything to cross the line and supply weapons or dangerous artifacts to the Fey or other brightbloods—" I shook my head.

Dawn said, "Those Fey Forest of Doominess jerks, they have a pretty big grudge against you, right? Maybe they are behind all this."

I sighed. "I don't know. Someone tried to manipulate the Forest of Shadows and the Silver Court into war, in the Other Realm *and* in our world.. It didn't add up that the Arcanites could influence things in the Other Realm, or that the Fey could have such influence in our world. But if they were working together—"

"This is crazy," Sammy said. "The Arcanites want to wipe out the Fey. Why would any Fey work with them?"

"Exactly! I don't know," I said. "Probably, each thinks the other side are suckers and plan an oh-so-surprising betrayal. In fact, I think the Fury attack today was maybe the start of that."

That sounds likely indeed, Alynon said in a voice that sounded like a yawn.

Well, look who's rejoined the party. Enjoy your nap?

Did you enjoy the protection I won you with the amulet?

Crap. Yes. Sorry, thank you. I'm not used to you actually helping.

Well, 'twould have served me little for you to get us both killed.

Fair enough. So, any thoughts on who might be working with the Arcanites?

No.

I waited for more, but Alynon remained silent. I sighed. If only I could compel him to speak the way I could compel a human spirit to.

That thought caused another worry to bubble up to the surface. Why had I not been able to summon the spirit of the Fury's host?

Hey, Drop Dead Fred, I thought at Alynon. *Do you think it's possible the brightbloods, or at least the Furies, have some way of protecting against my necromancy now?*

Anything is possible, but that is unlikely.

Because? I prompted.

*Because, should our vassals have some true means to protect against arcana magics, then there are many who would soon rebel against the order of the PAX."

What about that tattoo you put in my nether region? I asked.

At some point during my exile, Alynon had somehow added a tattoo to my body, hidden inside my butt cheeks.

Among arcana, wizards used tattoos to express their magic, replacing wands and scrolls as the wizard's method of choice for storing the form and potential of spells. They were totally rad. Think of the most awesome spells in any game or movie such as lightning bolts, fireballs, stoneskin, even stinking cloud, those are the kinds of things a wizard could do.

Way cooler than manipulating spiritual energy or talking to dead people.

But even though I in theory had the wizard's gift in my blood, my strongest gift by far was necromancy. ARC Law forbade me even a single wizard tattoo as a necromancer, for fear that I might use my necromancy to drain magic from others as fuel for my tattoo, or summon up dead arch-wizards to learn their most powerful spells.

Yet I had a tattoo after all.

Alynon's Fey butt tattoo summoned up a shield of sorts that absorbed magical energy attacks directed at me—shoot a fireball my way, and the tattoo would gobble up the energy and then spit it right back at you. Unfortunately, I had no conscious control over it.

Not that I was complaining, exactly. Having a defense against energy attacks didn't suck. I just wished I knew more about it.

*What *about* the tattoo?* Alynon asked warily. He had refused to discuss its origin or purpose. And unless I wanted to be stuck in ARC quarantine or to undergo butt cheek replacement surgery, I couldn't ask anyone for help in figuring it out.

You don't think the brightbloods maybe have developed something that protects against arcana summoning the way your tattoo protects against energy attacks?

Very doubtful, Alynon responded, and after a couple of seconds it was clear he wouldn't elaborate. Not that he would tell me anyway, I realized. As far as sides went, he was strictly on the Fey's.

I realized the others had been speaking, and I'd missed several comments.

"What?" I asked.

"I just want to go home," Mattie said. "I called Dad, told him what happened. He's activated the house wards and said he'd be ready for us."

"Good thinking," I said. Once again, Mattie had shown herself to be way more organized than I could ever hope to be, even after all that had happened to her. Though her extreme self-reliance and organization had begun to concern me as much as if she were an unmotivated slacker.

The ferry's speaker system beeped, then a voice told all drivers to return to their vehicles as we were close to docking. We made our way down to the car in silence, each lost in our own thoughts.

And then I remembered what Reggie had said about checking my e-mail.

"Smeg!" I said.

"What now?" Dawn asked.

"I forgot something is all." I climbed into the car, and pulled out my phone.

I opened e-mail, and spotted a message from "AuntyEntity"—Tina Turner's character from *Beyond Thunderdome*. That had to be Reggie.

I clicked on the video icon inside the e-mail, and after a second a video began to play on my phone as everyone but Dawn craned to see it. Dawn watched my reactions in her rearview though as she waited her turn to debark the ferry.

From the running time code in the corner, the grainy quality, and the fact that we appeared to be looking down on the scene from the upper corner of a room, I guessed it was security footage.

The spare, concrete room had clearly been built as a necrotorium or alchemist's lab based on channels in the floor to drain bodily or other fluids away from work areas. But there were no necrotorium tables or alchemist equipment. In their place stood a single metal table in the room's center with chairs on either side, as I'd seen up close in interrogation rooms.

At the table sat a hunched man who appeared to have been severely beaten, possibly over a long period of time given the overlapping and mottled shading of his bruises and wounds. He shifted, and I saw that he wore one of the restraining collars put on brightbloods and Fey changelings to prevent them from using their magic.

A young Asian man hung from the wall by chained manacles. He didn't look damaged, but also wore a restraining collar.

The sound of a door opening, and three men entered the room from below the camera's angle. The first was Grandfather in Justin's body, though he looked much younger than when I'd seen him today. Deputy Dolph was with him in an official enforcer suit, and together they escorted an older Asian man I recognized as an ARC magus from my visits to the Snoqualmie ARC headquarters, but didn't know his name or department. His hands were bound, and I guessed the binding restricted his magic as well.

"There is your son, Jing," Grandfather said. "Or at least, the filthy Fey changeling who's using his body."

"Stephen!" Magus Jing said, and crossed the room to his son's possessed body.

Dolph moved to grab him, but Grandfather raised a hand and shook his head.

Jing looked back over his shoulder. "Why is my son chained up here?" He seemed then to really see the man sitting at the table, to register his battered state. Jing blanched. "What is going on here, Gavriel?"

So he knew Grandfather's real identity.

"A little experiment," Grandfather said. Grandfather crossed to the bottom left corner of the screen, working with something just out of sight. He began to chant softly.

A line of energy shot suddenly to magus Jing from whatever Grandfather was working on, and remained flickering in the air. And from Jing, it leaped to his son's body.

Magus Jing fell to his knees, his eyes going wide, and his mouth opened in a silent scream.

The Stephen changeling yanked at his chains. "What are you doing to me?" he demanded. His voice held concern, but not pain, or terror. The ritual had no visible effect on him other than his distress.

Grandfather ignored his question.

When the ritual finally ended, the lines of energy faded, and Jing fell forward onto his chest. The fall turned his head to the side, and I could tell he was dead from his staring, vacant eyes.

Grandfather swayed and put a hand to his head. He clenched his other fist, and steadied himself, then said to the bruised and broken changeling at the table, "Now, dog. You may feed on his memories."

"Thank you, master," the changeling said, and rose as though afraid something might strike his head if he stood too erect, proceeding in a slightly hunched manner to the Stephen changeling. Grandfather had somehow broken him.

"What is this?" Changeling Stephen demanded. "Whatever you plan, it is in violation of the PAX. Cousin, if you harm me, your Demesne will demand—"

The broken changeling reached Changeling Stephen, and placed a hand on his head. Changeling Stephen's eyes went wide.

"What—stop. Those memories are mine! Don't—"

Then both changelings began to scream, and writhe. Broken Changeling fell to the ground, twitching and howling and scratching at his face until fresh blood began to run down onto the floor. Stephen Changeling flopped and kicked and wailed against the wall.

And then they both fell silent. Dead.

"It works," Dolph said.

Grandfather nodded. "We can poison the very energy that holds them together. It will spread like a plague."

The enforcer chuckled. "Shit, we'll be able to walk right in over their corpses and take control of the entire Other Realm."

"And then, *we* will be the immortals," Grandfather said. "*We* will control the magic."

The video ended.

Everyone in the car remained silent.

Blessed Aal, Alynon whispered at last. *He must be stopped.*

First we have to figure out how, I replied. *And we will.*

We had to. Otherwise, Grandfather really would rule the world.

And that would seriously suck.

My Casio read 5:27 P.M. as we drove into the small seaside town of Port Townsend. The late-afternoon light cast the town in a rich amber glow, not that the town needed much help to appear magical. You couldn't throw a fairy without hitting a quaint Victorian home, castle-like building, or wild garden; and the thriving arts community and wooden boat culture ensured plenty of creative flourishes everywhere you looked.

Port Townsend's founders envisioned it as one of the biggest port cities in Washington; at least until the Great Depression, unfinished railroad connections, and a nasty infestation of gremlins killed that dream. But when most mundies abandoned the town, the area's rich and important magical history made it an ideal home for arcana. Then the town got revitalized with the addition of a paper mill, and around the time I was born there came the influx of wealthy retirees and ex-hippies. During my exile, the town had shifted mostly to a tourism economy.

I still felt unsettled by the changes, and occasionally groused like an old man about the good old days when families would gather down at the tavern for cheap meals, when most of the town freely bartered with each other, and when the arcana community, though hidden, nonetheless celebrated the great turning of the wheel and our unique culture together. But it was also nice that the town had jobs, and the ability to support itself. And in some ways, the focus on tourism had helped the town to preserve some of its uniqueness. If Waterfront Pizza or Elevated Ice Cream were ever replaced with chain restaurants, then I would know that Ragnarok must soon be upon us.

Mattie called her father again to make sure the coast remained clear at home, and I could hear Mort's annoyed tone vibrating out of the phone's speaker, if not his words. Mattie gave the thumbs-up sign, and Dawn drove to her own home, which stood next door to my family's. We all climbed out of the car, and stretched, then walked through the break in the hedge to my family home.

Home. I felt a weight lift off of me at the sight of the large Victorian house. With everything that had changed in the world during my exile, with all of the uncertainty about my future, and the enemies I'd somehow made, this old house was a solid piece of continuity, of peace and safety.

We made our way past Mother's wild and tangled garden, overgrown and grumpy since her death, and up to the back door.

Boxes had been stacked on the back porch while we were gone—boxes filled with my stuff. I saw my books, my game journals, my Commodore 64, Sega Genesis and Super Nintendo, my Star Wars alarm clock, everything.

"What the hell?" I said.

The back door opened, and Mort stood behind the screen door, his hand on the handle. He'd regained some weight and health since being severed from his tie to Brianne, his succubus "spirit wife." He once again resembled Leonard Nimoy in his original Spock days, though with way more product spiking up his receding hairline, and a fashion sense that reinforced the worst stereotypes of necromancers.

"Dad?" Mattie asked.

Sammy waved at the boxes. "What ass-hattery are you up to now?"

"Sorry Finn," Mort said, and crossed his arms. "But you're no longer welcome here."

6

MAN IN THE BOX

I fought the urge to check on my Commodore to make sure Mort hadn't damaged it, and instead stepped up to the screen door, anger building as I reached for the handle. "Damn it, Mort, I—"

My hand hit the house wards and rebounded with a firecracker shock, like touching a doorknob after skidding in Raiden's socks across Tesla's carpet. "OW!"

"Sorry if that hurt," Mort said in a tone that sounded like he'd been taking non-apology lessons from Jack Nicholson in *A Few Good Men*.

I just stared at him, stunned more by surprise than the wards. If you have never come to that place that fundamentally represents home and comfort and safety in your mind, in your dreams, in your heart, and found yourself locked out and unwanted there, I can't begin to explain the feelings that swirled through me.

"Mort, this is the worst time for a stupid fight," I snapped.

"Who's fighting?" he said. "Mattie, come on inside. Sammy, you're welcome, too. Finn, you can take your stuff over to Dawn's if she'll have you, though I think it would be shitty of you to keep putting her in danger."

I ignored the accusation and said, "Father's still out with Verna, I take it?" Verna was a thaumaturge like Father, a creator of magical artifacts, and they had been spending a lot of time together these past couple of months.

Mort nodded. "And Pete and Vee are out at Elwha, playing at being Vice-Archons with the feybloods."

Great. The timing couldn't be worse. Not only was I worried about them being in danger, but that meant there wasn't much I could do about Mort's decisions right now. Sammy had long removed herself from the family decisions, especially ones about the home or business. Mort was the oldest family member beside Father, and I'd pretty much signed over control of the business to him. I just never thought he'd actually kick me out of the family home.

How long had he been waiting for just such an opportunity, just such an excuse?

Sammy crossed her arms. "Who do you think you are, Mort? Father—"

"If Father understood anything that was going on, he'd do this himself. Finn's brought nothing but danger to our family."

Sammy looked at me, one eyebrow arched. "Most of that wasn't his fault. He—"

Sammy's phone rang. She pulled it out, and answered it. "Fates, where are—" Her face went pale, and she activated the speakerphone.

A man's voice projected into the evening air, "*. . . make us use force.*"

"*I don't understand,*" Fatima replied. "*Why am I under arrest? I've done nothing wrong.*"

"*We have evidence otherwise,*" the man said. "*For the last time, hold out your hands, or we will subdue you.*" His tone and orders made clear he was an enforcer.

"*Fine. But when my father hears of this—*"

"*What makes you think your father will protect you?*" the enforcer asked, and I heard the sound of metal clicking. "*When he has failed his duty to protect us all?*"

"*What?*" Fatima asked. "*Hey, what are you—?*" Her voice grew distant as she moved away from her phone. She must have set it somewhere hidden from the view of the enforcers.

"*Put the evidence in the freezer,*" the enforcer's voice said to someone closer to the phone. "*Make it look convincing.*"

There was the noise of people moving around for a minute, then the sound of a door closing, then silence.

Sammy stared at the phone, as if waiting for someone to announce it had all been a joke. But after a minute, the only sound was the soft mewling of a cat and what sounded like scratching at the door.

Sammy hung up her phone with a shaking hand, and looked at me. "You said she'd be safe." Her voice vibrated with panic.

"I didn't know—" I shook my head. "This doesn't make sense."

"You said she'd be safe!" Sammy said again.

"You see—" Mort began, but Sammy wheeled on him.

"Shut the hell up and let us all in, Mort, or I swear on my soul I'm going to kick your balls into the Other Realm!"

Mort skipped right past frowning to scowling, then said, "You don't scare me, Sam*antha*. You can't even touch magic without breaking out in hives, so don't—"

"Magic?" Sammy snorted. "I don't need magic to drain your bank accounts, destroy your credit score, and make you the poster boy for necrophilia in every search engine and criminal database ever. Don't fuck with me, *brother*."

Mort glared at Sammy as if prepared to engage in the most epic sibling staring contest ever.

"Dad!" Mattie said. "Please! Stop this!"

Mort blinked, and looked at Mattie. His shoulders slumped slightly, and he shook his head. "I can't, Mattie. You just have to trust me, this is for the best. Enforcers were already here looking for *him*." He nodded at me.

"*Now* you tell us this?" I said.

"What, like it's any surprise?" Mort responded. "I'd be more surprised if we went a month *without* you getting us all into some kind of trouble."

I had no good response to that, so I turned to Dawn. "Is it okay if we figure things out at your place?"

"Of course," Dawn said. "I'll, uh, go clean up a bit." A good idea, given that she tended to leave most things laying wherever they landed after being used. She looked up at Mort. "You're being an ass, by the way." She marched off toward her house.

Sammy said, "Fine. I'll gather whatever wards and weapons I can find," and pushed her way past Mort into the house. "And don't even think about calling it stealing, Mort."

"Good luck," Mort called after her. "Finn's already used up or lost most of them anyway."

"The ones you didn't sell off," Sammy retorted as she disappeared through the basement door.

Mort glared after her a second, unable to respond, then turned back to us and said, "Mattie, aren't you going to help her?"

"If I come inside, you won't let me leave again," Mattie said.

"You always were the smart one," Mort said with a tired smile, confirming Mattie's suspicion. "Finn, you know it isn't safe for her with you, please tell her."

I wrestled with my response for a minute, then sighed. "He's right, Mattie. I'm sorry. You are safest with your father. You can't come with us."

Mattie frowned, then threw up her hands. "Whatever." She strode into the house.

Mort waited until she had disappeared down the hall, then said, "How kind of you to permit her own father to care for her."

I ignored the barb, and looked down at the boxes holding all my worldly goods. "I don't suppose you got the Kin Finder back from whoever you lent it to."

"No, and even if I had you couldn't take it with you. It's family property, not yours."

"Which is why I still can't believe you let someone outside the family use it."

"What I do to keep the family business from collapsing is none of *your* business. You signed—"

"—control over to you, yeah yeah, I know. But the only reason I can imagine you lending it out was just to keep me from using it for my dating service."

"Not everything in the world revolves around you, Finn. It hasn't in many, many years."

I shook my head. "You really need to get over the whole Talker thing, Mort. I didn't ask—"

"Didn't I just say not everything revolves around you? As much as you try to make it."

"Fine," I said. "But Grandfather is back and he's dangerous. He's kidnapped Mattie before to use against me, he might try again. If I were you, I'd take her and go hide someplace he can't find you."

"If you were me, Grandfather wouldn't be trying to kill us at all," Mort replied.

I felt suddenly exhausted, crushed beneath the weight of everything that had happened these past six months since my return, wrung out emotionally from all that had happened just today.

"Mort, look, I—you have good reasons to be mad at me."

"You don't say."

"I could have spent more time getting to know you again, more time helping you with the business—"

"Not what I asked for," Mort replied, and looked behind him impatiently, clearly wishing not to have this conversation, but also unwilling to leave the door unguarded and unable to send me away.

"No," I admitted. "But . . . I am sorry."

Mort shook his head, then said in a slightly less angry voice, his eyes not meeting mine, "You know, for like a second there after you came back, I actually was glad. I'd been taking care of Father, of Pete, of Mattie, of the business—for a second I thought maybe it would be nice to not have to do all of that alone."

I took a step toward him. "You're not alone, Mort. We're family. Brothers. We used to have fun together, before my exile, remember?" Well, before Mother died at least, before Mort grew more and more distant and angry.

Mort blinked, and looked at me. "What the fuck does that have to do with anything? Look around! We aren't kids anymore! And if your idea of fun is to go running after danger every—"

"I didn't *ask* to be used by Grandfather," I said in a tight voice, determined to remain calm and friendly despite my growing irritation. "And I haven't been 'running after danger'! I—"

"Just stop with all the damn excuses!" Mort snapped back. "You always have a perfect explanation for everything you do, but that doesn't change the fact you've hurt everyone in this family doing it."

Tears welled up in my eyes. "I know," I said.

"What?" he asked, clearly expecting some different response.

"I know," I repeated. "But you don't even realize how much I never asked for any of this. I swear I've only done what I thought I had to in the moment, what I thought was right, to try and *protect* this family, to—"

"The way you protected Mattie today?" Mort said sharply.

"She is exactly why we shouldn't be fighting right now," I replied. "She's hurting, Mort. She needs her whole family around her right now, together."

"How very Mr. Brady of you," Mort said. "But I have some news for you, Finn. Her whole family is either dead, mad, cursed, or dangerous, in no small part thanks to *you*. So you'll excuse me if I choose to keep you the fuck away from her for a little bit."

I felt as though he had just gutted me. I hadn't realized how much Mattie had become part of my life in the past six months. And everything he said about our family hit me like lemon-scented *Aliens* drool on an open wound, burning right through to my heart.

And there, it burst into an intense fire of determination.

I was going to put an end to all of this once and for all, put an end to Grandfather and his allies, and to their plots that were constantly putting me and my family in danger.

"I really am sorry, Mort. And . . . okay. Okay. I'll stay away, until this is done. But when—if—I can stop Grandfather and fix all of this, we're going to have this conversation again."

Mort snorted. "That right there's your problem. You keep trying to fix things, keep trying to play hero, to make everything right. And instead, you end up making things worse, destroying . . . destroying lives." He choked to a stop.

I winced. "Mort, look, I know you blame me for what happened with Brianne—"

"Don't," Mort said, his voice going flat. "I'm way past done with the heartfelt talk. I just want you out. And don't go trying to make me look like the bad guy to Mattie and the others, the way you do."

"Screw you," I said, irritation springing back up in me like Sonic the Hedgehog landing on spiky childhood arguments. Who was *he* to keep judging me? This was the guy who'd conceived Mattie and made sure she was a Talker just to secure his position as head of the family, then neglected Mattie for his succubus spirit wife. "I'm not you, I don't use Mattie to get what I want."

Mort was through the screen door and shoving me, hard, so fast that I had little time to react, and I stumbled backward down the stairs, falling back onto my butt.

"Fuck *you*!" Mort said. "When you move on, I'm still going to be here, I'm still going to be Mattie's father, and I'm done letting you make *my* life and *my* job any more difficult!"

Mort turned without waiting for a response and strode back inside the house, behind the protection of the wards, then marched off down the hall and out of sight.

I stared after him, shocked at the real anger I'd seen on his face, at the fact that he'd actually attacked me, at the fresh tears that welled up in my eyes at his words.

Your brother is an ass, Alynon said.

Yeah, I thought back. Then, *I wasn't exactly perfect, either.*

And yet, well do I know the difficulties a jealous brother may create.

"It's more than jealousy," I responded out loud. I felt the need to talk with someone, even if it was a voice in my head. "Hell, Mort and me, we've been fighting practically since I was old enough to argue over who got to eat the last bowl of Cap'n Crunch. But we've always made peace, and even had fun together in between the fights. We're brothers."

You say that as though the word itself holds some greater meaning, Alynon said. *In my experience, it is but a word, a space formed of sound, empty but for what you *both* choose to place within it.*

"Well, I don't know what life is like growing up Fey, but Mort and me, we share a lot more than just blood. A whole history of good times and bad that nobody else shares. I just wish *he* remembered that."

I wiped at my eyes, and climbed to my feet.

There wasn't much I could do about this now. I would have to try and mend things with Mort after I dealt with the little problem of my undead grandfather trying to destroy an entire world and name himself King of Everything.

I grabbed a couple of boxes, stacking one on top of the other, as Sammy emerged with a reusable shopping bag weighted down with objects.

"The sword?" I asked.

"Mort wouldn't let me take it," she said. "And if he's going to protect Mattie, I figured he should have it."

"Yeah, guess so." We headed to Dawn's.

Dawn stood in her kitchen making peanut butter and jelly sandwiches. For someone who worked in a café, she had a very limited list of foods she knew how to prepare, or at least that she was willing to prepare. Desserts, that was a different topic entirely. But when it came to meals, the microwave was Dawn's best friend. That, and cereal.

"Thought you might be hungry," she said, and licked the peanut butter off the knife. "I know I am."

"I—yes, thank you." I still felt shaken by Mort's outburst, and wasn't sure what I even wanted to do next.

We gathered in Dawn's dining room around the table—after she moved a teetering stack of mail, a small amp, two empty Amazon boxes, and a collection of small bags from The Spice & Tea Exchange to clear enough space for us. Dawn and I ate our sandwiches as Sammy lifted a crystal out from beneath her shirt and pulled it off of the cord necklace, revealing a USB dongle on one end. She plugged the crystal into her laptop, and began typing furiously.

The Arcana Ruling Council had sorcerers whose job it was to manage all information related to magic. As such, they'd created a kind of hidden layer within the Internet so that they could freely mess with information, hide things, post a bunch of fake information, all so the mundies wouldn't figure out the truth about magic, or brightbloods.

But Sammy was able to use their own "Infomancer layer" to tunnel into their systems and steal real information.

As she typed, Sammy said, "Make sure your phones are

off. Probably want to remove the chips as well, just to be safe. Until this is over, we can't contact anyone via our normal means."

"We've got to—" I began, or at least I tried to. The peanut butter made it incredibly difficult to speak.

Interesting fact, peanut paste was first created by Aztec alchemists to protect against a dangerous water brightblood, the ahuizotl, who would drag victims underwater and eat them. The Aztec would keep a leaf-wrapped ball of peanut paste in a pouch, and if attacked would stuff the ball into the creature's mouth. The peanut paste, combined with the creature's unique saliva, created a delicious glue that distracted the beast and made it impossible for it to bite anyone for hours. This trick was later adopted by other arcana as a cheap and easy way to stop many brightblood creatures whose voices were weapons, such as sirens, sphinxes, and leshies, not to mention evil wizards. In fact, soda crackers were invented solely to increase the stopping power of peanut butter—combine the two, and you could render a creature completely unable to speak as you escaped.

I finally managed enough moisture to speak clearly. "We have to figure out how the Arcanites are planning to use that spell we saw in the video, and why they went after me, and Fatima, and Reggie, but not the rest of you. Until we figure that out, I don't know what we can do. Any ideas?"

Sammy continued typing as she said, "ARC files say Reggie was arrested for possession of a Medusa's eye, and that it was used to stone an ARC Magus to death. Anyone want to bet on whether that Magus was an enemy of the Arcanites?"

"Oh frak," I said. Either of those crimes meant exile, but together they could lead to execution.

Sammy typed some more, and her face didn't so much pale as went a kind of ashy color as she looked up. "They claim Fatima had a blood star, and vials of blood from a number of arcana."

My skin prickled with goosebumps. "So that was the 'evidence' they were planting in the freezer." Not good.

Blood stars were artifacts from a dark period of arcana history. When blood was placed within the five-pointed star, it would separate out to the five points proportional to the gifts in that person's bloodline—alchemy, wizardry, sorcery, thaumaturgy, and necromancy. Any blood left in the center of the star indicated the amount of mundy blood the person had in their recent ancestry. The stars were used by a sect of arcana supremacists to weed out those arcana with more mundy blood than magical, and either kill them or lobotomize their gifts away. Although that had happened hundreds of years ago, there were, of course, extremists who still adopted the sect's beliefs due to ignorance, misplaced anger, and fear—or to control others using the same—just like mundies who became neo-Nazis, Klan members, or shock-talk radio hosts.

It was something of a cruel joke or bold irony that the Arcanites of all people had used a blood star to frame someone.

"This is crazy," I said. "Why would the Arcanites go after Fatima? Is it to get at us somehow?"

Sammy shook her head. "I don't think so. Maybe because her father works in the ARC? I need to get more info, look for patterns. And we should probably find someplace else to lay low while I do. Unless you want enforcers busting down Dawn's front door and mind-wiping her?"

Her tone suggested my answer wasn't entirely obvious.

Irritated, I said, "Of course I don't want that." Patterns. Pete was great at patterns. And while a brightblood steading wasn't entirely off the grid in arcana terms, it would be harder to find us lost among all that magical energy. "I say we head out to Elwha, lay low there."

"Sure," Dawn said. "What could possibly go wrong? Last time you went out there, you got involved in a conspiracy to start World War Fey."

"At least this time I got involved in a conspiracy first, *before* going out there. So, you know, I'm getting more efficient at ruining everyone's lives."

"Oh, stop with the pity party," Sammy said, packing up her laptop. "But we really should get out of here fast, before someone comes looking for us. I can't help Fatima if I'm dead or in a damn ARC hole."

"Hey!" Dawn said, and knocked on the table. "Don't jinx us further."

Sammy rolled her eyes. "Mind if I borrow clothes? Just in case."

"No, come on." Dawn rose and moved toward the hallway to her bedroom.

Sammy looked at me. "See if you can find some insect repellent. And flea spray if Dawn has any. Never mind, we can pick that up on the way. The sooner we get out of here, the better."

"Actually," I said, "hold on one second, both of you, I have something for us." I ran into what used to be Dawn's father's den, where I had stored a few things in his old safe for just such an emergency. I spun the tumbler, and pulled out three wax figures inscribed with runes and filled with colorful liquid. The figures had been reshaped from wax candy bottles by an . . . unconventional thaumaturge in town, and then charged by me with residual spiritual energy from three of the bodies that had come through our necrotorium. They hummed in my hand with that spiritual energy now.

I rushed back into the dining room, and handed the bottles out, yellow, green, and the red one for me. Red anything usually tasted best.

"Just stick a hair on its back." I plucked a hair from my head, and pressed it into the back of the figure for demonstration. "Then bottoms up."

Sammy set the wax figure down, and shook out her hand. "This thing is burning with magic. What is it?"

"It will mask our spiritual resonance for a little while. Hopefully, that'll hide us from the basic enforcer scrying and location spells."

Dawn held hers up to the light. "So it'll transform me?"

"No. Just create a sort of second aura around your own." I looked at Sammy. "The vessel has magic to hold the energy within, but the energy itself shouldn't bother you too much, I hope. It's mostly spiritual, not magical."

Sammy frowned down at the bottle, then rolled her eyes. "I've drunk worse." She plucked and pressed a hair onto its back, then in a swift move lifted it up, bit off the head, spat that out and downed the bottle's contents.

I held mine up like a toast to Dawn, then did the same. Dawn shrugged, and followed suit, pressing a hair into hers then downing it.

The spiritual energy tickled going down, like swallowing liquid laughter. I could sense the spiritual energy, bound and given specific purpose by the combination of thaumaturgical and necromantic magic, spreading like an expanding cloud, pressing out through my flesh to surround me like a second, invisible skin.

"Delicious," Sammy said, crushing her bottle beneath the heel of her green Converse and rubbing her hand furiously against her red jeans. "Now, can we get out of here before the ARC comes looking anyway?"

I realized there was something I needed to get before we left. I couldn't risk it being left for the enforcers to find. "You guys go ahead with the clothes. I'll be right back." I gave Dawn a quick kiss.

"Sure," Dawn said as I headed for the door. "But if you're thinking of sneaking off to keep me safe or something, just keep in mind how long you'll live if you try."

"Uh, right. No, I just need to grab something from next door."

I hurried out and ran through the break in the hedge to our garden. When Mother had been alive, she'd shaped this garden into a magical landscape. In her long absence, it had become a tangled and thorny beast shaped by leaked magic and, at one time, the evil manipulations of my grandfather and his accomplice, Felicity.

I grabbed a shovel from the back of the house, and made my way to the center of the garden, to the twisted, dried husk of its heart.

The ground had been dug up around the base of the gnarled bush.

"No." Oh gods, no. I dropped the shovel and fell to my knees, and dug at the loose dirt with my hands. But I knew I would find nothing.

That's not good, Alynon said.

"Oh, thanks, I thought I might be overreacting." I rested my head against the cool earth with my eyes closed, and groaned.

This was where I'd buried the spirit trap amulet that held the captured soul of Kaminari, a crazed and damaged jorõgumo. In itself, that wasn't too terrible since I had killed her in self-defense, and to save the lives of several others. But the means by which I had managed it, that was most definitely a problem.

I was nowhere near strong enough, or skilled enough, to rip someone's soul out of their body by sheer will alone, even with the aid of a spirit trap. I'd been exiled at the age of fifteen, before finishing my basic necromancer training, and I'd missed out on twenty-five years of apprenticeship and practice. So in a moment of desperation I'd resorted to dark necromancy to stop Kaminari, consuming a spirit already in the trap to create a kind of vacuum that sucked in Kaminari's spirit in its place. Dunngo, the dwarf whose spirit I destroyed, had given me permission; but still, nobody would be thrilled to learn the truth—not the ARC, not Dunngo's fellow brightbloods, not my family.

There was, generally speaking, a zero tolerance policy when it came to dark necromancy. I might as well have announced to a group of young orphans that Santa wasn't real—right after eating his liver in front of them with some fava beans and a nice Chianti.

It had been foolish to hold on to the amulet. But it had felt even more wrong to simply destroy it, or to dissipate Kaminari's damaged spirit beyond the Veil and ward her against speaking.

I had hoped instead to find some way to help Kaminari, as a kind of penance for Dunngo, and repayment for the death of Kaminari and her sister. They had both suffered terrible pain in their lives, and both fallen under the manipulation of the Shadows, who hardly saw it in their interest to heal psychological scars or temper bloodlust. I wished at least once every night before falling asleep that I could have found some way to help Kaminari rather than end her life.

So for the past month, when I felt strong enough, or brave enough, I came out to the garden and sat here at night, talking to Kaminari's spirit. She mostly cursed me, and promised inventive tortures. But I kept trying, sharing stories of my own experiences, or of others who had done terrible things only to find happiness and forgiveness later in life. Perhaps those talks had been as much to convince myself as her that there was hope of redemption and peace. But I also hoped that eventually, just by showing her that I cared enough to keep trying in the face of her anger and hatred, that she might eventually begin to talk with me rather than curse me, and maybe later even find some peace of her own.

And now, she was gone, her spirit to be used for the Fates only knew what purpose.

I opened my eyes, and as I began to lift my head I spotted something. I might have missed it had I not been so near the ground, but my perspective, and the low angle of the sun peeking between the vines and leaves, revealed tiny footprints in the soil.

"Frakking gnomes," I muttered.

Gnome families ruled the black market of the magical world. Stolen goods of a magical nature always seemed to find their way into gnome hands—usually because the gnomes were the ones who stole them. If you needed an illegal magical artifact, or a legal one that was too expensive to get legally, you could put a note under any gnome statue and an offer of payment, and if the gnomes accepted the deal you'd soon enough have the object in hand, no questions asked.

I'd seen a Godzilla gnome statue the other day, and a whole yard of zombie gnomes. I had no desire to test what would happen if I placed a note under one of those.

Generally speaking, gnomes did not steal from arcana, as that would quickly bring the Arcana Ruling Council down on their activities. But there were exceptions. If the item being stolen was itself illegal, for example, then the gnomes had little concern of the victim complaining to the ARC and explaining why they had the item to begin with. And I had a... complicated relationship with the Giardani family, the most powerful local gnome clan. Their leader, Priapus, saw me as bad luck at best, and dangerous to his family's health at worst.

But Priapus wouldn't have taken the spirit trap on his own. Someone had hired the gnomes to steal it, someone with power and wealth, and more importantly, someone who knew of the artifact's existence.

Grandfather. It had to be.

I stood, and brushed the dirt from my knees and hands, and swiped at my forehead with a forearm, to dry it. I headed back to Dawn's to help pack before the enforcers returned, trying not to think of what purpose Grandfather might have for the spirit of a psychopathic spider-witch, or an artifact that could get me convicted of dark necromancy—convicted again, that is, and this time for real.

7

AIN'T 2 PROUD 2 BEG

It was an hour and a half drive to the Elwha camp. We pulled into the parking lot of the Elwha River trailhead just past 7:30 P.M.

The Olympic National Forest filled the heart of the Olympic Peninsula, its snow-capped mountains and wild woods a dream destination for campers, fishers, and hikers, and a perfect shelter for brightbloods.

The Olympic Mountains appeared neon blue now in the evening glow, and a light breeze caused the spruce and cedar trees to sway gently. It was all so beautiful, so peaceful, so removed from the craziness of daily life.

"Finn!" Dawn said, and I realized she'd called my name a couple of times. I blinked, and looked at her.

"Sorry," I said. "Ready?"

"Yes."

We grabbed our bags out of the back of Dawn's wood-paneled Dodge Colt. Dawn had her guitar case, and Sammy her laptop bag, and I grabbed the giant hiking backpack stuffed with clothes and supplies. We made our way along a dirt hiking trail to the viewpoint for the Elwha Dam, a small hydroelectric structure of concrete walls and steel tunnels that filled a choke point in the narrow river ravine. The giant power generators were silent now, however. Construction crews were setting up machines and barriers around the dam, their shouts to one another echoing off of the forested hillsides. In a couple of weeks, they would begin the work of destroying the dam and restoring the river.

We left the main hiking trail, and made our way up to a hidden path that paralleled the river, and I led us as best as I could remember along the brightblood trails invisible to the untrained, or in some cases unmagical, eye. A cool, moist breeze drifted up from the river, and a rich loamy smell rose from the dark soil of the trails and the mossy earth to either side.

"Youselves halt!"

Sal the sasquatch stepped out from behind a tree. He stood nine feet tall, a mass of muscle and red-brown fur, and looked much as one might expect a sasquatch to look save for the fact that his feet weren't particularly huge. They would be quite impressive on a basketball player, certainly, but for a sasquatch they were rather small.

"Sal!" I said. "Good to see you. I see your hair's grown back." Last time I'd seen him, Sal had just shaved his hair and spun it into steely yarn to wrap protectively around the tree of Silene, his dryad love.

"And you got rid of the boots!" Dawn added.

I winced, but Sal just gave a shy smile and shrugged. "Iself not worried anymore what otherselves think. I know Iself's worth."

I smiled. "That's great, big guy." I looked at Dawn. "The love of a good woman is an awesome thing, for sure."

Dawn rolled her eyes. "Do you want some wine with that cheese?"

Sal's blush deepened. "Iself am very lucky, is big-true."

"Ack!" Sammy said, and made a *puh-puh-puh* spitting sound as she swatted at the air. "I just ate a gnat. Can we end the love fest and get someplace indoors?"

"Right," I said. "Sal, we need someplace to lay low for a bit, where the ARC can't find us."

Sal's smile turned to a slow frown. "I cannot offer youself shelter. Youself must speak with Silene. Iself will lead you." He waved for us to follow and led us uphill, away from the river, along narrow dirt trails hidden by overhanging ferns, up slopes with tree root steps. The sun's glow faded, and soon we had to use our phones' camera lights to find our way through the denser shadows of the forest. Sal had little trouble despite his beady little eyes, sniffing his way along. We hiked trails unfamiliar to me, and Sal would sometimes give us warnings to walk around a spot in the trail, or to take a side path marked only by a cluster of stones or mushrooms or some other subtle marker.

We emerged at last from the dense forest into an overgrown clearing.

"Wow," Dawn said. "Not what I expected."

I knew what she meant.

We faced a hot springs resort, or at least what used to be a resort, with a large central lodge and sanitarium surrounded by a scattering of lesser buildings built on the site of the natural hot springs.

The resort had been built sometime back in the early 1900s, originally intended as a gift from an ambitious waerbeaver lumber baron to his new bride. Unfortunately, his new bride called the sulfurous smell of the springs vulgar and the trip to reach it barbaric, and demanded that her husband build her a mansion on the sea instead. The lumber baron simply wandered off into the woods never to be heard from again.

The Silver Court brightbloods reclaimed the land as part of a pact after the last Fey-Arcana wars. Given the fact that the Silver Court had allied with us during the war, the Arcana Ruling Council was willing to chase off all the mundies, erase public records of the place, and allow the brightbloods to put up magical diversions so no hikers would stumble across it by accident.

Petey had gushed about the place after the first time he'd stayed out here.

The most impressive building was the 154-room luxury hotel, with the first story constructed of massive upright fir logs surrounded on three sides by a spacious veranda, and a checkerboard of windows.

Behind the hotel stood a second large building, originally a sanitarium with state-of-the-art (for the time) medical equipment, including an old X-ray machine that Petey swore looked like a death ray. And spaced around those two central buildings stood a large bathhouse, cabins, worker housing, an ice plant, steam laundry, and a gymnasium.

The golf course, croquet grounds, and tennis courts had long been reclaimed by the forest, but hints of the landscaping still peeked out between the ferns and saplings.

It was an ideal setup for a bunch of brightbloods, providing most of the comforts of modern living but in the wilds of the forest, and far from the eyes of the mundane world. Though it was not without issues.

The buildings had electricity in much the same way that the *Poltergeist* house had personality—there was a good chance someone was going to be shocked or burned at any moment. They also had steam heat, and hot and cold running water, but as Don Faun had informed me before, brightbloods were hell on plumbing. Just because a centaur could use a toilet didn't mean it was necessarily the best idea. I wasn't sure they even made plungers for that job.

It also looked pretty run down. Any paint had long worn away and many of the windows were boarded over. I spotted at least one collapsed chimney, and one gutted cabin had a tree growing up out of its center. Granted, a waersquirrel or dryad might love a nice tree growing in their house, but somehow I doubted it had been intentional.

Celebrating nature, furthering the interests of the Fey, and being stewards of the forest didn't exactly pay well. And while there was a brief period of time when many brightbloods found it easy to get credit cards—apparently even a faun whose only possessions are fleas and a healthy lust for life met the stringent requirements of some banks for a shiny new card (with interest rates that would make Scrooge McDuck blush with embarrassment, of course)—the ARC's infomancers quickly grew tired of having to step in and make the accounts, and the debt collections, disappear. So no more credit cards to brightbloods. Or their pets. Which meant trips to Henery Hardware were rare for these brightbloods.

Sal led us to the main resort building. The porch creaked ominously as he stepped up onto it, and he had to bend over nearly double to step through the door.

What had once been the hotel's lobby area boasted massive wooden pillars with gilt trim, and a river stone fireplace.

Hangers for what must have been impressive chandeliers now held simple bulbs strung from wires, the chandeliers long sold off.

But rather than a welcoming reservation desk, we found ourselves facing a low barricade made of heavy tables tipped on their sides and reinforced with stones. It created a nice kill zone inside the entrance, and a pair of fauns pointed crossbows at us from either side just in case there was any doubt as to the reason for the barricades. It was the kind of setup I might stick in a game dungeon, but didn't enjoy facing for real.

"Uh, hi," I said, raising my hands and stopping just inside the door, so that Dawn and Sammy remained outside.

"Theyself friends," Sal said, patting me on the shoulder with enough force I nearly fell to my knees. "Where yon is Silene?"

"And Pete," I added, rotating my shoulder.

The nearest faun lowered his crossbow, and said, "At the healing house."

Sal grunted acknowledgment, and motioned me back outside. I glanced back as we stepped down off of the porch. "What's with the barricades? Is that normal?"

"Weself must be fox-smart," Sal replied, and led us on a path around the hotel. "The shadowbrights have been on the steading, sneaky sniffing."

I frowned. "I thought there was a truce with the Shadows, after Silene won that duel with Barry and all."

"Theyself no longer seek revenge for the spiderbright's death," Sal's voice rumbled. "But theyself sense weakness maybe, and the Bright Lords and Ladies warn of war."

"Brilliant," Sammy muttered. "You brought us here just in time for a brightblood war?"

"It won't come to that," I said.

"How do you know that?" Sammy asked.

"Because," I replied. "If it did, Petey and Vee would get caught up in it, and that just can't happen."

Dawn took my hand, and squeezed it. Sammy, thankfully, didn't offer a snarky reply.

We passed several brightbloods going about their business. A centaur, two fauns, a woman who might have been a siren, or a nymph, or waer. I received courteous nods from those who recognized me from the events three months ago, when I had helped them in a battle against brightbloods pledged to the Forest of Shadows. I received suspicious glares from those I assumed, and hoped, were newcomers.

Sal made us carefully skirt hidden pits, bear traps, and clusters of deadly manticore quills. I caught movement on the rooftops from the corner of my eye. "Uh, Sal," I whispered. "On the roof—those are yours, right, not brightblood ninjas?"

"Theyself be Silverbrights," he replied, his voice taking on something of a growl. "Theyself will be getting a hard-talking. Should not be seen by weak arcana senses. No hurtfeels meant."

"None taken."

We reached the old sanitarium building, or "healing house," a basic two-story structure of gray wood that might have once been whitewashed.

The sanitarium entry was a simple room with wooden furniture, and double doors leading to the rest of the building. Garl the waerbear sat in a rocking chair in his human form, a ruggedly handsome Native American man wearing worn jeans and nothing else—I assumed to save the hassle of torn clothing when he transformed. He'd put on some weight since the last time I'd seen him, his belly now hanging over the top of his jeans, and his face a bit rounder. He looked up from watching something extremely fuzzy and wavy on a small black-and-white television that had an intricate metal sculpture of rabbit ears and wire hangers rising behind it like a schizophrenic's rendering of the DNA model.

"Garl!" I said. "How are you?"

Garl gave a puzzled smile and rubbed at his jaw as if waiting for the question to be translated by a Babel fish. Finally, he said, "I am good. Do you know this Ken Burns?" He waved at the television. I glanced in time to make out a wobbly picture of the PBS logo before the scene changed.

"Uh, no, can't say I do."

"Ah, too bad." He scratched casually around his belly button. "His movie about the Prohibition didn't say anything about the arcana fears of drunk brightbloods, or how Bacchus tricked—"

"Garl," I said, "we can't let the mundies know about brightbloods. You know what would happen."

Garl shrugged. "I know what you arcana say will happen. But I feel bad for this mundy, Burns."

My eyebrows pulled together. "What? Why?"

"Because I can tell the truth is very important to him, and there's so much he doesn't know. I know he can't show it in his films, but I still wish I could just tell him the truth. I like him."

"If you like him, then best if the Arcana Ruling Council doesn't care about him, right?" I said.

He gave a sad grunt of agreement, then perked up a bit as he said, "Did you bring any candy?"

"Uh, no, sorry. I was kind of rushed."

Garl looked sad again, and said, "Okay. Sal can show you in. I'm sure Heather will be happy to see you." He waved us toward the double doors.

Sal led us through the swinging doors into a wide-open room that filled nearly the entire bottom floor. Square brick columns were spaced every few feet as support, and there remained rows of metal-framed beds and lounge chairs facing the large windows along either side wall. Most were empty, but a few held brightbloods who looked sweaty and agitated, all being tended by a faun, and by Farquhar, a tall man with antlers on his head.

And in the near corner to our right, partitioned from the rest of the area with curtains, there were several chairs populated by brightbloods of widely varying ages, facing a chalkboard. In front of the chalkboard stood Heather.

Heather had been my high school crush, and the most talented alchemist I knew. And then, during my exile, she'd fallen in with my grandfather and his Arcanites. Granted, she'd done so to try and protect her son, who'd become Grandfather's new favored protégé, but the result had been the creation of a mana drug that the Arcanites used to enslave brightbloods to their will.

The last time I'd seen Heather, she'd announced her decision to become a brightblood as a means to avoid exile by the ARC and gain a chance at atonement, a chance to undo the damage she'd caused by curing the addictions caused by her alchemical creation.

That decision seemed to have done her some good. Gone were the pale too-gaunt features, haunted eyes, and aura of desperation. She looked tan and healthy, had put on weight, and her straw-blond hair was pulled back in a ponytail that didn't so much hang as explode out of its tie.

She was in the middle of a history class, apparently. "Can anyone tell me why the Feyblood Urban Resident Reduction program was enacted in the eighties? This is something that may have affected some of you, or your parents."

A young will-o'-the-wisp raised her hand, and Heather nodded at her. She stood, shimmering in the dim lighting, and said, "Because the mundy president put a lot of people out of their jobs and homes, and everyone was paying attention to all the new homeless people, and so the ARC was afraid the brightbloods wouldn't be able to hide so easy in the cities, and, uh—yeah." She sat down.

"True," I called out. "But puckish Robin, sir Billy, and Whoopi the Seer didst form a merry band to battle Prince Ron and his evil Sheriff of Trickeldown."

Heather looked over at the interruption, her initial annoyed expression replaced by a wide smile as I spoke.

"Finn! Sammy!" She walked past her brightblood students. "Holy Hades, it's good to see you guys! You too, Dawn!"

"Hey Heather," Sammy said, her tone more reserved than friendly. She raised her phone in the air, frowning at the screen.

I smiled at Heather. "You're looking good," I said, before realizing how that might sound. I shot a glance over at Dawn, but she seemed unfazed.

Heather harrumphed. "I've gained like twenty pounds! Granted, some of that was needed, but I didn't really think about the whole 'instinct to store fat for winter' thing when I let Garl bite me."

Dawn snorted. "Funny how they never covered that in sex ed, eh?"

"Hell," Sammy muttered as she turned in a slow circle, tapping at her phone, "I wish they *would* cover biting etiquette. I'd love to see how bad the parents freak out."

Heather glanced at the students, who were very clearly interested in the conversation, and said in a quieter tone, "Oh, believe me, crazy parents are one thing I do *not* miss about being a mundy school-teacher."

Dawn smiled. "You do look good though, Heather. A hell of a lot better than the last time I saw you."

Heather smiled back. "Thanks! You too. I think I've found the weight you lost. So what brings you fine folks out to Casa de Silver?"

My smile faded. "It seems the Arcanites are after us again."

Heather's face paled slightly. "Shit. Of course. They're like sharks, they can probably smell the blood in the water."

"You mean the Fey war that Sal was telling us about?"

Heather looked up at Sal. "Yeah. If the Fey are going to be killing each other, the Arcanites are going to want to help them along."

"This is all interesting," Sammy said in a tone of frustration, finally giving up on her phone. "But they took my girlfriend, and all I really want is to get her back. I don't suppose you have Internet?"

Heather shook her head. "We go down and use the Wi-Fi at the RV camp if we need it for any reason, but things are pretty primitive here. Relatively speaking."

The front doors slammed back open, and a dwarf entered. An elemental brightblood of rock and earth, the dwarf had a head, chest, and arms of granite mixed with colorful stones, which traveled on top of a moving mound of earth and gravel. The glimmer of life in the dwarf's obsidian eyes focused on me.

"You!" the dwarf boomed in a gravelly, female voice. "What happen to Dunngo?"

Oh, shazbasalt.

8

THE UNFORGIVEN

"Borghild," Sal growled in a warning tone, stepping between me and the dwarf. "Finn-mage is a friend. Heself fight to save Silene and I, and try to save your brother. Iself was there. Show respect."

Oh gods. Dunngo's sister?

Borghild slammed a fist onto the floor, causing the floorboards to jump. "Then why Borghild no allowed rituals for Dunngo? Something not right!"

"I—I'm sorry," I said, looking around Sal. "His body washed into the river. There was nothing I could do."

"No trust Gramaraye mage-men!" Borghild said. "If this one lies, Borghild will crush all Gramaraye!"

She rolled back out through the swinging doors, leaving a faint cloud of dust behind.

That went well, Alynon said.

An awkward silence had fallen on the room. Finally, Sal grunted. "Weself should go speak to Silene."

"If you really are cool with it," I said to Sal, second-guessing my decision to come here. "Not sure how much longer our spirit masking will hide us from the ARC, and the last thing I want is to bring a bunch of enforcers down on you guys."

"Not a problem," Heather said. "The basement is shielded from arcana tracking spells. If they're after you, then you should probably be down there anyway."

Sal didn't look happy that Heather had shared that fact, but he gave a grunt of agreement. "Iself . . . cool. Come."

Heather wished us luck, and returned to her students. Sal led us through a door in the back of the room to a hallway, and then into another room that look disused. The fading daylight glimmered through boarded-up windows, and light from the hall illumined a dusty table, broken chair, and empty bookshelves. Sal crossed to the middle bookshelf, and pulled on it. It swung out, revealing a doorway and descending staircase.

"Nice," I said.

"Yeah," Sammy muttered softly, "going into basements of abandoned sanitariums seeking supernatural creatures never ends badly."

Sal hunched over almost double to fit through the doorway, and eased down the stairs. "One at a time," he called back. As I took my turn, I understood why—the steps were smooth, seamless stone, easy to slip and tumble down. I reached the bottom safely and realized that this basement had not so much been built as carved out beneath the building, an addition created by the brightbloods themselves. When you had earth elementals like dwarves, I guess you didn't really need a hardware store or backhoe for some things.

The "basement" itself appeared to be a cavernous donut shape with the stairs in the center, and stone support columns spaced throughout. It looked like the Fortress of Solitude as designed by Batman, the walls a geometric puzzle of ebon and deep purple crystal. Black tourmaline, I guessed, good natural shielding against magical energies. Lanterns hung from the columns, burning bright yellow without any smoke that I could see, filling the space with a warm glow and causing the crystals to sparkle.

There were a few cots along the walls, as well as shelves stocked with supplies, and weapons—crossbows and bolts, spears, and swords. Brightbloods, even those considered "allies" to the arcana, were strictly forbidden the use of firearms or explosives. Still, the sight of all that deathiness made me uneasy.

But the uneasiness lifted as I heard my brother Pete say from somewhere beyond the curve to our left, "I don't think that's why the Fey made me and Vee Vice-Archons. The Archon made it very clear we weren't supposed to actually do anything."

A woman's voice responded, and I recognized Silene, the steading's leader. "You *must* take a more active role. We cannot rely on our Archon, that is clear."

A second woman's voice followed, softer but with a hint of firmness beneath: Vee, Pete's fiancée. "You don't understand. Just last week, Pete snapped at a young woman who didn't bring sausage with his waffles. She knew him, you see, and thought he was still vegetarian. Pete apologized, but he was up tossing and turning the entire night after, and the next morning took her a big box of chocolates. That's how much he hates confrontation. And I'm little better."

As Sammy and Dawn joined me at the bottom of the stairs, Sal led us in the direction of the voices.

"I know you did not ask for this burden," Silene said.

"But I believe the Aal has brought you to us in this time of need for a reason."

Pete said sadly, "Maybe the Archon just thinks nobody likes him."

"Nobody does," Silene said. "And for good reason."

"But maybe he started acting that way because he thought nobody liked him, and now nobody likes him because of the way he acts, and—can't we just invite him to sleep over here, get to know us? Maybe he'd like us if he got to know us. We could play Trivial Pursuit. He's a sphinx, I bet he'd like that. And I could make him waffles."

As we rounded the circular center, a table came into view with Pete, Vee, and Silene sitting around it.

Pete rose as he spotted us, a goofy grin spreading across my brother's round baby face. He stood head and shoulders taller than me, with the kind of naturally massive body that had made our high school football coach literally cry when Pete said he couldn't join the team because he didn't want to hurt people. Even with the changes the waerwolf curse had brought onto Pete, he continued to be the gentlest, sweetest dude I knew.

Vee rose beside him, standing nearly as tall. While I wasn't sure what the term "built like a ship" meant (and suspected it wasn't flattering regardless), she did look like she could have probably built, rowed, and even single-handedly destroyed ships alongside her Viking ancestors. Which again, like Pete, completely belied her gentle nature, a nature well-matched by her waersquirrel spirit. Well, gentle until you got her pissed off. In that and in most other ways, she and Pete were as perfect a match as could be.

"Finn!" Pete said. "What are you doing here?"

Silene rose last, with the grace as natural to her dryad nature as her green-streaked brown hair. She stepped around the table, her sinuous movement causing her green dress of leaves, grass, and cedar fronds to shimmer, and highlighting a pale silver scar that drew a line from her left shoulder down under her dress. "Indeed," she said, "and in our most secret chamber." Her tone made clear the unspoken question she aimed at Sal as her gaze shifted to him.

Sal blushed red. "Heather-bright told them where to find youself," he said.

I raised my hands. "I would never betray your trust, especially not when we are practically family." I nodded at Pete and Vee.

"And a caterpillar cannot fly," Silene replied. "But what is done is done. Come, and welcome. And Dawn, the woman who braided my hair and shared words of encouragement. You are welcome as well."

"Hiya, Silene," Dawn replied. "Still fighting the system?"

"I am fighting many things, unfortunately. It is good to see you, though again surprising that a mundane should be here."

"She's my girlfriend," I said.

"She is far more than her relationship to you," Silene said reproachfully. "Including a bard, if I remember correctly, and we are in sore need of inspiration and hope. I would love to hear you play, Dawn, and to learn more of you." She looked at Sammy. "And this one who looks like she wishes to weep?"

I looked over at Sammy, whose eyes were indeed red and teary. "This is my sister, Sammy—Samantha Gramaraye."

Sammy sneezed, a sneeze that echoed off of the walls and caused metal to hum in response.

Silene cocked her head slightly. "The name Gramaraye

has earned both curse and praise among my kin," she said. "But Samantha . . . are you she who fought against the unicorn Bishop Freedom?"

"Yes," Sammy said. I raised my eyebrows at her, and she said, "It was years ago."

"You defend women against both brightbloods and your own ARC," Silene added.

Sammy shrugged. "It's not their fault if they fall victim to the power of a unicorn or satyr. They don't deserve to have their memories wiped and their lives ruined."

Silene nodded. "You are one from whom I found inspiration. I am honored to meet you at last."

Sammy blinked, and wiped at her nose with the back of her hand. "I—thanks." She moved away from Sal. "You guys don't happen to have any kind of ionizing air filters around, do you? And maybe a bucket's worth of rose quartz?"

"The stone yes, perhaps, but I do not know what a lionizing air filter might be?" Silene replied. "Is this why you have come?" She looked at me.

"No," I said. "Sammy's allergic to magic, and I think she was just hoping to capture the free Mu particles in the air."

Sammy nodded, stepping even further from Sal. "If we're going to be down here for long, I'm going to have to dope up on Claritin, and that crap always makes me zonko."

"You're going to stay here?" Pete asked, excitement in his voice.

"That's up to Silene," I replied.

"What danger are you in?" Silene asked. "You would not seek to stay here without reason."

"True," I said, "but I think our danger and yours might be the same."

"What danger is that?" Silene asked.

"Sal told me that the Forest of Shadows are still making war noises. And it seems the Arcanites, the lovely folks behind the drug that you've been fighting against, are making some big move against the Fey as well. And they might be working together. Or at least, some group of Fey is working with the Arcanites, and perhaps manipulating the Forest of Shadows still."

Silene seemed to wilt a bit at the news, but then she took a deep breath, and stood straight again. "What is their plan?"

"To poison the Other Realm," I replied. "But we need time to figure out how, exactly, and why they are framing arcana for crimes."

"We need time *and* a decent cell signal, at the least," Sammy added.

A faun appeared from the direction of the stairs, and said, "Silene, a gnome brings a message for you, and says it is urgent."

"Very well," Silene said, "I shall be right there." She sighed. "Stay, visit with your kin, and we shall speak when I return."

She left with the faun, and as I turned back Pete nearly tackled me with a bear hug.

"I'm happy to see you," Pete said.

"Thanks, brother," I said with what little breath in my lungs he hadn't already squeezed out. But after my fight with Mort, the hug made me want to cry, and I was in no rush to escape it.

He released me, my heels falling back to the stone floor, and I smiled up at him. "It's good to see you, too, but it's not like we didn't see each other, what, the day before yesterday?"

"Yes, but that was only for a minute, you were going to that bonding ceremony."

"Ah, yeah . . ." One of the first persons I'd helped find

true love after helping Sal was a gentleman in the Department of Arcane Accounting, whom I'd connected with a local poet-sorceress burning through her trust fund. The two had enjoyed a whirlwind romance culminating in a bonding ceremony I felt obligated and honored to attend.

Pete continued, "And you've been so busy that I don't hardly get to see you, and—" he looked around as if someone might be listening, and then said in that loud whisper of his that could be heard just as easily as his normal voice, "They keep asking me to do things as Vice-Archon and I feel bad but I don't know what to do and . . . I just want to go home and things to be like they used to be." His eyes brimmed with tears.

"Ah Petey, I'm sorry, man. I didn't realize—tell you what, as soon as we figure out this current mess, it's going to be family time for me, one hundred percent. I won't leave your side."

"Well," Vee said, "that might get awkward. Pete's bed isn't that large to begin with—"

"Yeah," Dawn said. "Not that I don't dig a little variety and all, but that's not quite my thing."

"Ha ha," I replied, blushing slightly. "I just meant Pete is more important to me than most anything."

"Sarah says your heart is in the right place," Vee said, looking at the empty space beside her where she either saw or imagined her squirrel spirit, Sarah. "But I don't think there's much you can do. You cannot undo our waer . . . gifts."

"No, but I'm the one who got you named Vice-Archons. The Silver Court said they wouldn't expect anything from you in return for the titles. If they're asking you to do things for them now—"

"They're not," Vee said. "Not the Fey, anyway. But that

doesn't make it any easier to ignore what's going on."

"What's going on?" I asked.

Dawn laughed, and said in a singsong voice, "Twenty-five years and your life is still . . . trying to get up that great big hill." She grinned. "I never thought about it, but that's kind of your song, honey."

"What?" I asked, confused.

"Family sing-along time is great and all," Sammy said in an irritated tone, "but it isn't getting me any closer to helping Fatima."

Dawn raised one pierced eyebrow, but then said, "Sorry, Sam, I wasn't thinking. I guess Finn's rubbing off on me."

"Hey!" I said.

Dawn ignored me, and continued, "What were you going to say, Petey?"

Pete had hunched in on himself as Dawn and Sammy spoke, and looked miserable now as he said, "The Silver Archon won't confront the Shadows Archon about what they've been doing, and won't help Silene defend our steading, 'cause he doesn't want to look like he's provoking the Shadows. So Silene and the others, they're hoping we can do something, me and Vee."

"And that's only made things worse," Vee said. "The Archon must have heard rumors about the brightbloods coming to us for help, because he's begun to spread rumors about us, calling us ex-arcana who're just pretending at being brightbloods, willing to do whatever is easiest."

Pete blushed. "Maybe he's right," he said in a small voice.

Crap. "No, Petey, he's wrong. You didn't ask for any of this, but I know you. You always act from your heart."

Dawn rested her guitar case on the floor. "What is a Vice-

Archon *supposed* to do?" she asked.

Vee shrugged. "The titles haven't been used in hundreds of years, so nobody's got a good idea what exactly we're supposed to do, or what the rules are."

"Exactly," I said. "They're just honorary titles, from the Fey perspective anyway." Titles meant to give Pete and Vee protection from being declared rogue brightbloods, while retaining some freedom from normal brightblood restrictions. I'd hoped they could continue to live a somewhat normal life. "You shouldn't feel obligated to do anything just because of them."

*Yet the Archon *is* a fool and a coward,* Alynon said.

This region's Archon for the Silver Court brightbloods, their duly appointed representative to both the Fey Court and the Arcana Ruling Council, *had* in fact turned out to be more concerned with holding on to his position and covering his ass than doing what was necessary to ensure the safety and well-being of his brightbloods.

"Well," Sammy said, "like most politicians, he's pretty much making his own fears come true."

La, it makes sense now, Alynon said. *I had wondered why my sister so willingly granted you such a boon, when it was most certain to cause problems.*

Yeah? Care to share your revelation?

Indeed, since you are too addlepated to realize it yourself. My sister must have known that the Archon failed in his duty. But she could not simply remove him, not when the Silver Court was already under attack and any perception of weakness or lack of trust in our own Archons would be undesirable.

"Of course," I said, understanding blossoming.

"Of course what?" Dawn asked.

"Sorry, Alynon was talking to me. It seems Oshun hoped that granting Pete and Vee the Vice-Archon positions would force the Archon to rise to the challenge, and fulfill his duties."

La. And should he fail to do so, then the needs of our vassals would be met by two who she believed to have compassion and courage most abundant.

"Great." I looked up at Petey. "And if the Archon won't do what needs doing, maybe you would."

"So what *should* we do?" Pete asked.

"I don't know," I replied. "But I feel a bit used."

Silene's voice rang out, "That makes two of us." I turned, and saw that she had returned with Sal, antler-headed Farquhar, and three militant fauns, and none of them looked like they'd come to welcome us as roomies or explain the chore chart.

"Uh, is everything okay?" I asked.

"You tell me," Silene said, and one of the fauns held out a hand.

A rune-carved mouse skull caged in twisted metal fell from his hand and dangled by a cord: the spirit trap that had been stolen from Mother's garden. The trap I had used to capture Kaminari's spirit, by destroying Dunngo's—by destroying the friend and clan mate of these Silver brightbloods.

"Where'd you get that?" my mouth said before my brain told me the question wasn't necessary. I knew where. Grandfather had hired the gnomes to steal it, and to deliver it here.

"It came with a message," Silene said, ignoring my question. "That you used this to destroy Dunngo's spirit in order to capture Kaminari's, and he can never return to the Aal."

"Finn wouldn't do that," Pete said behind me, anger in

his own voice now. "My brother is not a dark necromancer, and I'll beat up whoever says he is."

I winced.

Damn you, Grandfather, I thought. *I'm going to make you pay for this.*

I turned and faced Petey, put a hand on his arm. "Pete, it's true. But I can explain."

"What?" Sammy demanded.

Pete pulled away from me, the hurt of betrayal clear on his face, and I felt my heart drop. I turned to face Silene again, because it was easier. I saw that Dawn had palmed her Taser out of her pocket. I gave her a slight frown and shake of my head, hopefully subtle enough that only she saw it, then met Silene's eyes. "Dunngo asked me to do it, begged me to. Kaminari was about to kill you, Pete, and Sal. I tried everything to stop her but I just wasn't strong enough. I told Dunngo the cost, that I didn't want to do it, but—" I shook my head. "I couldn't let Petey die."

I could see my words held some impact for Silene, and she hesitated before saying, "If your brother had died, if we all had died, then we would have returned to the Aal, and been reborn into the next life. But you took that away from Dunngo. You destroyed him forever. That is too great a crime to accept, even if it was done in my name, or the name of those I care about."

"Silene, please," I began, but her hand sliced the air.

"No. I am sorry, but there is nothing more to say. Though you have done much to help my clan, we know well the stories of dark necromancers, and have suffered much from the acts of your own grandfather. I cannot allow you on Silver Court grounds any longer. Return without invitation, and it will mean your death. Now take your cursed amulet with you, and leave."

The faun with the amulet held it out as though it stank like a dead skunk's colostomy bag, and stepped toward me.

"Is youself sure?" Sal asked Silene. "Not wise to give a weapon back to mage-men."

"Keeping it would prove even worse. And he would not risk the lives of all those here in a foolish attack, even if he were our enemy." She leveled her gaze at me. "Which I still hope he is not."

"I'm not," I said, my heart sinking even further at the cold looks that she and Sal gave me. After all we'd been through, it felt nearly as bad as losing family. Well, as bad as losing Mort, at least.

I reached out to take the spirit trap, and heard Kaminari's voice cackling from it, "Revenge is mine. On your bones they'll dine!"

I flinched back, but too late. My fingers brushed the amulet as it swung toward me, and there was a burst of energy like an ultraviolet camera flash. I felt Kaminari's mad jorõgumo spirit pouring into me, expanding my spiritual energy in a rush as it burned away to fuel a summoning spell.

The faun holding the amulet screamed.

His spirit began tearing from his body, pulled into the spirit trap, into the vacuum created as Kaminari's spirit was destroyed—as I consumed Kaminari's spirit, willing or not.

And I became more willing than not. I couldn't help myself. It felt as close to perfect ecstasy as I'd ever experienced, and my body welcomed it like a drink of water after days in the desert. My knees went wobbly, and I fell back onto my butt, laughing uncontrollably.

I realized that there was an easy solution, that nobody outside this chamber needed to learn about what I'd done to Dunngo. That if I consumed enough of Silene's little henchfauns, I would have enough power to make the rest of them do whatever I wanted. And then together, so perfectly united, we could surely destroy our enemies. I could keep them all safe. And wasn't that what they really wante—

Something hit me on the back of the head, and I slumped forward, falling into an abyss of mixed pleasure and pain as the flow of spirit energy abruptly cut off.

9

BEEN CAUGHT STEALING

I woke on hard cold stone, my head propped up on something soft. Opening my eyes felt like a bad idea on multiple levels, so I kept them closed. At least I wasn't dead, though the pain in my head and sudden wave of nausea made me think that sometimes, dead is better.

I realized that my head was not on a pillow, but on Dawn's legs. Not because I could feel them, but because I could feel her spiritual energy. I felt hollowed out, and dulled; but my body, my spirit, had a weird sort of lifting sensation, a yearning in the direction of Dawn, as if urging me toward her. I could practically taste her spirit, my body aching in anticipation of the rush of energy it would bring when—

I blinked up at her as she looked down at me, a worried expression on her face.

I raised my head to try and move away from her, from the pull of her spirit. I was still in the brightbloods' hidden basement. Dizziness made the crystal-walled chamber seem to spin though, and my head sank back down. I hadn't spotted anyone else I knew, just a couple of grim-looking fauns standing guard between the support columns. I heard one leave, probably to inform Silene I'd survived and was ready to be stoned to death. "What happened?" I asked.

"How are you feeling?" Dawn said.

"I feel like the Nothing has consumed my insides," I replied.

"Well then, Princess, let me give you a new name," Dawn replied. "How does . . . Ignacio P. Humpledinker sound?"

"I think it sounds like you're avoiding my original question. What happened with Pete, and Sammy? Why don't I have a bad case of sword-in-the-chest right now?"

Dawn sighed. "Well, for starters, the faun survived, though he didn't look good, otherwise you might be less alive-ish than you are now. But Sammy started choking and had to use her EpiPen—"

"Frak! Is she okay?"

"Okay, and pissed off. And—"

Sammy's voice cut across the chamber, "Pissed off doesn't begin to cover it."

I sat up with a moan and some help from Dawn as Sammy, Pete, Vee, Silene, and Sal all stalked toward me.

Gods, this was not going to be pretty. And I did not feel up to a confrontation just then, or defending myself intelligently. I felt irritable, twitchy, tired. But I had to try. I looked at Silene. "That wasn't me who attacked your faun. It was a booby trap of some kind, or—"

"We know," Silene said. "Your sister and brother have sworn before a luduan that there was power at work beyond your own. And even were you foolish enough to risk your own life to attack us, I still do not believe you would risk the lives of your family."

"I really wouldn't," I said. "I'd give my own life for Petey, or Sammy."

Pete just looked miserable and avoided my eyes, but Sammy said, "You idiot, you may have done exactly that. What do you think will happen if the ARC or Fey find out what you did?"

"Pretty much the same as I expected from Silene," I said, and looked at the dryad. "Exile, or death."

"For my part, it remains exile," Silene said.

I sighed. "I know I have no right to ask, but please reconsider. This is exactly what my grandfather—what Grayson—probably wanted." The truth of it hit me even as I said it, and I felt anger kindle in my gut at the full implication of it. "Why else send you the amulet? He's trying to break us apart so we don't work together to stop him." Was that why Reggie had been targeted as well? And it made me wonder too at Mort's sudden decision to kick me out, coming so soon after a visit from enforcers. Had they been Arcanites? Had they goaded Mort into that action? Son of a bitch!

Sal grunted. "Badbright mage-men not the ones who destroyed Dunngo."

The anger flared up, and I pushed myself to my feet, the sudden wave of nausea making me even more irritated. "Damn it, you were there, Sal. So were you Silene, and Pete. What would you have done to save your loved ones from Kaminari's torture? I saw you, ready to kill. So don't get all self-righteous on me now."

"Finn," Dawn said, putting a hand on my shoulder, but I shrugged it off violently.

"No. Most of you would be dead if not for me. You all tried to save each other. I just happened to be the only one with the power to do it."

Sammy said in a flat tone, "That kind of power never leads to good, Finn, you know that."

"Yeah?" I said. "So you're saying it would have been good if Pete died and that crazy jorõgumo had lived? You know what? Forget this. I don't need this hypocrisy."

I took two angry steps toward the space between Pete and Sammy, intending to storm out, but the cavern spun and I found myself on my knees, throwing up.

"Jesus," Dawn said, rushing to my side.

"Get Heather," Sammy said. "Please. I think he has a concussion."

As I passed out, I did my best not to fall face first into my own mess.

I woke to find Pete carrying me through the woods, cradling me on my back across his arms. Above us, through the dark silhouettes of tree branches and far from any city lights, the black of night was fuzzed out by the sheer number of visible stars, as if an irradiated Ally Sheedy had rubbed her hair over a black sheet.

I stared up at them in half-conscious blissfulness. Given the number of planets, it was a certainty life must exist somewhere else out there. I wondered if they, too, had breached the barriers between our universe and the Other Realm. In our world, the early Fey had taken their shape from the dreams, fears, and thoughts of the first humans who ventured into the Other Realm. What shapes might the dreams and fears of an alien take?

Then I frowned, trying to remember how I could have possibly gotten into this odd situation, floating along watching the stars, and whether this was another dream. But it was not. And memories returned in a rush—the spirit trap, the dead faun, Silene exiling me from the steading. Me throwing a fit.

"You're not going to toss me off a cliff or anything are you?" I asked Pete.

His face darkened. "Do you think I would?"

I felt like an asshole. "I'm sorry Petey. Just— Where are we going?"

Dawn's voice said from behind Pete, "Back to the car."

Sammy added, "And to a place where I can finally do something about Fatima, hopefully."

"You can put me down, I feel okay," I said. And I did, at least as far as the headache and spins went. I still felt like every cell in my body thirsted for more spiritual energy, the dull ache of it like exhaustion. And the hurt of Sal and Silene turning their backs on me, of my family's disappointment and judgment, came flooding back into my heart.

Pete shook his head. "Heather said to let you rest. So I'm going to let you rest."

"I don't want to tire you out or anything," I said.

"It's okay. You're not heavy," Pete replied.

And whether he intended it or not, I heard the phrase "you're my brother" after that. Tears welled in my eyes, but I blinked them away and just said, "Thank you. I was afraid you weren't talking to me again."

Pete stayed silent for a minute as he carried me along the dirt path between the tall fir and pine trees without any apparent effort. Finally, he said, "I used to think I was a waerwolf because you told me I was, back before I was one. And I told everyone you were not a dark necromancer, even though everyone told me you were. And then I found out that you lied to me about being a waerwolf. But then I became one for real. And then I found out you really did do dark necromancy. And—it's all very confusing. But it feels like you lie to me a lot."

"I know. I'm sorry, Pete. But I didn't do any of that to hurt you, or anybody. I was trying to help."

From somewhere behind Pete, Sammy muttered in her sarcastic tone, "So say missionaries and invading armies."

"And when they say that," I replied, irritation flaring, "it's because they're trying to get something, acting on some kind of master plan. I didn't *plan* on having to choose between destroying Kaminari or watch my brother be killed. I didn't plan to cause any of this."

"You never have a plan," Sammy retorted. "You've always had your head in the clouds, designing games, reading books—for jeebus sake, starting a *dating* service! Maybe if you paid a little more attention to what was going on around you, and *had* some kind of plan, you wouldn't just keep falling into trouble and dragging your whole family along with you."

"What's wrong with my dating service?" I asked, surprised, but before Sammy could reply, Dawn jumped in.

"I get you're upset and all, Sam, but maybe back off on Finn a bit. He's doing the best he can, and what's going on is not his fault."

"Whatever," Sammy replied. "Meanwhile, Fatima's in some ARC prison and we just wasted a whole lot of time thanks to Finn doing the best he can. Excuse me." She pushed past Pete, and a faun hurried to follow her.

As they turned around a bend in the hillside, Dawn said,

"She's just upset about Fatima."

"I know," I replied as Dawn pushed past us and sped up to talk with Sammy.

Upset was actually too mild a word. Sammy was one of the most even-tempered people I knew, dealing with most problems and crises with the calm of a robot. She thrived on solving problems, which is probably what made her so good with computers. So for her to be snapping at me and showing her emotions like this, she had to be near hysterical levels of upsettedness.

"I don't like it, either," Pete said softly.

"Don't like what?" I asked.

"The dating service."

"What? Why?"

"Before, when you were gone, me and Mattie helped Mort with the family business. But now, you're back, and I'm a—" his voice choked to a stop, and he squeezed my arm and leg where he held me a little too tightly. "And you have the special gift, the same gift as Mother, and you don't even want to use it, you act like it's bad, and yet you went and used dark necromancy—you should just be helping Mort more, that's all."

I didn't bother to tell him about Mort's kicking me out. That would only upset him more and, really, wasn't the point anyway. I understood why he was upset.

As a brightblood now—a being of our world merged with some form of Fey spirit—Pete was not allowed to have or use his arcana gifts. The Arcana Ruling Council had essentially neutered Pete's ability to use magic, and blocked his memories of his necromancer training. The PAX Arcana—

the truce between arcana in this world and the Fey of the Other Realm—had established peace between the two worlds, but that didn't mean there wasn't still a cold war going on, and constant plotting to gain the upper hand. A brightblood who could also use arcana magic was not something either side wanted, at least not openly and not without absolute certainty of the brightblood's loyalty.

So Pete had lost his magic, the magic he had grown up with and saw as part of his connection to Mother and Father and family; and here I was basically rejecting it by choice.

Gods, I was a jerk sometimes. I should have been more sensitive to that, but instead I'd been patting myself on the back for getting him named a Vice-Archon.

"Pete, I'm sorry," I said.

"You say that a lot," he said, sounding more sad than angry.

I sighed. "Yeah, I guess I do. But I mean it."

"Then help Mort. And save the family business. And don't do dark necromancy!"

I smiled despite myself. "The more you know," I said.

"And knowing's half the battle," Pete replied, a slight smile touching his face.

We marched the rest of the way back to Dawn's station wagon in silence. Once we reached the car, Pete lowered me to my feet and gave me a bear hug.

I squeezed his shoulder as we stepped apart. "Take care of yourself, little brother. Don't do anything you don't want to."

He shrugged, a resigned shrug, pulled a small cloth pouch out of his pocket, and handed it to me. I guessed it held the spirit trap amulet. Pete said in the saddest voice I'd heard him use in a while, "I don't think we can do what we want right now."

I pursed my lips. What could I say that wouldn't be a lie? In the end I gave what I hoped was an encouraging smile, then said, "Yeah. I guess you're right. Just be careful."

"You, too," Pete said, then turned and lumbered back into the woods, his footsteps heavy with his unhappiness.

Dawn put an arm around my waist as we watched Pete disappear into the forest, and I stuffed the amulet in my pocket. "He'll be okay," Dawn said. "He's strong in lots of ways. And he's got good people—or, uh, brightbloods—looking out for him." She gave me a squeeze.

"Yeah," I said. But I didn't feel any better, or less guilty for all the ways I'd hurt Pete, or failed to protect him, not only from danger but from all the things that had chipped away at his happy, innocent, caring nature.

"Come on!" Sammy said. "None of this is helping Fatima."

Right. Back to the fun.

Dawn drove, following Sammy's directions. Sammy worked on her laptop tethered to her phone, growing more and more agitated with each mile and each failure to get the information she wanted. Sammy had always been the type to go it alone, confident in her own ability to learn any skill or achieve any goal if she just used enough time and effort and the calm, even focus of a Vulcan. But at one point she made as if to throw her laptop out of the car window, and then slapped it back down on her lap with a loud "Aaaaahhh!" of frustration.

I knew better than to ask her if she was okay, or if I could help. I liked my head right where it was, and did not need it to be snapped off.

Though the distraction of having my head removed might have been nice right then, actually.

The low hum of the spirit trap amulet called out to me, and I finally pulled it out of my jeans pocket, feeling it through the rough cloth of the small pouch. The booby-trap spell had been interrupted when they knocked me out. I did not know if Kaminari's spirit had been destroyed, or if it escaped, but I did not sense it in the trap now. But the residual energy of the trap, and the memory it triggered of consuming both Dunngo's spirit and Kaminari's, brought to the fore the urge to consume a spirit, anyone's spirit, to feed my own energy, to feel that rush of power, of expanded self, just one more time. In fact, if Kaminari's spirit had merely escaped, I might be able to summon it back into the trap using the resonance of her residual energy within. That hardly seemed wrong at this point.

After all, Kaminari clearly still hated me despite my efforts to help her. She would destroy me if given the chance. And there seemed little value in allowing such a mad, damaged spirit to roam free, or even travel to the beyond. Wouldn't I just be passing this problem on to whoever or whatever waited beyond the Veil? Wasn't it better that I use her energy to do some good in our world, to make up for all the damage she'd done? If she were sane, and objective, surely that's what she would want anyway.

And my own spirit wanted it, so badly.

Dawn placed a hand over mine, the warmth and softness of it contrasting with the cold, hard amulet.

"You okay?"

I focused on her, on her eyes, on her touch, on my love for her. What would she think of me if I destroyed Kaminari?

What might I become, what might I do to Dawn, if I let this temptation consume me?

I enveloped her hand between mine, and forced myself to relive Pete's disappointment and Sammy's anger when they discovered I'd destroyed Dunngo.

And I remembered the memories that Kaminari's sister had shared with me, of Kaminari being horrifically abused as a young jorõgumo, of the horrors she'd witnessed. I had to believe there existed some hope for healing and redemption beyond the Veil.

I shuddered at the strength of my yearning, and handed the amulet to Dawn. "Here. Hold on to this, and don't give it back to me, even if I ask."

Dawn took it, and looked at it uncertainly, but didn't question me. She just nodded, and moved to put it in her guitar case, then visibly thought better of it. "I don't want bad vibes around Cotten." Cotten was what she'd named her guitar, after guitarist Elizabeth Cotten, one of her inspirations. Dawn put the amulet instead into her jeans pocket.

I closed my eyes and tried to meditate, seeking balance and calm, and to strengthen my will.

But my thoughts kept circling back around to Mort kicking me out, to Reggie and Fatima being arrested due to my grandfather's crazed cult, to Pete and Sammy and Silene and Sal and everyone else I seemed to have hurt or let down in some way. It was like trying to nap in the arms of your lover—while they struggled to carry you through the desert because you broke your foot kicking and spilling the last of your water in a tantrum. My guilt and hurt kept demanding attention.

I was jolted out of my semi-meditative doze a couple of hours later when Sammy said, "We're here." I glanced blearily at my watch. A little past one A.M.

Outside my window, a giant concrete troll leered at us as we cruised past.

We had driven to Fremont.

Fremont was one of the more quirky neighborhoods of Seattle. Self-proclaimed as the Center of the Universe, with signs pointing the direction and kilometers to other major points in the world and cosmos, it was filled with funky little shops and restaurants and artistic endeavors.

One of its primary attractions was the troll statue. Built four years after my exile, the massive concrete statue served two functions: the first, its publicly stated function, was to fill the space under the Aurora Bridge with something fun and positive rather than garbage heaps and sketchy drug dealers; and second, its less public function, was to commemorate the Great California Migration, when hundreds of gnomes, witches, unicorns, and other Shadows brightbloods, fleeing a mana drought, managed to blast a fairy path open from southern California to Fremont.

Thankfully for us, and unfortunately for them, the same reason that this end of the fairy path anchored here—the dense convergence of ley lines—also made this area popular with local arcana and brightbloods. No sooner had the California brightbloods emerged on this side of the path than a battle raged for the safety and soul of the area. The Washington forces nearly lost the battle due to a swarm of California ant lions. But a local bridge troll, immune to the creatures' bites, crushed the deadly lion-headed bugs and saved the day.

Since a giant troll statue crushing a swarm of California ant lions wouldn't have made much sense to mundies, the artists depicted him crushing a VW Bug with California license plates instead.

Sammy directed Dawn a few blocks past the troll statue and the touristy shopping section, and had her park across the street from the Theo Chocolate factory. I didn't know much about them except that Dawn called their chocolate true magic, but if they were in Fremont I suspected she was probably more right than she knew. Oompa Loompas and Keebler Elves didn't exist in the literal sense, but they weren't too far from the truth in some artisan candy factories.

Sammy led us cross-corner from the chocolate factory and through a pay parking lot to the side entrance of a basement garage. A sign declared it as ADD Motorworks. As we approached the door, she paused, and held out her hand for us to stop.

"The lady who's helping us, she's a sorcerer, but she's got a couple of . . . quirks. She's not so great with people, and so only talks with folks who can speak her language."

"Which language?" Dawn asked.

"You'll see."

Sammy knocked on the door, and after a minute, it cracked open and a young woman with jaw-length black hair who looked like Phoebe Cates's slightly mousy sister poked her head out.

"Hey, Helen," Sammy said.

Helen's eyes narrowed. "Are you really Sammy?"

"I hope so. I'm wearing her underwear."

Helen looked past Sammy at us, and then peered around as if we might be hiding a SWAT team in the shadows.

"Password?" she asked.

"Joshua," Sammy replied.

Helen nodded, and waved us inside. A Persona ID ring flashed as she did, holding an azurite stone, marking her as a sorceress, an illusionist like Kaitlin from BOAT.

As we stepped inside, the door slammed shut behind us, and fire sprang up between us and Helen, caging us in.

10

CONNECTED

The heat of the flames caused us all to flinch back, closing into a tight knot. Beyond the flames I got the impression of a garage with mopeds in various stages of assembly, and walls lined with cubbies that held parts and tools. But the brightness and heat of the flame wall made it hard to concentrate on anything except not being burned.

Illusions or not, it would hurt like hell if those flames touched us, possibly even kill us.

"Want to play a game?" Helen asked.

I looked from her to Sammy, and said, "Uh . . . the only way to win is not to play?"

Helen's eyebrows rose, and she looked at Sammy. "Is leet?"

"No, he's just a geek."

"Hey!" I said, then nearly coughed as the heat rushed into my lungs. Clearing my throat, I added weakly, "I'm not *just* a geek."

Sammy gave a noncommittal shrug, and scratched absently at her forearm. "He also hasn't seen any movie that's come out in the last twenty years or so, so you got doubly lucky."

Helen frowned at me through the flames, as if not sure

what to do with me. She looked at Dawn, and Dawn's Acolyte ring, and her eyebrows rose. "Girl's standing over there listening and you're telling him about our back doors?"

Sammy put a hand on Dawn's arm. "Hey, Miss Potato Head, I vouch for her."

Helen shook her head as if she'd just been tricked, and backed slowly toward the nearest open doorway. "You're fucking up my chi."

Sammy stepped between me and Helen, close enough to the flame wall that I could smell burning hair, and raised her hands. "Surprised that a girl with an IQ over seventy can give you a hard on?"

This oddly seemed to calm Helen down a little. She waved her hand, and the flames disappeared as quickly as they'd appeared.

I could see the room clearly now, with its curved bar-like counter to our right and a square metal table in the center of the room. It smelled of gas and chemicals. In the corner sat a red Nintendo cabinet that looked like a Star Wars droid and a Nintendo game system had spawned a love child. Two open doorways led to a back area, and I spotted a Ms. Pac-Man arcade cabinet through the nearest.

Helen eyed us suspiciously. "All of my filth is arranged in alphabetical order," she said, and waved at the old Nintendo arcade cabinet in the corner. "This, for instance, is under 'H' for 'toy.' "

Sammy waved her hand dismissively. "We won't mess with your stuff, promise. But I need the equipment I asked for." Helen began to get twitchy again, and Sammy quickly added, "A Sino-logic 16, Sogo 7 Data Gloves . . . you know the rest. Or at least, your version of it all."

Helen gave a single quick nod, and waved for Sammy to follow. She crossed the room, and opened what looked like an old iron-bound wooden door mounted a bit high in the wall. I spotted electronic equipment just inside the door, stacked along one side of what looked like a storage space that had pipes and levers running along its walls. Helen nodded sideways at the equipment. "We're sitting on the most perfect beach in the world, and all we can think about is . . ."

"Where I can hook up my modem?" Sammy replied, picking up the first item, a black box with several input jacks on it.

Helen nodded, and pointed down the nearest hall toward the back of the building.

"You're the best, Helen," Sammy said. "You sure the guys don't mind me squatting in their garage for the night?"

Helen shook her head. "So, what would you little maniacs like to do first?"

"Well, the beauty of the Gatekeeper system is that we can get in and out of the ARC like it's the public library."

"So it's both immoral *and* unethical?" Helen asked.

"Pretty much. We won't involve you, though."

Helen nodded, and climbed up into the narrow storage space, stepping over and around the equipment. She fiddled with the pipes and levers, and a hidden door popped open in the back of the space. I caught a glimpse of what looked like an old supercomputer.

Helen disappeared on the other side and closed the rear door.

"Uh . . . what was that?" I asked.

Sammy started to carefully sort and stack the equipment. "Helen was one of the sorcerers who helped develop the infomancer layer, before they figured out exactly how to interface their magic with the tech. Between using herself to test the dangerously flawed early constructs, and finding out how her creation was being used, it . . . broke her brain a little, I think. Now, she just likes to hang out here and help keep the infomancers in check."

Dawn's face took on that look she got whenever she saw a living creature in need. "That girl needs some loving human contact, not to be locked up with those dumb machines in a basement."

Sammy shook her head. "Humans aren't so great."

"We got our problems," Dawn acknowledged, "but I'd rather have a real live friend I can hug and have coffee with than some words on a computer screen any day. We're social creatures, babe, ain't no way around it."

Sammy snorted. "Anything bad you can think to say about computers is really just about the humans using them. Internet trolls, data collection, the infomancer layer, that's not problems of technology, that's problems of people being asshats and greedholes."

"Exactly," Dawn said. "And that's why having friends and loved ones is so important, to keep us from losing our shit, and keep us—"

Sammy rubbed briskly at her eyes and grabbed one of her neat stacks of equipment.

"Oh, shit sweetie," Dawn said. "Sorry. We'll get Fatima back."

Sammy just said, "Come on, there should be some food in the back. I can set up there. Grab some of this stuff, and be careful with it."

We hauled the stuff into the back area, and I blinked in surprise.

Classic arcade games and pinball machines filled the space.

"What kind of garage is this?" I asked.

"The kind they're turning into an arcade, from what I hear," Sammy said. "Though I question their sanity." She nodded behind us at the wall we'd just passed. I looked back, and saw a mural of Patrick Swayze's face floating in outer space.

"Are you kidding?" I asked. "This place is awesome!"

"You *would* think so," Sammy muttered as she began hooking up the various pieces of equipment to each other. She waved over at a mini fridge. "Fix me a mac and cheese while I take care of this, will you?"

"Yes, your majesty."

As I began to move toward the fridge, Sammy set out a large visor and what looked like a modified Nintendo Power Glove, then continued to set up and connect the various modules.

"What're those for?" I asked, resisting the urge to pick them up—Sammy did not like anyone touching her toys, that much hadn't changed since childhood.

"I'm going into the infomancer layer."

I frowned. "Normally you just do something fancy with Google. What's with the *Lawnmower Man* getup?"

"What I did for you before was just a simple data search. If there's a conspiracy going on, I'm going to have to get inside the Infomancer Core. These," she waved at the glove and visor, "will allow me to mimic the abilities of a sorcerer, at least enough to access the core and interact with its matrix."

"Uh . . . cool," I said. "But it uses magic?"

"Indirectly," she said, sliding a twisted gold headband over her hair. If the Borg invaded Final Fantasy and assimilated Rydia, she might wear something like it, with several inset red crystals and green microchips, and a cord dangling down behind her left ear. Sammy plugged the headband into a small black box now attached to her laptop. "I've found a way to route it through enough tech buffers that it doesn't set my allergies blazing, though I'll be needing some serious Visine when I'm done." She finished connecting all of the pieces together, and sat down. "Lesson time's over. Mac and cheese?"

I sighed. "Sure." I went to the long counter that lined the wall. A couple of silver beer kegs were stacked on one end. A microwave and a half-empty box of peanut butter and chocolate PowerBars covered the other. I opened the mini fridge beneath the counter. Sure enough, it had several boxes of Stouffer's mac and cheese in the freezer section. I grabbed one, opened it and popped it into the microwave as Sammy powered on her setup and slid on the visor and glove.

"So, what does it look like?" I asked. "Is it like Gibson's matrix, or—"

"Finn, I need to concentrate," Sammy said. "Go play some games or something. Keys are in the blue toolbox over there." She waved vaguely in the direction of the arched doorway between Swayze's space face, and an image of the flying Winnebago from *Spaceballs*.

I sighed. "Good luck." I looked at Dawn. "Play some doubles?"

Dawn moved to the microwave. "You go on, love. I'm hungry, too."

Sammy motioned with her gloved left hand and simultaneously typed something with her right as I began a quick tour around the room.

Smash TV, Street Fighter II Turbo, Ms. Pac-Man, R-Type,

Super Off Road, a Nintendo cabinet that displayed Gauntlet; a cocktail table–style JAMMA arcade game with Donkey Kong, Donkey Kong Jr., Frogger, Galaga, and Galaxian; and a NeoGeo cabinet that had several more games on it.

There was also a row of pinball machines that looked in great shape, including Baby Pac-Man, Indiana Jones, and Twilight Zone.

Their bright, pixelated displays and soft beeps, dings, and zaps were comforting. But I just couldn't bring myself to play them. I had too much weighing on my mind, and my heart.

I worried about my family and friends, and about the dull ache for spiritual energy that flushed over my skin whenever I got close to another person. I worried about how darkside Sammy might go if anything happened to Fatima.

"I found something," Sammy said, and lifted her visor.

I shivered, then said, "What?"

"I confirmed Fatima wasn't taken because of us. She was taken because of her father."

I frowned, and crossed back to Sammy and her pile of tech. "Because he's an ARC magus?"

"Yeah. And a real a-hole. But I've done some cross-checking, and it looks like there was a ton of arrests this past week, and most of the people arrested were somehow connected to someone in power at the ARC."

"That doesn't make any sense," I said. "If the Arcanites are targeting their opponents in the ARC, why frame relatives, why not just frame their opponents directly?"

"Blackmail?" Dawn asked.

"No," Sammy said. "If it was blackmail, the Arcanites would have framed them quietly, and held just the *threat* of arrest and exile over their heads."

My grandfather had sent me into exile originally so that he could draw raw magic out of the Other Realm through our spiritual bond, in order to fuel his immortality. But if the Arcanites were trying something similar on a large scale, they would be sending their own relatives into exile, not the relatives of their enemies.

"Are you sure Fatima's father isn't an Arcanite?" I asked.

"He's a big enough jerk, but as much as I dislike him for the way he treated Fatima, I'd have to say no. You weren't around for it, but for a while there the ARC's Department of Education went off the rails worse than Texas and Kansas combined. Only instead of pretending science and safe sex were dangerous myths, they tried to whitewash arcana history and push an official view of the Fey as non-sentient."

"That probably made the Arcanites happy," I said.

"Yeah, well, Fatima's father was one of those who fought back against it. He made this big speech that made him popular for a while, about how only by pushing out into the uncomfortable unknown would we continue to grow, yadda yadda. Real Captain Kirk shit."

"And that worked?" I asked.

Sammy snorted. "That, and he pointed out that while we were raising ignorant arcana, the Fey and feybloods wouldn't be flinching from the truth, and that would give them an advantage in developing future magics more powerful than ours."

Indeed, Alynon said. *Many Demesnes considered secretly lending what support we could to such self-imposed ignorance on your part. But ignorant enemies are . . . unpredictable. And the Silver Court threatened to treat such education as a violation of the PAX Arcana, since declaring us non-sentient would make any treaty with us meaningless."

Ah. Now, that *I can see making an impact on the ARC,* I thought back. The ARC would want to avoid anything that threatened their trade for raw magical energy with the Other Realm.

"So, Fatima's father's not an Arcanite then," I agreed. "But why would the Arcanites send the relatives of their *enemies* into exile?"

Dawn licked her fork, and said, "They're certainly not doing it to teach the Other Realm to sing, and buy the Fey a Coke." She set a finished Mac next to Sammy, and began prepping a new one for herself.

"The video," Sammy said. "From Reggie."

Smeg. "They are going to poison the Other Realm somehow through the connection between the people they've arrested and their relatives." That had to be it.

The leather VR glove creaked as Sammy's hand clenched into a tight fist. "That bastard is not going to use Fatima for anything."

I frowned, thinking. "In the video, Grandfather used changelings for his spell. Which means the Arcanites probably have to spiritually exile all of the prisoners first, make them all changelings to create a connection to the Other Realm for the spell to work."

We have set up barriers against such attacks, Alynon said. *After Verona's spirit bomb.*

Katherine Verona had sent her daughter into the Other Realm, and used the connection between them to close the breaches between worlds and stop a Fey invasion. Unfortunately, it had caused her daughter's spirit to overload with raw magic and explode like a nuclear bomb.

"They must believe this is different," I said, then remembering the others couldn't hear Alynon, added, "different from Verona's spell, that it will get through any barriers somehow."

Sammy gave a grunt of agreement. "We need to find where they're keeping Fatima, and stop them from sending her, and the others, into the Other Realm if it isn't too late. That's the first thing we can do." She slid the visor back over her eyes, and waved in the direction of the shelves. "Turn on the radio, will you? Helps me concentrate." Then she went back to navigating whatever virtual obstacles she saw.

Dawn turned on the radio, and tuned it to KEXP, the public music station, then pulled me away from Sammy. "Hey," she said quietly. "What's wrong?"

"What, you mean besides being hunted by a group bent on world domination, and realizing that same group plans to use people I love to commit genocide? Nothing at all."

Dawn touched my cheek gently, a comforting touch.

Then she slapped me gently. "You have worse things to worry about right now."

"Like what?" I asked startled, wondering what terrible thing I had forgotten now.

"Like how I'm going to crush you at pinball." She walked over to the Indiana Jones game.

"I'm actually not feeling in a game mood now."

"Since when? You're always in a game mood."

I shrugged. "This just doesn't seem like the best time."

"What else are you going to do? Stare anxiously at Sammy?"

Sammy grunted. "Please don't. That'd be creepy."

"Fine," I said. I grabbed the arcade keys from the toolbox,

and figured out how to add several credits to the pinball machine, then stepped back, waving at it. "Ladies first."

Dawn waved in return. "Age before beauty, booty, and brains, babe."

I smiled despite myself, and stepped up to the game. As soon as the silver ball began bouncing between the bumpers and rolling down toward the flippers, I was deeply engaged. The ball finally snuck between the flippers and disappeared. "Damn it!" I slapped the cabinet and stepped back with a groan of disappointment.

Dawn gave me a light hip check to push me aside, and said, "Let me show you how it's done."

As Dawn played, I watched her more than the game. Each and every day her beauty was like a revelation. The light freckles across her nose and between her breasts like a sprinkling of stars across a tourmaline sky. Her hazel eyes that seemed to have their own internal glow. That damned mischievous smile she flashed at me as she passed my score and kept going. I smiled back. And that was exactly what she'd intended, to make me smile, to distract me.

My love for her filled me like awareness after sleep, like the morning sun pouring into a mossy hollow and banishing the fog.

I gave her shoulder a kiss.

She waggled her eyebrows, but didn't look up from her game. "Hey, Dr. Jones, no time for love. I'm about to get a free ball."

At that moment the DJ said something that turned both of our heads to the radio.

"And here's a little something off the new EP coming out from Volvur Records, a local artist named Dawn Taylor. The song is, 'Godzilla Buys Swimsuits Too.' "

Dawn and I looked at each other, the game forgotten.

"Oh my god!" Dawn said. As her song began playing, her eyes widened and started to tear up.

I grinned at her. "Holy frak! I'm so proud of you. This is awesome!"

Dawn pulled out her phone. "I have to tell *every*—" she stopped, and her smile faded as she looked at the dark screen.

"Shit," I said as my own smile faded and realization struck. "Frak. I'm so sorry, Dawn. I—shite."

"What's wrong?" Sammy asked, not pausing in her work.

I put a hand on Dawn's arm and gave a squeeze, not sure she would want a hug from me just then. "Dawn's song is playing on the air, and she can't announce it or call anyone because—" I trailed off.

"Shite," Sammy said. "Give me just a couple of minutes. I think I've almost found the heart of this stupid web. Once I get what I need to free Fatima, I can help you post the news without being traced or—"

Sammy froze and seemed to go more alert at the same time, like a meerkat spotting a predator.

"Hey, you okay?" I asked.

Sammy replied in a grim voice, "The bastards laid a trap. A damn good one. I didn't even notice until now, but I think they traced me! Damn it. Stupid, sloppy, I was in such a rush—"

The room shimmered. Dawn and Sammy disappeared. The tables, moped parts and equipment became digitized, the objects becoming 8-bit glowing representations. The counter where the beer kegs, microwave, and fridge had been stationed became a conveyer belt carrying pies and silver barrels.

Several arcade screens flared, and with TV sci-fi sound

effects, three figures projected and expanded out of them until they stood fanned out in an arc before me as living, glowing neon creatures.

Donkey Kong hopped from foot to foot and beat his chest. Inky the light blue ghost from Ms. Pac-Man hovered back and forth as though confused for a second before his squared eyes fixed on me. And Sagat, the seven-foot scar-faced Muay-Thai fighter from Street Fighter, crossed his arms and laughed at me.

"Shazbyte."

11

WICKED GAME

I whipped the steel baton out of my pocket, extending it in the same motion. But instead of the blue glowing baton, a digitized lightsaber extended.

Alynon, are you seeing this? I asked.

Countdown, humanoid, he replied in a robotic voice. *Countdown, intruder!*

Great. Even my perception of Alynon was affected.

In a combined roar, the video game creatures charged.

I turned and fled.

The garage's two large rooms were connected by two halls, like a fat-ended Roman numeral II, forming a kind of mini-maze. If these creatures were as predictable as actual two-dimensional game characters, hopefully they would chase me in a straight line down the first hallway. It might at least choke them up and slow them down. If lucky, I could lead them in circles until I figured out what the hell was going on.

It appeared to work, at least to start. Inky floated down the hall after me, and then Sagat, and then I was into the front garage area. It too had been transformed into a smooth-walled digital room with stomach-height blocks and walls like a 3-D Pac-Man maze, and a smiley-face clock on the far wall. The door to the street was nowhere to be seen. Not that I would abandon Dawn or Sammy anyway.

As Inky emerged from the hall, I swung at him with the baton-lightsaber. Maybe I could take them out one at a time at this choke point.

The baton passed right through Inky as though he were, well, a ghost.

As my hand followed through and contacted Inky's body, an electrical shock burned my skin, and made my fingers spasm. The lightsaber fell to the floor, and I backed quickly away, retreating into the room's maze.

This all had to be another illusion. Wizards could shape magic into any potential, but could not alter reality. Thaumaturges could give a semblance of life to inanimate objects but could not create 8-bit beings of energy. Despite Inky being a ghost in theory, I sensed no spiritual energy from him, so these were not spirits summoned by a necromancer. An alchemist could probably make me hallucinate with some gaseous potion, but I felt clearheaded. Sorcerers, on the other hand, could make reality appear to change, make Sammy and Dawn appear to vanish, and create the illusion of video game creatures come to life.

Which didn't help me much. My best bet would be to sit down and try to force the sorcerer out my mind in a battle of wills. But I had neither the space nor time to do so, since even illusions might cause actual damage—as Inky had just demonstrated. The mind's power over the body and all that, damn it. Not to mention that any one of those illusions could be hiding a real person or creature.

*Lead on, adventurer . . . * Alynon said in the voice from Gauntlet. *Your quest awaits!*

I'm moving as fast as I can.

"Helen!" I shouted. "Is this your doing?"

I wove my way through the room's maze, trying to buy time to think of a plan.

A doorway flashed into existence on the wall to my right. Out of it stepped a young man, somewhat heavyset for his short height, with long, lanky blond hair. I recognized him—her—by her dress.

"Helen?" Whatever illusion I was in must be canceling out the illusions Helen normally used on herself.

"Don't try and bend the spoon," Helen said. "Instead, try to realize the truth."

"What?" I exclaimed as Sagat joined Inky in chasing me around the table-sized block at the center of the room.

"All that is visible must grow beyond itself," Helen said, "and extend into the realm of the invisible. You must—oh my!"

Sagat leaped at Helen and threw an elbow strike. Helen pulled back inside the maintenance room, slamming the door closed just as Sagat struck it.

So this wasn't Helen's doing.

I ran down the second hallway back into the arcade room.

Donkey Kong was trying to squeeze into the first hallway, blocking it now. I couldn't keep running in circles. I was trapped.

Donkey Kong turned to face me, beat his chest and gave an electronic roar.

Frak.

I reached out with my necromancer gift, felt for spiritual energy. Maybe I could sense the sorcerer. Or at least find

Dawn and Sammy and make sure they were okay.

Faint vibrations whispered to me seductively, but I couldn't lock onto them, couldn't distinguish them. Whoever was in my head—besides Alynon—had managed to confuse my magical perception as well.

Donkey Kong grabbed a silver barrel from the conveyer belt and threw it at me. I dropped into a low squat that killed my knees and made my thighs burn, barely dodging the barrel. If I had not been working out the past couple months, I probably would have had a face full of keg, or be collapsed on the floor. As it was, I wished for the thousandth time since returning to my body that being forty didn't mean trading aches and strains for better muscles and brains.

Inky appeared from the second hall, his cyan-colored sheet of a ghost body floating above the floor.

Crap. I had to do something to fight back. But what? If I couldn't find the sorcerer and stop them physically, I had to break through their illusions somehow.

I sprinted in the direction of the nearest arcade game. Maybe it was as simple as unplugging—

"OW!" Pain exploded in my groin as I ran into what I assumed was an invisible table corner. I almost fell down from the waves of nausea and sudden discomfort.

For those who have never experienced a blow to the testicles, it basically feels like when you eat a plate full of jalapeño poppers, washed down with a large creamy milkshake followed by several shots of hard alcohol—or rather that tight, nauseating, sweat-inducing pain that follows in your lower guts an hour or so later.

Except, you know, in your groin.

"Frak me!"

Inky rounded some invisible object and floated toward me, his large eyes shifting in my direction, as Sagat emerged into the room.

Donkey Kong lifted a pie, and flung it at me.

I lurched to the side. The pie smacked into Inky coming up behind me, knocking him back.

I continued as quickly as caution and my huddled limp allowed to the arcade game, and looked behind it, but it did not appear to be plugged into anything.

Sagat slammed his knee into the machine, and I barely moved my head in time to avoid getting it crushed between the arcade cabinet and the wall.

Smeg!

Bad move, Space Cadet! Alynon offered, helpful as always.

I made a desperate backhand swing at Sagat as I stumbled away from the arcade cabinet, just to hold him off for a second. He threw out a cloth-wrapped arm to block, and my fist was knocked aside by solid flesh hidden beneath the pixelated skin.

The sorcerer! He must be hidden inside Sagat! If I could find a way—

Sagat's kick sent me flying back to crash into a half-assembled light cycle.

I moaned, and rolled across the floor away from him. I pushed to my feet and continued to back up in a defensive side stance as I struggled to simultaneously remember my limited Wing Chung training and what I'd been taught in Arcana School about dealing with illusions.

Sorcerers weren't allowed to meddle in your mind without permission, and if the ARC did want to get in your mind they didn't want to teach you how to block their tampering, so my training in blocking sorcery was pretty limited. All I really remembered was that my own mind held the true source of these illusions, so I also held the key to defeating them. Real Yoda stuff. Very helpful.

Inky made his way through the maze of invisible obstacles toward me again.

Sagat shouted, "Tiger!" and threw an energy attack at me. I jerked to the side, feeling the heat of the fireball as it flew by—and was knocked forward to the floor as an empty steel barrel smashed into my left shoulder from behind.

Donkey Kong gave a mocking electronic bark of laughter and stomped his feet.

With my face pressed to the cool concrete floor, my body a mass of aches and pains, my magic having abandoned me, my entire life pulled out from beneath my feet, I considered just saying screw it and lying there.

I was pretty well done with life dealing me problem after problem.

But I was not alone in all of this. And if I quit, it would be on my terms, not because some bastard hiding behind a bunch of illusions beat me down. I hadn't let the Fey break me in all those years of feeding on my memories. I wasn't going to break now. Well, not as far as my will went anyway. My bones, they were a different matter.

I made some very manly whimpering noises at the pain, then crawled away from my opponents and back to my feet one more time.

I took a gamble and launched a front kick at Sagat. He sidestepped and blocked the kick, knocking it aside. But rather than turn and re-engage as my foot hit the floor, I kept going, charging at Inky. At the last minute, I veered away from the ghost as well.

As I'd hoped, Inky turned to my left and floated toward the corner of the room, obeying the pattern not only programmed into the Ms. Pac-Man machine but luckily into my conception of who Inky was.

Then I turned to confront Sagat. I had little confidence I could beat him physically—even if the sorcerer wasn't actually as great a fighter as Sagat, he could trick my brain into thinking he was—and I didn't trust Alynon's Fey butt tattoo to protect me from Sagat's energy blasts since they were likely illusions, not true balls of magical fire. Which left only one option I could think of. After all, illusions operated on something closer to dream logic than the rules of reality.

I squatted into a warrior stance, pressed my wrists together with my palms facing out, and shouted, "Hadoken!"

Nothing happened.

Sagat shouted, "Tiger!" and launched another energy attack back at me. I dropped flat to my stomach, letting the attack pass over me in a wave of heated air. Then I pushed quickly back to my feet.

Bad move, Space Cadet, Alynon said again.

I frowned. "Not helpful."

Chicken! Fight like a robot!

My eye twitched. Alynon and this entire situation *was* enough to drive me berserk. But as I dodged another energy attack from Sagat, and a pie from Donkey Kong, it occurred to me what he might mean by fighting like a robot.

I faced Sagat, squatted straight down, then moved up and forward in a rising arc, and thrust my joined hands forward again, mimicking the joystick movements needed for the attack. "HADOKEN!"

Air exploded out of the area in front of my hands as a blue-white ball of vacuum energy formed and shot straight for Sagat.

Sagat fell apart faster than *Ab Fab*'s Edina and Patsy at a detox clinic.

But no sorcerer waited beneath the dissipating pieces of Sagat.

Rather, Dawn stood blinking at me. In a frilly pink dress.

"What the—Dawn?" I asked.

"Finn? What the hell's going on. One second you were one of The Gentlemen trying to steal my voice—"

That was definitely Dawn. I rushed over to her and gave her a hug.

As soon as I embraced Dawn, a giant 8-bit heart appeared above us, and Donkey Kong gave a loud digitized growl of anger and flipped over onto his head. With an electronic trill of music, he melted down into the floor.

Dawn's pink princess dress disappeared, replaced by her own brown jeans and gray T-shirt.

"Can you see Sammy, or anyone else?" I asked Dawn.

"No," she replied.

"Damn it." Inky began moving toward us. Dawn followed my gaze, and startled.

"Is that seriously a Pac-Man ghost?"

"Yes, and it seriously might hurt us." I pulled Dawn after me and ran down the hall to the garage's entrance room again. It should be easy enough to keep avoiding Inky, but eventually I'd get tired or make a mistake, and I wasn't sure what—

"Intruder alert!" a robotic voice announced from above. "Intruder alert!"

The yellow smiley face clock dropped from the wall and began bouncing toward us.

Someone wasn't interested in giving me time or room to figure out what to do next. I led Dawn back up the second hall to the arcade room.

Warrior needs food badly, Alynon said in his digitized voice.

"I'm not that hurt," I said.

"What?" Dawn asked.

No! Red warrior needs food badly, Alynon repeated.

Did he mean literally? What food? The mac and cheese? Or—

I looked at Inky. It seemed ridiculous, but no more so than anything else that had just happened.

I dragged Dawn to the conveyer belt, praying there were no unseen obstacles between me—or my groin—and my goal. I reached the belt, felt the counter's edge dig into my lower stomach.

Aly, if you can understand me, and can see the actual PowerBars, I need you to take control and grab one!

Prepare to Qualify! Digi-Alynon responded.

My hand jerked up of its own volition—or rather by Alynon's control—and grabbed a pie off the belt. It transformed in my hand into an 8-bit candy bar.

*You're all clear, kid . . . * Alynon said, his voice winding down like a robot running out of power, the last word distorted and low.

I peeled open the candy bar wrapper to reveal a glowing bar that pulsed with white light. I took a large bite.

As soon as I did, I tasted chalky chocolate and peanut butter.

But more importantly, Inky turned dark blue.

Regardless of what Alynon might say, my mouth was not large enough to chomp a four-foot ghost. But I'd seen the Pac-Man cartoon, and in that all he had to do was remove the ghost costume from the invisible spirit.

I charged at Inky, grabbed a handful of digital ghost sheet, and yanked.

Inky flashed for a second, and then his eyes floated away to the far corner.

In the cartoon, whenever a ghost died, its eyes floated back to its master, Mezmaron. In this case, I hoped my deeper mind was aware of where the sorcerer stood despite the illusions, and had directed the eyes there.

"Reveal yourself!" I demanded in the direction of the eyes, as much an order of mental will as a request.

"FINAL LEVEL," boomed a digitized voice.

The ghost eyes faded, and an illusory Tron materialized in their place. He reached back, and grabbed the identity disc from between his shoulders. The Frisbee-like disc lit up with neon blue lines, illuminating his grin. "Give it up, Finn One," he said. "Don't make me bring in the logic probe." He cocked back his arm to throw the disc.

"Finn!" Dawn shouted. She ripped one of the digitized hubcaps off the wall and tossed it to me. As I caught it, it turned into an identity disc with neon red lines as Tron's disc flew at me. I grabbed mine with both hands and held it in front of me like a shield just in time to deflect Tron's attack. I flinched at the force of the blow as it rang through my wrists. Illusory or not, he had a heck of a throwing arm. His disc bounced off of mine, ricocheted off a wall and flew back to him trailing a tail of ghostly blue light.

I cocked my arm back, took aim, and threw my disc hard in a vertical slice at his head.

Tron raised his hand, and my disc bounced off of it and went spiraling away somewhere behind me.

"Surrender," he said. "Or face immediate deresolution."

"Screw this game bullshit," Dawn said, and charged at Tron.

"Halt!" Tron shouted.

"Dawn!" I called in warning.

Dawn ignored us both. At the same time, my disc zigzagged back to me, and I snagged it out of the air.

Dawn plowed into Tron with open arms to tackle him—but she passed right through him. As she did, she screamed, and fell to the ground, twitching and gasping for air. If her entire body had just suffered the kind of freezing shock I'd felt when punching through Inky, her heart and lungs could well be frozen—or at least, she believed they were. And she might not survive that illusion.

"Damn you!"

I'd thought Tron was finally the sorcerer, but he was just another decoy. Another weapon.

Tron smiled. "Your user can't help you now, program."

Finn One, Alynon's voice said groggily, *get your disc into the heart of the MCP.*

"I'm trying!" I said, and threw my disc at Tron again, willing it to break through his defenses, trying to believe that it would succeed, to make my will the illusion's reality.

Tron deflected my disc again, and threw his disc at me.

I did my best to spin out of the way, but the disc grazed my right side, and my rib cage spasmed in fiery pain as 8-bit squares of blood and cloth fell to the floor.

"Aaahh!" I fell to one knee. My disc ricocheted off of the nearby wall and flew back to me like a red comet. I reached up to grab it and nearly passed out from the rush of searing agony that flared out from my injured side. Tron's disc zigzagged through the air back to him, its glowing blue tail almost cartoon-like—which didn't make it any less deadly.

"There's nothing special about you," Tron said. "You're just an ordinary program."

"I'm also better than you," I replied.

Get your disc into the heart of the MCP! Alynon said again, frustration clear in his tone now.

"I told you, I'm tryi—" I blinked, and looked over at the Tron game cabinet.

All of the other games had been there in reality. But there had been no Tron cabinet before the illusion.

And on the screen, the small Tron figure was blasting away at a rainbow barrier as he tried to enter the MCP cone.

"Stop!" Tron said. "I'm afraid you—"

I threw my disc at the Tron game screen. At the same time, Tron threw his disc at me.

My disc struck the game machine just a second before Tron's disc reached me.

The illusions shivered, wavered. I saw a stocky man with a goatee holding his chest and wincing in pain, overlaid with the image of the Tron arcade cabinet.

Tron's disc shattered into a thousand tiny square bits as it struck me.

"End of line, asshole," I said as I charged at the sorcerer.

He fumbled at his jacket pocket as a wall of fire erupted up out of the floor between me and the sorcerer as a desperate, reflexive illusion. I plowed through the flames with barely a tingle and saw the sorcerer leveling a wand at me. I gave the sorcerer a front kick to the gut just as he had begun to speak the activation phrase for the wand.

He collapsed to the floor, gasping, and the illusions vanished altogether, the room and its contents returning to normal.

I snatched up the wand from him, then looked to Dawn. Her spasms calmed, and she sucked in a deep breath like someone emerging from a dive.

I scanned the rest of the room, but saw no other sorcerers. Sammy still sat at the makeshift desk, her left hand twitching slightly in the modified Power Glove, but she appeared otherwise frozen.

I kicked the sorcerer hard in the gut again so that he fell forward onto his elbows, retching. I rushed over to Sammy, and lifted up the visor.

Sammy's eyes were blank, staring at nothing.

"Sammy!" I said, and gently turned her head to look into her eyes. Still nothing. I could sense her spirit, but her consciousness was another question. I felt panic rising in my chest, but I pushed it down and marched back to the sorcerer, my empty fist clenching, the wand shaking in the other.

12

FREE YOUR MIND

The sorcerer sat against the black wall between two arcade game cabinets, his goatee quivering, and he waved one hand between us as if trying to push me away with the Force. I grabbed his wrist. I didn't know any fancy submission holds or anything yet, but I pushed him back, off balance, and said, "If you don't answer my questions, I'll rip out your spirit and compel the answers out of your corpse." A total bluff unless I was willing to use the spirit trap and more dark necromancy to do so. A terrible idea on several levels. Though if it meant saving Sammy's mind—

The sorcerer shook his head. "Anything you can do to me, your grandfather can do far worse." He clearly tried to utter that bad TV dialogue with something like conviction, but his voice wavered uncertainly.

"What happened to my sister?" I demanded.

He pressed his lips together and looked away.

I summoned his spirit, just to give my bluff some teeth.

Or at least, I tried. It was like trying to grasp a beam of light. I just couldn't hold on to the summoning.

Frak!

I kicked him in the gut one more time.

When he was done gasping, I shouted, "What happened to my sister, damn it!"

"She was snooping where she shouldn't," he said, his words becoming slurred. "And now her mind is trapped."

Dawn stepped up beside me, her breathing still a bit raggedly, and put a hand on my shoulder. "You okay? You're not, you know, going darkside or anything?"

"I'm fine," I said, irritated at the question—or more honestly, irritated at the perfectly real need for the question.

"Go help Sammy," she said. "I'll keep an eye on Mind Games here. If he—"

The sorcerer gave an ape-like grunt, and waved at Dawn. "Want!" He stared at her.

"Excuse me?" she said.

Great. "He's in caveman mode," I replied. "It's a kind of mental backlash from using so much sorcery. His higher brain functions basically shut down for a while." Sorcerers who pushed too far could even suffer a complete shut down to the point where they basically forgot how to breathe, and died. "Don't worry though, that usually means he's too wiped out to actually act on any of those lizard brain impulses."

Your sister remains trapped, Alynon said in a tired voice, *and time is short. Mayhap you should end this sorcerer, and question his spirit.*

I'm not killing a defenseless man, or a defensed man for that matter if I can help it. And I wasn't sure I could summon his spirit regardless.

He would have killed you. And you can claim it was self-defense if you but—

Drop it, I thought. "If he starts getting too active, let me know," I said to Dawn.

At least knock him out to be safe, Alynon urged.

I'm not up for hitting him in the head repeatedly, either, I thought as I crossed to Sammy. As well as that might work in the movies, I knew enough from my experience in the necrotorium—and more recent personal experience—that any blow hard enough to knock him out might also kill him, or cause serious damage. And as much as I felt the burning desire to strangle the little mind weasel, I couldn't bring myself to beat a guy over the head repeatedly, not when he was just sitting there.

And, I realized, that was probably what Alynon wanted. If I killed the sorcerer, there was a good chance I'd be exiled for it—and Alynon would get to go home. Assuming we survived the current crisis, of course.

I moved to Sammy while Dawn kicked the sorcerer hard in the groin, causing him to collapse into a fetal position on the floor. She saw my frown, and said, "What? He looked like he was getting up."

I sighed, but didn't say anything.

I sat down next to Sammy. On her laptop screen, a glowing purple sphere pulsed within a cage made of golden bars.

My hand hovered over the keyboard for a second, then closed into a fist. I had no idea what to do, how to help.

Helen peeked out from the hallway, once again appearing like a young woman with a Cleopatra cut. She looked around the room, and then frowned at Sammy.

"Connection status?"

"Her mind is trapped," I said. "Some kind of infomancer spell."

"You're either a one or a zero. Alive or dead. She must become one on her own."

"Uh, okay. How?"

"She can carry nearly eighty gigs of data in her head. Gain data access."

I frowned. "So . . . we need to help her reconnect with her memories, her consciousness?"

Helen nodded.

"Can you share my memories with her?" I asked. "I can use those to lead her back to herself."

Helen shook her head. "Not my game."

Meaning she didn't have the mind reading gift. Damn. I turned Sammy in her chair so that she faced me, so that her eyes were at least aligned with mine even if they didn't seem to see me. I took her ungloved hand in mine.

"Hey, brat," I said, and tried to think of what I could say that would reach her. "Remember Fatima. Fight this, for her."

Helen said, "Insufficient data."

I sighed. "Okay. I— Sammy, do you remember when I first met Fatima? You two—" I stopped. That was just a passing moment. A great moment, but I needed more, to set a trail James Burke Connections style that Sammy could follow back to herself. I leaned back a bit, and took a deep breath. "I remember not long before I was exiled—so you were just shy of twelve going on bratteen—and Grandfather let me, Pete, and Mort each have a friend over for the day. Pete's friend, Amanda, was just a year older than you, and you followed her around all day, while she followed Petey around." I chuckled, and shook my head. "Poor Petey. He had no clue that she had a crush on him, and wouldn't have known what to do if he had."

Dawn snorted. "Like you were any better, chasing Heather around all day."

"*Any*way," I said to Sammy, "you and Amanda were in the cottage for a while, and then she took off. Pete was mad at you, Amanda seemed mad at you, but nobody dared ask you what happened because you had that look you get, that look that says the first person to speak to you would regret it.

"Monday, at school, pretty much everyone knew what had happened. You'd tried to kiss her. You beat the crap out of Darren V. for some joke he made about it, and got sent to the principal's office. Grandfather was not amused, and grounded you for a week. But that night, I snuck my TV into your room, and we stayed up watching old monster movies until the crying Indian finally came on, and you said, 'I'm never going to cry again, and I'm never going to fall in love. It's just stupid.'"

"Far as I know," Dawn said, "she didn't have any real girlfriends most of the time you were in exile. At least not while she was in Port Townsend, or that she ever brought home."

I nodded, and squeezed Sammy's free hand. "I'll bet if you hadn't found Fatima, that might have remained true. But I remember the first time I met her. It was Brian and Ernesto's wedding, with that horrible DJ. You refused to dance, the way you do. But Fatima sat with you, wiggling in her chair to the music despite the awful songs, obviously wishing to get up. And finally, you somehow hacked into the sound system with your phone and played some song that made tears come to Fatima's eyes, and you two danced. And not just danced, but she actually got you to take off your shoes and dance barefoot on the grass—that's when I knew you must really love her."

I felt Sammy's hand twitch in my own. Encouraged, I

continued, "Fatima is the only person I know who can make you smile. You. Smile. Laugh, even. And she doesn't do it with potions, or by beating up a lecherous unicorn, or offering you a new computer. She—"

Sammy blinked, and her left hand moved within the Power Glove, her fingers making a series of motions like a ninja focusing her powers. On the laptop screen, several of the cage's golden bars dissolved or drew apart, forming a gap. The glowing sphere flew out of the cage, and a second later, Sammy blinked and shuddered.

"Sammy?" I asked.

"The one and only," she said.

"You okay?"

"I'm Rocking the Casbah," she replied, then looked at me, and her tone softened slightly. "Thanks, brother."

"Of course," I said.

Sammy looked around the room, her eyes fixing on the sorcerer and Dawn. "We have to get out of here, now." She nodded at the sorcerer. "He was just responding to the alert triggered by my hack, but they didn't know who tripped it. I'm sure he reported us, and reinforcements are on the way."

"Where are we going?" I asked.

Sammy looked at the sorcerer. "How about we not discuss our plans in front of Mysterio over there?"

"Oh, uh, right. Are you okay to move?"

"I'm fine," Sammy said, disconnecting her laptop and stuffing it into her messenger bag, along with a couple of the components Helen had provided.

We left the sorcerer drooling on himself, and we all passed down the hall to the front of the garage arcade. Sammy and Dawn headed for the exit to the street, but I paused by the door to Helen's hideout.

"What about Helen?" I asked.

"She can take care of herself, trust me," Sammy said.

We exited, and made our way across the parking lot to Dawn's car. As we marched, I said, "So, where are we going?"

"I have to go free Fatima. You have to stop the Arcanites. Which, as luck would have it, involve the same thing."

"So you figured out where they're doing the transfer?" I asked.

"Maryhill Stonehenge."

I moaned.

"What's wrong?" Dawn asked.

"Gods, where to start," I said as we piled into the car.

Sammy leaned forward from the backseat and said, "First, we need to go to Green Lake. I have a friend there who can hook us up with supplies, and mask us from the ARC's location spells, at least temporarily. And hurry, before enforcers find us."

Dawn started up the car, and took off. Dawn generally drove responsibly to avoid any possibility of a police stop. But when in a hurry, she treated stop signs and traffic signals more like suggestions than rules. Only her preternatural sense for police cars and traffic cameras saved her from getting busted faster than Smokey and the Bandit in a Geo Metro. And those Air Force flight simulators that tested g-forces had nothing on the passenger seat of Dawn's old station wagon when she started whipping around corners and changing lanes like she was Automan. I waited until we hit the freeway and I was (somewhat) safe from being pressed against the glass of the passenger window before I tried to explain my reaction to the Maryhill Stonehenge.

"Did you know that Seattle is the only city to have officially mapped its ley lines?" I asked.

"Yeah," Dawn replied. "I remember hearing that."

"Well, there's a reason. There's a group of mundies—not the group who actually did the mapping, but the group behind that group—who suspect the magical world exists. And they view it as their sacred duty to watch for magic and stand ready to defend against it."

"Ooo," said Dawn. "Please tell me there's one girl chosen every generation to wield superpowers and stand against the magical forces of darkness? Because if so—"

"Um, no. The Gedai don't have any real powers."

"Jedi? Seriously?"

"Genuine Earth Druids Against Inhumans. Gedai."

"Ugh. I briefly dated a guy who thought he was a druid, but mostly he just liked to camp and take mushrooms."

"Well, these guys are a little more serious about it than that. Granted, they have their share of whackjobs, but I'd say the core group are at least as serious and organized as a good weekly gaming group."

"So what do they have to do with the Arcanites?"

"I don't know. But the Gedai keep on top of anything that might possibly be a part of the magical world, hoping to capture proof of our existence."

"I thought the Maryhill Stonehenge was just a replica, a bunch of concrete pillars?"

"Built over a major ley intersection, with crystals and runes at their heart that focus and direct the ley energies. They have real power."

"Of course they do," Dawn said. "When will I stop being surprised?"

"If the Arcanites *are* using Stonehenge Junior for something," I said, "then either they've found a way to hide their activities from the Gedai, or they've eliminated the Gedai in the area. Either way I think I know a way in."

"George the Druid?" Sammy asked, her face lit by the glow from her laptop.

"He goes by Merlin now," I replied, and nodded agreement.

"Whatever he's calling himself, think he's forgiven you?" Sammy asked.

I turned sideways in my seat to face Sammy. "I don't know. And not sure we have much choice anyway. So why Stonehenge? It doesn't make sense."

"It is a fixed portal spot," Sammy said.

"Yeah, maybe if the Arcanites were trying to illegally breach the walls between worlds I could see it. But they seem to have control of the ARC at this point. Why not just sit back and let the ARC send everyone over from the Snoqualmie facility?"

"Maybe they don't have as much control of the ARC as you think," Sammy replied. "Or they are afraid of backlash from the cubicle grunts there. I mean, if the Arcanites can arrest and send whoever they want to the Other Realm, what's to say you're not next, right?"

"Or maybe they need to do something special with the spiritual transfer that will create the link they need for the poisoning ritual," I thought out loud.

Sammy shrugged. "I don't care, really, as long as we stop them."

I moved to put a reassuring hand on her arm, but thought better of it, and just said, "We'll stop them, Sammy. We'll get Fatima back."

"Oh, I know," Sammy said. "And then, we're going to burn Grandfather's little asshole club down, once and for all."

Dawn drove us south toward the Washington-Oregon border and Maryhill Stonehenge. I rode in the front with her, and as the streetlamps and mile markers flicked by, I told her what I knew about our destination.

Maryhill was founded by a man named Sam Hill. He'd intended it to be a utopian experiment, to build a town perfectly situated between the dry heat of eastern Washington and the rainy coolness of western Washington and populate it with Quakers. In support of it, he became a pioneer in road building, and funded a highway along the Columbia River to the area. He was a man of wealth and vision who helped to shape an entire region.

Unfortunately, the land he bought was a bit too far on the dry heat side of the line for good farming or comfortable living, and no Quakers followed his dream.

He did, however, leave behind several monuments to his vision, including the river highways, and the Peace Arch between the US and Canada. The fortress-like mansion he had begun to build for himself in Maryhill he instead converted into a museum. And, of course, there was the Maryhill Stonehenge, a to-scale and astronomically aligned replica of the actual Stonehenge, dedicated as a monument to the fallen of World War I and Hill's desire for peace.

But that was not the whole truth, of course. It was not just Quakers, but arcana and brightbloods he hoped to bring to Maryhill to live together in peace. In that land between extremes, Hill had hoped to build a bridge to peace between our world and the Other Realm, and the Maryhill Stonehenge was to be the bridgehead—a portal not only capable of allowing spiritual transfers, but actual physical crossing between the realms.

But the wounds of the last Fey-Arcana War were too fresh, and the various factions in power too invested in the status quo to easily be moved toward true peace.

Also, summer in Maryhill sucked weather-wise. Stepping outside is like the heat wave of an opened oven hitting you in the face, more likely to inspire irritation than peace. And the land is all hills of brown grass, dust, and stone ill-suited to paradise.

Hill had originally been close to buying a much more ideal location west of Maryhill, with fertile farmland and a hill with quartz deposits perfectly situated both geographically and on the ley lines to open a portal to the neutral wildlands of the Other Realm far from any single Fey Demesne. But just as Hill was about to close the deal, he whipped out his whiskey flask and proposed a toast to the deal—and the uptight teetotaling couple who owned the land canceled the sale.

If not for that one impulsive act, who knows whether Hill would have ultimately succeeded in his dreams. Some have even suggested that it was actually an act of sabotage by agents of the Arcana Ruling Council, or some trickster Fey from the Shores of Chaos, that led to the collapse of the sale.

What can be said for certain is that distances in our world versus the Other Realm are tricky. While the distance in our world between that original property and Maryhill was not so great, the Maryhill Stonehenge opened a gateway not to some equally close part of the Other Realm wildlands, but rather to a far, dark corner of the Forest of Shadows.

And that, unfortunately, had been the last nail in the coffin of Hill's dream for peace.

"Huh," Dawn said. "Someday it would be nice to go someplace with you and not find out it has this whole secret history I know nothing about. You know, just so I can feel like I know something for real."

"Sorry," I said. "Maybe we can go to Disneyland when this is over."

"Wait, Disneyland is the most magical place on Earth," Dawn replied. "It's right in the tagline."

I shrugged. "There you go. No surprises."

Dawn punched me in the leg.

"Ow!" I exclaimed.

"Big baby."

"Speaking of magic," I said, "what exactly did you see back at the arcade?"

"You were one of the Gentlemen, from *Buffy*. And you controlled a bunch of those creepy Dig Dug dragons."

Which explained why she kept chasing and attacking me. For some odd reason, she'd always found the little green dragons on Dig Dug creepy, with their "empty eyes and tiny red feet." And she had occasional nightmares about one of the Gentlemen stealing her voice.

I gave her my version of events.

Dawn glanced over at me, and said, "You know what I find interesting about that?"

"My amazing skill as a storyteller?"

"No."

"My amazing skill at video games?"

La, Alynon said. *You mean your amazing skill at playing with your joystick?*

You're just jealous.

"Nuh uh," Dawn said. "It was that you were the bad guy in every match."

"What? No I wasn't. Ms. Pac-Man's the hero of Ms. Pac-Man. Mario's the hero of Donkey Kong. And if anyone's the hero of Street Fighter, I'm pretty sure it's Ryu."

"Sure. Do you remember that conversation we had—no, of course you don't, it's one of those memories of us that you lost. Well, in one of the many instances where I proved what an awesome friend I was, and incidentally the one time we tried pot together out behind your mother's cottage, I listened to you go on and on about video games and how the heroes were really all bullies and bad guys."

"Really?"

"Really. You gave me this whole crazy theory that Inky was supposed to be a shy ghost, who just wanted to get away from it all and felt forced into fighting Pac-Man to avoid being eaten."

"Oh. Uh, yeah, I guess I could see saying that." That fit his profile from the Pac-Man cartoon anyway.

"Uh huh. And you said that anyone who'd watched King Kong knew that humans were the real bad guy in that movie, and Donkey Kong was no different, and the reason there was a timer on each level was because if Mario didn't get the princess away soon enough, she'd realize DK was really the one she loved."

"Oh."

"Yeah. I'm pretty sure you believe Tron is the hero of

Tron, so no surprises there. But Street Fighter wasn't around back then, so I have no idea what your thinking on Sagat is. Maybe you feel bad for him or something? Anyway, I'm guessing you made yourself Ryu for some other reason than you think he's the hero."

I opened my mouth to ask what reason that might be, then closed it. I'd read that Ryu struggled with inner demons, an "evil intent" that if he let it take over would turn him into "Dark Ryu."

Did I really see myself as the bad guy? Or truly in danger of becoming "Dark Finn"? I *knew* the reasons why I had destroyed Dunngo. They weren't evil.

"I don't know," I said. "Maybe it was the sorcerer controlling my choices, and casting himself as the good guy."

"Maybe," Dawn said in a dubious tone. She reached over and squeezed my leg. "I'm just worried about you."

"Me too," I said.

"Oh? Do share," Dawn said.

I sighed. "I'm worried something's . . . wrong with me. Or broken. Or . . . I don't know. But my magic isn't working."

"It seemed to be working when you almost killed that faun at Elwha," Dawn said, and I could hear in her tone all of the fear and worry that she was holding back, how much that had disturbed her.

"That wasn't me, in any sense," I replied. "That was a trap, a spell set by my grandfather that just used me as a conduit. But when I tried to summon a spirit on my own, it just . . . nothing happened."

Dawn arched an eyebrow. "Well, from what I know about performance issues—"

"Can we not call it that?" I asked.

"—they're either physical or psychological. I don't know much about how you do the voodoo you do, but I know a bit about psychology—at least, I've read enough self-help books to deserve a master's degree in pop psychology—and you've had enough crap happen that I wouldn't be surprised if you're all clogged up in here." She rapped on my forehead. "And that's without having Aly ride shotgun."

I frowned. Magic required will, which was just a short way of saying mental and emotional discipline, focus, strength, and desire. For it to work, your mind, body, and spirit needed to be one. But I *had* wanted to summon those spirits. I'd been willing, I felt certain. "I don't think that's it."

Dawn shrugged. "The mind's a mysterious thing, my love. It may not want what you think it wants."

"Maybe," I said. But I worried about a darker cause. Dawn squeezed my hand.

Had my use of dark necromancy damaged me in some way? Or . . . changed me? Could I no longer summon one spirit except by destroying another? I'd never heard of that happening to dark necromancers of the past, but then nobody really taught the details. Maybe—

I would go crazy if I kept thinking about it. So I just squeezed Dawn's hand in return, and said, "I'll be fine."

Dawn turned on the radio, and I soon dozed off, doubts and fears swirling through my dreams and taking dark winged forms.

We arrived at the home of Merlin at 5:32 A.M., an hour or so before sunrise.

Merlin lived in a mobile home on the Oregon side of the

Columbia River, in a trailer park just a half-hour drive away from Maryhill Stonehenge. It had a fabulous view of the Dalles Dam, which looked pretty cool all lit up at night.

The dam sat on what once was the prime fishing grounds of the local Native tribe, not to mention the former home of a number of river feybloods, some of whom had been depicted in pictographs that were now mostly underwater being erased forever. Add to that the fact that the Gedai had somehow guessed a connection between hydropower facilities and the magical world—arcana liked to build our secret facilities under either moving water, or power stations, or both, since the shifting energy helped to shield from scrying and Fey magics—and it was not surprising that Merlin had plopped himself down with a view of the dam.

I took a deep breath, then walked up and knocked on the rattling metal door.

A dog began barking and growling inside the trailer so loud that the metal siding rang from the reverberation. I braced myself to face the dog's owner. Hopefully, he wasn't still angry with me about—

The door opened. Merlin stood there, a six-foot-tall and rather wide Samoan-American in a voluminous Jedi bathrobe, staring groggily at me as he held a waist-height slobbering beast of a dog to heel. He blinked, and recognition sharpened his gaze. "Finn Gramaraye?"

"Yup. And, uh, I need your help."

"As a druid, I do not visit violence upon others," he said.

"Oh, well, that's . . . good?" I said.

"That's why I have a dog," he added, and released the beast at his side.

13

THE EMPEROR'S NEW CLOTHES

The dog tackled me to the ground, and I saw Dawn from the corner of my eye fumbling her Taser out of her pocket. The back of my head hit the gravel roadside with a painful thud, and the dog lunged for my face.

I flung up my arms to protect myself, and to maybe summon the dog's spirit. If I could.

Slobber and warm dog tongue smeared my face as the dog licked me excitedly.

"Heel, Lancelot," Merlin said, chuckling.

Merlin—aka George Mills, aka George the Druid—was a sixty-year-old alchemist who had been sent under deep cover to live as one of the Gedai about forty years ago. But after the first twenty years or so, he came to believe he was Merlin reincarnated.

Nobody, not even the ARC I suspected, knew what had caused this revelation. Some said he tried one too many sacred mushrooms with the other Gedai druids. Some said it was just the mental strain of pretending to believe in magic despite all doubt and ridicule, while at the same time pretending that magic wasn't actually real and therefore his belief in magic (which as an alchemist he knew was actually real) was wrong, despite his (pretend) belief to the contrary. I got a slight headache just thinking about it myself, I couldn't imagine living it for forty years.

But whatever the reason for the belief that he was indeed Merlin, it appeared sincere. He had legally changed his name to Merlin Emrys. He carried a twisted oak staff, and often wore brown druid robes and a fitted metal helmet like Merlin from the film *Excalibur.* And he claimed to possess ancient druidic knowledge lost since Merlin's time.

But here's the thing—he didn't run around trying to use the charm of summoning, or looking for King Arthur, or preaching the doom of Camelot on some street corner. Rather, he organized fundraisers and signature campaigns for nature conservancy groups and naturopaths. He led groups of fellow believers in Solstice rituals to heal the Earth. He attended public meetings of local government to speak on behalf of the environment and pagan religious equality.

If Merlin *were* reincarnated into a three-hundred-pound Samoan-American alchemist, he just might do the exact same thing. Hell, Merlin did a lot more good with his (probably) imagined birthright than most people did, arcana or mundane.

On the other hand, he also held some rather unfortunate beliefs. For example, he believed that marijuana was the dragon's breath, "as proven by the song 'Puff the Magic Dragon.'" And that the Lady of the Lake now lived in the golf water hazard of the Dalles Country Club in order to be close to him. So he'd been arrested for possession, and for entering the water hazard nude at night hoping to... reconnect spiritually with the Lady, among other similar offenses that had harmed nobody, but left him with a spotted record as far as mundy law enforcement was concerned.

And then there was the fact that he came to me two months past hoping that I could find his long lost love Morgana so that he could mend the breach between them and have true happiness at last.

He had learned of my dating service somehow, perhaps through the Matchmaking for Magicals website Sammy made for me on the arcanet. I tried everything to get rid of him. As long as he was a member of the Gedai and calling himself Merlin, official ARC policy was to treat him like a mundy. For all we knew, he could be wearing a wire and one of those tiny button cameras or something, sent in by the Gedai to try and get proof of magic. In the end I told him the website was some joke I'd made for my D&D group.

But I am a lousy liar, and he was determined. And, damn it, I *wanted* to help him. Arcana or not, crazy or not, he was so sincere in his desire for love, so clearly lonely, that he tugged pretty hard at my heart strings. But I couldn't use the Kin Finder or other magic to find his true soul mate. So I told him I'd help as best I could, sent him home, and created a profile for him on a couple of online dating sites with Dawn's help. We sorted through the results, and sent Merlin the profile we thought the most promising.

Apparently, they went on one date that went horribly, horribly wrong. He hadn't shared the details, but had informed me that he considered it a deliberate act of sabotage on my part.

As I stood and wiped the dog slobber from my face, I was grateful that druids were, in the end, pacifists.

"Very funny," I said to the dog, and touched the back of my head to feel for blood.

"And now you know a bit of what my date was like," Merlin replied. "So why are you here?" He looked past me to Dawn and Sammy. "Would you claim one of these to be my Morgana?"

"You wish," Sammy said.

"Afraid not," I said. "Actually, I need your help."

Merlin laughed. "And so the wheel turns. Come inside, and we shall discuss what Merlin may do for you." He patted at his thigh. "Come on boy, inside."

The dog returned inside the trailer. After a glance at Sammy and Dawn to make sure they were willing to follow, I led them after him.

The interior of Merlin's trailer looked like a Greenpeace office run by the Society for Creative Anachronism. Maps and posters highlighting areas of environmental concern and potential magical activity, interspersed with Green Man figures and neo-pagan artifacts prominently featuring crystals, runes, and pentacles. A worn-looking guitar leaned against a coffee table covered in books, empty beer bottles, and a blown-glass bong shaped like a dragon.

Merlin waved us to a sofa covered in a sheet. "How may I help you?"

"A group of, uh, dark druids are going to be using the Stonehenge to exile a bunch of innocent souls to the Other Realm at sunset," I said. "We need your help to stop them."

The druids believed in an Otherworld, a place that can be visited by dreamwalkers and the spirits of the dead, so whatever Merlin's state of mind with regards to his arcana nature versus Gedai beliefs, I hoped my description fit within his frame of reality.

Merlin blinked at me, then said, "Dark druids?"

"Yeah."

He frowned. "I don't know of any dark druids. That is like saying dry water."

"Well, they exist. And they are the enemies of all that you stand for."

"So you say," Merlin replied. "But it matters not. It is not the druid way to do battle. That, we leave to the warriors, and always we counsel against war."

"This is not Gaul," Sammy said. "And you aren't a goddamn druid, George. War is here whether you want it or not. Pick a side."

"I pick the side of wisdom and love," George said.

Sammy threw up her hands. "I knew this would be a waste of time." She pulled her phone out, and slammed out of the trailer, saying, "I'm calling in some muscle."

George sighed. "She has a lot of anger."

I nodded in agreement. "Her girlfriend is about to be exiled to the Other Realm, and likely killed or trapped there in a plot to destroy the Fey."

"The Other Folk would not let that happen."

"It seems that at least some of the Other Folk are helping the dark druids."

Merlin shook his head. "First you say these dark druids wish to destroy the Others, then that the Others are helping them."

"It's complicated. So what *can* you do to help?"

He raised his hands. "I can call a moot between the local grove and your group of, ahem, 'dark druids,' and seek to guide all to a path of peace and mutual happiness."

Dawn picked up the guitar and turned it over in her hand, examining it with a wistful look on her face.

I shook my head at Merlin's suggestion. "I don't think that would work out for you, or your grove." At best, the

ARC would call in infomancers to erase their memories. At worst, the Arcanites would simply erase *them*.

But his suggestion gave me an idea. A terrible idea, but I had to try.

"Or, actually, that would be great. A moot between me, and the leader of the dark druids, mediated by you in a public place."

"Very good," Merlin said in an approving tone. "And how shall I contact this dark Arch-Druid?"

"I'll take care of that, if I can borrow these?" I picked up a pen and a piece of junk mail off of the coffee table. "You just give me the time and place, and I'll make sure he shows up."

"Of course." Merlin gave me directions to a local diner.

Dawn began strumming the guitar, and Merlin looked over, his round face lighting up. "Are you perchance a bard?"

"You could say that," Dawn said, smiling. "Never been to Skara Brae, but I like to think I capture the tale of the times in my songs."

"Then come! We shall drink beer and I will tell you my tale."

"Um," I said. "I'm not sure—"

"I'd kill for a beer right now!" Dawn said.

"Excellent!" Merlin rocked himself to his feet. "And you, Finn?"

"Uh, no, thank you." All beer tasted like fizzy pee to me, and I didn't care enough to pretend otherwise just then. "I need to go get a message to the, um, Arch-Druid."

"Very well. I am more than happy to treat with the bard here."

La! Merlin's hoping to wake the dragon with your girlfriend!

I'm not worried, I thought back as I stepped outside. The distant waterfall noise of the dam filled the pre-dawn air, and a bracing chill breeze blew up from the dark river below.

I stepped over a low picket fence and found what I needed in the corner of Merlin's garden, as I knew I would—a weather-worn gnome statue. I scribbled a message and an offer of payment onto the junk-mail envelope:

For gnome delivery to Gavriel Gramaraye, Necromancer, last seen in possession of the body of Justin Gramaraye. Offer of payment: Standard mana rate, negotiable for extra costs, plus 1/2 Thoth of mana if delivered by local sunrise.

Begin

Dear Grandfather,

I'm willing to trade myself for Fatima. Meet to discuss at Big Jim's Restaurant at 8AM this morning.

Phinaeus Gramaraye

End

In addition to message delivery, I request the following artifacts, cost to be negotiated and secured against the Gramaraye account:

Wand of Sleep

Wand of Freezing

Amulet or other artifact that protects against necromantic possession.

Then I slipped the note under the metal sculpture.

Sammy marched up the road toward me, hanging up her phone and taking a drag on her clove cigarette.

"Get your muscle?" I asked.

"Maybe, some help to hide us once we have Fatima if nothing else. What are you up to?" She took another drag of her clove and exhaled a cloud of sweet-smelling smoke.

"Plan A," I said.

"You know, I think the only thing that scares me more than you always running into danger without a plan is when you start making plans."

The gnome statue tipped over, and a real gnome hat poked out, this one blue and resting above a pair of narrowed eyes that scanned the surroundings before Priapus, don of the Giardini gnome family, sprang up and out of the hole. He immediately whipped his deadly-looking scythe out of his belt, the corded muscles of his bare arms flexing.

"Priapus!" I said. "Greetings. I didn't expect you to respond, not so far south."

"Gramaraye," he replied. "I ain't staying long. This is Prato family territory. But I been watching for you to make a gnome request, so's I could talk at ya alone-like for a bit."

"If you think I owe you something—"

"Nah," he said. "But I wanted to let ya know, there's been a temporary change in management of the Giardini family."

When last we'd spoken, he'd been surprised to find some gnome within his family had been undermining him, working against him to destroy records and even kill his loyal gnomes, and they appeared to be doing so in league with whatever force in the Other Realm was pitting the Silver and the Shadows against one another. It seemed things had escalated since then.

"So . . . what does that mean?"

"It means don't trust no gnome from the Giardini family until I'm back in charge, and don't go passing important messages by them, capiche?"

"What about this Palto family?"

"Prato, and they ain't nothing to worry about. Never had much power, so don't see as why anybody'd care much who's who in their zoo."

"Look," I said. "My Grandfather and the Arcanites have something big planned, I'm guessing it's somehow tied to what's been going on with the Fey, and you, and everything these past months. Don't suppose you can do anything to help me stop him?"

"Ha! Funny guy! Me and my boys, we're laying low, magus, while I figure out who's loyal and not, and who dies and not."

"Sure," I said, and my shoulders slumped. "I understand."

"But here." Priapus drew a sigil in the dirt with the handle of his scythe. "If it's a real End of Times–type thing, and I mean seriously end of times, you put that there on a note and leave it under a statue, and I'll know to come, see?"

"Wow. Um, thanks!" I said.

"We can work out fair compensation once we see how hard me and my boys'll have to work to save the world and all."

I sighed. "Of course." How silly of me to expect a gnome to do anything out of the goodness of his tiny little heart. "So who do *you* think is behind all of this?" I asked. "On the Fey side, I mean?"

"Buddy, if I knew that, I'd go over to the Bright Realm and introduce them to the sharp end of Mister Tickle Sickle here. And since you wouldn't be askin' me if ya had a clue, guess share time is over like."

And with that, he hopped back into the hole, and the statue magically righted itself.

"Shit," Sammy said. "If the Giardini gnomes are working

for the enemy, that's like North Korea hacking every database in North America. They can snoop in all our messages, dig through all our dirt."

"That sounds pretty North Bad," I agreed.

Big Jim's diner was empty except for Merlin and myself. Merlin had use of the place as a favor from one of the members of his druid grove. The main lights were off, the dining area lit obliquely by the bright morning light slatting in through the windows.

I sat at a booth facing the door, toying nervously with the utensils on the table, my nervousness only partially offset by my annoyance at the letter in my pocket.

Phinaeus Gramaraye:

Message delivered, payment expected within 24 hours or penalties will be accrued and enforced.

Regarding the artifacts requested, it has been made clear that you are no longer authorized to offer payment from the Gramaraye account. As our records do not indicate any significant personal wealth or mana stores, we must respectfully decline your request.

Pala, chief of the Prato family.

Mort. The jerk had made sure I couldn't even access the family's mana stores. One more thing I had to work out with him.

But I had more immediate problems to worry about.

I attempted to twirl the butter knife between my fingers

as I glanced down at my watch. It was five minutes past eight A.M. If Grandfather didn't show—

A knock on the glass door made me jump slightly in the seat and drop the butter knife with a loud clatter.

Merlin moved to the door, and glanced back at me with raised eyebrows.

The man outside was hard to make out, silhouetted against the bright sunlight. But after a second he visibly sighed and placed his right hand against the door, the black stone of his arcana persona ring clicking on the glass.

I nodded to Merlin. "Let him in."

Merlin unlocked the door, and opened it.

Grandfather strode in as if taking possession of the place, pausing only long enough to give Merlin a disapproving frown before crossing to me.

He looked even worse than before. Perhaps escaping the Fury had taken a toll on him, or whatever evil magics he had been performing in preparation for his big Spell o' Doom. He looked seventy going on *Evil Dead*, his hair mostly fallen out, his flesh gaunt and pale, papery skin stretched thin over his bones.

"Finn," he said. "Time to put an end to this. For good."

14

SO WHAT'CHA WANT

Well, this could have started better, Alynon said. Grandfather stopped a foot away from my booth.

Please save all comments for the end of the ride, I thought.

"Grandfather," I said. "You look great. Been working out?"

Grandfather's lips went even thinner for a second, then he said, "When I take possession of your body, it is a great relief knowing that your sense of humor shall be destroyed along with your spirit."

"That hurts!" I said. And I was surprised to find it genuinely did. "I used to make you laugh. Sometimes. You know, before you went all evil."

"Evil?" Grandfather said. "Don't be so dramatic, boy. This isn't one of your silly games or movies. And I am done trading barbs. Your time has come."

"Actually," I said, "you're going to leave here, and return Fatima to us unharmed."

The corner of Grandfather's mouth turned up in a condescending grin before he said, "Really? And why would I do that?" He nodded back at Merlin. "Because of this pathetic excuse for an arcana?"

"For one, yes," I replied. "He is a Gedai leader, and druid. If you—"

"If nothing," Grandfather said. "George Mills is a failed experiment, nothing more."

Merlin's face went red. "Now look here—"

I raised my hand and urged him with my eyes to remain calm. "*Merlin* has druids and Gedai both converging on this diner right now," I lied.

Grandfather snorted. "The Gedai are mundies for all their watered-down Templar nonsense. And druids are even less a threat, with their New Age peacenik idiocy. A single arcana is more than a match for them all."

Merlin's eyes narrowed. "You are a fool. You would upset the natural order—"

"Natural order?" Grandfather asked sharply. "The natural order is that arcana are the superior race—we are better than creatures dreamed up by primitive minds or magical perversions, and certainly better than humans lacking even the ability to *sense* the magical realm."

Merlin stood straighter. "There is more magic in a single act of compassion than you have in your entire body."

Grandfather snorted. "Compassion won't stop the Fey from making slaves of us all."

"It worked for Gandhi," I said.

"There are many paths to peace," Merlin added, looking at Grandfather with something like pity now. "War is the worst of them."

Grandfather sneered. I had read about people who sneered, of course, and seen it characterized by cheesy villains in movies and such, but never really thought I'd actually see a live sneer in nature. It was one of those words like "discombobulated" that seemed too cartoonish to be seen in reality.

But Grandfather definitely sneered, and said, "That is exactly the kind of nonsense I'd expect from a literal tree-hugging loony. Even if you've somehow forgotten the last Fey invasion, George, you're still old enough to know better."

Those last words resonated with me. "You're old enough to know better" was the kind of thing Grandfather had said to us kids all the time as we were growing up, and really drove home that this wasn't some unfamiliar lunatic. This man destroying our lives was family, a man who helped to raise me.

During my childhood, his supremacist views peeked through in the occasional joke or complaint, but he hadn't exactly been homeschooling us with a bunch of Arcanite propaganda about Fey Creationism and arcana superiority, or drilling us like little soldiers. He'd been fiercely proud of the Gramaraye name, and of our arcana heritage, always pushing for us kids to be proud as well.

"Who are you doing this for?" I asked.

Grandfather turned to me. "I did not come to explain myself."

"No. You came to destroy me. Me, Petey, Sammy, Mattie, you're destroying the lives of your family, of everyone you claim to be defending." I leaned forward, putting genuine care in my voice. "Grandfather, don't you remember what it was like to sit around the dinner table with Mother and all us kids? Do you remember that story you used to tell about seeing Mother for the first time in Grandmother's arms, and then seeing each of us for the first time, how happy you were that Mother's children had the necromancy gift to continue the family line?"

Grandfather's lips went razor thin and he turned away. "I remember," he said, his tone sad. "I remember your grandmother every day. And that is why you should believe that what I do is necessary. If I could live the simple life of a family man free from worry, I would." He turned back, and his tone sharpened again. "But I know too much to sit idly awaiting the doom of my world. And I have chosen to sacrifice my happiness so that others won't suffer."

"Funny, so far the only people you've sacrificed, and who have suffered, are the people closest to you." I waved at his worn-out body.

"It is— This too is my gift to the arcana, my sacrifice." He straightened, standing even more stiffly than before. "But if the cost of victory were cheap, then it would not require someone of my conviction to pay it."

Merlin said, "Yet you are not the one to truly pay it, are you."

"Go lick some mushrooms and mind your own business, druid," Grandfather snapped.

"So . . . no chance you'll stop, then?" I asked. "Maybe just come home for some waffles?"

"I see you have not outgrown the habit of avoiding hard truths by making jokes," Grandfather said.

"Maybe." I shrugged. "And maybe if you saw the humor in things a bit more, you wouldn't be running around destroying lives and starting wars. Seriously, Grandfather, how can you not see that what you're doing is wrong?"

"Because I see more than you."

"And you're proving true every fear that people have of necromancers. *You* are the real danger here."

That got past his arrogant calm. His face went splotchy red, a vein pulsed on his temple, and he leaned in to slam a fist onto the table, causing the place settings to clatter noisily. "Respect!"

"Earn it!" I snapped back. "That's what you always taught us, that respect had to be earned. Do you think anyone's going to respect the monster you've become?"

"History will judge me a hero," Grandfather spat back. "Just like Verona. Just like my—" he stopped, and visibly gathered himself, taking a deep breath and tugging at his shirt to straighten it. In a cold, mocking tone, he said, "You are very self-righteous, yet you destroyed a spirit and used that power to win your own victory. If I am a monster, then so are you. But I am a monster for a greater cause, not some momentary need."

That was like a punch to the gut. But I pushed forward. "I had no choice in that. You do have a choice here. Nobody is forcing you to do this."

Grandfather gave a pitying shake of his head. "You are a child wandering the dark forest with a flashlight. You see only a tiny patch of reality. But in the trees wait terrible creatures, Finn. And beyond the woods—" he stopped, and chuckled. "I have made alliance with some of the Fey, as you know. Fey who seek to gain access to our world, to use us just as we would use them. Do you think if I lay down and die, they would not still be plotting to consume our world?"

"Who?" I asked. "Which Fey? The Forest of Shadows?"

Grandfather smiled. "Once again, I must disappoint you. I am still not so foolish as to reveal the details of my plans before they are fulfilled."

"No, see, getting the Baron von Joy GoBot for Christmas when I asked for an Optimus Prime Transformer, that was a disappointment. What you're doing now, this is a heinous crime."

"Well, then, let us put an end to your suffering,"

Grandfather said, and stepped toward me, one hand rising. I felt the tingle between my eyes that warned of rising magic.

"Smile," I said. "You're on Hidden Camera."

Grandfather froze, and said, "What?"

I pointed over my left shoulder to the restaurant counter, and the kitchen behind it. "There's a hidden camera recording everything we said. And through the wonders of modern Samology, my sister can send those recordings to the ARC, the YouTube, and a bunch of other places I've never even heard of."

Grandfather shrugged, a bit too nonchalantly. "The infomancers—"

"Can't hold an If statement up to my sister. It will be seen. By a lot of people."

"Maybe I shall still take possession of you, and hunt your sister down," Grandfather said. "I can deal with this video after."

"Sammy says you guys have only arrested about half the people you plan to. You may control the local ARC, but I'm guessing the other regional ARCs being alerted to your conspiracy now would be rather inconvenient. Are you sure you want to risk it?"

Grandfather's thin lips pursed to the side and his eyes narrowed. Finally, he said, "What is to keep you from releasing the video regardless?"

"My word, as a necromancer, and as a Gramaraye, if that still holds any meaning to you."

"They of course hold meaning to me. I am just not convinced they hold such meaning for you. You always did seem to have your foot half out of the door, ready to abandon your family and duties both, even before exile."

"Wow. You know, a hippo who rolls all ones has got nothing on you."

"Excuse me?" Grandfather asked.

"You do hear yourself, right?" I said. "The guy who's literally destroying his family with necromancy is questioning *my* honor?"

"Perhaps if you had done anything worthy of living, your death would be a crime," Grandfather replied. "As it is, I will be judged a hero and my family simply a footnote."

Damn it if that didn't sting. Why I still cared even a little about what this maniac thought, I didn't know; but I had to stop myself from trying to argue the worth of my choices, the value of my accomplishments. I guess an entire childhood spent trying to please him had left its mark on my psyche.

"Fine," I said. "I swear upon the spirit of my mother, and *her* honor as a necromancer."

Grandfather gave a slight bow with his head. "That, I believe." He stared at me a long silent moment, then said, "Where did you say this camera was?"

"Hidden," I replied.

"Very well." He glanced back at Merlin, then looked in the direction of the kitchen behind me. "Samantha, you were always a disappointment to me, and to your mother."

"That's enough" I said.

He ignored me. "You weren't a Talker like your mother. With your allergies, you weren't even a true arcana."

I stood up. "I said stop it. Now!"

Grandfather smiled, still looking toward the kitchen. "And then you couldn't even fulfill your duty to carry on the family line, choosing perversion over—"

I shoved him.

At least, I tried. He simply raised a hand between us and my nervous system flared. I writhed in more pain than Howard the Duck being roasted on a spit while watching *Leonard Part 6*. Grandfather summoned my spirit, and I'd walked right into it, let my anger disrupt my mental focus and my defenses.

I fell to my knees, my hands and jaw clenching against the pain, my entire body shivering.

"Merlin!" I called.

Merlin took a step toward us. "Please stop this. By hurting him, you only injure yourself."

"No," Grandfather said. "I feel confident that Finn is the one being injured."

My burning nervous system agreed with him.

"As a worker of spiritual energy, you must see that we are all connected," Merlin said, frustration clear in his tone. "Violence to another only—"

"Damn it, Merlin!" I shouted through my pain. "*Do* something!"

I fell to the ground, convulsing now into a fetal position as my muscles spasmed and my skin felt like I'd gotten a thousand paper cuts before soaking in Agent Orange juice.

Grandfather gave a derisive snort. "You were a fool to rely on a druid for protection. Especially this one."

"I am not here as muscle, Gavriel," Merlin said. "I am here to offer witness, and wisdom should you accept it."

"Go sell your nonsense to the hippies," Grandfather said. He closed his hand, and the pain stopped.

Did he waver on his feet for a second, or was that just my own dizziness?

It couldn't be easy maintaining possession of that body.

And to exert control beyond it at the same time—

Grandfather cleared his throat. "I think I shall deny your request for the life of Samantha's lover," he said. "Instead, I shall grant you your life, for now. And as insurance, I shall hold on to the dyke sorceress—her body at least. Should you release the video, or make further attempts to interfere in my plans, then I shall have to kill her. And there would be no reason to further spare you."

He turned away, and gave a dismissive wave at Merlin. "Remove yourself from my path, meat wall."

Merlin's face went red, but after a second he stepped aside, and let Grandfather march out of the diner.

As the jingling of the doorbell faded, I pushed myself up into a sitting position.

"Looks like we're doing it the hard way," I muttered.

15

RUNAWAY TRAIN

Merlin offered me a hand, but I waved it away, annoyed, and pulled myself up using the edge of the booth.

"What the hell was that?" I asked, my voice still shaky. "I mean, I know you're all about the non-violence, but couldn't you, I don't know, hug him real hard or something? I might be dead now!"

Merlin looked sad but not remorseful as he said, "If walking the Path were easy, then everyone would do it."

"Damn it, Merl, it isn't a question of easy. Do you think it's easy to fight my own grandfather, or to nearly have my spirit ripped out of me? No. It's about doing what is right."

"Death is just part of the cycle," Merlin replied. "But violence is a choice."

"If you can stop violence but don't, isn't that a choice to support it?"

Merlin sighed. "I do not expect you to understand. And I did not come knocking on your door at the crack of dawn. If you do not wish my counsel, then you may go elsewhere."

Sammy pulled up in front of the diner in Dawn's Woody wagon.

"Come," Merlin said. "Let us return to my home. I need a beer."

I grabbed Sammy's camera and transmitter setup from the kitchen, then we closed up the diner and climbed into the car. I joined Dawn in the backseat, and Merlin took shotgun. Sammy looked ready to murder someone, pulling out of the parking lot like a stunt driver on too much coffee, and Merlin had the poor luck of being the closest target for her anger.

"You godsdamned delusional bastard, you were just going to let Finn die. I don't give a crap if you want to dance in your bathrobe chanting nonsense at the moon, but there's no excuse for that kind of bullshit cowardice!"

"It is not cowardice," Merlin replied with an edge to his tone. "It is conviction. True conviction, not Gavriel's madness."

Sammy snorted. "A conviction to let the Arcanites kill people and Fey without doing anything to stop them, long as they don't piss on your petunias. Unbelievable."

Merlin was silent for a minute, then said, "Your home is upon the doorstep of the Olympic forest, is it not?"

Sammy rolled her eyes at me in the rearview mirror, but didn't respond to Merlin.

"Yes," I said.

"For many years, the rangers suppressed all fire in the national forests," Merlin said, watching the moonlit landscape speed by. "They wished to save the trees and avoid destruction. A seemingly noble cause. But in time, they came to realize that fire is a natural part of a forest's lifecycle, a necessary one. Without it, the ground becomes piled with dead wood and leaves. Without it, certain trees and plants grow up unchecked, while those that have evolved to use fire in assisting their reproduction die away. With so much thick coverage above and growth below, the water cycle is changed, affecting even the weather. And when a fire finally does ignite naturally, the heat and fury of it is difficult to control, let alone stop."

Sammy shook her head. "That's fascinating. But what the fuck does that have to do with standing there like a frakking lump while my brother is killed?"

Merlin shrugged his massive shoulders. "Stopping your grandfather might save lives. But who in this car has the wisdom to say with certainty the world will be better for it? To see all the lives touched, the futures shaped, the positive changes no longer inspired?"

I could hear the creak of the steering wheel as Sammy's hands tightened around it. "I think I can say with pretty damn certainty that my girlfriend being murdered is not going to make our lives any better."

"She's right," I said. "Doing nothing doesn't guarantee a better future any more than doing something. But at least by fighting back, we might keep innocent people from being killed."

"Death is inevitable. But their spirits continue on, you know this," Merlin replied.

"Death is inevitable," I agreed. "Murder is not. If everyone felt like you, then there would be nothing to stop my grandfather from taking over the world and making everyone's lives suck."

"If everyone felt like I did, then your grandfather would see the wisdom of peace."

"News flash," Sammy said. "Our grandfather is no druid. So while you spit out your philosophical hypothetical bullshit, those of us who live in reality have to deal with the actual facts."

"Whose facts?" Merlin replied. "Might your grandfather's acts be evil? Perhaps, depending on your views. But if he is evil for visiting violence upon others, then let that stain be upon his spirit. Do not put a stain upon your own by matching his violence with violence."

I gave up. Sammy wasn't finished, however.

"Pretty convenient to pick and choose all the pacifist earth warden bits there, Sir Inconvenient Truth, and ignore that druids practiced human sacrifice."

Merlin shrugged. "It was a different time, a different place, when we were the law for our people, guiding them to order and balance. We led by authority and by example. Now," he sighed. "Now, we must lead by example alone."

"Whatever," Sammy said.

We rode in a silence more awkward than Refrigerator Perry in the Super Bowl Shuffle, until Dawn finally leaned forward and said, "So, is this Stonehenge a spiritual place for you?"

"Of course," Merlin replied. "It is tied into the spirit of the earth."

"Well, isn't it putting some kind of stain on the spirit of the earth if the Arcanites use Stonehenge to hurt people or cast dark magic or whatever?"

Merlin was silent a while. Finally, he said, "Very well. I will summon the Gedai knights."

"Seriously?" Sammy said. "You'll help save a bunch of rocks, but not people?"

"Knock the leaves from a tree and it survives," Merlin said. "Poison the roots, and the whole tree dies."

"Unbelievable," Sammy muttered.

Your sister clearly does not understand the nature of human religions, Alynon said.

What would that be, oh wise one? I thought back.

To justify whatever it is they want to believe anyway, Alynon said.

Wow. I thought you were going to say—

And of course, to justify whatever sexual perversion one may enjoy.

Yep. There it is.

That used to be their one redeeming quality, Alynon went on, probably because he sensed it would irritate me. *Though sadly so many of the modern religions have abandoned the orgies and sex rituals, and instead practice self-loathing. Still, from what I've observed, making most kinds of sex taboo and sinful only makes it hotter, yes?*

Uh huh. Do you mind if we discuss something else? Like how we're going to stop my grandfather and rescue Fatima, and not get ourselves killed?

La! I look forward to the battle.

I frowned. *I know I'm going to regret this, but why, exactly?*

Because fighting always seems to get your lady rather . . . excited.

I sighed. *Thanks for not disappointing me there, Aly.*

A Gedai knight was waiting for us when we arrived back at Merlin's trailer.

He stood leaning against an old Volkswagen Rabbit, wearing a black duster and Aussie-style cowboy hat, reading a comic book in the morning sun.

Merlin gave an introductory wave of his hand and said, "This is Jay. He's the only knight who lives close by."

Jay grunted without looking up from his comic. "Don't

go pumping me up too much now, Merl."

I stepped up beside Merlin. "Uh, hello, Jay. Thanks for helping us out."

"It's just J," he replied, still not looking up. "No *a* or *y*."

"How can you tell the difference?" I asked. "Don't they sound the same?"

He looked up at me with one eyebrow arched, then looked at Merlin. "So what's the deal? Some punks planning a party around the stones again?"

"No," Merlin said. "It's a bit more serious than that. Some, uh, cultists are planning some dangerous rites. They may even be the real deal."

J lowered the comic and raised both eyebrows. "Well well, seems like it's a g'day to be in the Order."

Merlin sighed. "I appreciate your tenacity, but we are not changing the official pronunciation to G'Day Knights."

J harrumphed sharply through his nose, and said, "It's better than sounding like we're a bunch of Star Wars fanboys and girls. And when they make movies about how we broke wide the whole magic thing—"

Merlin put a hand on J's shoulder. "I tell you this as your friend, J: give it up. This isn't one of your lawsuits."

"Lawsuits?" Sammy said, looking up from her phone. "You're not the druid who tried to sue Marvel Comics for portraying Doctor Strange as a fictional character, are you?"

J's eyes narrowed. "That's right."

"Wait," I said to Sammy. "He what?"

J tossed the comic into his car, making me wince at the poor treatment of a sacred text, and said, "There's more than one way to fight the powers that hide the magical world with their lies and illusions."

"Sure," Sammy replied. "But you filed, what, two thousand lawsuits last year? Against everyone and everything. Julian Assange, Paul the Octopus, the *Clash of the Titans* remake, even the Old Spice guy I think, right? How exactly is that fighting the powers?"

"It isn't," Merlin said.

J ignored him, and said, "The conspiracy to hide the magical world is as wide as it is deep. Assange withheld any leaked files on the government's Magical Investigations squad. The 'octopus' clearly had predictive powers, was probably even a mer-creature of some kind, but then suddenly dies of 'natural causes'? Right. And the *Titans* remake was just so people wouldn't watch the original and find the clues hidden within it about the truth of magic."

I frowned. "I've seen the original a hundred times, and I didn't notice any clues."

J gave a dismissive snort. "It takes a trained eye familiar with the world of magic to spot them. And how else can you explain such a crappy remake when the original was so perfect?"

"I haven't seen the remake yet," I said.

"Smart man," J replied.

"Yeah," Sammy said in her trademark deadpan. "And magnets, how do *they* work?"

J glowered at Sammy, but Dawn said, "And the Old Spice guy?"

J blushed. "He's clearly some kind of siren or succubus, out to make it harder for human men to get girlfriends."

"Uh—" Dawn began, then obviously thought better than to try and come up with a response.

Merlin moved beside J and put a massive hand on his shoulder. "J is a good man, and a good fighter. He can help."

"Damn straight," J said, sweeping open his duster to reveal what looked like Boy Scout Batman's utility belt covered in pouches, canisters, and at least one Taser.

He also wore a collection of necklaces that would have made Mr. T jealous, each holding an amulet of some kind. I spotted silver mirrors, crosses, a David's star, even an Eye of Agamotto.

Held in cloth loops inside the jacket itself hung two silver sais, the three-pronged weapons flashing in the sunlight.

"Right," I said. "Okay. So what's our plan?"

"First, we eat," Merlin said. "Then, we rest."

"And then?" J asked, clearly not thrilled at the first two.

"Then," I said, "we save the world."

I held on for dear life as Dawn careened down the road in her wood-paneled station wagon. We crashed through two wooden sawhorses with CLOSED TO PUBLIC signs that the Arcanites must have placed on the road, the broken boards clattering behind us on the pavement.

Unfortunately, there was no good way to sneak up on Maryhill Stonehenge, especially with the sun still floating above the distant line of hills. The monument sat on an open plateau, with low hills on one side and a slope dropping off on the other, both entirely lacking in thick forest or secret tunnels or anything actually useful in a sneak attack. And the road that led to the monument's parking lot was certain to be watched and guarded. Which meant daylight or not, we would be spotted well before reaching the monument.

So Dawn simply drove as fast as she could to make us a difficult target.

And a target is exactly what we wanted to be. So we

towed some pans and cans on a rope to make a nice, loud, clattering cacophony.

Because there was a road that ran below the monument as well. Merlin, J, and Sammy were in theory marching up that right now. They, too, would be easily spotted, unless everyone's attention was elsewhere, like on a crazed couple barreling at the monument in a station wagon making one hell of a racket.

It was vital the others not be detected. Apparently, Sam Hill had requested his public grave be down-slope of the monument, with a gravestone of his own design that, Merlin insisted, had some connection to the monument via the ley lines. Though the ARC had replaced Hill's original gravestone with one of their design, Merlin still felt confident he could use it to shut down whatever portal or other magics the Arcanites attempted with the monument.

Merlin would not be happy to know our own plan—smash into the monoliths and damage as many as we could in hopes of disrupting the ability to easily create a portal. There would be hell to pay afterwards with both the ARC and the mundy authorities—and I would feel as guilty as hell about damaging a public monument to peace—but that was a problem for tomorrow. With luck, the ARC would cover it up and repair the damage.

J believed Merlin was simply there to help ferry away any hostages they rescued. He thought he was going to be doing the bulk of the work, protecting Sammy as she freed Fatima, while Dawn and I would hopefully distract the Arcanites long enough for them to get away.

I had tried multiple times to get Dawn to join Merlin's team, arguably to protect him, but really to protect her. She had of course refused.

It was all a terrible plan. My inner gamer craved some clever, multilayered plan involving feints and fake-outs and flanking, and maybe some other f-words besides fatalities.

What we had instead was a deranged druid, a paranoid mundy knight, and a rattling Dodge Colt.

We turned off the paved road onto the gravel drive of the monument's parking lot, skidding around a small maintenance building. The sky grew fiery orange over Stonehenge as the stones came into view, the surrounding landscape growing golden in the last light of the day.

Stonehenge looked much as you would expect it to, except fully intact and clean-edged, a circle of upright gray monoliths supporting lintel stones, with additional free-standing monoliths and a stone altar inside the ring.

But blocking our way to the monument stood an imposing figure in the kind of fitted black suit favored by the FBI, Mormon missionaries, and Hollywood hipsters. I saw the eye-bending swirl of darkness around his throat, like a band of interstellar space torn from the sky and made into a dickey—an enforcer wizard with a tattoo primed and ready.

White flickering energy began to dance around the man's outstretched hand.

"Lights!" I shouted.

Dawn threw on her high beams.

The enforcer threw up one hand to shield his eyes and turned slightly away, and the lightning bolt that leaped from the other hand narrowly missed our car.

"Hit him!" I said, blinking against the after-image of the lightning bolt.

"I know!" Dawn replied, her irritated tone failing to mask the edge of panic beneath. She must have floored the gas pedal, because the engine revved and the car leaped forward, plowing into the enforcer.

There was a neon blue flash of light around the enforcer like an awesome 80s music video effect as he bounced off the front of our car and went spinning off to the side, tumbling into the dirt and gravel.

"I'm so going to jail," Dawn said.

"He'll survive," I replied as we fishtailed then continued speeding toward the circle of concrete monoliths. Enforcer uniforms were enchanted to protect against physical and magical strikes. Suits by Armorni. I just hoped the force of a driving car was enough to leave him stunned for a bit at least. "He won't be reporting this to the police, trust me."

The sun touched the hills to the west, spreading like liquid fire along their tops, spilling along the brown rolling landscape and reflecting sharply off the rearview mirror into my eyes.

"Damn it." The Arcanites would open the portal at any moment.

Another enforcer stood guard in front of the monument, a neckless barrel of a guy who looked like a grim Fred Flintstone stuffed into a suit. Beyond the upright monoliths I could see movement, a group of people gathered within the central altar area. They began to scramble back as we careened toward them.

Dread Flintstone raised his hand, the stellar darkness of wizard ink sworling up around where his neck should have been.

"Dawn—"

"I see him, damn it!" She leaned slightly forward, her elbows splayed and hands twisting on the steering wheel as if trying to push the car into just a bit more speed.

The hairs on my arm stood straight up a second before lightning leaped from the enforcer's hand and flew at us. Dawn tried to swerve to avoid it, but the forks of dancing light struck the car squarely.

I squeezed my eyes closed against the blinding light. The radio squealed, and my hair danced around my head as if in a wind. My butt cheeks twitched as Alynon's Fey tattoo stirred at the presence of arcana energy being directed toward me. Dawn cried out and I peeked over as she jerked her hands off of the steering wheel, shuddering, but neither of us burst into flames or began smoking. The lightning faded, flickering away over and around the car and into the ground.

"Woo hoo!" Dawn shouted.

The engine died as we skidded sideways through the gravel and came to a stop. We'd missed the enforcer and the monument entirely. Damn it.

The enforcer began marching cautiously toward us, approaching from Dawn's side of the car.

Dawn turned the key, but the engine didn't respond. She looked from the enforcer to me.

We were somewhat protected from lightning in the car, but there were a lot of other ways the enforcer could kill us.

"Come on!" I said, and opened my door on the far side of the car from the enforcer. Better to have some maneuvering room, and at least some hope of fighting back.

I scrambled out of the car, and Dawn scooted across the seat and followed me out, then paused to grab her guitar case out of the back.

"Dawn!" I shouted at her.

"I'm not leaving Cotten! What if the car blows up?"

I decided it would be foolish to argue further with her.

She would, as always, do whatever she wanted anyway. And if the car did blow up, I wasn't going to be held responsible for Cotten's destruction.

The enforcer had nearly reached the car by the time we'd both climbed out onto the gravel. And a second enforcer had emerged from the stone circle and marched toward us as well.

Great.

The sky turned that eye-bending gray-blue of twilight. As I fumbled to pull out both my Taser and baton at the same time, I felt a hum, a keening barely on the edge of my normal senses, similar to what I sometimes felt when I walked into a room with an old television set on.

The portal had opened. We were out of time.

16

THIEVES IN THE TEMPLE

The Flintstone enforcer marched at us around the smoking obstacle of Dawn's car. The paint of the old Dodge wagon was scorched black in spots, and the vinyl wood paneling had bubbled and melted. I owed Dawn big time. Again.

Hopefully Rattley Wood would be the only victim today.

Dawn had her Taser out, but looked a little shaky. I whipped the baton into full extension, and it lit up with a phosphorescent blue glow.

Dorks are near! Alynon said.

Not the time, I replied.

I handed Dawn my Taser, and pulled out the wand taken from the arcade sorcerer.

"I'll distract the nearest one," I said. "Aim for their heads."

If we could come at the enforcer from two directions, then we might have a shot.

Dread Flintstone made a whipping motion, and his own baton extended, lighting up. I motioned for Dawn to wait and stay low as I straightened, and marched defiantly around the back of the car. Flintstone followed my movement, and the second enforcer changed his trajectory to back up his partner. I felt pretty certain Grandfather had told them all about me and Dawn, and they would consider a necromancer who'd battled a jorõgumo a greater threat than a woman without magic.

They'd obviously never seen Dawn pissed off.

I squared off against the Bedrock Bouncer, and raised the wand. "I'm going to assume you guys know you're working for Gavriel Gramaraye, Arcanite asshole and wannabe Bond villain?"

To his credit, the enforcer didn't engage in pointless banter. He just raised his hand and shouted something.

Are you sure about this? I thought.

A lightning bolt leaped at my head.

Hold fast!

My butt cheeks twitched, and a ghostly shape like Pac-Man with a tribal tattoo appeared floating in front of me, mouth open.

The Pac-Man shield swallowed the lightning, and transformed the energy. I felt it coursing into me, overloading my senses. I swung my baton like a second wand, pointing it at the enforcer, and the energy channeled out along my arm to spew in a stream of purple-tinged darkness at the enforcer.

The enforcer scrambled back, throwing up his arms in a cross before him and shouting something.

The blackness struck the enforcer, and his suit began to melt right off of him like body paint in a rainstorm.

"Now!" I shouted.

Dawn stood up from behind her car, and fired her Taser at the enforcer. The darts glinted in the black-light glow of twilight as they sped through the air, thin silvery lines uncoiling behind them, and punched into the enforcer's now unprotected flesh.

The thick-bodied enforcer fell to the ground, spasming, and a song from *The Flintstones* ran through my head, "Twitch, twitch," I said.

The second enforcer paused just beyond his partner, looking more cautious and less cocky now. I pointed the real wand at him, and shouted, "*Dormio!*"

A globe of light shot from the wand like a photon torpedo. The magical missile hit the enforcer's suit, and burst into fragments and sparks that floated harmlessly down to the gravel.

Smeg.

The enforcer regained his aggressive demeanor. New black lines sworled up around his throat, and he shouted something. Nothing obvious happened, except he appeared to drop slightly into the gravel as if landing from a jump.

Dawn came around the front of her car, guitar case in one hand and the second Taser now in the other, and fired the Taser at the enforcer's head.

One of the silver darts struck him in the neck—and bounced off with a flash of sparks as if ricocheting off of stone.

"He increased his density!" I told Dawn. "Stay back." He wouldn't be able to maintain it for long—it wreaked havoc on the body's organs and systems. And he would be slow and inflexible. At least, that's what I assumed based on my reading of comics—general arcana training was purposefully vague on the weaknesses of enforcer magics for obvious reasons.

I raced to meet Dawn on the far side of her car, placing its smoking bulk between us and the heavy hitter.

He must have felt confident that I couldn't strike him

from a distance, not without him first firing at me. He would expect me to close in, to try to use my necromancy or the baton. And if I did, he'd Hulk Smash me.

"What now?" Dawn asked, looking down at the expended Tasers in her hand and holster. They could still be used as contact Tasers, but it would be suicide for either of us to get within striking distance of the enforcer now.

"We run for Stonehenge," I said in a low voice as we moved slowly toward the front of the car, matching the enforcer's pace toward the rear, keeping maximum distance. "He won't risk damaging the stones, and they'll give us—"

The enforcer kicked at Dawn's car, and the tail end swung around, the rear tires sending up a cloud of dust. Dawn managed to scramble out of the way, but the station wagon caught me square on the hip, sending me skidding across the gravel. The small sharp stones bit into my palms, elbows, and side as I ground to a halt, coughing and blinking against the dust.

The enforcer took ponderous steps toward me, each stomp sending shivers through the earth.

"Run!" I shouted at Dawn, and struggled to regain my feet before the enforcer reached me.

And of course, Dawn ignored me.

"Hey! Density's Child!" she shouted.

The enforcer glanced at Dawn—and got a stream of pepper spray in the eyes.

He shouted a curse, and threw an arm up over his eyes, too late. Neither his increased mass nor his Elven Klein suit of Protection Against Magic stopped the chemical burn.

I pushed to my feet, and limped after Dawn, my hip screaming in protest with every movement.

We rushed at my best speed to the concrete columns. The enforcer continued cursing, and stomped after us, his stomps growing softer and quicker as he released his density spell.

Maryhill Stonehenge had an outer ring of upright slabs, squared columns holding a ring of lintel stones. I directed Dawn ahead of me, and we passed through into the inside of the monument.

Within the outer ring stood a number of slightly shorter slabs in a horseshoe pattern, and within their curve sat a rectangular altar stone.

Above that altar stone now floated an eye-bending hole in reality, a portal to the Other Realm. And in front of the altar, all was chaos.

A group of prisoners—or hostages—huddled in the watery glow of the portal, a dozen men and women old and young, all wearing the loose gray outfits of convicted exiles. I spotted Fatima in their midst, also dressed in the gray.

Interesting fact: Back in the late 1970s, one exile had worn a T-shirt with an image of the Brady Bunch on it. When the Fey changeling took possession of the body, he was instantly offended. It turns out that a Fey from his Demesne had assumed the identity of Mr. Brady, treating his fellow Fey as his own children and offering continuous and often unsolicited advice. The resulting competition for his favor and wisdom sparked a bloody internecine war that the changeling's Demesne had barely survived. Thus, the changeling thought that the ARC was mocking him, and demanded an immediate apology and compensation for the offense.

So after Mr. Brady nearly started a global Fey-Arcana war, all exiles were required to wear the featureless, and supremely unflattering, gray uniform during the exchange.

In addition to their bland gray garb, the prisoners also wore silver bracelets meant to inhibit their magic and prevent them from fleeing—and to prevent the incoming Fey changeling from using the portal to launch an attack.

A battle raged now around the exiles and the shifting portal.

Grandfather had squared off against Sammy on the far side of the exiles, his back to us. He stood between Sammy and the exiles, and as he moved, the exiles shifted to always remain behind him, compelled by the magical shackles. So Grandfather must be wearing the control bracelet.

Sammy had a selfie-stick with a protection amulet attached to it extended in front of her, shielding her from Grandfather's necromancy while minimizing her allergic reaction. But Grandfather had come prepared. He had two leather bands strapped around his calves and each had holster-slots for multiple wands. Between that and his black tactical outfit, he actually looked pretty badass, something I never thought I'd say about Grandfather. Of course he ruined the effect by wearing his pants pulled up way too high, and a black silk ascot stuck out at his throat. But fashionable or not, he held one of the wands now, looking for an opening to fire it at Sammy.

Sammy used the concrete pillars for cover, dashing from column to column attempting to goad Grandfather into using the limited charges of his wands. The mixed success of this tactic was evident in the two scorch marks on the pillars, and the two on Sammy. She held her free hand against a nasty-looking burn on her side, and the selfie-stick wavered as she struggled to continue holding it upright. She wasn't going to last much longer. On our side of the exiles, J battled

Deputy Dolph, the six-foot-plus brute, who had apparently recovered from his short stint as a Fury's host. If you had asked me whether a mundy could stand up to a wizard toe-to-toe, particularly an enforcer trained in combat magics and wearing a bulletproof suit, I would have said no way. And, it turned out, I would have been right.

The fact that J was still alive and not a pile of messy ickness on the ground spoke well of his skills, or his dumb luck. But his situation did not look good. His duster was dust, and his shirt and jeans had been largely burned away, revealing strange white undergarments that I realized were Mormon underwear, at least the parts that weren't blackened holes, which probably was not a sign that he believed in the religion itself but rather had donned them for the same reason as the amulets: just in case rumors about the underwear's magical properties proved true.

Several brass Thai penis amulets hung from a cord in front of his groin area, also meant to ward off harm aimed at his genitals. And tattoos peeked through the remains of his clothing. I saw what looked like a Key of Solomon, an Auryn, and a stylized black pair of Siouxsie Sioux eyes among them.

This guy really was the Mikey of magical protection: he'd try anything. And none of it had stopped the enforcer's magic.

But to his credit, or perhaps his lack of sanity, J had not fled, and his magical undies were still white—at least, in the spots where they weren't scorched. J stood now waving one of his silver sai daggers in one hand, and grasping at the collection of amulets around his neck with the other. The enforcer advanced, clearly unconcerned. In fact, I worried the enforcer might simply be toying with J at this point, like a cat with a three-legged mouse.

Despite J's surprisingly successful distraction of getting himself slowly toasted, the rescue of the sentenced arcana was not going well at all.

"Come on," I said to Dawn, and ran to the group of exiles, toward Fatima, steering well clear of the battle between J and Deputy Dolph.

"But Sammy—!" Dawn said as she followed me.

"I know." I reached Fatima, without Grandfather noticing as far as I could tell, though my view of him was partially blocked by the rest of the exiles. The portal hummed and glowed behind and above me now, making me want to hunch my shoulders as if some Fey warrior was going to leap through it at my back.

The portal was not the usual stable, oval window between worlds that I'd (unfortunately) seen several times in the past. Or at least, it didn't remain one. Rather, it was stretching and shifting in shape, like a clear elastic sheet being tugged at by many hands; changing from an oval with a glowing blue edge one second, to a square with a red aura, to a rounded star shape with green glowing edges; cycling between them and other shapes as well; and the hum that resonated like a vibration in my spiritual bones shifted up or down in frequency with each change in shape.

The shifting must be Merlin's doing, as he attempted to find the right frequency to close the portal. The different shapes and frequencies served different purposes. The star shape and frequency could be used to cross physically into the Other Realm rather than transfer spirits, I knew. But locking it to that shape might not stop Grandfather's plans; Merlin needed to close the portal entirely. Hopefully, we could hold out and keep Grandfather distracted long enough.

Fatima looked between me and Dawn, confusion in her expression. "What is this? Who are you?"

I felt a chill.

"Damn it! We're too late." Fatima's spirit had already been exchanged with a Fey changeling.

"Finn!" Reggie said, pushing through the crowd to me.

"Reggie! Thank the gods!" At least that part of my plan wasn't completely hosed. I looked to Dawn. "Watch my back!"

I pulled out my skeleton key. I pressed the enchanted thief's finger bone against Reggie's manacle. There was a soft click and a seam appeared in the silver band, but it remained on his wrist. I reached out to try and pry the damn thing apart, but there was a flash of red light, and a shock that caused me to jerk my hand back reflexively.

"Ow! Damn it!"

"What's wrong?" Dawn asked.

"The manacles have some kind of spell that repels magic, even the magic inside me."

"Oh, well . . ." Dawn reached over, and tugged at the manacle. It came apart, and fell to the ground. As my eyes rose from watching them fall, I saw that Density Dude had joined Dolph and knocked out J, and both Arcanite wizards now stalked toward us.

Reggie rubbed at his wrist. "This was a dumb move. But thank you."

"No problem, Gandalf," I said, and handed him my extending baton as I moved to Fatima. "Get it? Because you're in gray, and you're a—"

Reggie pushed past me and flicked the baton into full extension.

Right.

I turned to the next exile. "Who are you?" I asked.

"Finn!" Grandfather shouted before I could judge whether the exile was friend or Fey. At the same time, Reggie engaged the two enforcers.

The remaining exiles began shuffling and lurching as Grandfather maneuvered them away from me.

I took a step to follow, to keep them between me and Grandfather, hoping to free more.

Four more Arcanites shimmered into view squatting atop the concrete outer ring, invisibility masks dropped.

I froze.

Aal's balls.

"TRAP!" I shouted. The four Arcanites leaped down from the columns, hitting the gravel with grunts and small bursts of dust. I backed up with Dawn until my heel hit the altar stone.

Grandfather had us.

Reggie began to fight his way back toward us, but two of the new Arcanites advanced on him as the other two moved toward Dawn and me.

The spiritual energy of the remaining human exiles called out to me, whispered promises of power, of escape. If I just took it, I would have the power to stop the enforcers, to stop Grandfather here and now. Their sacrifice would mean nobody else would suffer their fate.

I licked my lips, reaching out with my necromancer senses—

"Finn!" Dawn shouted, and grabbed my arm.

Her spiritual energy burned bright, familiar, delicious as fresh baked cookies. I wanted to devour it. I turned to her—

Her eyes were filled with fear.

My heart lurched, ached to calm that fear, to protect her.

I shuddered.

"Reggie, get out of here!" I shouted. "Take Fatima!"

I looked in the other direction. I met Sammy's eyes, shook my head in the direction of Fatima, then motioned for Sammy to leave. I took Dawn's hand.

"Do you trust me?" I asked her.

"Of course," she said.

I turned and faced the portal.

"Phinaeus Gramaraye!" Grandfather called. "Don't you dare!"

I waited for the portal to shift and stretch into the star shape, and then plunged my hands into it.

The portal grabbed hold of me, and pulled both me and Dawn into it faster than an episode of *Twin Peaks.*

Grandfather's shout of fury and frustration warped and faded as the world swirled away.

PART II

17

COME AS YOU ARE

Colors streaked, light bent, and my body felt like it was being squeezed out of a Play-Doh Fun Factory.

Then the squeezing stopped and the weird pressure began. My head felt ready to implode and at the same time there was a kind of vacuum around me that sucked the air out of my lungs.

The swirling colors and light resolved themselves into a forest of black trees as massive as those redwoods that have car tunnels cut through them, and each more gnarly than a Klingon sex tape. A black-light moon bathed it all in an eye-bending glow that made the umbrella-sized pale mushrooms shine neon bright, and made Dawn and me stand out like Tron rejects with the white stripes and patches on our clothing lit up.

Dawn collapsed to the ground beside me, gasping.

I was somewhat prepared for this—at least in the sense that as soon as it happened I remembered that this was something that would happen. I willed the environment around me to conform to my needs.

The pressure around me lessened, and sweet, cool air rushed into my lungs.

"Dawn!" I said, and extended my will to cover her as well. I felt the strain of it, to control so much of the environment. Dawn gasped in air.

At the same time, I noticed that the sting of the many scrapes I'd gained on the rough gravel of the Stonehenge lot had faded considerably, perhaps because despite willing air in my lungs, there was no actual air to irritate my injuries.

NOOoo! Alynon shouted in my head.

Oh frak. Alynon.

He was still trapped in my head.

When I had traveled in spiritual form to the Other Realm last time, Alynon and I had been separated into our own Fey bodies, though still spiritually bound together in some way. One theory about how to permanently separate us had been to try traveling physically to the Other Realm to force a true separation. If I wasn't in a Fey body, perhaps the link between us would be severed.

Another hope crushed.

Damn it! I'm so sorry. I didn't want him in my head any more than he wanted to be there.

Save your apologies. They do less than little to change our situation.

Dawn sat up, and as she took a deep breath I felt again the strain of maintaining the reality of an atmosphere around her.

"Dawn, you have to control the air around you with your will. Tell it to be what you need it to be."

"I need it to be hot and steamy," Dawn said, pushing to her feet. "As in my shower, at home. I don't suppose there's an easy way to get out of here?"

"I don't know. But please, concentrate on the air. Believe that the air around you is normal, breathable."

Dawn frowned, but after a second I felt a lessening of the strain on my own will, of the weight of belief in a reality that extended beyond myself.

"What happens if I stop thinking about it?" Dawn asked, her eyes unfocused as she concentrated on the air in front of her. "Or go to sleep?"

"Once your brain makes the connection between willing there to be air you can breathe, and actually breathing, it will just take over, the way your lungs work without you having to will them to."

"How about instead of that we just go home?" Dawn asked.

No! Alynon said. *Long have I fought to reach the Forest of Shadows, and now that we are here I will see my heart's purpose realized!*

Oh man. Alynon's true love. I was fuzzy on the details, but apparently he'd been involved in some kind of Romeo and Juliet affair with someone from the Forest of Shadows.

Aly, I'm not sure that's going to be possible. If we are caught here—

I have watched you play matchmaker to every magical sob case rather than concentrating on freeing me. And now that my love needs only for us to reach out and secure it, you would deny me even the attempt?

"Finn?" Dawn asked, concern and annoyance both growing in her tone. "You *do* know how to get back, right?"

"Uh—" I replied.

Okay, so I may have been distracted working on a game map in Arcana school while the teacher talked about Corporeal Portal Traveling. Not that "corportaling" was discussed much at all, since it was pretty much forbidden.

And because it usually led to snickering, as someone inevitably suggested what kind of sex act "corportaling" might be. But hopefully I wouldn't have to figure it out on my own—the actual portaling, not the sex act worthy of the name, that is.

"Not exactly," I added.

"Great," she said, and hugged her guitar case.

If only she knew how much better this was than the alternative. Not just the "being captured and killed" alternative, but the "Finn goes dark necromancer and drains the life from everyone" alternative. In fact, I heaved a huge sigh of relief as I realized that the constant tempting buzz of spiritual energy was gone now. We had come to an entire Other Realm devoid of earthly spirits, other than Dawn's. Hers blazed like a lighthouse beacon to me now, but after being surrounded by crowds of humans and a world filled with life energy, her sole soul was less a temptation and more a reminder of why I loved her.

"It will be okay," I promised. "If we can find our way to the Silver Court, or the Colloquy—"

Lines of purple energy sprang up around us like a cage, and solidified into nasty-looking black branches covered in thorns the size of a mutant cat's attitude.

Holes opened up in several of the great trees like doorways to a Bauhaus laser show, filled with warped shadowy images painted in negative colors. From those doorways stepped four Shadows Fey.

Behind us emerged a Viking in dark furs, bearing an axe. To our left emerged a knight in full black plate, and on our right emerged a medieval highwayman, wearing dark leathers and carrying a crossbow.

And before us emerged a Greek warrior, with a bronze muscle cuirass on his chest, leather skirt, and greaves on his legs. A purple wool cloak swept down from his bare shoulders, and he carried a bow as tall as himself that looked more like something a giant would use than a man.

Odysseus.

Odysseus was a fictional character of course, but the Fey built much of their appearance and identity on memories taken from human visitors to the Other Realm. The Fey also apparently had little ability to tell the difference between fact and fiction. Or perhaps they just found the fictional more interesting. So if a fictional character lived in someone's memory with enough richness and detail as to seem real, then memories of that character were just as likely to be used to create a Fey personality as real human memory.

In fact, there were probably hundreds of Odysseuses running around the Other Realm, each unique depending on the particular version of Odysseus remembered, the mix of other memories each Fey had incorporated, and their own actual experiences. And not all would choose to dress or appear like Odysseus.

This Odysseus approached from our front while the other three Fey kept a safe distance behind and to the sides of us. He held an arrow loosely nocked on the bow, and pointed it at Dawn. "Disarm!"

"Okay okay!" Dawn said, and pulled the Taser from its holster, tossing it down.

"Do not mock me," Odysseus said, and motioned at her guitar case. "Disarm!"

"He means Cotten," I said. "Set her down."

"What?" Dawn said. "Listen, buddy—"

Odysseus drew back his arrow with a great creaking of the bow.

"Jeez, okay!" Dawn said, setting her guitar case gently down on the ground. "But if you damage her, we're going to have a real problem."

The highwayman dashed in and snatched up Cotten then moved back. Odysseus slackened his draw, and swung the arrow around to me. "Who ventures to our world in body against the will of both men and the Aal?"

Don't tell them your name! Alynon said.

I'm not an idiot.

The last time I'd ventured into the Other Realm—or at least my spirit had—a Shadows Fey named Chauvelin tried to imprison me for my supposed crimes against the Fey. Granted, he'd done so with Alynon's help, but that was a whole other issue. Right now, the important thing was to avoid revealing my true identity to the Shadows Fey as long as possible; and given the rivalry between the Shadows and the Silver, I would definitely hide the fact that I had a Silver Court Fey sharing my body.

"We, uh, came here to help," I said.

"Everyone seeks to help," Odysseus said. "Though when you dig to the heart of their intent it is most often to the benefit of themselves. I ask again, who are you, strangers, and what purpose have you here? Speak true, or die."

"Well," I said, "would you believe that I came here because you've been tricked with a kind of Trojan horse?"

Odysseus frowned. "And if that were true, why would you reveal the plot to us?"

"Uh," I replied. Good question. "Well, war isn't good for anybody, all that death and destruction, right? So"—I looked around—"where *are* the spirits that were exiled here?"

"They are far from this place. As you soon shall be."

Damn. Whatever Merlin had done to destabilize the portal must have caused its destination point to jump around. Or perhaps there was something about traveling physically that shifted the portal's end point. In either case, Fatima's spirit was out of reach for now.

"Hey," Dawn said. "Far away sounds good to me. How about you set us down right outside Waterfront Pizza? I'll even buy you a slice."

Odysseus frowned. "You have come to the Greatwood in mortal form, an act forbidden by treaty and the will of both races. Whatever your true intent, your fate lies not in your world but in the Black Lodge." He waved his hand, and two thorny branches swept in like striking snakes to whip around our necks, the thorns close enough to tickle our skin. "Move any way but the one I wish, and you shall lose your head. Come."

He beckoned for us to follow, and the vines began to float in his direction, the thorns of mine biting painfully into the back of my neck and forcing me to move with them.

Odysseus marched us toward the tree he'd emerged from, and as he approached it the gnarled lines of the bark spread apart to form a new doorway.

Dawn hissed as one of the thorns bit into her neck, then said, "I don't suppose he's taking us to Halloween Town?"

"Uh, no," I replied. "He's taking us to their court, of sorts."

"Great," Dawn said. "Think we can get Daniel Webster as our lawyer?"

My eyebrows rose. "Actually, that might be possible."

Then I sighed. "But somehow I don't think we're going to exactly get a fair trial by an impartial jury. And besides, the Black Lodge isn't that kind of court. I meant more like a royal court, or at least the local castle. No outsiders are allowed into the true heart of the forest."

"Is there, like, a human embassy there?"

"No. The best we can hope for is an ambassador from one of the friendlier Fey Demesnes is present."

We reached the massive tree with its human-sized doorway opening onto a mind-bending light show. Odysseus stepped to the side, and waved us forward.

We had little choice but to follow his direction.

As my foot crossed over the door's threshold, I felt the vine release its hold around my neck, and my body was pulled forward into yet another portal. I managed to grab Dawn's hand just in time to make sure we weren't separated somehow.

We emerged not from another tree, but rather out of an actual doorway into a room that looked something like the entry hall of a rich medieval hunting lodge where Tim Burton and David Lynch had waged an interior design war. The wall and ceiling had exposed beams of black, wet-looking wood, or perhaps bone, since they seemed to rise up and meet the central ceiling beam like ribs to a spine. In between hung tapestries depicting what I assumed were scenes from the Shadows' history, the woven images dancing and moving through a looping animation of sorts. Glowing roots hung down from the ceiling, their bluish light casting everything in a surreal twilight.

There was a second doorframe to our left, but no door within it, just lines radiating out from the center like a giant asterisk.

One section of the far wall stood out from the rest, holding a tiered tree of brass award plaques. And before it stood a pedestal holding a rounded crystal flame the size of a mini fridge, which served as a display case for three golden golf trophies.

Golf, it turned out, was one of the major crazes in the Forest of Shadows, and performance in the sport had some complex impact on power hierarchies within the Demesne. Of course, being in a forest, the game had been adapted somewhat, the type of iron and the force of the stroke still determining distance, but the player's will and mental reflexes were then used to guide the ball safely through the trees, weaving between them to reach the clearings that served as putting greens.

"There's no windows," Dawn said, looking around. "And no guards." She stepped beside the doorway. "Maybe we can jump him when he comes through."

Already looking for a way to escape. She was so much better at this than me.

I wouldn't tell her that the building in which this room existed quite possibly had no actual outside in the Other Realm, no way to leave it except through the magical portals of the Greatwood. The laws of our world did not always apply in the Other Realm.

In fact, a popular story said the Forest of Shadows was one large beast slumbering away the centuries, the trees being like quills atop this sleeping titan's head. Certainly, the Shadows Fey had some kind of connection with their forest, an ability to control it in some ways, or at least use its nature to their advantage. And wherever we were now might well be within the titan's body, or even its dream, in a place where no road traveled and no human could reach without a Shadows Fey to guide them.

Indeed, a low susurration filled the air, like a mountain breathing slowly, and the air smelled like the shed skin of an old snake.

But I didn't want to take away what little hope Dawn held on to. If for no other reason than I needed her hope to keep me from giving up myself.

So all I said was, "That's a bad idea. Trust me."

Dawn sighed, and stepped back as Odysseus emerged from the portal.

"Hey there," I said, looking around at the decor. "Is Gargamel home, or is he out trying to catch those darn Smurfs again?"

"I know not of this Gargamel," Odysseus said.

"Well, whoever's in charge, take us to your leader."

"You make no demands here," Odysseus said. "But as fate would have it, it is to the Echelon that I take you."

"Ah. Lucky us."

Dawn shot me a worried glance at my tone, but I rolled my eyes at her and gave her a reassuring smile.

I wished I felt so certain of what awaited us.

Odysseus walked toward the door to our left, and the asterisk lines opened up like an orifice, revealing a hallway.

"So," I said, "who *are* the Triums in these parts? Just curious."

Odysseus chose not to reply.

The hallway felt much like the entry room, with ebon beams or ribs rising up to an arched ceiling, and between those ribs were doorways that when closed appeared seamless with the wall, differentiated only by their slightly darker color. I eyed the few open doorways as we passed them, but sadly none of them opened onto a yellow brick road with a sign that said CONVENIENT ESCAPE ROUTE THIS WAY. I just had to play along, and use whatever value being an arcana might have in order to ransom, or bully, our way to freedom.

Dawn leaned close and whispered, "So what's the plan?"

"I'll know once my mouth starts moving," I whispered back.

"Great. We really need to work on your planning skills."

"Says you, my family, and every teacher I ever had."

"Hey!" Dawn said as we passed an open doorway. "Was that Hannibal Lecter?"

"Or Van Helsing," I said. "Either one has the traits of cunning and deception that the Shadows prize."

We arrived at what appeared to be membranous double doors, which opened like sideways eyelids to reveal a narrow passage into a large chamber beyond.

A pale man in a black fur cloak rushed out of the passage, wringing his hands. Odysseus frowned as though tasting something sour.

"te'Wormtongue," he said. "What is it?"

"The Trium request that the prisoners be held a short time until an ARC ambassador from the Colloquy arrives to deal with them."

I blinked in surprise. This was better than I'd dared hope.

Of course, not everyone in the ARC currently had my best interests in mind. But even if they were aligned with Grandfather, he would want me back physically in our world. I could deal with whatever situation I found there better than I could anything here.

Odysseus sighed. "Very well. Send word when they *are* ready."

"Of course." Wormtongue bowed, and retreated back into the passage.

Odysseus guided us to a doorway across the hall which

opened as we approached, and led us into a room with several chairs and a pedestal holding a platter of fruit. The room was otherwise featureless and black except for the ghostly light emanating from the dangling root-like lights. "Wait here," Odysseus said. "Do not attempt anything foolish." He then left, closing us inside.

"So," Dawn said, pacing around the room as if she might find an exit they'd forgotten about. "How screwed are we?"

"I don't know," I said. "It all depends I guess on who the ARC ambassador is, and what the Shadows hope to gain from capturing me."

"Don't you mean capturing us?" Dawn asked.

"No. You should be set free. I can't imagine why even the Shadows would risk the ARC's retaliation by holding a mundy captive."

"Lucky me," Dawn said. "So what are we looking at here? I mean, who's in charge? Sauron? Pat Robertson? An HMO board? How evil are we talking?"

"It's . . . complicated. The Forest of Shadows isn't technically the Demesne of evil, it's the Demesne of cunning, deception, and personal power."

"So more like politician evil," Dawn said.

I shrugged. "Most of them probably convince themselves they need power to do good things for their fellow Shadows—even if they never actually use it for that. And some of them, like Odysseus, probably try to use it for something other than personal gain. I mean, if they were all purely selfish and evil, none of the other Demesnes would deal with them."

"Still, if they're all about power and cunning, then for all we know, Hitler could be in charge. That's better how?" Dawn asked.

"Well, it means they won't just kill or torture me for fun, not if they can gain some advantage from keeping me alive, or letting me go. And the one person I'm pretty sure won't be in charge is Hitler."

I shared what I remembered from my Arcana school lessons about the Forest of Shadows' political structure, which made the late Roman Empire look positively enlightened and stable, and Gordon Gekko look like a rank amateur.

The Forest of Shadows, like all Fey Demesnes, had many different regions, or versions of itself, that each touched the different major land areas of Earth. Each Shadows region had a black lodge controlled by a triumvirate of leaders, and beneath them a body of senators who were ranked in influence and power.

Though specifics of the Fey internal politics were not well known to arcana, stories of the Shadows maneuverings had reached us. There was the Year of the Three Hitlers, for example, which had seen an escalation of plots and assassination attempts that had embroiled the Forest of Shadows in civil war and nearly brought about its collapse. Since then, there were no te'Hitlers to be found in the Forest of Shadows, for much the same reason there were no divas allowed in the Summerland.

"So if we're dealing with senators, does that mean we can buy off a few of them?" Dawn asked.

"If we were Fey, maybe. But they won't take bribes from humans. It's kind of like how Congress sells their votes to American companies, but not Russian or Chinese, at least not openly. Makes them feel patriotic, I guess." I picked up an apple off of the tray. "But maybe—"

"Stop!" Dawn said.

I paused in the middle of polishing the apple on my T-shirt. "What?" I asked.

"Isn't fairy food supposed to be enchanted? Like, if you eat it, you're trapped here forever?"

I smiled. "Actually, Fey food is one of the few things I enjoy about the Other Realm. Here, try it."

Dawn looked at me dubiously, but then bit into the apple. She frowned at it. "It tastes . . . weird. Sort of a bitter edge."

"That's because it doesn't taste how an apple tastes to you. You experienced how it tastes to whoever's memory its Fey creator used as a template."

Dawn blinked down at the apple. "Wait, so even though you hate lentils, if a Fey took my memory of lentils and made some for you, you'd think they were delicious?"

"Well, I'd taste them the way you taste them, yeah. I still don't understand how anyone can like the *texture* of beans."

"That's because you're crazy," Dawn said.

The door opened, and Odysseus waved us out of the room. "Come, it is time."

Dawn tossed the apple back onto the platter, and we crossed the hall and moved through the double membrane doorway. The passage beyond opened onto a round stage at the chamber's center, with seats rising in tiers on three sides: a theater-in-the-round layout shaped like the radiation warning symbol. All sides looked equal in every way, which probably had less to do with any noble ideals of equality and more to do with keeping anyone from taking offense at a perceived slight.

The tiers of the Echelon held space for sixty-three Fey senators—a number I knew from my lessons, not from counting chairs—and most seats were filled already. Every

Fey there had some element of a famous deceiver in them. And while not strictly evil, I did not expect to find any friends here.

Odysseus waved his hand as we reached the center of the circle, and glittering black manacles appeared around our wrists, with chains running down into the ground, holding Dawn and me in place.

"We await the Triums," he said. "Do not think to test your strength against the might of this chamber, nor speak you words of insult or challenge to any here."

"Wouldn't dream of it," I said. I had little desire to be turned into Finn Jelly.

"Well, you could at least *dream* of it," Dawn whispered to me.

Fey were still arriving, rising up from the ground in their cushioned seats, though it appeared less like they were rising from trap doors and more like time-lapse videos of growing plants as they basically willed themselves to be in this place. Platters holding food and drink waited between the chairs, and as the senators appeared, they began grazing on the delicacies.

The lowest tier with the fewest seats held the most powerful senators, each subsequent tier above them holding progressively lower-ranked senators as measured by their length of service, the number of personal favors they were owed, the number of other members they had blackmail material on, the number of other members they could easily kill, and their golf ranking. The lowest tiers with the highest ranks were mostly filled with Fey whose persona had been around longest, reflecting the amount of time it took to actually achieve such a rank and, I supposed, a good golf handicap.

I didn't recognize most of the senators, their core identities taken from times and cultures I had no exposure to, or from someone not particularly famous. But I recognized a few. I quietly pointed them out to Dawn as I gave her a quick overview of Shadows politics.

In the front row sat a Rasputin with his oily hair and rat's nest of a beard. Higher up I spotted a Saci-pererê with his red hat and pipe, and a Paul the Apostle—at least, that version of Paul perceived in someone's memory to be a cunning deceiver, presumably. Higher still sat a Jareth the Goblin King, looking bored as he twirled glass globes in one gloved hand; and a Fey I thought might be the magician Prospero, exiled Duke of Milan, in flowing robes and tempest-tossed white hair.

Dawn frowned. "If I fought so hard to advance to the top, I'd want to be, well, at the top. I'd want my enemies in front of me."

"There's no direct physical attacks allowed in here," I said. "Both by strict tradition, and I'm pretty sure by deadly magics. Deception and cunning are the only weapons allowed."

"Damn," Dawn said. "I was hoping maybe you could trick them into destroying each other with that mouthy-wordy thing you do, *Doctor Who*–style."

"Sorry. Fey do still get killed in here, though. They just can't attack each other."

"Whahuh? How does that work?"

"Well, for example, all that food and drink was prepared outside of the chamber before being manifested in here. So if poison was introduced to it outside the chamber, that doesn't strictly violate the chamber's rules or protections, see?"

Dawn frowned at all of the Fey chowing down. "Why not just avoid the food then?"

"I guess that would imply they aren't clever enough to outsmart a poisoner."

"A really clever person wouldn't feel he needs to prove himself by being an idiot."

Odysseus scowled, but didn't say anything.

I think she's talking about you.

Stuff it.

"Maybe," I said. "They do use poison tasters. It's become part of the whole game though, like everything else they do here. You know, taste a senator's food today, and they owe you some small favor in the future. Gain a bunch of little favors and it might add enough to your power and influence that you could secure a senator's seat yourself—maybe by, say, poisoning an existing senator."

"How very circle of strife," Dawn replied, and rolled her eyes.

"Hakiller Murdata," I agreed.

A sharp scream of pain drew our eyes to the upper tier in front of us. A Fey manifested, and as he appeared he divided into two, peeling off to either side and curling down in a mess of Fey protoplasm. His scream died away.

The Fey to either side of him sprang to their feet, and one, a fellow who looked a bit like Colonel Sanders but wasn't, said in a Southern accent, "Dadburn it all to Hades! Look at this mess all over my shoes. I thought we agreed not to sabotage entrances."

"No," said a man in red Inquisitor robes on the next tier up. He lifted his robes, and floated down to the spot where the Fey had just died. "We agreed it had become impossible. But I have just proven that with great faith and moral conviction, the Aal makes anything possible."

A seat rose up beneath the Inquisitor as he took his new position in the chamber. After a brief exchange of looks, all of the senators above him shifted to fill in the gap, some advancing a tier behind him, leaving an empty spot in the uppermost tier. Sanders's eyes narrowed at the Inquisitor for a second, but he withheld whatever comment he had, and instead retook his own seat, causing the remains of his former neighbor to evaporate with the wave of his hand.

Dawn looked a bit shaken. "That wasn't poison," she whispered.

"No," I agreed. "But I guess since he was entering the room, not *in* the room, it was allowed."

Three bells rung, and at the top of each tier one of the Triumvirates appeared.

On the left sat a gnomish man I guessed to be Rumpelstiltskin. His gray beard and hair were braided through with golden thread, and his red doublet and flopping pointed hat had the shifting brightness of thick velvet.

On the right sat Lucifer, because, well, of course. He was beautiful, the kind of man I might consider putting on my list of men I'd be willing to sleep with, but would be uncomfortable if Dawn did so. He wore white robes trimmed in gold and crimson, and a nimbus of light surrounded his head, a halo of bright starlight that occasionally flickered and went fiery red in time with an eye twitch.

Above the row directly in front of us sat a gray-haired gentleman I didn't immediately recognize, wearing a dark Victorian suit and a solemn look upon his thin face.

Any advice? I asked Alynon.

Remember that each is interested first and foremost in the gathering of power and influence, or else proving themselves cleverest of all here. Look for ways to play that to your advantage.

Well, they won't be able to do much with that power if the Fey they rule over are all dead. Hopefully they're clever enough to see that.

La, the protection and prosperity of the Forest of Shadows may run a close second to their own success where it benefits them, but the interests of their fellow Aalbrights outside the Shadows at best limps behind at a distant third. Unless you can prove a direct threat exists to them personally as well as to their Demesne, they will care little, I fear.

Right. And maintaining the peace of the PAX Arcana and their relationship with the ARC was so far behind their other concerns it might as well be the last runner in the race. That runner being a turtle. With a handicap of being severely dead.

In other words, my chances were somewhere between slim and none, and that was only if they didn't find out who I—

"Phinaeus Gramaraye," the Victorian gentleman above us said. "We have been warned of your coming."

Doh!

18

DOWN IN A HOLE

"Your honor," I addressed the grim-seeming Victorian Fey gentleman. "Or, uh, highness, or—"

"Lord Cadmorius te'Moriarty," Odysseus snapped beside me.

Moriarty. Great. Of course an amoral sociopathic genius was in charge of our fate.

"Lord Moriarty," I continued. "I don't know what you've been told about me, but—"

"Lack of knowledge is your weakness, not mine," Moriarty said. "I have been told enough to know what charges may be laid against you. And to know that your fellow arcana are most eager to bring their own charges."

"What—"

I heard footsteps clicking in the passageway behind us, and turned to look, the chain to my wrists pulling tight and forcing me to step around it for a better angle.

A figure approached, silhouetted black against the light of the doorway behind him. But from the tri-corner hat and the arrogance of his stride, I guessed his identity before he reached the light of the chamber.

"Chauvelin," I muttered.

This could be bad, Alynon offered helpfully.

I leaned over to look past him, hoping to see the ARC ambassador, but Chauvelin walked alone.

"Who's Chauvelin?" Dawn whispered back.

"The Fey who tried to get Silene killed and me held prisoner last time I visited the Other Realm," I replied. A Shadows ambassador to the Colloquy—a sort of Fey United Nations in the Other Realm—Chauvelin's persona was based on the villain from the *Scarlet Pimpernel* novels, a cruel French citizen ruthless in enforcing his beliefs.

Chauvelin strode out onto the round floor of the chamber, and smiled like Sylvester finding Tweety trapped inside a microwave.

Make that definitely bad, Alynon amended.

Chauvelin made a sweeping bow to the three Triums, then said to me in a voice entirely lacking his usual French accent, "Hello, brother."

Double frak.

"Mort?" I asked. "You're the ARC ambassador?"

He smiled. "As soon as Grandfather confirmed that the Shadows had you, he arranged for me to exchange bodies with a Shadows ambassador and come here."

"Hold," Lucifer said. "You are family? How can you be trusted to hold justice above kinship?"

"I assure you, good lords," Mort said, looking up at the tree Triums. "I am here to offer you both Finn and Alynon in permanent exile."

His words were a punch to the gut. Whatever fleeting hope I'd held that he would still act as my brother died.

"You don't have the authority to offer anything!" I said,

and looked up at the Echelon. "He's not a real ambassador, just someone who's angry at me."

"I am, in fact, an official representative of the Arcana Ruling Council," Mort said. "Grandfather arranged a quaestor position for me."

Well of course he did.

Quaestor was an entry-level position in the ARC often given by senior members as favors to important supporters. It held little real power, but the status had probably appealed to Mort's ego regardless. And the nice extra paycheck probably didn't hurt.

"Jesus, Mort," I said, equally hurt and angry. "This isn't a fight over who gets the most ice cream. This is serious. They will hold me, feed on me, forever."

"Don't be a dick, Morty," Dawn said. "Mattie—"

"Don't!" Mort said. "Don't bring Mattie into this, or Father, or anyone else, either of you. This is about Finn, period." Mort looked up at the Triums. "What are the charges?"

"We had first intended to address those crimes previously laid against this arcana by te'Chauvelin in the Colloquy," Moriarty replied.

"Wait," Dawn said, looking at me. "What crimes?" I could see the worry in her eyes. Not just for our current situation, but that there was something else she didn't know about me, some other secret I had withheld from her like my use of dark necromancy to stop Kaminari.

Moriarty said in a formal tone, "The charges laid against Phinaeus Gramaraye include the death of two wardens during his release from exile, the trapping of an Aalbright within his body, and the murder of the jorõgumo Hiromi, pledged to our Demesne."

"And what punishment does the Shadows seek?" Mort asked.

"Punishment?" I said. "Uh, shouldn't I get a trial or something before we jump to punishment?"

"Your guilt is known," Moriarty replied. "And once we begin to consume your memories, I suspect we shall find many more offenses to justify punishments far greater in number and method than your mortal body will bear. There is no need for a trial."

My memories?

Oh, shazballs.

Bright's buttocks! Alynon agreed.

Normally, when an arcana traveled into the Other Realm, they had blocks put on their memories to hide any sensitive knowledge of the arcana world or magic from the Fey just in case their memories were read. But I didn't have any such blocks. And neither did I have protection as an ambassador under the PAX that forbade my memories from being shared with the Fey. Basically, I was an open buffet, and the Shadows Fey could very well learn things from me that would put arcana in danger, that would put the Elwha brightbloods in danger. That would put my family in danger.

There's got to be something we can do to block my memories from them? I asked Alynon, though I knew the answer.

You miss the full danger here, Alynon replied. *They might gain access to *my* memories as well.*

What? But I thought . . . ah, crap.

Any of Alynon's memories of his time spent in my body as a changeling that had imprinted on my brain were locked away behind a wall of Fey magic. No arcana was able to access them. But with my physical brain here in the Other Realm—

Double shazballs.

"Your honors," I said. "You do remember that the last time I entered your Realm I came to make you aware of how you were being played like pawns in someone's game? And in return Chauvelin tried to violate the PAX to hold me captive. If anything, you should be rewarding me, not punishing me."

"We had no need of an arcana's help," Lucifer replied.

"Yeah? That's funny, because you've been fooled again, and here I am again trying to help you."

Mort snorted. "I told you that you were a fool to come here before. You're twice the fool to come back knowing what happened last time."

"Then I guess we're *both* twice the fool," I said. "What is that, like, a Rube's Cube?"

"Always ready with a joke," Mort said. "But that doesn't change that I was right."

What could I say? He had a point. I hadn't really thought things through. Again. It might just have been better to die at the Stonehenge, even if Grandfather had taken control of my body. And I'd dragged Dawn into this, confident she'd be safe—

"Wait," I said. "Dawn is innocent, and a mundane. She should be returned to her world."

"And yet," Moriarty replied, "she brought a weapon into the Greatwood."

"Weapon?" Dawn said. "You don't seriously mean my guitar?"

"They do," I said. "Musical instruments are forbidden in the Other Realm."

"Jesus." Dawn shook her head. "Music is illegal? What is

this, Feyloose? If this is all heading toward a prom, just kill me now. My first prom was bad enou—"

Moriarty raised his hand, and said, "Despite this violation of the PAX, we will be releasing the human to her world. Just as soon as we have established both her innocence, and her lack of magic."

I felt a flood of relief, even as I understood the real motives. They would feed on her memories under the guise of proving her innocence before releasing her. And they would release her, but only to appease the Arcana Ruling Council as a "compromise" for condemning me. Regardless of all the ways in which Dawn was amazing, her lack of magical knowledge made her of little value to them.

But she would be safe. Somehow, that made facing whatever came next bearable. And if Mort's being here had helped ensure Dawn's release, then I was grateful, whatever his intent toward me.

I opened my mouth to thank them, but stopped. For all I knew, my gratitude would make them change their mind out of fear of appearing to compromise in any way with an arcana.

Lucifer stood. "I propose he be sentenced to a lifetime as a memory feeder."

Rumpelstiltskin stood. "Of course you do. Your faction controls the memory farms. But we can draw memory from any exile. How long since we have had a mortal body to play with? And one bonded with an Aalbright?" He rubbed his long, knobby fingers together. "I propose he be subjected to study and dissection. And possibly breeding experiments."

"Oh hells no!" Dawn said, and jerked against her chain as if trying to rip it out of the ground, but both her remark and efforts were ignored.

I looked at Mort, to see if any of this was registering with him. I couldn't believe he'd actually allow me to be physically tortured. But he deliberately turned away from me, and said nothing.

Lucifer's eye twitched as he regarded Rumpelstiltskin, and his halo flared red. "You would use him up and waste him in but a cycle. Think of how many offspring we may create from his memories over his lifetime."

Rumpelstiltskin barked a laugh. "You speak of offspring to me?" Several of the senators shifted uncomfortably in their seats as he continued. "Consider if we might branch offspring who are able to enter the mortal realm without the need to inhabit a body from that world? Consider if we might strengthen the benefits and control of the bond with our brightblood cousins, the offspring of our ancestor's folly? You are shortsighted as ever."

Lucifer's halo became a roiling bonfire now, like the Eye of Sauron. "And you would teach the humans every secret of the Greatwood if it gained you a single new vassal today."

Rumpelstiltskin giggled, and did a little capering dance. "Oh what a weak and desperate accusation, Lucy my boy," he said, then continued in a singsong. "Ad hominem, you're lobbin 'em, but I be rubber and you be glue, they bounce off me while you sniff your own goo."

Lucifer glared coldly at Rumpelstiltskin. "Ware, Imp. You overestimate your power here."

"Perhaps," Rumpelstiltskin said, his voice suddenly as cold as a serial killer's while speaking to his victim. "But Chauvelin rose from my faction, and it was he who laid the charges, so my proposal outweighs yours, unless you have something besides taunts to back yours up?"

Moriarty stood. "You both forget an important fact. It was indeed Chauvelin who laid the first claims against Gramaraye on behalf of the Greatwood. Gramaraye, however, outwitted him and made him seem the fool—"

A Grinch-like smile spread across Lucifer's face at Moriarty's words, but Rumpelstiltskin cleared his throat loudly and said, "My lord te'Moriarty, what is your point?"

"Simply that no single faction has priority on this claim. It must be decided, and the rewards shared, by us all."

And Moriarty had managed to pit Lucifer and Rumpelstiltskin against each other, which helped his position.

Mort raised his hand. "Please, your honors. The ARC also has claim on Finn for his crimes in our world, including the attack that brought him here."

Lucifer's eye twitched, and his halo burned red again. "Twice has this arcana escaped Shadows justice for his crimes against us. And twice did the ARC claim the privilege of jurisdiction, holding him safe in your world. Do not think to come here and snatch justice from our grasp again."

Mort raised both hands now in a gesture of offering. "I'm not here to take Finn anywhere. Not his spirit, anyway. What I propose is that I take his body back, but that his spirit may remain here, with you, in exile. Permanently. Just as I promised."

"Jesus, Mort," I said. "Didn't you just hear what they were saying?"

"Don't blame me," Mort snapped back. "I warned you not to keep getting involved with the feybloods and their wars. I warned you to stop putting Mattie and the family business in danger. You brought this on yourself."

"Uh huh," I replied. "How convenient that this is also exactly what you want."

"You have no idea what I want. You haven't bothered to ask me once since you stormed back into our home dragging danger with you. You've hurt everyone around you, including the woman you supposedly love." He waved at Dawn.

"Bullshit!" I said.

"Really? Name one family member you haven't hurt since you've been back."

"I—" I stopped. I couldn't. "That isn't fair, Mort. This is all Grandfather's fault.

"He's the one who exiled me, who caused most of these problems. He's the one who treated you like crap. So why are you so desperate for his approval still?"

"You're wrong," Mort said. "Grandfather is the only one willing to do what is necessary to truly protect our family, and to keep Mattie safe. To even protect you from yourself. I see that now. *You* showed me that."

"Are you serious?" I shouted. "Don't you remember what he did to—"

"Enough squibble squabble!" Rumpelstiltskin said.

"Agreed," Moriarty replied. "This is not a court of family grievances. Ambassador Gramaraye, while this lodge wishes to offer the ARC all possible respect in this matter, we shall not relinquish your brother's body. Phinaeus Gramaraye is not its only occupant, and as fellow Aalbrights we cannot allow Alynon to be returned to exile in your world."

How thoughtful of them, Alynon said with a complete lack of sincerity.

"Right," Mort said. "About that, I believe there may be a way to separate Alynon Infedriel's spirit from its bond with my brother."

"What?" I asked.

What? Alynon said.

"Indeed?" Moriarty said. "So you propose to allow us both the spirit of your brother and of the traitor Alynon Infedriel in exchange for your brother's body?"

"Yes," Mort said.

"What?!" I said again.

"I am still of a mind to decline," Moriarty replied. "You must understand, this is not a trade negotiation, nor an ARC trial. This is the Echelon of the Greatwood, and we shall decide what is a fitting punishment. However," Moriarty said, and raised a hand to cut off the clearly coming protest from Mort. "There is a way we may be able to satisfy both the need for a fair trial, and allow the ARC to claim Finn Gramaraye's body."

"And what is that?" Mort said.

"The accused may attempt to prove himself innocent through trial by combat."

Of course. Why did it always come down to something like this? "So what does that mean?" I asked.

Moriarty inclined his head. "If you win, all charges laid against you by Chauvelin shall be dropped."

"And should I lose?" I asked.

"Then you would be subject to what punishments this Echelon deems fit."

"Wait," I said. "How does trial by combat allow the ARC to claim my body?"

Moriarty smiled, and steepled his fingers. "Why, if the one who defeats you in combat is a representative of your ARC, of course. Then might we grant the request honorably to them as victor."

"Wait, you mean—" I looked at Mort.

"You can't be serious!" Dawn said. "You're going to make Finn fight his brother?"

Mort did not share my expression of surprise.

This is a setup, Alynon said. *They planned this entire exchange.*

Yeah, I picked up on that, too.

It was just another political power game being played with my life. If I won the duel against Mort and escaped Chauvelin's charges yet again, it would be an embarrassment for the ARC, and weaken the position of Rumpelstiltskin's faction aligned with Chauvelin. If I lost the duel, it would still earn Moriarty points for pitting two arcana against each other, increase resentment of the ARC, and probably be used to push whatever anti-arcana agenda Moriarty had.

But the Shadows power plays were not my concern. Getting out of here with both my spirit and body intact was. And if nothing else, this would buy time to either escape, or be rescued somehow.

I was worried I didn't have that time to waste, however. Whether Mort really believed Grandfather would help protect Mattie, or whether Grandfather had held Mattie's safety hostage to gain Mort's allegiance—whether Mort truly believed he was doing what was best for me and the family or not—I knew the reality of what Grandfather was capable of.

Do you see a better option? I asked Alynon.

Alynon was silent a minute, then, *Fa, not really, no.*

"Dawn will still be freed, regardless?" I asked Moriarty.

"Yes," he replied.

I sighed. "Very well, I accept," I said. "On the condition that whether I win or lose, you honor the promise made to Alynon Infedriel by Chauvelin, and reunite him with

Velorain." I looked to Mort. "If you really can free his spirit from my body, that is, and aren't just lying."

What? Alynon said in a genuinely shocked tone. *What are you doing?*

The right thing.

Rumpelstiltskin spat. "We owe Alynon Infedriel nothing. He failed to deliver you to us as promised."

"No," I said. "Alynon delivered me to Chauvelin. He held up his side of the bargain. Chauvelin just failed to hold on to me, and I forced Alynon back into my body. Neither of those things are Alynon's fault."

Rumpelstiltskin made a whiny growl sound, then said, "If te'Chauvelin made promises on behalf of the Greatwood, then they shall be honored."

Moriarty smiled. "Indeed, and I quite look forward to studying the mechanism by which you two are joined."

I— Thank you, Finn, Alynon said quietly.

Don't thank me yet, I thought back. *Somehow, I don't think Moriarty will be quick or gentle in honoring that promise.*

Still, it is more than I deserve after what I did to you.

You didn't ask to be trapped in my body, in exile. Believe me, I understand that.

Moriarty looked to Mort. "Ambassador Gramaraye, do you accept the terms of the contest, to fight your brother for the rights to his body?"

Mort looked from Moriarty to me. I could practically hear the thoughts running through his head as he weighed the risk of me winning versus the risk of failing in the mission Grandfather had given him, of failing yet again to earn the respect he felt he deserved from Grandfather.

"I accept," he said. "But I too have a request. In addition to Finn's body, I wish to take the spirit of one who was sent here three months ago, a . . . succubus spirit, named Brianne."

I sighed. "Oh, Mort," I whispered. Of course there was more in this for him than simply pleasing Grandfather or, sadly, more even than protecting Mattie and the family. In fact, getting Brianne back was probably one of the things Grandfather had promised Mort to win his support.

"You make a demand on top of your demand?" Moriarty asked.

"I am offering you two spirits, and taking only one body," Mort replied. "This would simply balance the terms."

Lucifer said, "I know of the spirit you seek." His tone said that he held something back.

Mort took a step toward Lucifer, his mask of feigned indifference truly breaking for the first time. "Where is she? Is she—" he caught himself, and continued, "Can she be made ready for transfer?"

"I'm afraid that's not possible," Lucifer said. "She is no longer in our Demesne."

"But," Moriarty said, "we can offer you her location. Clearly, she holds some personal meaning to you."

Emotion warred clearly on Mort's face—relief that Brianne was alive, frustration and disappointment that she remained out of reach.

"Fine," he said at last. "I accept the duel, in exchange for Finn's body and the location of Brianne's spirit should I win."

Dawn strained against her chain, reaching toward Mort. "Mort, you asshole, you can't be serious! You're going to take away Finn's body and leave his spirit to be tortured here?"

"You don't understand, Dawn," Mort replied. "Finn's

messed everything up, including your life, you just can't see it."

"Excuse me?" Dawn said.

Rumpelstiltskin scowled. "I still protest. We can learn so much from his body."

Mort crossed his arms. "You deserve better than him, Dawn. When we get back, the ARC will erase all memory of him, so you can have a normal life again, without almost getting killed every other day."

"Who are you to tell me what I fucking deserve?" Dawn said, anger welling in her voice, and I knew her well enough to hear the edges of fear as well. "And who are you to mess with my memories? My *mind*?" The fear was much clearer now. "Do you know how hard I had to work to get my shit straight to begin with? If you want to fuck with my love *or* my mind, Finn's not the one you'll have to fight!" She stretched her arms apart, straining. She gave a long, slow shout of effort.

"Dawn—" I began. I didn't want her wasting her efforts only to bring the wrath of the Shadows Fey down on herself.

Several links bent and stretched.

"Holy—" I said.

The chains shattered, sending shrapnel flying in every direction.

19

HARD TO HANDLE

Mort turned to Dawn, his shocked expression a match for my own as the broken remains of her chains dropped away and evaporated. Dawn charged at him, and he made a belated attempt to swing at her, but she knocked it aside and slid behind him, grabbing him in a choke hold.

Odysseus, I noticed, did nothing, watching the entire thing stoically.

"Okay," Dawn said to the gathered Fey. "Here's the real deal. You're going to let us go, or I snap Mort's neck."

"Go ahead," Moriarty called from above in an amused tone. "He is no vassal of the Greatwood that I should protect him."

Dawn pulled at Mort's neck, dragging him back a step. "I'm serious. Let us out of here, or you'll have to explain to the damn ARC how you let their mouthpiece die. That can't be good for you."

"Enough of this," Moriarty sighed. "te'Odysseus?"

Odysseus advanced on Dawn.

I pulled at my chains with all of my might, willing them to break. I felt them begin to flex, their resistance to my will like trying to press down a trampoline with my hand alone.

Then the pressure snapped back my will, the chains unbroken, causing a momentary dizziness.

Damn it! I gathered my focus, prepared to try again.

Odysseus waved at Dawn, and snaked up around her once again, this time looping over her shoulders and around her arms, sealing her in a cocoon of Fey steel and yanking her back from Mort.

Mort, red faced, turned toward Dawn with fists clenched and shaking.

"Ambassador, halt," Odysseus said.

Mort looked up at Odysseus with something like disdain on his red face. "She's a mundy, so she's in my jurisdiction, right?"

Odysseus shook his head. "This mortal did naught but that which any proud woman might, who has the heart to defend what is hers. And, in truth, I fear that if I let you at her, I will but have to save you once more."

A wave of chuckles in the Echelon made Mort's face go from an angry deep red to an embarrassed fiery red.

He looked at me, and muttered, "You won't be 'hers' when the ARC is done with her." Then to Dawn he said, "Whether you believe me or not, this is for your own good."

"My fellow lords," Lucifer said. "This woman did break her bonds. Surely that calls for some small investigation into her memories, to discover the source of such strength."

Rumpelstiltskin snorted. "And of course your own faction would receive the king's share of any such memories, and the strength they offer."

Moriarty waved his hand. "We must carefully weigh the benefits of such action against the cost in the ARC's trust, which is paramount to our greater plans. Such calculations are not to be made lightly. Let us consider them carefully during the duel, and revisit the question of the mundane's fate after."

"Agreed," Lucifer said with clear disappointment.

"Agreed," Rumpelstiltskin said, his tone and distant expression making clear his mind already sought the best advantages for himself.

"Very good." Moriarty waved his hand. "te'Odysseus, escort our guests to the Room of Contest."

"Yes, my lord," Odysseus replied. He faced Dawn. "There is no hope of escape, and no place you may escape to even should you overpower every Aalbright here. It would be like jumping from a ship in the midst of the dark sea. So do I need to drag you, or are you once again in possession of your calm?"

"He's right," I said. "This is not the time to fight."

Dawn rattled the chains around her, and gave Odysseus a petulant look, but said, "I'm calm as I'm gonna get."

Odysseus waved his hand, and the chains disappeared from Dawn, and from my wrists as well. "Follow," he said, and left the chamber the way we had entered.

We marched up the passageway, and back into the many-doored hallway.

"Are you okay?" I asked Dawn.

"Me? You're the one about to play gladiator!"

"I'll be fine," I said with far more confidence than I felt. "It won't be to the death or anything. They still want to have a Finn Memory Buffet, don't forget."

That is *true, isn't it?* I asked Alynon.

Mostly, Alynon said, not sounding very positive.

So, what, I'll be mostly not *dead?* I asked.

Each time you "die," you will lose something of yourself, a memory. For you, that will be an inconvenience, perhaps a slight change to your personality. But we don't know how it will affect me if you die, since we are connected. For me, for any Fey, losing a memory is to permanently lose a part of what makes us . . . alive. We cannot share our own memories with each other without losing something of ourselves and risking true death. That is why a Fey child is both rare and a true commitment of the parents, a merging of key memories from each of them.

What about Mort, in Chauvelin's body?

His risk is no greater than yours. Less, perhaps, since while you were in exile, he received his full arcana training.

Thanks for the pep talk, coach!

Alynon sighed. *Like many things here, the duels will really come down to a battle of will, at least within the rules and limitations of whatever setting you choose. Is that what you wish to hear?*

Better, I thought. *Though I was hoping maybe you could find some way to give me the memories of a master duelist, or, I don't know, that we could go to a pocket space in the Other Realm where time moves slower and I could train for several months.*

Hold! Alynon said, excitement in his voice. *You mean like "Superman versus Mohammad Ali"?*

Exactly! Why? Is *there a way?*

La! . . . No! Alynon said in a tone that suggested I was an idiot. *Your only chance is to use whatever greater experience you possess in focusing your will learned from your time in exile, and the advantage that choosing the duel's settings may give you, to overcome his arcana and fencing training.*

I moaned. I'd forgotten that Mort took fencing training at some point during my exile. It used to be mandatory for all arcana when the threat of war with brightbloods and the Fey was more common, and still was something of an Arcana Merit Badge to do so.

"Well, at least my memories of necromancy training weren't blocked before coming here."

Exactly so, Alynon said. *And his surely have, for your Grandfather and the ARC would not have risked his memories to be taken. With any luck, that will give you some kind of edge, or surprise.*

I took several deep breaths, and tried to practice the mental exercises Grandfather had taught me to focus my will. *Any other helpful advice?* I asked.

Alynon sighed, and after a moment of silence said, *Tell me, do you think that's really air you're breathing?*

No. I don't know, I don't think so. Why?

La, I don't know either, actually. I think it is intended as one of those Zen koan-type riddles, Alynon said. *Just remember where you are, and that you are not necessarily limited by the same rules that apply in your world. You can be better, faster, stronger here.*

"Well, that will come in handy if I have to battle a bionic bigfoot," I muttered.

Sorry. That is the best I can do. I have not exactly engaged in many duels myself, you know.

Really? I thought you'd have been in plenty, as popular as you seem to be.

Odysseus stopped before a door. "This is the Room of Contest. Gramaraye, you will enter here. I shall take your woman to join those who observe."

"She's not my woman," I said, giving Dawn a smile as my eyes teared up. "She just tolerates me."

"Damn straight," Dawn replied, her own eyes growing watery. "Kick his ass, and let's get out of this place."

"Sounds like a plan," I replied. I pulled her into a kiss. I wasn't afraid I might die, at least not based on what Alynon had said. But I was terrified that this might be good-bye, that the Fey might choose to haul us each off to separate fates, whatever happened in this room.

"Don't leave me here with these jerks," Dawn whispered.

"I won't," I replied. "I promise."

Odysseus put a hand on my shoulder. "It is time, Gramaraye. Enter, and fight well."

The Room of Contest was entirely green, so perfectly green and evenly lit that when the door closed behind me, removing the faint column of light from the hall, I had a hard time determining where the floor ended and the walls began.

Mort stood facing me, a good ten paces distant. He still wore Chauvelin's tight-fitting black clothes, looking like the fifth French musketeer, Dar'ninja, with his hair pulled back into a small ponytail, his pants ending at the knees and his smile ending well before his eyes.

"It's been a while since we've had a real fight," Mort said. "I was afraid you were going to back out."

I crossed my arms—not so much out of defiance as to hide the shaking of my hands.

"You *should* be afraid," I said in a melodramatic voice. "For I am the terror that flaps in the night. I am the deep scratch on the DVD of your soul!"

"Always with the jokes," Mort said, clearly upset I wasn't playing along with whatever script he had imagined for this moment. "That's your problem, you don't take anything seriously, just dreaming and joking your way along, leaving us to clean up your messes. But now I'm the one who—"

"Is about to condemn your brother to eternal brainfuckery? Excuse me if I don't respect that choice."

Mort's borrowed body actually appeared to slump for a minute under some weight, and he shook his head.

"As much as I'll enjoy knocking that smirk off of your face, do you *really* think I wanted all of *this*?" he said, waving his hand around him. "I tried, Finn, I did. I warned you what would happen. Do you even have a clue the things I did to make sure you all—"

"Knew how hard you were working?" I said. "Yeah, you told us pretty much every day. And as much as I'd love you to have your big martyry monologue moment, brother, I'd rather just get this over with. I've got such a tight schedule and all."

Another door opened to my left, and Hannibal entered the room. Not the cannibal, but Hannibal Barca the Carthaginian general, in bronze breastplate and red cloak, looking like a buff version of Kid from Kid 'n Play, though with a horse-tail helmet in place of his high top fade, and a nose that might have been broken several times and reset into a hawk-like curve.

"The terms of the duel have been set," he said. "Three battles, the nature of which shall be selected from the memories of the accused. Prepare for the first exchange."

"Wait," I said. "I haven't chosen the setting yet."

"The conditions of three duels have already been gathered from your most present memories upon entering the room," Hannibal said.

"Uh, okay, so—"

The room changed. I stood suddenly upon an uneven rocky bluff overlooking the sea, littered with the remains of a long abandoned castle or fort. Not Fort Worden. This had the look of a movie set, something familiar, something I'd watched recently with Dawn.

Mort remained in black, though now he looked like a buccaneer, with sea boots and a sash, and a black cloth mask that covered his head. A rapier appeared in his gloved hand. I looked down to find myself in a tan shirt, brown vest, and brown leather pants, and a rapier appeared in my hand as well. It was a beautiful sword, a true work of art.

Ah.

"Well," I said. "Looks like I'm on the losing side of this battle."

"En garde," Mort said, raising his sword in a salute, then stepped forward in a fencing stance, his rapier held ready in front of him. Mort's confident smile did little to improve Chauvelin's weasely little face.

Crap. Even if he hadn't been cast for some reason as the winning character in this little scene, Mort knew how to duel. I did not.

"Hello," I said. "My name is Finn Gramaraye. You're a dumb ass. Prepare to die."

"Bring it," he replied.

I did not, in fact, bring it, but backed away, keeping my distance from the pointy painy deathy end of his rapier.

Mort shuffled forward and made two quick strikes, beating aside my own blade. He smiled, and came at me more aggressively, striking my blade once, twice, three times, and then I felt pain slice across my thigh. I stumbled back, holding up my sword in an attempt to keep him distant, and looked down. My thigh had been slashed open, the pants and flesh separated in a clean line, and blood trickled down my leg.

"Come on, Finn," Mort said. "Don't make this too easy."

"Screw you, Mort."

I tried to will my wound closed, and to replace my vest with a nice shirt of mithril mail. For a brief second, the change flickered into existence, but then the brown vest and throbbing agony of the wound snapped back into place.

The rules of this duel are set, Alynon said. *You cannot change them. You must use them.*

Mort smiled, and advanced.

"Shouldn't you be fighting left-handed?" I said, as I tried to buy time to figure this out.

Mort frowned. "Why? I'm right-handed. Or did you conveniently forget that same as you forgot all the ways you've screwed over our family."

He gave a quick exploratory beat at my blade.

"You know, you're not nearly as witty as the real Wesley," I said, shuffling back and trying to stay out of cutting range.

"I don't know who Wesley is," Mort said. "But I would rather cut you with steel than words."

And then it occurred to me that Mort didn't know the source of our setting or roles, while I did. I supposed I shouldn't have been surprised. If a film didn't feature explosions or naked women or both, Mort probably hadn't seen it.

But how could superior knowledge of the source material help me?

I retreated. I edged around a low stone wall, and then kept moving to keep the stones between myself and Mort.

Mort watched me, an amused grin on his face, clearly enjoying the fact that I was running away from him and outmatched. "You're only going to drag this out."

Damn it. He was right. While I was dressed like Inigo Montoya, I obviously had not inherited his skill with the blade. And even if I had, then Mort would have gotten Wesley's, and I'd still be screwed. Maybe, if this had been the battle with Fezzik I'd have stood a chance, might have been able to beat Mort in a wrestling match. With swords, I—

Wait!

I turned and fled, running up the stony path to higher ground, and jumped across a gap between two sections of wall.

Mort watched, a patient expression on his face. "Higher ground is a good choice, but only if you know how to use it. And you can't escape the room." He began climbing a second path to where I stood, his pace slow but determined.

I switched the rapier to my left hand and picked up a chunk of broken stone wall the size of a grapefruit. Not the boulder that a gentle giant would have been able to hurl, but large enough to create a new part in Mort's hairdo if it struck his head.

Screw dueling, and wrestling for that matter. I felt no need to prove anything to Mort except that I could beat his butt.

I threw the stone at Mort as hard as I could.

The rock flew through empty air as Mort ducked and slipped on the gravel. "You—!" He scrambled back to his feet and toward me. "That's cheating!"

I ran up higher in the ruins, grabbed another rock, and lobbed it at Mort.

This one hit him in the shoulder and knocked him sideways. He cried out in pain.

"He's cheating!" he shouted. "Do something!"

"Do something yourself!" I shouted back. I picked up another rock and threw it. This one missed as he ducked behind the base of a fallen wall. He emerged and threw a rock back at me, and as I dodged he ran up the hill toward me.

Crap. I dropped the rapier and picked up a giant slab of granite the size of one hell of a headache. I lifted it above my head, and turned toward Mort.

Mort lunged, overextending and practically falling on his face, but I felt his sword point slide into my gut. My knees went wibbly wobbly.

The hernia-heavy slab of stone slid from my hands and crashed to the ground behind me, and I fell forward, toward the smug grin on Mort's stupid little face.

"Victory!" Hannibal's voice declared. "The duelists shall separate now."

The landscape, weapons, and wounds melted away, lowering me to the bright green floor.

Mort knelt down to smile at me as I uncurled from the phantom pain of being skewered. "This is fun, huh? Let's make the next one last a while." He turned and walked back to his side of the room from where he'd started the duel.

"Arcana," Hannibal said, motioning to my side of the room.

"Great."

I moaned as I rose to my feet, then walked back to my starting point. A memory flashed sudden and vivid across my mind, of my mother handing me and Mort each one of the mixer beaters covered in chocolate cake batter, and saying, "A treat for my two handsome little men."

I felt the memory being pulled from me, and tried to hold on to it, but then it was gone.

I stumbled, and almost fell to my knees at my starting point. I felt as though I'd lost something more than just a fight, I'd lost some part of myself. I didn't know what it was, but I knew I didn't like the feeling, that I never wanted to experience it again.

And I had two more fights to go. Well, only one if Mort killed me again. Yay?

I turned to face Hannibal and Mort.

Hannibal raised his hand. "The second duel begins."

20

IT AIN'T OVER 'TIL IT'S OVER

Hannibal lowered his arm, signaling the start of the second duel, then disappeared.

"Wait," I said. "Can I have—"

A broad, pebbly stream filled the center of the Room of Contest, separating Mort and me. The stream looked too swift and deep to wade across, but was bridged by a broad log whose top had been worn flat by the passage of feet and the occasional axe.

A staff of blackthorn appeared in Mort's hands.

I looked down, unsurprised to find myself clothed in Lincoln green, a freshly limbed oak staff now in my hand.

I looked at the river, and shivered in response. I had gotten over the worst of my fear of water that had begun after drowning in Grandfather's underwater villain lair. Ironically, nearly drowning in an attempt to save Dunngo in the Elwha River had helped. But the thought of Mort sending me tumbling into that water, possibly to drown me, still made both my knees and my stomach unsteady.

"I wish a different setting," I called out.

"The setting and rules have been chosen," Hannibal

responded. "They cannot be changed."

Mort climbed up onto the log bridge, and began advancing toward me, his staff held in both hands to aid his balance.

I remained where I stood, on good old solid ground. I started retreating to put my back to the tree line, then realized I would be giving up my one chance at an advantage, and instead walked up to the end of the log bridge. If I waited for him there, I would have a good shot at hitting his legs out from under him when he reached my end of the log.

Mort stopped at the center of the log bridge. "Let's go," he said. "I know this scene. You're Robin Hood, right? That makes me Little John, and I need to send you for a swim." He turned the staff slowly in his hands.

Damn it.

I couldn't win this, any more than Robin had. Any more than I had won the last fight. And I doubted that Mort would be happy with simply knocking me off the log, or willing to embrace me as friend and leader afterward as John had done. He would go for the kill.

Mort thumped his staff against the log. "I'm not going away," he said.

"You and the common cold," I replied.

Mort waved at the scene around us. "You know, Costner made a horrible Robin Hood, but there was that bit about how Robin Hood's father totally screwed over his other son to treat Robin as his favorite, I could totally relate."

"Oh, get over yourself," I replied. "I didn't ask Grandfather to be a dick to you. And I'm certainly not the one doing his dirty work now."

"I'm not an idiot," Mort said. "In fact, I finally wised up. I'm going to get everything I can out of this mess with you and Grandfather before it all falls apart."

"Yeah, you're a regular Joseph Donnelly ya are, lad."

"What?"

"*Far and Away*? Never mind. How is it that I'm more up on movies than you?"

"Because some of us had to raise a child and run a business rather than sitting in their room with the television all day."

Hannibal's voice echoed from above, "This is a battle, not a conversation. If one of you does not advance to victory soon, then both shall forfeit."

"Come on, let's get this over with!" Mort said, waving at me again to advance.

"Toe pick!" I heard Dawn shout from somewhere above. "I lo—"

Her voice cut off. Apparently the Fey didn't approve of a cheering section.

Focus. Right.

There had to be a way to hack this game, a cheat code to give me invulnerability or skip a level or something. The setting and the rules were set by me, by my memory of this duel. That had to give me some advantage, right? Except I knew how this story went. I remember being surprised the first time Mother read it to me. Robin was the hero, so how could he lose? And she'd explained—

Wait. Maybe I did have one chance.

"Mort, I won't come out onto the log to fight you. And if you come to me, I'll just wait to knock you from the log when you reach this end. I don't suppose you'd trust that I'll let you come to this side without attacking—"

"Nope," Mort replied.

"Then let me meet you on your side. If you give me your

promise on Mattie's life that you'll allow me to cross the log and step safely onto the other shore, I will cross, and then we can see who wins this duel fairly."

Mort's eyes narrowed. "Why should I?"

"Surely you're not afraid that me and my buck-and-a-quarter quarter staff will beat you on even ground?" I goaded.

I could tell he was trying to find the trick in my offer, but he also must have realized there was little choice. Either he did as I asked, or he would have to come at me and give me the advantage. Or we would both lose. "Fine," he said. "I promise, you can cross safely to my side. But as soon as you step off of the log, you're fair game."

"Sounds fun," I replied.

Mort paused a second longer, then nodded, and carefully back-stepped to his side of the stream. He jumped to the rocky ground and took several steps away from the log, then motioned for me to proceed.

I stepped up onto the log, and crossed with the care of Indiana Jones navigating across a greased pole over a pit of snakes. Every time my eyes fell to the water, my legs went wobbly and I had to slow way down, bending over in case I fell to my hands and knees. As I neared Mort's side of the stream, I prepared to defend myself. "Okay. Here I come," I said.

I hopped off of the log, away from Mort. My feet hit the stream's stony bank with a crunching of pebbles.

Mort advanced on me, and I raised my staff, prepared to retreat to the trees—

"Victory!" Hannibal announced.

"What?" Mort demanded, and held his staff to the side. "Who? How?"

The scene melted away, as did the staves and medieval

clothing, and Hannibal reappeared.

"Me, I believe," I said, looking to Hannibal. He nodded in acknowledgment, the horse tail on his helmet swishing, and I continued, "The point of the duel between Robin and Little John was that both wanted to cross the stream, and neither wanted to give way. It was a contest to see if one could get past the other. I reached your side of the stream, therefore I won."

"You cheated! Again!"

"No. That's diplomacy," I replied. "I should think you would be good at diplomacy, being a big important ambassador and all. Huh." I rubbed my chin. "That must be embarrassing."

Mort advanced toward me. "I'll shove embarrassing up your—"

"The duel is done," Hannibal said, raising a hand between us. "Honor the outcome."

Mort stopped in his tracks, and looked from Hannibal to me, then glanced briefly up in the direction of our invisible audience. "Fine, whatever," he said at last, "have your victory. But I'm not falling for your crap again."

He strode back toward his side of the room.

He stumbled mid-step, and placed one hand against his head, almost falling to his knees. But his hands closed into fists; he straightened, and finished walking stiffly to his side of the room.

"Arcana," Hannibal said, motioning to my side of the room. I nodded, and returned to my starting point.

The ground became an arena of light brown earth, surrounded by a circle of brown stone trilithons. In the center glowed what looked like a fire pit full of honey-colored crystals, and beside that a green metal obelisk. The sky turned blood red.

A weapon appeared in my hands, a polished wooden pole with a cone-like steel weight at one end and a fan-shaped blade at the other. The same appeared in Mort's hands, who now wore black pants and a blue shirt.

I looked down, and saw that I now wore black pants and a yellow long-sleeved shirt.

"Amok Time"! Of course this would be one of the duels my mind conjured up. Kirk, a man out of his element, the environment itself his enemy, facing an opponent stronger and native to this world. Granted, native only in body, but then Spock had been of two worlds as well.

It could have been worse, I supposed. I could have been Monty Python's Black Knight facing King Arthur. Judging by Mort's face, he'd have been happy to give me quite a few flesh wounds. But this battle still hadn't worked out too well for Kirk.

The all-too-familiar battle music began pounding from all directions.

"Ah, Gorn crap," I muttered. And then Mort leaped at me, his fan-shaped blade swinging down for my head.

I stepped back and raised my own weapon to block him. Or at least attempted to. Mort powered through my block, and the blade sliced down my shirt.

Agony screamed along my chest, and I stumbled back further.

Mort twirled his weapon casually, and said, "Nowhere to run, no way to cheat this time."

"Uh," I said.

I fled. I ran around the edge of the arena, past the trilithons to place as much space between Mort and myself as I could. I needed a minute to concentrate, to think.

Boos and mocking jeers came from above.

What would Kirk do? Alynon prompted.

Kirk would have a doctor friend who could give him shots to help him adjust to the environment and fake his own death.

Kirk would also get into a grappling, shirt ripping, karate chopping fight with the guy. But Kirk rarely won fights mano a mano against Spock.

My lungs were starting to feel the strain of all the running. I stopped on the far side of a trilithon, and played ring-around-the-rosy with Mort, trying to catch my breath while keeping the stones between us.

Mort pushed at a trilithon, toppling it toward me, and I had to dodge out of the way. The stones fell with the sound of Styrofoam. I resumed sprinting, but Mort closed on me.

Damn it! I said to Alynon. *Are you sure there's nothing you can do to help me here?*

Alynon remained silent for several heartbeats, then said, *Why was Kirk the hero?*

What? Because he was Kirk, I don't know. He was the best fighter, strategist, diplomat, ladies' man, all of that.

Those were his qualities. A villain could have those qualities.

I appreciate your sudden interest in Star Trek, but is this really necessary for you to help? I asked.

Yes! Why was Kirk the hero?

Fine. I thought back, narrowly dodging a stone Mort kicked in my direction and gaining some distance as I did. *Kirk was a hero because . . . he fought for something, for the safety of his crew, of his* Enterprise *family, for life, liberty, and the pursuit of happiness, all the good stuff. And he was willing to sacrifice himself or break the rules to do it, but he still stayed true to the principles of the Federation. Is that a good enough answer? Can you help me now?*

So what have you been doing if not fighting for the safety of your world, of your family? And while you broke rules, you did so for good reason, didn't you?

That's what I keep telling myself. But even I'm not sure any more. I'm not fighting some Fey here, I'm fighting *family. And maybe he's right. I . . . it felt—*

It felt good to use dark necromancy. It felt deeply satisfying to see Barry defeated, Kaminari no longer a threat, Mort embarrassed. Was I a hero? Or just a weaker, unfocused version of my grandfather?

For all that is holy, get over yourself! Alynon shouted. *You're a damned hero! And believe me, I wouldn't say it if it wasn't true. So start acting like it! Release the Kirken!*

I winced. *Really? Release the—*

**You* of all people do not get to judge me on wordplay!*

Yeah. Okay. Fair enough.

I didn't know about me being a hero, but one thing was true: right now, I was Kirk, damn it! The most badass of Starfleet captains. And he was definitely a hero. As long as I played the role, I would live up to it.

I stopped fleeing, and turned. I advanced on Mort in a fighter's crouch, holding the weapon ready as I tried to replay the fight scene from the show in my head, to remember Kirk's moves.

"That's more like it," Mort said. He leaped at me again, swinging the weighted end of his weapon at me like a great mallet. I hopped backward, my arms raised, my hips and stomach pulled back. The swing whooshed by me.

I tried to punch him in the stomach with my own weapon

as he recovered from his swing, but he, too, jumped back out of range.

We circled each other, and then he jumped forward and thrust his weapon two-handed against mine so that we were locked in a contest of strength.

Even though he was smaller and thinner, I could feel myself losing the battle as he pressed me back, and down, so that I began to bend backward.

I bent my knees, straightened my back, and thrust up with all my strength.

Mort stumbled back.

I threw my weapon at him like a spear. Screaming, I leaped after it.

Mort knocked my weapon aside, and I crashed into him. I grabbed for his weapon. If I could just twist and do a judo throw thingy—

Mort twisted the weapon around, which twisted me so that my back was to him, and I suddenly found the wooden shaft across my throat, pressing in.

I began choking.

Do you think that's air you're breathing? Alynon shouted.

Seriously? I shouted back.

Whether or not there really was air, I was choking. Maybe it was the rules of the contest. Maybe it was just my inability to both believe I didn't need air here and provide my body the oxygen it needed. Either way, I could not release Mort's weapon to fight back without him crushing my throat. I tried to thrust back with my hips, tried tripping him up with my feet, tried anything I could to get him to lose or loosen his hold as I gasped for air.

I maneuvered him toward the fire pit, and pushed backward, stumbling back with him until he tripped. He managed to miss falling into the pit, but at least we were separated. I rolled across the ground, coughing, then rose slowly to my feet. A torn flap of my shirt hung down now from one shoulder, the cut across my abdomen burned, and my lungs ached.

Mort began to rise, his hand grasping for and finding his weapon.

I screamed "RELEASE THE KIRKEN!" and charged at him, tackling him back to the ground.

We landed hard together and rolled, each trying to get on top of the other. He tried to push me away and stand, and I tackled him back to the ground, and wrestled him underneath me, then sat up on his chest and started beating at his face with my fists as he did his best to stop my blows.

I lost myself. I suddenly felt all of the anger and frustration and fear of the past few days, of the past months, swell up in me like a marshmallow in a microwave, a ragemallow, boiling hot and billowing out until my body felt too small to hold it.

Flashes of all the hurts and frustrations of the past months played across my mind like a projection illumined by fire. The terrible moments when I realized that my own grandfather had sent me into exile, of Heather's betrayal, of the deaths of Zeke and Jo and finding Felicity's corpse. Of dying in the freezing water. Of trying to adjust to a world that had moved on twenty-five years beyond me. Of trying to make me and Dawn work, trying to figure out if it was wrong for me to even try. Of fighting to protect Pete and Vee from a Fey war and failing at every attempt.

Of Mort's betrayal.

My strikes slowed down, until I was more just holding Mort down than beating on him.

Mort's betrayal.

Was it a betrayal when he really had warned me constantly that it would happen? When he had shouted his anger and frustrations and hurts at me, and I had just thrown up my hands in exasperation or given a token attempt at reconciliation?

I had placed Mort's issues, his needs, pretty much at the bottom of my list of concerns. That had made sense at those times when I'd been running for my life, or fighting to stop a war and save Petey and others. But in the months between, I had more or less avoided him, and told myself it was what he wanted. At first, because it had been easy to dismiss his complaints to the same problems of jealousy and small-mindedness that had caused our fights before my exile, when we were just teenagers, not considering that maybe he had new reasons now, or at least that his jealousy and small-mindedness had new cause. Not *wanting* to consider it, really, since some of those reasons might have been my fault. And then the Brianne incident happened, when I accidentally banished his spirit wife to an unknown fate, and I definitely kept my distance.

But that distance, that avoidance, was not what he *needed*. It was not what we had needed, our family had needed, from me.

I pushed away from Mort, and stood, wavering, physically and emotionally spent. Mort groaned, and rolled away from me, using the ledge of the fire pit to pull himself up.

What are you doing? Alynon demanded. *Finish him!*

It's better if I lose, I said, looking for an explanation he would accept. *If I win, the Shadows and Mort will still find some way to keep me here even with Chauvelin's charges dropped. You know they will. But if I lose, if Mort takes back my physical body, Pete and the others can at least use it as an anchor to pull my spirit back, like they did before with the Summoning Simon.*

Your body will be taken over by your grandfather before that happens.

Maybe. But if I beat Mort, you also stay trapped in my head. If Mort wins, he sets you free.

Alynon didn't respond to that. What could he say? That he would sacrifice his life for mine? I couldn't blame him for his silence.

And he hopefully wouldn't blame me for not sharing my other reason, perhaps the most important reason. I would throw this fight because Mort *needed* me to. He needed to win, needed to let out his own anger before it destroyed him and hurt Mattie even further. There was no guarantee even if I won that I would get out of this mess whole and in control. The one thing I could control was whether I caused even more damage to Mort, or if I instead tried to help my brother and my family this one last time.

"Yield!" I said. "Or are you too stupid to give up?"

Mort-Chauvelin's face was a green-bruised mess. But he struggled to his feet, and spat green blood onto the sand at my feet. "Fuck you."

"You're pathetic," I said. "You couldn't beat me with a—"

Mort screamed and charged at me, knocking me to the ground this time. We fell hard, and I could have rolled with it, maybe gotten on top, but I let him wrestle his way to straddling my chest. It was his turn to beat the hell out of his brother.

Despite my best intent to let him have his go at it, I couldn't help but try to stop the blows as the pain started. Funny how blinding pain will do that. But at the same time I did my best to let blows through. Not that I had to try that hard. Fists pounded into my jaw, my mouth, my neck, my temples, until I was dizzy with pain and possibly a concussion.

"You're an ass!" I said as best I could.

"And you're losing!" he said.

"*You're* losing," I replied between blows. "You need to—ow!—get over your stupid—uhn!—grudges already! For Mattie. For yourself. Look what they're turning you—OW! Jesus, that—"

A hard punch sent my ears ringing, and the world collapsed into a narrow tunnel before expanding again. I blinked against the pain, dimly aware that Mort was screaming as though he was the one in pain. His hands trailed a thin stream of blood droplets through the air now as they pulled back from my face before coming in for another strike.

The world went black.

And then exploded back into prismatic painful existence again as Hannibal dragged Mort back off of me, and said, "Victory!"

Mort jerked and pulled against Hannibal's grasp.

"Hold, arcana!" Hannibal said. He might have been more a master strategist than a hulking warrior, but Hannibal still towered over Mort and looked as though he could easily break the smaller Fey body that Mort possessed in half. "Hold, or forfeit your victory!"

Mort settled down, then held up his hands, still covered in my blood. He stared at them with a dazed look.

The landscape and uniforms melted away for the last time, replaced by the green room. I was back in my jeans and

Space Invaders T-shirt, and Mort in the frilly French Goth outfit. The wounds and the blood all disappeared, and with them the cloudiness of near-death.

I rose to my feet. "Mort—" I began, my voice shaky.

A memory rose up unbidden, filling my awareness: Mort, Sammy, Petey, and I all gathered in excitement on the library carpet before the television, as Mother carried in a tray with Mexican hot cocoa and Father set a giant bowl of popcorn down in front of us just as *The Year Without a Santa Claus* came on.

The memory evaporated even as it played out, lifting up and carried away to some Fey collector.

I felt a moment of sadness, of strange disconnected loss, as though I'd just discovered the death of a good childhood friend that I'd not talked to in decades.

"Come," Hannibal said, slapping Mort on the back. "We shall go and arrange the conditions of your reward."

"And well fought, both," Odysseus said, entering the room behind me, before I could call out to Mort. "Phinaeus Gramaraye, if you will follow me?"

"But—" I began, and turned back to find Mort already leaving through a side door, a deep frown on his face. I sighed.

Odysseus led me back out to the hallway, where Dawn stood waiting. She threw her arms around me.

"Thank you for not dying," she whispered. "At least not for real. You idiot."

"I, uh, you're welcome?" I looked behind me, though Mort was no longer in sight. What would happen now? Had I reached Mort at all?

She leaned in close, her breath warm on my ear. "You threw the fight didn't you. Why?"

Two figures approached along the hall. One dressed as a Frankish knight from the crusades, and one as an impeccably groomed businessman in a tailored suit.

Before they reached us, I whispered quickly, "They aren't going to just let me go, whatever I do. But if Mort takes back my body, he might be able to free my spirit as well with Pete and Verna's help. Stick with him, try to convince him—"

Odysseus gave a slight bow of his head to the approaching Fey, and said, "I must go prepare for the lady's return to her world. te'Godfrey and te'Bateman shall guide you both to a holding room until I am ready."

Godfrey of Bouillon I recognized, a Frankish knight and leader of the First Crusade. The businessman I did not, though he had sharp, lean features and an intense gaze that was unsettling.

"Forget it," Dawn said. "I am not leaving without Finn. Or at least his body."

"Your freedom has been secured," Odysseus replied to Dawn. "You would be wise to accept it. The ARC ambassador won the right to claim Gramaraye's body over our right to hold him for those claims laid by Chauvelin. But Phinaeus is now to be held for his more recent crimes."

"What crimes?" I asked, not even able to muster fake surprise at this news.

"The killing of the younger jorõgumo, Kaminari, and the unauthorized travel to our Realm, which were not among those offenses laid against you by te'Chauvelin, and thus not resolved by your duel."

Dawn shook her head. "You cheating bastards—" She advanced on Odysseus with fists clenched.

A wall of black brambles covered in wicked-looking

thorns sprang up from the hallway floor between us and Odysseus, followed by a second wall behind us, separating us from the other two Fey.

"Make another aggressive move," Odysseus said, "and you both shall be pierced more thoroughly than a hundred enemy suitors."

21

GOOD VIBRATIONS

The thorny walls on either side of us shivered and moved in, forcing Dawn and me close together to avoid being punctured.

"When I get out of here—!" Dawn practically growled at Odysseus.

"Fight and be impaled," Odysseus said. "Or calm your fury, and allow yourself to be taken to a room where you may at least spend some moments with your man here as I prepare your passage home. It is your choice."

Dawn looked at me, and clenched her fists, but didn't say anything more.

Odysseus looked past us at the other Fey, and said, "Take them by the prescribed route, lest you disrupt important events."

"Of course, captain," the knight, Godfrey, said.

"I know my job," Bateman added in a tight voice that belied his creepy smile. "Just don't be late relieving us, I have important business."

Godfrey's mouth quirked up in a smile, and Odysseus gave Bateman a sharp glare. "Ware, te'Bateman. You may be rising rapidly through the ranks here, but you have far to go before you would be wise to offend me."

"As you say," Bateman said.

Odysseus nodded, and said, "I shall fetch the woman once the way is prepared." He marched off.

"Come," Godfrey commanded, and began marching off in the opposite direction. Bateman glared murder at the knight's back for a second, then flashed us a salesman's smile and said, "Come." He walked double pace to catch up with the knight, and moved slightly ahead of him.

The thorn walls moved after them, forcing us to keep pace or be skewered.

"I know of you, Gramaraye," Bateman called back. "Exiled from your world in nineteen eighty-six. I have . . . memories of that time, of the music."

Dawn looked at me with an arched eyebrow. "I thought they couldn't handle human music," she whispered.

"They can't," I replied as softly. "The vibrations and emotion interrupt their control of reality here."

"I haven't heard the music played here, of course," Bateman said, as if overhearing us. "But I have extensive memory of it, and would love to discuss it. I particularly enjoyed Robert Palmer's 'Addicted to Love.' Are you familiar with it?"

"Of course," Dawn replied. "I'd be happy to play it for you."

"Very funny," Bateman said. "Did you know that the dancers in his music video for that song were based on the paintings of Nagel? And that for several years it was the height of fashion in a number of Demesnes to make one's features appear washed out and stylized like the women in Nagel's paintings? Different Demesnes had different reasons of course. The Heart Lands because they felt it was a distillation of lustful beauty. The Emerald Fortress because they felt it reflected the pure, simple clarity of logic and order. The Summerland because—"

"Great," Dawn muttered to me. "We're getting escorted by a psycho Casey Feysem."

Bateman looked back. "What was that?"

"Nothing," I said.

Dawn snorted, and said, "If you're going to bore us, can't you at least do so with good taste? Rattle on about The Smiths or even Lionel Richie, please? Unless you *mean* to torture us."

Bateman's face flushed red, and veins leaped out on his temples as he shouted, "Disrespect me again, and I'll torture you until you beg me to kill you, you goddamned filthy human!"

"te'Bateman," Godfrey said in a warning tone.

Bateman's eyes snapped to the knight, then he shuddered, and his face changed—a ripple actually passed over his features instantly transforming them from furious to charming. "But I live to serve the Greatwood, of course." He continued marching in silence.

"Dawn," I whispered, "just stay cool until you get out of here. Your best bet for helping me is still reaching my family."

"I don't know," Dawn said. "I—ouch!" A thorn caught her on the arm, and she sucked at the wound, then continued. "Here, I actually seem to have some magic like you for once. And I have half a mind to go Red Dawnya on their asses."

*Her will *is* uncommonly strong.*

"Will, not magic," I replied. "You've always been strong-willed, Dawn, it's one of the reasons I love you. But it isn't enough to take on the whole Shadows Demesne. Please, just trust me. Going home is your best chance to help me."

"Fine, but don't think I won't come back here with every strong-willed musician I know armed with guitars, sitars, and scimitars if they don't— Ah! Damn it!" Dawn hissed in pain as another thorn found her rear, and said, "This is one situation where being bootylicious isn't helpful."

"I don't know," I said. "When Odysseus gets back, maybe you can distract him with some flirting and I can knock him on the head or something. He does have a thing for beautiful women with sexy voices."

"Except they won't let me use my voice. And you just think I'm beautiful because you love me."

I took her hand. "No, I love you because you're beautiful, in a thousand different ways."

She didn't respond, but walked in silence beside me.

"You okay?" I asked. "Did I say something wrong?"

"Yes. You told me to leave you here."

I sighed. "We covered this."

"Still— Hey! That's my guitar!"

The door to our left swung open as we passed it, and in the room beyond, rotating slowly in the air above a glowing white stone, floated Dawn's guitar.

"Great," I said, raising my hand to my collar. "Except—"

Dawn grabbed the collar around her own neck. I could see the muscles on her arms and jaw stand out as she strained against both the strength of the Fey steel and the pain that shot through her body at the attempt. The thorns stopped moving, but not before several dug into her back, causing her to give a long, angry shout of pain.

"No!" Bateman shouted. "This is not how you are supposed to behave!"

There was a high-pitched metallic keening that made my teeth hurt, then Dawn's collar snapped, and she launched herself in a stumbling sprint for her guitar.

The thorn wall between me and our two Fey escorts shrunk away, and a broadsword appeared in Godfrey's hand. He charged after Dawn.

Bateman advanced on me. "I have all the memories of a human being within," he said as he strode toward me. "But I have never seen a true human opened up." A chainsaw flickered into life in his hands.

"Uh," I said, scrambling backward away from him. "I don't think your bosses will be too happy if you kill me." I tapped my head. "There's lots of valuable stuff up here."

"te'Chauvelin was a fool to let you escape the Colloquy," he replied. "I won't risk such failure." He raised the chainsaw, and revved it up, charging at me in earnest.

I didn't question why he hadn't simply paralyzed me with the collar, I just thanked all the gods for the break and ran after Godfrey and Dawn, hoping there was more space in the room to dodge a chainsaw.

As I stepped in the doorway, a wave of music washed over me. Literally. The strumming of Dawn's guitar caused ripples in the air, the sound waves forming actual waves in the fabric of reality that rolled outwards as she sang, "Get back! Get back! Get back to where the Fey belong!" Godfrey was pushed back into me, and I was pushed back toward Bateman. Bateman staggered back a step, then grinned and pushed forward as if against a windstorm, both my body and Godfrey's obstructing the flow of sound waves through the doorway, weakening the music's effects on the chainsaw wielding maniac.

"The weapons!" I shouted. "Will them away!"

Dawn strummed a few more times, then sang, "Disarm you with freestyle, and cut you like you fucking deserve!"

Godfrey's sword shattered, the razor shards slicing through his armor and flesh. Nothing struck me thanks to either Dawn's will or the shielding of Godfrey's body, but my control collar disintegrated. Behind me the sound of the chainsaw stuttered and died, and Bateman cursed.

Dawn stood smiling radiant and triumphant, looking a bit like Galadriel as played by Tina Turner unveiling her power. "Awesome," she said. And then she sagged to the floor, her eyes rolling up into her head.

"Dawn!" I called. "Shit." Godfrey fell to his knees from the damage Dawn had done him, but Bateman staggered into the room after me, still wielding the dead chainsaw. Even without the blade spinning, it wouldn't feel great to have that thing swung at my head.

I looked around the room, but there was nothing in it except the pedestal and white stone over which the guitar had been suspended. I could go for the guitar, but Bateman would reach me before I managed to strum it.

I tried to will a sword to appear in my hand. One flickered into being for a minute, and I felt a great drain on my energy, but then it disappeared.

"Idiot," Bateman said. "You have no power here."

You're not in a Fey body this time! Alynon said. *You're an arcana!*

Holy batballs! He was right. All my years of experience in the Other Realm had been in a Fey body, and I was trying to control reality as if that were still true. But I was an arcana physically present in a Realm where raw magical energy floated through the air like pollen. And my memories were not blocked.

I had my magic!

The only problem was, I wasn't a wizard. I was a necromancer, and necromancy didn't work on Fey spirits—one of the many facts that people like my grandfather argued to support their belief that Fey weren't true living beings. And there were no bodies laying around for me to raise as a zombie defender, even if such an act wasn't considered dark necromancy.

Bateman has his powers though, I thought at Alynon as I continued to back away from the crazed Fey. *Why hasn't he just caused an anvil to fall on my head yet?*

He is too new to his form. He is angry, and acting like an angry human would.

Angry, huh?

"Jesus, Bateman," I said. "You're a joke! I can see why you're a low man on the totem pole."

"Fuck you!" Bateman shouted, and lunged at me, swinging the chainsaw blade like a sword for my head.

I dove and rolled across the floor as I'd practiced a thousand times on the mats in class, and came up near the pedestal. I lifted the white stone off the pedestal and threw it at Bateman. He batted it out of the air with his chainsaw, but whatever floaty powers the stone held acted like a repulsion field against the saw, and the rebound caused Bateman to spin away from me.

I knelt down beside Dawn, placed my hand on her chest, and sent a jolt of life energy into her.

Dawn jerked up into a sitting position with a gasp, and looked around herself wide-eyed.

"Hey, beautiful," I said. "Can you sing a little something

to make the angry psycho go away?"

"What?" Dawn asked, but I stood and moved away from her as Bateman advanced toward us again, drawing his attention to me.

"Gramaraye," he said, "I'm going to make this slow."

"Funny," I replied. "That's what I said to your mom last night."

Dawn reached her feet, and raised her guitar. Bateman's eyes shot to her, and I saw the realization and alarm in them just before Dawn struck her first chord.

"And you're Fey," she sang. "Fey falling."

A hole opened in the floor beneath Bateman, and he plummeted into it, his fading cry filled with anger and fear.

"Come on," I said. "Before he figures out how to fly back to us."

Dawn grabbed my outstretched hand, and we ran from the room.

"What now?" Dawn asked.

"We find Odysseus," I said, turning in the direction the Fey had been leading. "You make him take us to Fatima, and then send us all home."

"And how do I do that?" she asked as we began springing down the hall.

"I don't know. Sing him a love song?"

"After what you told me about that alchemist and the love potion?"

The memory of a stubbly cigar-flavored kiss rose sharply.

"Uh, okay, good point. Love magic is bad. Maybe . . . threaten to turn him into a woman. His personality is traditional enough that he'd probably rather face glorious death than be emasculated."

"Wait, do you think I could actually do that? Turn him into a woman?"

"From what I've seen of your strength of will and the power of your music, yeah, I think it's possible."

"Hmmm . . ." We sprinted in silence for a few seconds, then she said, "A shame we can't stay here a while. It might be interesting to play around a bit."

"With what?" I asked.

"With us," she said.

"What, you mean . . . ? Oh. Uh . . ."

Dawn laughed. "You can't tell me you've never fantasized about doing it as a woman. Or at least wondered."

I blushed, and said, "I don't know, maybe wondered once. That's natural."

She laughed again. "I love that I can still make you blush. And if we ever find a chance to visit here without being in danger, I'll make you do a lot more than blush."

"I believe that," I replied. "But what I can't believe is that you could think about . . . that, when we're running for our lives."

"Oh baby, that's so cute. Don't you know me by now?" Dawn asked.

I would be happy to know her, Alynon offered, generous as always.

I ignored him.

We spotted an opened door ahead on the left. We slowed, and approached it cautiously. I edged up to it, and gave a quick peek inside.

"Frak!" I stepped fully in front of the room.

"What is it?" Dawn asked, joining me. "Oh. Frak."

It was the pedestal room where we'd battled Godfrey and Bateman. We'd pulled a *Labyrinth*.

"I hate the Other Realm," I muttered.

"Maybe we just need to start looking for the hidden side passage?" Dawn suggested. "Or a Hoggle?"

"No," I replied. "I think it's because we don't know where we're going. The hall was being formed by the expectations of our Fey guides. Or something like that. So unless we know where we are going, we can't get there."

"Then let's head back to that first room, where we arrived in this place," Dawn said. "If there was a way in—"

"There might be a way out. Okay. Just believe that that room will be at the end of this hall, and let's give it a try."

We sprinted again, the doors passing quickly on either side. Until we came back to the same open door that had held Dawn's guitar.

"Oh for dog's sake!" I said, panting.

"Start opening doors?" Dawn asked.

"I guess—"

In the room, a figure reverse-melted up out of the floor. Bateman.

"Damn it." I jerked the two membranous sides of the door together, where they sealed with a wet suction sound.

"Maybe we can use him to take us where we need to go," Dawn said.

"I'm not sure he can be reasoned with," I said, my back against the door.

An axe blade punched through the door beside my head.

The door across the hall opened. Odysseus stood framed in the doorway, and waved us inside. "Come! There is little time."

"Why would—" I began.

"Velorain secured my aid," Odysseus said.

Velorain?! Alynon said.

I blinked, then said, "Dawn, come on!" I ran across the hall, making sure that Dawn was with me.

The door opened not into another room, but another hallway. Odysseus closed the door behind us, and placed his hands on it for a second, eyes closed as we all stood in the new hallway.

"Velorain?" Dawn asked. "As in Aly's lost love?"

I nodded, and said to Odysseus, "Why did Velorain not help us herself? And why would you help us for her?"

Odysseus reopened the door, and said, "She is far from here. And I owe her a favor."

She is not here? Alynon asked. *Where is she?*

"Where is Velorain?" I asked.

"She is lost to you, Alynon Infedriel," Odysseus said. "More I cannot say."

Alynon did not respond, but I thought I could sense his pain, like a low moaning hum.

Yet another new hallway ran from the door rather than across it now.

"It's like the Keymaker," Dawn said.

"*Ghostbusters*?" I asked.

"No, *Matrix*," Dawn said. "*Ghostbusters* was the Keymaster."

"Oh, right," I said. "I really need to watch this *Matrix* movie. This is like the hundredth time someone's mentioned it."

"Well, it's a few months early, but I suppose if you get us out of this—"

"Come," Odysseus said. "Make your plans on the move."

He strode out into the hallway, and after a quick exchange of looks, Dawn and I followed.

"So," I said, "if Velorain wanted us free, why did you

bring us here in the first place?"

"She did not request the favor until after your arrival here was known. And even had she asked such a boon earlier, I am not certain I would have granted it."

"What changed your mind?" I asked.

He glanced back at Dawn. "The lady. Or more truly, her power, and yours as well."

"Is that why you had those two steroid cases attack us?" I asked. "To eliminate us as a threat?"

"No. I merely provided you a means of escape that would reflect poorly on two whom I hold in little regard."

Dawn scowled. "You used us to fight your enemies."

"I opened an opportunity, and returned to you your weapon. How you used both was up to you."

Dawn hugged her guitar to herself. "Well, I *am* grateful to have Cotten back. Thank you."

Odysseus gave a nod to Dawn, and led us around a turn into another hall.

"I don't understand," I said. "Aren't you afraid we'll turn our power against this place now that we're free?"

"You misunderstand me," Odysseus said. "I do not fear what you may do with such power, but what those with too great ambition and too little wisdom might do with it. Understand, I serve the Greatwood above all else. Often that means I must find clever ways to achieve the Senate's goals without sacrificing our Aalbrights or too great a number of vassals. And sometimes it means steering them away from wars that would hold too dear a cost to our Demesne."

"So you're a Sean Bean kind of Odysseus," Dawn said.

"I am unfamiliar with this kind of bean you speak of," Odysseus said. "In what way do I resemble such a plant?"

"Uh, never mind," Dawn said. "So you're sending us home?"

"No. I am sending you to the Silver Court."

Oh Bright, Alynon groaned.

"You're what?" I said. "Wait, we need to go wherever you sent the spirits that were transferred into exile at the same time we crossed over."

"La, and that is the Silver Court. Following the revelation in your last visit that the Greatwood's vassals had been manipulated into killing or defaming the Silver Court's vassals, we offered to tithe our share of exiled spirits for one full cycle of the wheel as a gesture of goodwill."

My eyes narrowed. "That does not sound like the Forest of Shadows, or Moriarty, to offer such a thing freely."

Odysseus grunted. "I too found it suspicious. The news that some outside force has been manipulating the Greatwood and the Silver Court toward war was disturbing enough, but I fear that even with eyes opened the Senate freely marches in step with those plans still, as they have ever sought a path to victory over the Silver. Hold. We have arrived."

Odysseus stopped beside a door of brushed black steel bound in twisted black iron, with three large silver bars across it.

"I shall open the door, and you will step through. Do ought else, and I shall strike you down."

I raised my hands. "No complaints here."

"No offense," Dawn said, "but how do we know you aren't just tossing us into a meat grinder?"

"I swear by the Aal that this door shall lead you to the edge of the Silver Demesne."

Dawn looked at me, and I nodded. Odysseus waved his

hand, and the three bars lifted one at a time from the door, and stacked along the wall. With another wave, the door itself opened, revealing a swirling blue-gray portal.

"Thank you," I said to Odysseus. "You are a man of great honor."

"I am an Aalbright of great duty," he replied. "But I pray you are a man of great honor, Gramaraye, and hope that you discover the truth of the conspiracy and end it before ruin finds us all."

"Uh . . . I'll do my best," I said. No pressure.

"Go," Odysseus said.

I took Dawn's hand, and we met each other's eyes as we took a deep breath. Then together we stepped into the portal.

22

TWO PRINCES

We stepped out of a gray stone trilithon onto a grassy hill at the edge of an emerald lake. From the center of the lake rose shining white cliffs, and atop those cliffs stood the gleaming castle of the Silver Court.

Dawn and I looked at each other for a minute, then grabbed each other in a hug, holding each other as close as we could.

Now that we were free, or at least free of the Shadows Demesne, I could admit the fear of losing Dawn forever that had been looming over me since our arrival in the Other Realm. We were not yet free, but for the first time I had real hope we might both get out of this alive, hope that wasn't one-half self-deception, one-quarter false bravado, and one-quarter gut-wrenching guilt.

We finally stepped apart. Dawn looked behind us at the trilithon, the portal now gone.

"That was surprising," she said.

"What? That we survived?" I asked.

"That Odysseus helped us like that for Aly's girlfriend."

"I don't know," I replied as I examined the trilithon for

convenient written instructions or a big shiny Portal button. "Maybe the Odysseus part of him remembers what it was like to be parted from his love for decades, and sympathized with Alynon."

The trilithon held no clues as to how to reopen a portal within it, let alone open a portal back to Earth. Damn.

"Maybe," Dawn said, looking up at the castle on the cliffs. "I assume that's not just a model. So how do we get up there? Or do we even want to?"

"I think we do," I said. "We still need to find Fatima, and figure out what is being done with the exiles, why the Shadows are sending them to the Silver Court, and how to stop them from becoming weapons."

"Do we?" Dawn asked. "Not to be selfish, but now that we know Fatima's with the good guys, can't we just go back home and send them a warning? Won't they send her back once they know?"

"That's not selfish," I said. "If I could send you home, I would. But I don't know how to open a portal from this side."

"Send *me* home?"

I sighed. "I need to find Fatima, to free her. It's my fault as much as anyone's that she's here. And I just can't face Sammy again unless I have Fatima with me. *That* is selfish, I know, but—"

"Well then," Dawn said. "On to Camelot then." She began marching, and sang, "Weeee're . . . knights of the round table!"

I watched her a second, taking the moment to appreciate how lucky I truly was. Then I sprinted to catch up with her, singing, "Let's hope this isn't fatal." And with that, we began our hike down toward the lake, singing increasingly ridiculous lines as we went, our voices sending ripples out through the ether of the Other Realm. Which, I thought, would also serve as a warning of our approach to any Fey we encountered.

Yet nobody appeared as we crossed the shining white bridge that led to the island at the lake's center, or hiked up the winding trail past glimmering groves of exotic silver willows, past structures of gleaming standing stones, past arches behind which rolling green hills and stone cliffs rose to meet the sky. It reminded me of Ireland, or at least the pictures I'd seen, with touches of Rivendell and entire stands of Ellcrys trees.

We crested a hill, and the Silver Court castle stood ahead of us. We fell into silent awe.

In a flash of light, four knights in shining silver armor appeared around us, causing me to startle. The knights were nearly blinding in their mirror-bright armor, casting glimmers like lens flare with every move.

"Halt!" the knight in front of us shouted and flicked his hand.

I felt the cold metal of a collar form around my neck, and looked over to confirm that a silver collar had appeared around Dawn's neck as well. Great.

I sighed, and raised my hands in a show of peace. "We come as allies to the Silver."

"Set you down then all weapons," the knight replied.

I looked at Dawn. "I think he means Cotten again."

Dawn frowned, but set the guitar down and said to the knight, "I'll tell you what I told the other guys: if you damage her, you'll regret it."

One of the knights stepped in from the side and snatched up the instrument, then returned to his position. The first knight said, "You are here in violation of the PAX, bearing illegal weapons. State your names and purpose, or face immediate penalty."

Déjà vu.

"I'm Phinaeus Gramaraye," I said. "You might know me from such movies as *Saving the Elwha Brightbloods*, or *Host to Alynon Infedriel*. And this is my lovely partner, Dawn 'boom bard' Taylor."

The knight frowned as I spoke, then said, "You bear the spirit of Alynon Infedriel?"

"Yes. Unless you're one of the many beings he's managed to annoy, in which case, maybe?"

Nice, Alynon muttered. *Thanks.*

A smile quirked up the corner of the knight's mouth before he restored his stern glower. "You know him well indeed. Follow us, and do not stray."

He began marching back toward the castle, and I felt a tug on my collar, forcing me to follow.

Alynon sighed in my head. *It's not too late to try your skeleton key and run.*

My skeleton key! I felt like an idiot. I hadn't even thought about using it in the Forest of Shadows, again conditioned by all my years of exile to operate on will alone here.

But fleeing would get us, literally, nowhere.

Yeah, I responded. *I think it is too late, actually.*

I took Dawn's hand as we continued moving in the direction of the castle walls. The walls were made of silver stone, the bright, uneven surface traced through with darker veins of tarnished silver. And before the walls ran a reflecting pool with a large star-shaped platform at its center, out of which rose a golden crystal-like monument. It took me a second to recognize it as the monument from the Justice League's Hall of Justice.

My eyebrows rose, as did my hopes. *Why is there a Justice League symbol here?* I asked Alynon. *I thought the Silver Court was modeled more on Camelot than anything.*

Insomuch as my father's core persona is King Arthur in his prime, our Court has been shaped thus, Alynon replied, his tone subdued, distracted. *But this is the Demesne of justice and wisdom, and you will find many manifestations of those ideals here, not just the one.*

Something occurred to me that never had before. *If you're the son of Arthur, your core persona isn't Mordred is it?* I asked.

No, Alynon said, without elaborating.

Well, that was good at least. *So there's a chance your father will listen to us?*

Alynon was silent a second then said, *Let us but hope my father is in a listening mood, and that my brother is away chasing some sport.*

You think your brother wouldn't help us?

I think my brother would see us in chains. His grievance was key in my leaving, and ever was my brother one to remember a wound and the one who gave it.

Shazbot.

"There's no gates or anything," Dawn said as we appeared to be walking right for the unbroken wall.

"No," I confirmed. "You know those deep-sea fish that have the little glowy ball things floating off their head that they use to lure in prey?"

"Yeah."

"What you're seeing is kind of like that glowy ball thing. It's what the Silver Court projects as a result of its existence.

But the real Silver Court is hidden, like the giant fish."

"So, we're about to be eaten?" Dawn asked.

"Hopefully not," I replied.

As we approached the wall, a blue light flickered to life above our heads where four stones intersected, and then shot out along stone seams to form a rough arch. With a brief flash, the stones inside the arch disappeared, and what looked like a throne chamber became visible on the other side.

No small talk, no foreplay, just right to the being screwed, Alynon thought.

Hey, I thought back. *At least* try *to be optimistic. They might be happy to see you after all this time. You did help save them from a Shadows conspiracy, after all.*

No, you uncovered the conspiracy. I nearly defected to the Shadows to be free of you.

I was trying to be generous, I thought back. *I know how hard it can be to deal with family after a long absence. Especially when you left under a dark cloud.*

*La, but that I left under a *mushroom* cloud,* Alynon replied as we were led through the gateway.

The chamber looked like Camelot on Krypton. Great crystal columns supported the vaulted ceiling, light radiating from them, and braziers spaced around the room held glowing flower-like crystal formations. Blue and silver tapestries hung at intervals from the walls, depicting scenes much like those in the Shadows tapestries. And across every visible surface of the floor, the walls, the ceiling, the columns, fine silver script ran in branches like interwoven lightning, light pulsing along the script and changing it in chains and cascades, as if a million possibilities were being explored and updated and recorded in a cross between Elvish script and flow charts.

There were no golf trophies here, instead owls roosted atop pillars and along a ledge that circled the room, their eyes all turning to fix on us as we entered. I heard a familiar metallic whirring and whistling, and looked up to our left to spot Bubo, the golden owl, flapping his wings at us.

From the archway where we entered, it was a straight march along a blue and silver carpet to the foot of the dais on which sat two male Fey, and one lady Fey.

The center Fey had to be Arthur, for above his throne a silver grail floated in a halo of golden light, rotating slowly. He matched the image of Fey royalty I'd imagined as a young man, dressed in chain over a blue shirt and wrapped in a red and gold cloak, and wearing a woven silver crown. He looked part Arthurian legend, part Tuatha Dé Danann, nobility and grace exuding from his features, though he sat now looking somewhat bored and lost in his own thoughts.

To his left sat a Fey Lady who I guessed was queen, her appearance clearly Egyptian. A loose red linen dress left her bronze shoulders bare, a shawl of green feathers hung from her arms, and a gorgerine of red, black, and turquoise stones covered her chest. A silver headband that was a thinner version of the king's crown held a single ostrich feather, standing straight up. The goddess Ma'at, goddess of justice.

And to the king's right sat a haughty-looking young man, a loose white robe held over one shoulder by a brooch leaving his well-muscled arms and chest exposed. Between his perfect physique, olive skin, sharp nose, and the crown of silver laurel leaves holding back his wavy brown hair, I would have guessed him a Greek god, and the fact that he sat plucking casually at a lyre confirmed him as almost certainly an Apollo. His apparent disinterest in us was betrayed by the rigid tension that radiated from his body. He appeared ready to leap from his seat.

A fourth Fey stood before the dais, a white-haired man in voluminous blue robes that I guessed was some version of Merlin. As we approached, he announced, "Phinaeus Gramaraye, Dawn Boom Bard Taylor, and Alynon Infedriel. Welcome you to the Silver Court. You face Inerius te'Arthur, king of the Silver Court, forger of the Great Truce, shining hand of Justice. His Queen, Nyria te'Ma'at, fourth bonded to Arthur in time and first in the light of his eyes. And William te'Apollo, First Prince of the Demesne, first heir to the throne, and voice for the king."

Shazballs.

I gave an awkward bow, and said, "An honor, your majesties."

The queen gave a small, gracious nod of her head. The king frowned, and I was reminded of my own father's expression when his confusion was upon him.

Oh no, Alynon said quietly in my head.

Please not oh no, I thought back.

Apollo leaned forward in his chair. "In what way, honor?" he demanded.

"Uh," I said, and mentally rolled a *1* on eloquence.

Dawn said, "An honor to meet such gracious and polite royalty, of course."

The queen laughed. "Well said. Apollo, be not rude."

Apollo gave a dismissive wave of his hand. "These are not ambassadors or allies, Nyria, they are invaders bearing with them one who has brought naught but pain to this court."

Care to say anything? I asked. *We could use some help here.*

Alynon remained silent, and I began to fear he would remain so—a fear I never thought to have—when he finally said in a soft voice, *Ask what happened with Velorain. Why did he not marry her? Why did he not keep her safe?*

I frowned, but said, "Alynon would like to know what happened with Velorain, why you didn't marry her?"

Apollo stiffened. "Velorain te'Uriel left of her own choice. I am convinced that her entire purpose here was to lure my foolish brother into betrayal, and to make me appear equally the fool."

Tell him that jealousy ill suits him.

Dude, I really don't think—

If you want me to speak, then repeat what I say, or don't ask at all.

"Uh, Prince Apollo, Alynon says that jealousy ill suits you."

Apollo stared at me a second in surprise, then laughed. "Jealousy? May well as claim I envy the lowest beast of your realm. What cause, jealousy, when I am me, and he is but a disgraced and displaced voice?"

Because Velorain loved me. And until my brother was so quick to believe the worst in me, I loved him. Nobody made a fool of Apollo but Apollo.

I repeated Alynon's words, and Apollo shook his head, sinking back into the chair. "Ever you spoke of love as if it were some power that erased all reason or reality, that it was the highest form of good. Yet it was in the name of your love that you betrayed me, our father, our Demesne, and Velorain. In the end, you loved only yourself."

Alynon snorted in my head. *As if anyone could love themselves more than him,* he said.

"As if—" I began.

Don't repeat that! Alynon said. *Are you addlepated?*

Well excuse me! How am I supposed to tell the difference?

Alynon sighed. *Say this: I was framed by the Shadows. The real betrayal was how easily you believed their lies. But I forgive you.*

I took a deep breath, and repeated Alynon's words.

"Framed by the Shadows you now claim?" Apollo asked. "Deception ever came easily to you. It is no wonder that you offered to defect to the Shadows. And now you would betray them as you betrayed us." He shook his head. "Careful brother. You shall soon run out of Demesnes to betray."

Forget it, Alynon said. *He is so full of himself, there is room for naught else, especially reason.*

This is kind of important. Can't you just be nice and make up long enough for us to rescue Fatima and get us out of here? If not for me, then so we can stop whatever the Shadows and my grandfather are up to?

La, of course. I'll just convince him the way you convinced Mort.

I winced. Okay, maybe we *were* screwed.

Still, I had to try.

"Look," I said, raising my hands. "I'm sorry, Prince Apollo. Obviously, you and your brother have some bad blood, or, uh, bad bright? And while I am happy to be your go-between—I owe him that much—we really just want to leave." I looked to the king and queen. "We only came because our two worlds are in danger."

The king squinted at me, then shrank back and shook his head violently as though I'd dared him to lick the men's toilet in a troll high school on Taco Tuesday.

Oh, Father, Alynon said.

What's going on?

He is unstable. He must have branched again after I left, and given too much— Alynon fell silent.

The queen prompted, "Of what danger do you speak?"

I blinked, and looked from the king to her.

"The, uh, Shadows are being used by some other Demesne, and you are being played by them both, and it is all tied to some plot by arcana extremists to use exiled spirits as a weapon."

Apollo rolled his eyes. "Your words are so vague as to be useless. As well say the ARC wishes more magic. Ever there have been plots and pacts, and plans for war."

"This is different," I said. "Whoever tried to pit your Demesne against the Shadows—the plot that your sister Athena died to help expose—they're still manipulating the Shadows. The Shadows think they are merely playing along, but—"

"Athena died, and yet you and my brother escaped unharmed," Apollo said. "And as reward was your own brother installed Vice-Archon among our vassals. In truth, I see as much reason to suspect you as the Shadows. For wherever you go, trouble follows, and few seem to benefit but yourself."

Now he really does sound like Mort, I thought angrily.

But part of me also heard something my mother used to say: "*When one person says you are wrong, you must weigh the value of their opinion. When everyone says you're wrong, you must weigh the value of your own.*"

If everyone I knew felt in some way or another that I had made their lives worse these past few months—

Do not listen to him, Alynon said. *And tell that pompous ass that Athena gave her life not to save you, but to save him, this Demesne, and our brightblood vassals because she at least had the wisdom to trust you and to see the true threat.*

I don't know—

Say it!

"Um, Alynon says to remind you that Athena didn't sacrifice herself for me, she did so for all of you, because she trusted me and she saw the real danger."

"And her sacrifice is honored," the queen said in a gently reproachful tone toward Apollo.

"I do not question Athena's wisdom," Apollo said. "Nor the reality of the danger that she prevented, only your role in it. But that danger has passed. And the Shadows are paying wergild."

"Exactly," I said. "Doesn't that set off any alarms, that they would do that so easily?"

"And what alarms should it raise?" the queen asked.

"There's something wrong with the exiles they're sending you as wergild," I replied. "Or at least, there's something more going on. They were chosen by—"

Apollo held up his hands palms upwards, and moved them like scales as he said, "Which would wisdom recommend us? That the Shadows would jeopardize our pact even as they lend us greater strength, and whilst they are under the close watch of the Colloquy? Or that you and my ever-inconstant brother, known to have some enmity of the Shadows and having gained some small reward for uncovering past plots, have returned to paint the Shadows as enemy once more, hoping to draw further reward like a fool seeking to milk Glas Gaibhnenn dry?"

Dawn looked at the queen. "I thought this was the Demesne of wisdom. If Finn is saying you're all in danger, doesn't it make sense to at least look into it? I mean, better safe than sorry, right?"

Queen Ma'at gave a slight nod of her head. "Well said."

Apollo glowered at Dawn. "Ill said, I say."

"Come now, Prince," the queen replied. "Let not the pain of past hurts divert you from the Silver Path. While we must yet judge the truth of his claims, wisdom teaches that we all are bound together, and any disturbance in the harmony between Demesnes or with the arcana will affect the order of our Demesne in some way."

Apollo waved his hand. "And let not your compassion blind you to my brother's tricks. His nature is as like to Chaos as any from that Demesne. What I do, I do to protect the Silver, from him."

Ma'at put a hand on the king's arm. "And what I do, I do to protect the Demesne *and* the dignity of your father's legacy. And I suspect your resistance 'gainst your brother's words has as much to do with protecting yourself from further injury as protecting the Silver."

"You trespass well beyond the borders of your knowledge or right where I am concerned," Apollo said.

"And you act with less courage than your brother and your Demesne deserve," the queen replied.

A flash of anger crossed Apollo's face, but he looked away a second, then laughed. "How can I have less courage than you, who would challenge me so?" He stood, gathered his white robe in one hand, and walked down the dais to me, his stride regal and confident. But when he faced me, there was something of uncertainty on his face, or was that fear? He looked into my eyes for a second, then said, "Brother, why? These long cycles have I thought long upon this question, and still the answer does elude me. It . . . bothers me, no matter how I wish it not so."

I met his stare uncomfortably, wondering if he could see Alynon behind my eyes, and waited for Alynon's response.

And as I stood staring into Apollo's gold-flecked brown eyes, his power emanating off of him, I saw a touch of vulnerability there—

Tell him . . . tell him I state clear and simply that I was not in league with Chaos, that I was not in league with the Shadows, that I had no intention of betraying Velorain or him. I swear upon the Aal that it was a Shadows conspiracy.

I relayed Alynon's words. Apollo looked even more troubled.

"Is it possible, brother, that you have gained the ability to speak outright lies?" Apollo asked thoughtfully. "Was that always your ability, your birthright? Or can I trust these words, and in trusting know that I betrayed *your* trust?"

You did as your nature dictated, and I chose not to give you any reason to do else, not then. But now, with Velorain gone and danger present, I beg you to—

The doors behind us swung open once again, and two Silver Guards each escorted a Fey into the chamber.

The first Fey was a man with bushy gray sideburns dressed like a Victorian lord in black suit and high-collared cape sewn with arcane-looking symbols in gold thread. He carried a silver-headed cane, and a ruby-encrusted dagger glinted at his side.

At least it wasn't Mort. I hoped.

The second Fey—well, I'm rarely attracted to the supermodel type. The more "perfect" a girl's features, the less they seem to hold my interest. Maybe I just found perfect symmetry boring, or maybe I'd met too many beautiful girls growing up whose beauty went only skin-deep. Who can control all the reasons for attraction?

Yet this woman—this Fey—was the next level of perfection. She made me feel as though I had discovered colors and shapes that were normally too perfect for mere human perception. Her green eyes glittered as she looked at me, and her black curls appeared to dance in a wind all their own, brushing along her shoulders and the top of an emerald feathered cape. And her gossamer green dress clung tightly enough that I could see the smooth movement of muscles beneath her tan skin—

"You like my dress?" she asked softly as she neared, and my eyes snapped back up to hers.

"Uh," I replied. "I'm—" I added, just to ensure there was no mistake as to my level of cool. I looked at Dawn on the other side of me, and found her regarding me with one eyebrow cocked. I blushed. "What?"

"Oh, nothing," Dawn said.

As long as you're in trouble anyway, would you mind looking back to the lady?

Don't push it.

"My lords and lady," the first Silver knight announced. "Proxenos Oscar te'Oz the Great and Powerful, from the Forest of Shadows, has come on urgent business regarding these humans."

The second knight said, "And Proxenos Telloraine te'Lerajie from the Shores of Chaos requests immediate audience as well."

"Proxenos," Apollo said to the Shadows Fey. "You are welcome to the Silver Court." Gone was any hint of uncertainty in his manner. He stood straight and regal once more, looking the part of a prince, and Apollo. And was that a slight glow to his skin as he turned to face Lerajie? "Chaos especially has been missed in this court. I hope that we can bring our . . . Demesnes closer together once more."

"Indeed," Lerajie said, "it is to that end that I am come."

"Great Prince," Oz said, as the prince continued to smile at Lerajie. "I am Oz, the Greatest and Most Respected Proxenos of my Demesne, and I come to warn you against the lies of these two humans, who invaded our Demesne and attacked two of our Aalbrights. As a sign of goodwill toward your Demesne, I am willing to take them away. I'm afraid they are quite dangerous indeed."

"That's not what happened!" I said.

Apollo looked over at me, and whatever hint of openness that had been there before melted away like snow off of a marble statue, leaving only a cold, hard visage. "Did you enter the Forest of Shadows without permission?"

"Yes," I said. "But not—"

Apollo held up a hand. "And did you attack two of their Aalbrights?"

"No!" I said. "Well, I mean, we had to fight to escape. They were going to imprison me. And Alynon."

Oz shook his head and made a *tsk*ing sound. "He did indeed face sentencing for crimes against the Greatwood and our vassals, crimes recognized by the Colloquy. I'm afraid they are quite serious."

"This is crazy," Dawn said. "You can't take this guy's word over your own brother's! I mean, Oz is a con man!"

Oz laughed. "Oh my dear, I am not even a man, pro or con, and a good thing that is, too. You humans all tell lies with more frequency and finesse than a unicorn poops, I'm afraid. But don't you worry, you will be returned home safely, just as we promised."

"Oh, will I?" Dawn said in a falsely sweet tone. "Though if you expect me to actually believe your word, maybe you should be offering me a brain instead, since you clearly don't think I have one."

"Prince," I said, trying to regain control of the conversation. "If we can just finish the conversation we started before the Proxenos arrived, I—"

Apollo raised a hand to stop me, looked between me and Oz, and then to Lerajie. "And what of Chaos? What may Silver offer you?"

"A fair hand, Prince," Lerajie replied. "When last your brother did upset this court, 'twas Chaos that was blamed. I am here to ensure such mistakes are not made again."

"Which mistakes?" Apollo asked with an amused half-grin. "Alynon's mistakes in getting caught, or your Demesne's mistake in using him?"

What are they talking about? I asked Alynon, but he did not respond.

"Alas," Lerajie said, " 'twas your mistake in believing we had any part of it."

"Well, we clearly have a disagreement on that point," Apollo replied. "Perhaps we can work out our differences once we are done here."

"I look forward to it," Lerajie said.

Apollo gave a smile of confident success, and climbed the dais back to his throne. "Well then, let us conclude our business here. te'Marduk!"

The lead knight who had escorted Dawn and me to the castle stepped forward. "Yes, Prince."

"Take the humans to the holding chamber. We shall summon our own Proxenos from the Colloquy that we may judge the merit of the Shadows' claims."

"Prince—" Oz began, but Apollo held up a hand.

"While we would maintain goodwill between our two Demesnes, so too we have our own claims against these humans, and against the Silver Aalbright with them, and little desire for releasing them to Shadows justice before the Silver has satisfied our claim."

Oz considered Dawn and me for a second, as if weighing whether he might sneak us out under his cloak before anyone could stop him. "Very well," he said at last. "I only meant to say I had intended to suggest just such a course myself. But know that the Shadows will be satisfied with nothing less than the return of these two humans once the Silver has verified the truth of our claim."

"I know many things," Apollo replied. "Including what is best for the Silver. te'Marduk." He nodded to the Silver knight, who gave a sharp bow of his head, then signaled to two other knights.

"Prince," I said. "Please. You must believe me. The Silver are in danger—"

"Indeed they are," Oz said. "From you." He looked at Marduk. "Bind the woman well, knight. She has uncanny strength of will."

Marduk gave Oz a cold look.

Apollo said, "Instruct not our knights, Proxenos, they know well their duty." He looked at me. "And as for believing you, we will of course give your warnings due consideration—though it seems clear you came to seek rescue from justice rather than to offer it."

"Come," Marduk said, and turned once again to march Dawn and me back along the blue and silver carpet. I felt the tug of the silver collar around my neck again.

As I turned to follow its lead, Lerajie said, "Here, that you may dream of me." She plucked a feather from her cape, and tucked it behind my ear, letting the back of her hand brush along my cheek as it lowered.

"Uh," I said, but she had already turned her stunning smile back toward Apollo.

Dawn cleared her throat. "Come on, Kirk, you can seduce the space babe later."

Marduk and two knights escorted us to the double doors, which opened as we approached, revealing now a mirrored hallway of polished silver.

Damn it, I thought to Alynon as we were lead down the hallway. *I thought for a second maybe your brother might actually listen, might believe you.*

Yes, Alynon said in a subdued tone. *As did I.*

I'm sorry.

You tried. And if we can force a trial here, rather than a return to the Shadows Demesne, we might yet prove the truth to my brother, on many points. There was hope in Alynon's voice. Faint, the hope of someone who'd had hope betrayed in the past, but it was there.

Marduk halted us before one mirrored panel among many in the hallway, and I studied it, trying to see anything special about it. Having learned the lesson of the Black Lodge's labyrinthine hallways, I was doing my best to figure out how to retrace our steps to escape if needed, and if possible. But I could see nothing unique marking this spot.

Facing the mirror, with the mirrored panels behind us as well, it had that infinite reflection effect, as though we stared down a new hallway of ever-shrinking doorways. But behind us the near-black gray of badly tarnished silver seemed to rush at us, swallowing each nested reflection as it grew. I turned, startled, to see what rushed at us, but saw only the mirrored panel on that side of the hall showing the same thing, a growing darkness behind me.

When I turned back, I found myself not in the hallway, but in a room made of the tarnished silver, with what looked like a door-sized window behind me opening onto the mirrored hallway.

"You will remain here for the even' cycle," Marduk said. He gave a wave of his hand, and two simple beds with silver frames rose from the floor, followed by a small table bearing fruit and a pitcher. "We shall return for you come brightrise."

"Great," Dawn said. "And if I can't hold it until then?"

"It?" Marduk asked.

"Yeah. What if I need to use the restroom."

"You have beds for resting," he replied, frowning, and turned to leave.

"She means urinate," I said.

"Ah," Marduk said, turning back with a look of distaste. "I had forgotten." He waved his hand, and a large silver pot rose out of the floor. "Until the morrow," he said, and moved to the door-window.

"Seriously?" Dawn asked. "You clearly haven't had to share a bathroom with this guy when he's under stress."

"Thanks," I said. "Wait, Marduk, can we just—"

Marduk ignored us now, and walked into the window. He passed through it, into the hallway, and then the window vanished.

"Well," I said. "At least this time we might get a fair trial."

"Yeah," Dawn said, clearly not convinced.

"It *has* been a crazy couple of days with little rest."

Dawn plucked Lerajie's feather from behind my ear, and said, "I'm way ahead of you." She moved to the chamber pot, and dropped the feather in. "Just go over there for a minute and turn your back. Let's maintain the mystery a while longer, shall we?"

"I am so with you," I replied. I went to the far corner and made loud *la la la* noises until Dawn threw an apple at me to let me know she was done. We switched places, and after I was done we willed ourselves clean, moved the beds close together, and went to sleep, my hand on hers.

I woke, and rubbed at my face. It felt sticky. Had I drooled on my pillow again?

My eyes opened, and I remembered I wasn't in my bed, or even Dawn's.

Nor, I saw with surprise, was I in the room of tarnished silver.

I sat up, looking around me.

I lay in the center of a large four-poster bed with hanging curtains of red and silver. Above me, another mattress rested on the ceiling, I guessed to prevent injury when defying the illusion of gravity in this place. My impression from Alynon was that Fey did not experience the physical pleasure that humans did from sex, but obviously they still got something out of re-creating the act.

Beyond the bed I caught vague impressions of a giant floating sphere of water filled with gently swirling rose petals, a peach tree growing downward from the ceiling offering its fruit for easy plucking, and a fireplace that ran the length of one whole wall filled with blue and silver flames that sang softly in a hundred-voiced chorus. But I barely registered them, and ignored the other wonders calling for attention.

Because next to me lay Apollo, Prince of the Silver Court, with a ruby-hilted dagger in his chest.

No! Alynon thought.

"Oh, fu—"

The chamber doors slammed open, and Marduk rushed into the room, spiked mace raised and ready to cave someone's head in. He looked from me to Apollo and back, and his mace flickered with blue-white lightning as he shouted, "Murderer!"

23

POLICY OF TRUTH

As Marduk advanced on me with his mace flickering brightly, I did the only thing I could think of. I held my empty hands above my head, and said, "I didn't do this!"

Marduk cocked back his mace to strike, then swung it down viciously—at the empty air. "Bah!" he exclaimed, and waved his other hand, which bore a sprig of some kind of plant. Manacles with chains manifested around my wrists and ankles, and it wasn't until I felt the cold hard edge of a collar manifest around my neck that I realized I had been freed somehow from the last one.

"I don't—" I began, but Marduk gave another wave of his hand, and a gag choked my next words.

"Chant the praise of the Aal, arcana, bow to your luck that this is the Silver Court. Were it any other Demesne, your spirit would be ten steps into death already. But you are in the Demesne of justice, and justice shall you face."

He motioned, and I was jerked up to my feet, then forward to follow him as more Fey poured past us into the room.

As Marduk led me through mirrored halls, I thought to Alynon, *What happened? Do you know if Dawn's okay?*

I do not know, I remember only blackness after you fell asleep.

I hesitated, then thought to him, *There's not a chance you took control, is there? Maybe unconsciously, or—*

I will say this but once, Finn. I did not wish my brother dead. I wished to knock his ego down a peg or two perhaps, and I wished him to know and believe the truth of what happened between us, but that is all.

Okay. So any idea how this might have happened?

As it was Oz's dagger used to do the deed, suspicion shall fall on the Shadows, and me as being their agent.

Which is obviously what someone wants.

Yes.

But if the Shadows really were behind the attack, they wouldn't be stupid enough to leave such an obvious clue. Unless they wanted to make a statement?

Were they the Mountains of the Mind, ever ready for open contest, perhaps, but the Shadows avoid direct and honest war. They prefer to work through deception, and only strike when they have clear advantage.

The queen will see that, right? She'll see that someone's obviously trying to frame us?

Perhaps. She has great wisdom. But she will see it is also possible you simply did not escape the scene and it was by luck that the dagger was discovered. Or possible that the Shadows, knowing that nobody would believe them foolish enough to use their own dagger, used their own dagger so as to ultimately shift the blame away from themselves. Or . . . that I used you, not caring for your fate.

I moaned. *Could someone in the Silver Court be behind it? Someone who wants to take over, maybe? Or held a grudge against your brother? Gods, it's not the queen, is it?*

I find it more likely that it was the Chaos Proxenos, Lerajie. I think it is safe to assume she had access to my brother's private chambers.

I thought of the feather she had placed behind my ear, of her touch, which had felt electric against my skin. Had that been more than a flirtation? Had she done something then that allowed her to control me, or at least locate me to work some magic?

I supposed that would make more sense than that she was flirting with me. I sighed. Dawn said women flirted with me all the time, but I never noticed it. So of course the one time I notice, I should have realized it was something else.

I thought back to the events of the past few months, of the plot to pit the Elwha Silver brightbloods against the Shadows brightbloods, part of a larger plot to maneuver the two Demesnes into a war that would weaken both. There were not many clues as to the identity of these puppet masters, except that they were perhaps working with the Arcanites. And they had somehow used the gnomes to deliver forged orders in the names of both the Shadows and Silver.

Alynon, who do the gnomes pledge to?

What?

Which Demesne do the gnomes pledge to?

Alynon sighed, then said, *Most often, the Shores of Chaos.*

And you didn't feel it necessary to share this earlier, when we learned someone was using the gnomes in these plots?

In case you have forgotten, arcana, I am an Aalbright of the Sil— he fell silent a second, then said, *I am not of your realm. I do not offer you information freely unless it is to the benefit of myself or my realm. This should not come as a surprise.*

But this affects your realm.

I considered the possibility that Chaos was to blame, but did not see enough evidence to make it likely. After all, even your grandfather found a way to make brightbloods work against their own Demesne through his drug. And the Chaos Aalbrights and their vassals have ever been for the progress of our realm, and our race, free from our ties to humans and your realm. They would not ally with the Arcanites, or seek a war with humans. At least, I believed not.

But war is *chaos,* I thought back.

Battles are chaos, Alynon responded. *War seeks to direct that chaos to reach a purposeful goal.*

You're splitting hairs. War breeds chaos. And change.

Fine. I may have been mistaken in dismissing the Shores of Chaos. Congratulations. You win, and my brother is still dead.

I winced.

Sorry. We'll figure out who did this, and bust their ass.

Marduk rounded a corner in the hall, and jerked me around it by my invisible tether.

Yes, we are off to a fine start, Alynon said sourly.

I didn't respond. What could I say?

I thought about the Shores of Chaos, Demesne of change and entropy. They had such beings as Loki, Typhon, and Ahriman, known troublemakers. And when I imagined what personalities might be there, names like Charles Manson or the Joker came to mind, though, I realized, I had no idea how accurate that was. They couldn't be all about destructive chaos, since they were also said to have been instrumental in the early evolution of the Fey out of the formless chaos.

And where the Silver had in some ways aided arcana in

ending the last Fey-Arcana war, Chaos had remained truly neutral in all of the wars on record. More, they had sought neither favor nor recognition from the ARC for that.

In fact, I now remembered a story I'd heard as a child. "Mira, *interesting fact*," my mother had said. "*Once, when the Demesnes were planning for war against our world, they knew that Chaos would not join. For Chaos claimed that all Fey life began in the great Sea of Chaos beyond their shores, and that it was the will of the Aal that Chaos should remain untouched by the war: for if the Fey should be utterly defeated in war then Chaos would be left to once again fill the Other Realm with life.*

"*The other Demesnes, however, did not like the idea of Chaos waiting to take their place in defeat, or the arrogance of Chaos, and so planned both a trap and a punishment. They gathered together a Quorum of all the Demesnes, and argued it was only fair that Chaos should prove the will of the Aal by the drawing of stones from within a blazing Fey Flame, one stone inscribed with the symbol for war, the other blank. The Fey Flame was a fire willed by all Fey to be eternal, so that the Chaos Proxenos could not quench it in the supposed name of the Aal. If the Aal truly willed Chaos to remain apart and uncommitted, the other Demesnes argued, then the Aal would allow the Chaos Proxenos to draw the blank stone from the flame.*

"*But, led by the Forest of Shadows, the Quorum secretly placed within the flame two stones both with the symbol for war.*

"*The Chaos Proxenos, seeing little choice in the face of the combined will of all there, drew one of the stones, even though it left his hand horribly burned and forever disfigured beyond even a Fey's ability to reshape. Suspecting the Quorum's simple trickery, however, the Proxenos instantly devoured the stone before any could see it, claiming it as an act to the glory of the Aal, that the stone should also be part of him forever just like the flame's mark.*

"A cry of protest arose. 'Now we must do this again, for you did not show us what you drew!' the Quorum's leader declared.

"'Not at all,' the Chaos Proxenos said, 'for I drew the blank stone. And if you do not believe me, then you have simply to reach into the flame and withdraw the war-marked stone for proof.' Of course, none took the offer, knowing well that the remaining stone was marked for war. So Chaos had their way, though some say the Chaos leader never forgave the other Demesnes for the loss of his hand."

That story certainly lined up with what Alynon said about Chaos not wanting anything to do with the human realm. And further, as I thought about it, that fit with what had been happening these past months as well. If Chaos truly believed it was their destiny to repopulate the Other Realm when the other Demesnes had fallen, might they not seek to speed up that fall by pushing both the Demesnes and the arcana toward war? And had this invisible enemy not outwitted the other Demesnes?

Add to that the fact that Lerajie did seem the most likely suspect, at least out of the very limited number of suspects I knew of, and that the gnomes had been instrumental in the last plot—

Is it possible that there's an extremist group within Chaos doing this, like my grandfather among the arcana?

Alynon didn't respond.

Aly, look, I'm sorry. This sucks. But if we work together, maybe we can actually stop all of this once and for all.

Alynon remained silent for several steps. Then he sighed. *Possible, yes. Though it is much less likely. Aalbrights of any Demesne are part of that Demesne in ways that go beyond simple loyalty. We draw something of our nature, our reality, our sustenance from the Demesne, and shape the nature and reality of the Demesne in return. It is somewhat a symbiotic relationship. Not all within a Demesne share a single nature, but the natures of all are felt on some level, and a Demesne always acts as one through their leadership. We are not so inconstant as humans.*

Not to start a fight or anything, but you don't seem very constant, or tied to your Demesne. Is that because you were a changeling, or some other reason?

Alynon went silent again.

Great.

We reached double doors, and Marduk said, "Enter the Chamber of Counsel, and be judged."

The doors swung open, and Marduk led me into a room that reminded me of the Quorum chamber in the Colloquy, a great round chamber that rose several stories, with gallery-style balconies ringing the room at each floor above us. Faces peered down over the railings. I spotted the Dalai Lama, Helen Keller, Martin Luther King Jr., and Susan B. Anthony, as well as Mary Poppins, Mr. Miyagi, Gandalf, several Ma'ats and Minervas, and other figures who had lived in memory as figures of wisdom and justice.

The room itself held a curving table, a half circle with the ends pointing toward me like horns, at which sat a string of Fey who looked like the committee for a World Culture Festival. Queen te'Ma'at stood, pacing agitatedly behind her own chair at the table's center, the gold bands on her arms flashing.

Within the curve of the table stood a woman dressed in white robes and a silky white blindfold.

Is it just me, Alynon said, *or is that blindfold kind of hot?*

I didn't respond. I could tell his heart wasn't in the comment. It held an ironic edge, as though he were commenting to himself on the ridiculousness of his own Earth-influenced reactions here, in the heart of his true home, in the midst of such a terrible moment.

And besides, I barely registered him or the other Fey as my eyes fixed on Dawn standing next to the woman in white, flanked by two of the Silver Guard. Dawn heaved a large and obvious breath of relief when she spotted me, and I did the same.

I knew she felt what I felt—that as long as we had each other, everything would be okay.

"Explain yourself, arcana!" Ma'at said as Marduk pushed me to stand beside Dawn and the lady in white. The queen's face blazed with furious emotion, her eyes flashing bright within the contrast of dark kohl. "What could you hope to gain from such poisonous treachery?"

"Mmmph-rr-mumble!" I replied.

Marduk frowned, and waved his hand, removing the gag.

"Thanks," I said, wiping my mouth against my shoulder, then said, "I didn't do it, majesty. I'm being framed."

The lady with the blindfold, who I realized must be Justitia, Lady Justice, held up her hand and said, "This is not the way. We must follow the Silver Path to wisdom and justice, not the path of anger and judgment."

The queen opened her mouth as if to protest, but did not, perhaps because she heard her own words spoken to Apollo now echoed back to her.

“So it shall be,” she said, and took her seat. “Please call for the Terms.”

Justitia nodded and said, “Let each Counsel propose the terms of punishment for the accused should he be found guilty. The accused shall choose which Term to accept, and should none be accepted, then final decision shall fall to the queen.” She turned to the left-most Fey seated at the table.

“te’Ecne, what are your Terms?”

Ecne wore a thin band of gold on his head, matching the tiny gold balls that hung on his long braids. He stroked his forked beard, and said in a thick Irish accent, “If the arcana Gramaraye did kill Prince te’Apollo, then for ten thousand cycles shall he be made to live the experience of being murdered fresh each cycle, or until his natural death, even so he may contemplate and truly understand the loss that death brings to not just the murdered, but to the murderer, and to all lives touched by both.”

“Oh hell no,” Dawn said.

I had to agree with her. Nobody else spoke, and I realized this was my chance to accept Ecne’s Terms. Even though I felt pretty certain I was innocent, at least of *intentionally* killing the prince, I had no desire to be murdered every day for ten thousand days if they found me guilty anyway. But for all I knew the remaining Terms could be even worse, so I didn’t dare reject them outright, not yet. I remained silent, and after a couple more seconds Justitia turned toward the next Counsel at the table.

“te’Lao-Tzu, what are your Terms?”

Lao-Tzu, an elderly Chinese man wearing pale yellow robes, gave me a sad smile, then said in a soft voice, “If the arcana Gramaraye killed Prince te’Apollo, then there is a great imbalance within him to drive such an unnatural act, and he should be exiled from all contact with others to contemplate the source of that imbalance, empty himself of ambition and harmful desires, and return to harmony with himself and the Aal."

Sentenced to a lifetime of solitary exile in the Other Realm? Not the worst of possible fates here, but I held out hope for something better.

Justitia turned to the next Counsel, a Germanic woman in white robes.

"te'Frigg, what are your Terms?"

"If the arcana Gramaraye killed Prince te'Apollo, then we should seek to weave the best destiny for our Demesne from the threads of tragedy, and . . ."

So it went.

Frigg, Zarlîk, Mandanu, and Shamash all proposed some variation on exile for life in the Other Realm with a delicious side order of mental torture, for my own good of course.

The last Counsel was a Fey who'd adopted the persona of Obi-Wan Kenobi.

"te'Kenobi," Justitia said. "What are your Terms?"

I expected him to respond in Alec Guinness's cultured voice, but instead he said with a Sean Connery accent, "You have the manners of a goat, Gramaraye. But I hear you've gained at least some knowledge of your potential."

The words were familiar—not just from the *Highlander* movie, but from my years in exile. Only one Fey had ever really spoken to me outside of giving commands, let alone quoted back bits from the memories he fed on.

"Blobby?" I asked.

"Indeed, Highlander," he said, and winked.

I'd named him Blobby McFerrin first because, like any Fey visiting me in exile, he had appeared as a giant gelatinous blob to mask his true identity in the wildlands. But more importantly he had been the only Fey to share a memory back with me—a music video from after my exile for "Don't Worry, Be Happy." Both the message that happiness was in my mind and my control, and the reminder that there was a whole world of new music and entertainment waiting for me upon my return, helped get me through those early years of exile.

Justitia prompted, "Your terms, te'Kenobi?"

His voice did change now to the fatherly tone of Alec Guinness as he said, "If Finn killed the prince, then he shall be held as a guest until such time as Alynon Infedriel may be safely separated from him, and then we shall re-evaluate at that time the appropriate fate for each. It is unjust to sentence two for what is possibly the crime of one."

I blinked. "Accepted!" I said.

Dawn grabbed my arm. "What? Why?"

"Trust me, that's about as good as I can hope for." Especially with Queen Ma'at glaring daggers at me.

I had my doubts about the ability to separate Alynon and me at all, despite Mort's earlier promise, which meant that I might be held as a guest, in decent quarters, for the rest of my life rather than being fed on in exile. And if we *were* separated, then we would each get a second chance to make our case for innocence. Either bought me more time to escape or argue my case.

"Accepted," I said again.

Justitia nodded once. "So the Terms are set, and agreed to. We shall now offer the accused the chance to swear an oath of innocence."

Oath?

If you swear you are innocent, then the charges are dropped.

Wait, really? That easy? Why—

The queen stood. "I ask that the human not be allowed the Oath," she said. "For while an Aalbright may speak truth by our nature, a human does not, and may swear to innocence he possesses not."

"From all I've seen," Dawn said, "I'd trust Finn's word over some Fey's."

"Nonetheless," Justitia said, "it is agreed, the Oath cannot be held as certain when given by a human. We therefore shall withhold the Oath—"

"Wait," I said. "In the Colloquy, in the Quorum chamber, they said anyone who spoke a lie there would suffer great pain. Can't you do the same here?"

Justitia looked like she'd just sucked a lemon-flavored algebra problem. "Such methods are distasteful to us. It implies coercion toward a desired answer, and when coercion is used even an Aalbright may find ways to deceive. Particularly one pledged to the Shadows."

"I'm not pledged to the Shadows," I replied. "And trust me, being forced to tell the truth is nowhere near as distasteful as being punished for a crime I didn't commit. I know from experience."

Justitia cocked her head as if listening to something beyond normal hearing, then said, "If the accused is the one requesting a compulsory truth-telling, then we see no reason to refuse it. Counsel, please commune and Shape the room, Aal willing."

"Our will is Aal," the others replied, and then fell silent

for a minute. I felt a slight pressure growing in my ears, as though in a swiftly climbing airplane, then there was a flicker as if reality were a worn VHS movie finding its tracking. Nothing seemed to have changed though.

"Now, arcana," Justitia said. "Speak you any word of deception, and you will suffer great pain. Did you kill Prince te'Apollo?"

"Not that I know of," I said, causing a stir among the Fey. "I mean, if I did, I don't remember it, and it would have been someone else controlling my body."

"So Alynon Infedriel may have done it?"

"He says he didn't, and I believe him," I replied.

Thank you, Alynon said.

"But you do not know for certain whether he took control of you?"

"Well, he's never been able to before. I mean, not for more than a couple of seconds. And that sort of knocks him out a while."

"In your world, and that you know of," Justitia said. "But are you certain he does not have greater control in his native Realm?"

"Uh, no," I admitted.

"And do you have access to his thoughts? Are you able to know when he speaks true?"

"No." Damn. "But your honor, we do think we know who framed us. If you could just summon—"

"Out of order," Justitia interrupted. "We cannot accept your claims of another's guilt until we have proven the truth or lie of your own guilt, so that we may judge the possible intent and worth of your claims."

"Seriously?" Dawn said. "Would it help if he filled out

form twenty-seven B stroke six?"

Justitia cocked her head in Dawn's direction, and her brow furrowed above her blindfold. "I'm afraid I do not understand the question."

"Well then," Dawn said, "let me explain about a little thing called bureaucratic bullshi—" I grabbed her hand and squeezed it.

"It's okay," I whispered. "We'll figure this out." Louder, I said, "What she was asking is, why won't you listen to my charges? You would know if I was lying, right?"

Justitia replied, "It is not certain that yours is the innocence in question. You are two spirits in one body, which presents a unique puzzle that we must solve. We cannot know whether your actions were yours, or Alynon's, or some combination. We cannot trust your charges if they were influenced by one who might themselves be guilty. And we cannot hear Alynon's words nor compel him to truth while he is within you."

"This is crazy," Dawn said. "Why would Finn *or* Alynon kill the prince? We were trying to get his help!"

"An excellent question," Blobby-Wan Kenobi said, and rose to move around the end of the table. He placed a reassuring hand on my shoulder. "Perhaps, if we cannot prove Alynon innocent of the act itself, we can prove him innocent of the will or want to commit such a crime. Can we not try Alynon through the old way of Proof against Cause?"

Justitia tilted her head a second, then said, "Though not a certain proof of innocence, it may be taken as proof against guilt, if three proofs are given." She looked around at the other Counselors. "What cause may be laid upon Alynon Infedriel that he should kill the prince?"

Ecne said, "Alynon had the cause of Revenge against the Silver: revenge for his exile, and the reasons such exile was imposed."

Lao-Tzu nodded. "Alynon had the cause of Selfishness, as his nature has never been true to the Silver, but rather true only to his own desires and ambitions."

Shamash said, "Alynon had the cause of Jealousy against his brother, who won that which Alynon desired, and was the favored prince."

Justitia waited a beat, then said, "Three good causes, Revenge, Selfishness, and Jealousy. Alynon, do you wish to prove against them?"

Do you think I can get her to punish me privately if I do not? Alynon said, though he again sounded more ironic than lascivious as he did.

You need to take this seriously, I thought back.

La, now here is a day to mark indeed, when you are the voice of reason.

I sighed, then said out loud, "Alynon says yes."

Justitia nodded. "The Causes are presented, and challenged." She frowned. "But can Alynon's memories be shared as Proofs?"

Blobby looked at me, and held his hand up, palm facing me, his Jedi robe sliding down his wrist slightly. "May I?"

I sighed. "Yes."

He placed his hand on my head—not a necessary act to read my memories I knew, but something he had always done for me as a reassurance of when he was in my head and not. He stood in silence a moment.

"I believe so," Blobby finally said, to my surprise. "The barriers against Alynon's memories were woven by the Silver, after all, and though their nature has been corrupted I should be able to get past them."

I groaned as it really hit me what this meant—I was about to go inside Alynon's head. Bad enough to have Alynon in my head, but for me to go inside his? "Why do I feel like I'm in for a violent prolonged transformative psychic episode?"

"Just relax," Blobby replied. "Pretend you are going to see a moving picture."

"Except I don't have to live with the characters in my head afterward," I muttered.

Clearly, you don't pay attention to half the things you say, Alynon replied. *I sometimes think you are little but the characters collected in your head.*

"Ready?" Blobby asked.

Just focus, and get us out of this mess, I thought back. I closed my eyes, and practiced the mental exercises Grandfather had taught me long ago for clearing the mind of distracting thoughts and worries. Then I gave a sharp nod.

THERE, a voice echoed in my head. A shift, similar to what I felt when Vee had read my memories, except I could feel it physically, like I had one of those little brain crawly bugs from *Wrath of Khan* squiggling and burrowing between my brain lobes.

Uh, Finn, Alynon said. *There's some things I probably should have told you—*

And then, a memory bloomed. It wasn't mine, yet I experienced it as if it were.

24

GROOVE IS IN THE HEART

Alynon watched as Apollo performed the maze dance for their father, te'Arthur.

The maze glowed upon the floor, a circular pattern representing the five rings of mastery leading to perfect harmony and wisdom, and all princes of the Silver had to dance its pattern.

A bard stood in the corner, chanting a poem, punctuating the words to create a rhythm:

"Make grow your wisdom, make it grow,
Like a tree reaching for sky;
Roots in learning, ourselves to know,
And a trunk of fail and try;
Let past pains go,
Reap as you sow,
And so shall judgment blossom
Upon your bright branches to show
For all, your wisdom awesome."

The bard beat out a rhythm with his hands and by making

percussive noises with his voice for several beats, then resumed his chanting.

"Seek you justice, seek you the true,
Without bias, be you fair . . ."

As the bard continued, Apollo stepped with the grace of a cat in splints, stiff and proper, his movements fluid despite the seeming rigidity of his back and legs.

He reached the end of the pattern, and bowed.

"Perfection," Arthur said, and Apollo's chest swelled with pride. Literally. It swelled up, like he was one of those bright-chested birds doing a mating display, or Pamela Anderson on Mars. Arthur clapped once. "Now, Alynon."

Alynon moved to the start of the pattern, and waited for the bard's chant to begin anew.

"Make grow your wisdom, make it grow,
Like a tree reaching for sky . . ."

As the words flowed through Alynon, he began the pattern. But the steps felt confining, like a too-tight jacket, and while he was always willing to suffer a bit to look good, in this case it did not seem fitting. And so he let the words guide him.

He transformed into a flaming spirit, silver flames in place of hair, his skin burning white hot.

He rose up like a tree for the sky, spreading his arms, sending branches of blooming light upwards and swayed, then rotated to the next ring.

He leaped. He spun. He grew through trial and pain into

a glorious tree. He swept like a shining wave across the realms, bringing justice to all.

And then, he ended with the splits.

There was a long moment of silence after both the bard and Alynon had finished. Alynon floated upward and settled back onto his feet.

"That was everything I might hope," Arthur said at last.

Apollo stepped forward. "But you said *I* did perform it perfectly."

"Truly, not even the Aal could find fault with the smallest part of your performance."

"But if perfection is the highest state that may be strived for, how then could Alynon have done better? He did not even attempt the traditional steps."

"I made no comparison, nor does the merit of Alynon's achievement blemish any part of yours, but rather each is worthy of praise separate in nature. Forget not the purpose to which Alynon's nature was conceived."

Apollo frowned at his brother. "I do not think—"

"Lord te'Arthur," a herald called, entering the chamber.

"Speak," Arthur said, as Apollo glowered at the intrusion.

"The Proxenoi from the Shadows have arrived."

"Please, show them in," Arthur said. "I shall receive them here."

The herald bowed, and glided from the room.

A minute later he returned, followed by two Aalbrights of the Shadows. The first was a meticulous and aristocratic-looking man in a long-tailed black jacket and sharp white ruffled shirt, wearing the halo of a Proxenos, an ambassador of the Colloquy. And the second—

Alynon felt a heart form in his chest just so it could beat

rapidly, like a bellows that stoked the sudden heat which coursed through him.

The second Aalbright had the appearance of a young woman, with impossibly large, dark eyes, and lips that curved up into a warm smile. Her hair cascaded down in dark waves, past an elegant, slender neck adorned with rubies, and down the back of her sheer gold dress with its delicate red patterns. She did not have the halo of a Proxenos, but she shone with her own light, like polished brass during a golden sunset.

"I bring greetings from the Shadows and the Conclave," the Proxenos said. "I am Canubrius te'Vilovain, and this"—he motioned to the young woman—"is my apprentice and assistant, Velorain te'Uriel."

"You are welcome, both, to the Silver Court," Arthur said. "These are my branches: William te'Apollo, first chosen to succeed me; and Alynon Infedriel, First Knight."

Canubrius arched an eyebrow at the speaking of Alynon's name, but was diplomat enough not to raise the obvious question regarding the lack of a te' prefix.

Velorain was less constrained. "You are without persona?" she asked Alynon.

"I have plenty of personality," Alynon replied, and pulled a sterling rose out of the air, presenting it to her. As she reached for it, it exploded into a hundred miniature rabbits, hopping wildly away in every direction, including over the top of Velorain's head.

She burst out in laughter. And Alynon felt as though he had just conquered the entire Bright Realm.

Arthur cleared his throat, and said to Canubrius, "My hands shall see that you are fed and made comfortable, and then we shall speak."

A servant stepped forward into the room, but Apollo raised his hand and said, "I should be the one to take them. It is only appropriate for such important guests."

Arthur arched an eyebrow. "Very good."

Alynon cursed himself for not thinking of offering first. But it would be too much for them both to act as escort—too much of an honor, and at the same time too much danger they would appear untrusting of their guests.

Alynon almost offered regardless. But the opportunity passed as the two Shadows Aalbrights made their bows, and Apollo swept past him with his sun god grin.

Blur . . .

Alynon and Velorain floated over the Lake of Infinite Moons, their dangling toes skimming the mirror-like surface and sending out ripples that appeared to be fractal waves of crystal, reflecting and refracting back the countless celestial lights. Crystal pillars rose from the water at intervals, supporting square platforms with lush green and silver gardens overhanging them. As Alynon and Velorain floated between the gardens, the pale flowers bent toward them and whispered vibrations that hinted at growth and death and rebirth.

Velorain tilted back her head, exposing her long slender throat, and watched the moons that arced overhead. "This all is so different from our Demesne."

"And is that good or bad?" Alynon asked.

"A little of both, I think," she replied.

"Is it something you could perhaps get used to?"

Velorain looked at Alynon, an amused smile spreading across her face. "Why? Would you have me stay?"

"I think you know my heart on this matter."

Her smile turned mischievous. "Do you possess a true heart, then?"

"I have that for which a heart may be both blamed and praised, that glowing affection that is as like to love as to be love."

"I see. Your brother did profess love to me as well, you know."

Alynon gave a dismissive wave. "Professing love is as natural to his persona as feeling love is not. Ware should you chase his promises, lest you end but another trophy claimed and then cast aside."

"I have met Apollos before, and know well their love of the chase. But you, even had I met every other Aalbright ever there was, you would remain unique among them all, and your nature remain a mystery to me."

"And what think you of my nature?"

"What makes you suppose I think on you at all?"

Alynon laughed. "Well enough. But if my nature did detract even the smallest share from what affection you might feel toward me, then I would count it a curse."

Velorain reached over, and brushed her hand along Alynon's, causing ripples of light and pleasure to spread out from it across his skin like the glittering waves below. "It is no curse."

Alynon smiled, and felt as though he could swell to encompass the moons and all that their light touched.

"What is it like?" Velorain asked. "To have no dominant persona?"

"Having never had a dominant persona, I cannot measure the lack of it."

"It seems to me that without my chosen persona I should feel adrift, without compass or the surety of knowing my own nature."

"I think perhaps you overestimate your persona. You are more than the sum of those memories whose form and content gave you substance. Uriels have I met in our Demesne, and they are in no part you. And Uriels have visited our court from out-Demesne, yet none were so enchanting, nor enchanted with the Silver, as you."

Velorain waved her hands as if presenting herself. "And yet Uriel I am, and by my persona all know the truth of me, may better judge which private counsels or important tasks to entrust to me."

Alynon nodded. "And all may know that poetry is your truest love."

Velorain smiled. "Indeed, you have been most prolific these past cycles, and most creative in the delivery of your words. Though Canubrius was less than amused when he received my firstbright meal by mistake, and the fruit began to dance and praise the inspiring curves of his body."

Alynon laughed. "La, I fear I shall be smoothing over that breach of etiquette for some time."

Velorain's smile faded. "Yet, Alynon, you were created most from those memories your parents formed themselves. Any memories of Substance used in your creation are more the stuff of mortar than architecture, more note than nature. You may love . . . poetry one day, and hate it the next and I cannot know which and when."

"I am not so inconstant as that," Alynon replied.

"Those from the Shores of Chaos created such as you were are said to be wild and unpredictable spirits."

"My parents were not seeking to breed chaos," Alynon said. "They adopted the method of that mad Demesne, but not their purpose."

"But you cannot yourself branch?" Velorain asked, and there was something of sadness in her tone.

"No. Having no core memories of Substance, I have not that within me which may create a stable offspring."

"And does that not make you sad?"

Alynon floated in silence for a minute before saying, "I think it matters not. Were I my brother, then what memories of Substance I might lend to the enterprise of branching would be the same memories that any other Apollo might lend. Therefore, might I not simply adopt the offspring of some other Apollo to equal effect?"

Velorain was silent for even longer before responding, "I suppose, though that feels somehow wrong. And what of your mate? You would permit her—or him—to branch with another?"

"I . . . I had not thought of that aspect before, but I must admit that it does not please me to imagine it now."

Velorain smiled, clearly happy at the response.

Alynon looked up at the moons. "But perhaps we need neither branch. The Chaos Demesne has survived by converting and adopting defectors from other Demesnes to balance the loss of true offspring, and by all reports they continue to thrive, in their own way. We—that is, my mate and I—might do the same."

Velorain glanced sideways at Alynon. "And have you any desire to defect to the Chaos Demesne, being of similar nature?"

"I have never been given cause to consider it," Alynon said. "Even if their ways and goals were not so shrouded in mystery, I feel no particular draw to them. As I said, my parents adopted the method of Chaos, but not their purpose."

"And what *was* your parents' purpose?" Velorain asked, her too casual tone telling Alynon how important this question was to her. Did that curiosity come from her role as a Shadows agent, or from her care for him? He preferred to believe the latter, and even if that were not true he was happier to live in a fiction of her caring than a reality of her not.

"They feared that our race are limited by our dependence on human memories and personas, and to truly grow and evolve we must needs be able to create our own ideas free from any influence of human nature."

"Limited how? We grow, we learn, we have nearly defeated the humans in war several times. We have created beauty such as this," she waved at the lake around them. "Well as say a human is limited to being a beast for taking in the flesh of beasts and making it part of their own."

"It is not the same," Alynon said. "Humans do not play the role of the beasts they eat."

"I am not so sure that is true," Velorain said.

"La. Then take my brother—"

"Are you sure that is your wish?" Velorain asked with a grin. "That I take your brother?"

"A clever jest, but no, that is most definitely not my wish."

"Very well. What were you to say of your brother, then?"

"My brother, he has incorporated memories from many forms of Apollo in order to be the fullest expression of that persona possible. Apollo Phoebus. Apollo Loxias. He has even incorporated modern forms in order to match the knowledge and growth of humans, such as Apollo Creed. For my part, I find him more tolerable since he gained some measure of nobility and responsibility from Apollo of the

Galactica, whatever great nation is that. And yet, for all that, he will never be other than Apollo, not in any great way."

"So do you feel you would be a better king than he?"

"Bright no!" Alynon shuddered. "That would be awful. Of course, the power is shared equally with the queen, so if I had the right queen I might be able to manage it a while. But no, my brother is born to be king, and I can think of no being better suited to that burden besides my father."

Apollo leaped down from a nearby garden as they passed, stopping just above the water to float beside them. "Why thank you, brother! And may I say, you are most suited to praising me."

"Then I shall praise your great timing, and even greater humility," Alynon replied wryly.

"And I will humbly accept your praise," Apollo said, and winked at Velorain. "My lady, the Shadows Proxenos demands you return to court. May I offer you a ride back in my chariot?" He raised his hand, and from the sky descended a golden chariot pulled by three pegasi.

Velorain could not refuse, of course. And there was no room for Alynon in the chariot. Alynon frowned as Velorain said to Apollo, "Happily will I return with you." Then she put her hand on Alynon's arm, and he shivered from the pleasure of it once more. She leaned in close, and said for only Alynon to hear, "Alynon Infedriel, I leave you my heart. Or that which it holds in seeming. Care for it well."

Alynon grinned, and his smile wasn't the least diminished by Apollo sweeping Velorain away.

Blur

* * *

te'Arthur summoned Alynon to his private chamber, and Alynon entered past the guards. His father stood waiting with his brother, and with his sisters, te'Athena and te'Oshun. Their presence meant nothing good for Alynon, he felt sure. His mother had passed into the Aal while he was young, made instable due to his branching, and since then his father had recruited his sisters' aid whenever there was some important decision to be made for the Demesne, or some difficult news that required a more delicate handling of Alynon than Arthur's nature allowed. He guessed this was the latter case.

Sometimes, Alynon liked to give his father a hard time about this difficulty. He would visit his father and say things like, "Father, I do not understand these feelings of loneliness. Can we talk about them?" or "Father, how do you know when you are ready to branch with a mate?" or "Father, what is a good size to make my genitalia?"

But this was not one of those times. Alynon could sense that he was not going to like whatever discussion approached.

"Father," he said, bowing. "Sisters." He nodded to each in turn.

Athena had been a Proxenos in the Colloquy since before Alynon was branched, and Oshun nearly as long. Athena wore flowing white robes as clean and sharp as her reason, and her golden aegis glowed upon her chest like a shield meant to deflect any attempt to reach her heart.

Oshun moved with a flowing grace in her gold robes and peacock feather headdress, her eyes the swirling gray-green of a deep and swift river. They watched Alynon enter now with a sympathy that made him wary.

Arthur wore his kingly robes, signaling that whatever news came next, it came from Alynon's king, not his father.

"What news?" Alynon asked.

"Your brother has made a formal request," his father said, motioning to Apollo. "He wishes to be bonded to Velorain te'Uriel in order to strengthen the ties between our two Demesnes."

Emotion rippled through Alynon like a quake, expanding out through the air so that two of the moonglobes overhead flickered, and died. Alynon looked to his brother. "But she loves him not!"

"Be reasonable," Athena said. "The benefits of this bonding far outweigh any that may be gained from a bonding with you. You may not branch heirs, nor—"

"Has she given response?" Alynon asked.

"Not yet," Arthur replied. "Though the Shadows Proxenos has assured us the bonding would be happily approved, and that her delay is only to lend her answer the weight of a considered response."

"But I love her!" Alynon said.

Apollo smiled. "As do I. Come, little brother, be not a sore loser. There will be other—"

"This is no game to me," Alynon snapped. "Velorain is not a prize."

"What is love if not a game?" Apollo responded.

Alynon looked to Oshun. Of them all, she had always shown the greatest compassion. In truth, Alynon had taken advantage of that in the past. But now, he needed her understanding, her emotional wisdom. "Sister, can you not see it? I hold something deeper, truer, than some memory of feeling within me. I hold feeling itself, true love and affection for Velorain."

Oshun's eyes went dark, going from river green to the light-kissed blackness of a night sky. "I see within you that which exceeds seeming, it is true. But I have not the wisdom to understand it, nor judge its nature."

"Enough," Arthur said. "I have expressed my blessing for this bonding. If there is some contest or conflict between your nature and my decisions for the benefit of this Demesne, then it is your nature that is flawed. And for my part in your nature, I will apologize if you wish, but I offer no apology for this decision."

"What of justice?" Alynon demanded. "We are the Demesne not only of reason, but of justice, and I say it is not a just act to bond someone against their will."

"Nobody is being bonded against their will," Arthur said. "And even were it so, it is not reasonable to expect our Shadows cousins to abide by our definition of just."

Alynon felt something like the collapse of a star within his chest, and his form wavered. He did not want to believe Velorain would agree to the bonding. But he knew her nature, and nothing felt certain or stable in his world.

"By your leave," Alynon said, and bowed. His entire form vibrated with his emotions as he turned and strode away.

Wait, Blobby's voice sounded. *We are interrupted.*

I was jolted out of Alynon's memories back into the reality of the Chamber of Counsel, and became aware of the Shadows ambassador's angry voice demanding entrance behind me. I blinked, and turned away from the row of Silver Counsels to see Oz blocked by the two guards at the chamber entrance, his face quite red between his bushy gray sideburns.

He flicked his high-collared cape in a gesture part agitation, part showmanship, and said, "I demand to know what is going on. I have been treated more like a criminal than an ambassador. And this court has had more than enough time to see the wisdom of sending these two true criminals back with me to my Demesne for trial there. Instead I learn you are holding a trial here—"

Ma'at stood, and said, "I am curious how you learned any such thing, as you were to be confined to your rooms until sent for."

Oz stood up straight, and said in a great booming voice, "I am Oz the Great and Wise. I know many things and you cannot hold me—"

"Then you surely know why they are here, but your dagger is not," Ma'at said.

Oz looked startled. "My dagger?" He glanced down at his hip, as though surprised to see it not there.

"Proxenos te'Oz," Ma'at continued, "I promise you that should these two be found innocent of the charges we bring, then we shall consider the merits of sending them to the Shadows to face justice there as you have requested, as well as other considerations of justice. Guards, please return the Proxenos to his rooms."

Oz was forced back from the doors, and they swung shut once more. And their clanging felt like the shutting of a prison door on my hopes. Even if Alynon could prove reasonable doubt about our guilt, would the Silver just send us back to the Shadows to face a much less forgiving justice there?

25

PRICE OF LOVE

"Alynon, do you wish to continue?" Justitia asked.

Yes, Alynon replied, his tone one of restrained emotions. *I must. We have not yet addressed all charges against me.*

"Alynon says yes," I translated.

Dawn put a hand on my arm. "Are you okay? What did you see?"

"You couldn't see the memories?" I asked, surprised.

Blobby shook his head. "She could not. Only the Counsel may perceive them. We have no wish to reveal even more of our world to a mundane."

I sighed. "I'm okay," I said to Dawn. "Don't worry. This will all be over soon."

"Very well," Justitia said. "te'Kenobi?"

Blobby-Wan placed his hand on my head, and I fell into Alynon's memories quickly this time.

A flash of silver light.

Alynon looked into Velorain's eyes and asked, "You would

say yes to my brother's proposal? For all that is sacred, why?"

They stood in the Silver Grove, beneath the canopy of a star willow. The tree's tarnished silver trunk stretched two hundred feet toward the moons above, its branches made of flickering, flowing light that fell like curtains of sparks and shooting stars all around them.

"We spoke of this," Velorain said, radiant in her gossamer red dress and diamond-netted hair. "It was in Apollo's nature to claim me. It was in your father's nature to do what is best for his people. And it is in my nature to seek the greatest power for mine."

"But you also said you love me," Alynon said.

"And I do."

"Yet you would bond with my brother?"

She frowned at Alynon. "I—what would you have of me?"

"I would have *you*."

Velorain looked at Alynon in silence for a minute, her face lit silver in the glimmering light of the willow. "To marry your brother would place me in a great position of power and influence, and would gain much for my Demesne. To turn away from such an opportunity—I would instead likely lose much of the power I have gained, and may well be exiled."

"And should I defy my father's clear desires, I too may be exiled," Alynon said. "So let us go into exile together."

Velorain took a step back. "To what gain?"

"The gain of each other," Alynon said.

"The gain of an uncertain future in return for the injury of all that I have known," Velorain said, "of all that I have built for myself."

"And to what end, all that you have built?" Alynon asked. "For what purpose do you play this game of power?"

"What end? To no end: no end to my life, no end to my freedom."

"And what use 'life' or 'freedom' if you do not employ them to your happiness?"

She smiled. "You assume that the game itself is not what makes me happy."

Alynon shook his head. "I assume nothing. I *hope* that you might consider life with me a life indeed, and the freedom to love me the greatest freedom."

Velorain watched the light cascading down for a long silent time, then said, "Where would you have us go?"

"Wherever you may feel happiest with the choice," Alynon replied. "The Summerland, Demesne of creativity and art, where you may be surrounded by poetry every day. Or the Heart Lands, Demesne of passions and desires, for surely they would accept us."

Velorain considered her hands for a moment, then said, "I know that I love you. I have all the thoughts and feelings that commend themselves to that name in the memories given me. And there is in my nature that which yearns to be consumed by this love as in a great fire. But also I am Uriel, and shaped by and for the Shadows to a Shadows' purpose. I cannot abandon my ambitions nor my duty so easily. I am sorry." She looked up. "Would that you were the elder brother, that I might be bonded to you, then all of my desires would be fulfilled in one body."

"Let me fulfill all your desires yet," Alynon said.

"How?"

"I—we may go to the Shores of Chaos," Alynon said. "Whatever is in me that surpasses like and proves real—whatever in my nature allows for love to conquer all other impulsive needs that my makeup recommends me—it is surely tied to the manner of my branching. And that method comes from Chaos. Let us see if they might alter that fixed part of your nature that binds your will to memory, and in alteration find love's truth."

Velorain looked into Alynon's eyes for what felt like an eternity before saying, "If I might indeed be freed from the compulsory and oft tyrannical law of mine own nature, to pursue my heart's desire—to pursue love for love's sake as I willed—that would be a kind of power worth such risk."

"Truly?" Alynon asked, barely daring to hope.

"Yes," Velorain said, and then with more conviction, "Yes. I will go with you to the Chaos Demesne."

Blur—

Alynon faced Apollo in his brother's private chamber, a room as grandiose yet soulless as Apollo himself.

Apollo rolled his eyes, and flung one leg over the arm of his throne-like chair, leaning back. "Give it up, brother," he said. "Find some new entertainment."

"Have you not heard me, brother?" Alynon replied. "She has agreed to leave with me in exile. But I would not see her stripped of home and title. Relinquish claim to her, find some other Shadows match to pursue, that she may withdraw from the proposal with the lesser shame and come with me not as an exile, but as an ambassador. A thousand beautiful Lydas will I find you for this one Velorain."

Apollo laughed. "My appetite is for a Velorain. A thousand Lydas tempt me not."

"Why can you not understand that I truly love her, brother?"

"I understand well. And I declared my love equally."

"That which you hold is not love," Alynon said. "It is a passing desire shaped by your nature."

"It indeed holds the shape of love, and the feel of love, and all other forms and aspects of love," Apollo replied. "How then is love not love?"

"When it allows not for the happiness of the one you claim to love."

Apollo grinned, settling into an even more relaxed stance across his chair. "Oh, I have never had complaint of my love before, and I feel quite certain Velorain shall not differ in this regard."

"Perhaps," Alynon offered generously, managing to keep his tone, and his form, steady. "But I ask you, brother to brother, to believe me when I say that there is naught in your nature that can love her as I do." Apollo snorted, and Alynon raised a hand. "This is no flaw in you, but rather a happy curse for me. But if love shall be the wind that drives your course, let it be whatever familial love you do hold for me, and grant me this request. I will grant you in return any boon you ask."

Apollo sat up, his expression growing serious. "Enough, brother. I do love you, as I love Father and all of our Silver Aalbrights. It is to all our benefit that I take Velorain as mine. And more importantly, it is what my heart compels me toward. I will speak no more on the matter."

"This has naught to do with love, or duty," Alynon said angrily. "You would simply take that which I desire most."

"Believe as you will," Apollo replied. "It changes my answer not at all."

A sword flickered briefly into existence in Alynon's hand,

but he quickly regained control of his emotions—or at least the outward expression of them. "I came to you as a brother, hoping for a brother's love," Alynon said. "I leave without a brother, and a love that is truer than any you shall know."

Alynon marched out of the room, already making plans for a swift escape to the Shores of Chaos.

Blur—

Alynon motioned Velorain to the side as he stood before the trilithon and prepared to invoke the portal to the Shores of Chaos Demesne. Behind him, he could feel the presence of the Silver Court like a weight upon his shoulders, and could not face it, could not face the home he was about to leave and possibly never see again.

He raised a hand. "Yl thein ghlach'lorahn mich anthon—" As he spoke, the trilithons began to glow, and hum.

But before Alynon could complete the first pattern, a dozen rainbow-edged blurs of light streaked down from the Silver Court walls and resolved themselves into the Silver Guard, each armored in gleaming silver plate with a silver diadem holding back his or her braided locks.

Arthur and Apollo appeared as well, and Alynon's heart quivered.

"Father—" he began.

"Do not address me so," Arthur said, and held up his hand. A rotating black crystal appeared above it, radiating an ultra-violet glow. A communication crystal. "We uncovered your conspiracy before its damage could be realized."

Alynon frowned. "Love is not a conspiracy, Fa—my lord. I tried—"

Arthur's fist clenched, and the crystal vanished in a dark flash. "I know what you tried!" he said. "And speak not of love. I viewed the messages from your Chaos patron. You would have betrayed our Demesne, and your brother, to bring this Shadows Aalbright as sacrifice to the Chaos Lords, a trade to gain you position and power in their ranks."

"What?" Velorain said, stepping back from Alynon.

"What?" Alynon said at the same time. "I have had no communication with the Chaos Lords, nor any desire to join their ranks."

"Indeed?" Apollo asked. "And to where was this portal meant to take you?" He waved at the trilithon.

"Father," Alynon said, ignoring Apollo and raising his hands in a pleading gesture. "It is true, we were defecting to the Shores of Chaos, but only—"

"Enough!" Arthur said. "Knights, take him. I will escort Velorain te'Uriel safely back to the company of the Shadows Proxenos myself."

"No!" Alynon said, and reached for Velorain. But she stepped back from him, her face and form rippling with signs of hurt and confusion and anger.

"You were but using me?" she asked.

"Never!" Alynon said. "Someone went to much trouble making it seem so, but—"

She shook her head. "In the Shadows, we learn to assume every word and act of another is part of some larger game toward their own advancement. But I had hoped—you made me believe else."

"Velorain, please—" Alynon said. But four knights

surrounded him and extended their will to bind him between them as in a cage. Apollo moved to Velorain's side.

"You failed, brother," Apollo said. "You have failed us all. Accept your punishment." To Velorain, he said, "Come."

"No!" Alynon said. "Brother, Father, please—"

But Apollo led Velorain away, and the four knights of the Silver Guard forced Alynon in the opposite direction.

Blur—

Alynon paced the containment room until a doorway appeared. The door always appeared in a different location on a random wall so that Alynon could not easily ambush whoever came through, even if his control over anything beyond his own body weren't blocked.

The Shadows Proxenos, Canubrius te'Vilovain, swept into the chamber and fixed his dark eyes on Alynon. The door closed behind him.

"You did this," Alynon said.

"Did what, exactly?" Canubrius asked. "Took Velorain in defiance of your father's wishes, and tried to steal her away to Chaos? That was you, I'm afraid."

"You created the false record of my messages with Chaos. Deception is a Shadows weapon."

Canubrius arched an eyebrow. "You say that with disdain in your tone, and while I admit no deception, you are there, and I am here, and which is the better position?"

"This isn't a game!" Alynon said. "And when next I speak to Velorain, I shall—"

"You will not speak to Velorain," Canubrius said. "You tried to steal her away to her destruction. I shall not allow you to see her."

"There will be a trial," Alynon said. "Whatever deception you have woven will be destroyed upon projection of my memories."

"Again, I admit to no deception," Canubrius replied. "But I have a terrible foreboding that denying your guilt will not end well. For you or anyone you love. Why put them through such a . . . torturous ordeal?"

Alynon froze. Had Canubrius just threatened his family harm if Alynon did not go along with this charade? No. He had not the power to harm Arthur or Apollo. If he did, the Shadows would have done so long before.

He spoke of Velorain.

He would torture or destroy Velorain.

"You bluff," Alynon said. "You would gain nothing by harming Velorain."

"I said nothing of harming Velorain," Canubrius said. Alynon grit his teeth. Though it was normally impossible for an Aalbright to outright lie, they could dance around the truth like Fred Astaire on pixie dust, and none were better at it than the Shadows.

"Your intent was made clear, nonetheless," Alynon said.

"Intent?" Canubrius replied. "I am not the one who nearly took Velorain to Chaos to be sacrificed. Yet had you succeeded in your plan, perhaps it would have been best that she be sacrificed. For having failed that purpose to which she was pledged in coming here, and should the Shadows Senate believe her to have gone willingly with you," he shuddered. "One might fear she would be seen as a disappointment at best, and a liability at worst. I am just glad I was able to spare her from such a fate. And I think it villainous of you, sir, that you persist in trying to destroy not just her honor, but her very existence."

Alynon had backed against the wall as if trying to escape Canubrius's words, and he slid now to sit on the floor.

Canubrius was not bluffing. He would destroy Velorain. Perhaps even frame Apollo for her death. How much advantage would the Shadows gain in the Colloquy and in their constant campaign to bring low the Silver Court if both princes of the court had made an attempt on the life of a Shadows ambassador? It seemed foolish, when even more advantage might be gained from having Velorain bonded to a Silver Prince, but there were plenty of Shadows who preferred war with the Silver to any lasting peace or profit, and Canubrius might just be among them.

Alynon didn't care about his own reputation, or about exile. The former had never been sterling, and the latter he had been prepared to impose upon himself already.

What he did care about was Velorain's life.

"Very well. I shall not contest the charges."

"La, wise choice," Canubrius said. He rapped on the wall, and the door appeared. A guard opened it, and Canubrius left.

Blur—

The door appeared once again, and this time it was Anansi, Master Strategist of the court, that entered. He wore robes that hung from just below his armpits and across his chest, robes of bright red, yellow, and blue in zigzag and geometric patterns that told a story, though Alynon had never learned the secret of reading it. Anansi's four extra limbs, still in spider form, wrapped around from his back to cross his mid-section.

"Come to gloat?" Alynon asked. "For never have you held me in favor, I know."

"I come to offer you the chance to regain honor, and serve your people," Anansi replied.

Alynon snorted. "Apologies, dear friend, but ritual suicide went out of fashion generations ago, and you know I do nothing out of fashion. I'm afraid you'll have to exile me."

"If you stay, you will die. If you go to exile, you feel it is death, but that is feeling only. So you may as well go forward, for that is the path to new things my friend," Anansi said.

"La, I have so much to look forward to."

"Perhaps you do. I have come with a way you might turn this into an opportunity, not a punishment."

Alynon blinked in surprise. "You are the last I would have thought on my side."

Anansi shrugged. "I am not entirely convinced of your guilt. I know something of trickery, after all."

"And what would you have of me?"

"That you truly work as an agent of the Silver while in the human realm. We have much work to do, much power to gather."

"You wish to challenge the arcana?" Alynon asked, surprised.

"Not unless necessary. But should there be another Bright-Arcana war, it would be best that we defeat the Shadows and their allies without the aid of the arcana. For as much strength as the arcana lend as allies, that alliance also makes us appear weak and disloyal in the minds of many Demesnes."

Alynon frowned in thought for a second, then said, "What would you have me do?"

"Help to strengthen our web of contacts and resources there." He smiled. "And help us develop our own magics in that realm."

Blur—

Alynon danced shirtless in the club—in Finn's twenty-something body—the heat of the crowd making the place feel virtually steamy. The Fastbacks were blasting through their last song, and a band named Alice in Chains were up next. A tightly packed crowd of young men and women in T-shirts and denim and flannels jumped and bumped against each other in front of the low stage, but Alynon stayed back, close to the crowded bar.

Alynon pounded back the last of his Zima and pushed through a heavily-tattooed couple to set the empty bottle on the bar. He'd become practically addicted to wine coolers—he was convinced that Bartles and Jaymes were in truth mighty alchemists—but few of the clubs in Seattle carried the delicious concoctions.

While Zimas were a poor substitute, beer tasted like bitter puddle water to him, and few other things mixed well with absinthe in his system—as he'd learned after an amnesia-riddled night spent with another Silver changeling who'd looked like a Viking biker; a night whose events were only hinted at by a blurry Polaroid, running mascara, a stack of empty whipped cream cans, and a boa constrictor hungrily eyeing the live chicken flapping about his apartment.

A night that had, apparently, also left him with a magical butt tattoo.

Alynon resumed head-banging to the rapid-fire joy of the music, and his eyes were drawn to a woman standing beside a pillar to his right. She perfectly filled a black lacy dress that left little to the imagination, and her hips wove a figure-eight pattern as she danced to her own internal beat. She watched the band, but Alynon could tell she watched him as well from the corner of her eye, her bangs swishing lightly as her head moved side to side. A slow smile spread across her bright red lips, and Alynon guessed—or perhaps hoped—it was because she'd noticed him watching her.

The song ended, and the audience applauded.

Alynon made his way over to the woman. The PAX forbade any actual relationships or sexual contact with humans, but Alynon had discovered that he quite liked the flirtation part at least, the thrill of the hunt. Perhaps he had absorbed something of his brother's nature somehow.

"Greetings," he said. "This may seem an odd question, but are you Wiccan?"

She smiled. "I'd say more wicked than Wiccan, why?"

"You look amazingly like that Wiccan photographer in the new Doors movie. Have you seen it?"

"No," she said. "Why go watch a fiction of magic when the world is full of real magic?"

Alynon's smile froze on his face.

Pox! Another glance down confirmed that she didn't wear an arcana ID ring. But if she were from the magical world and recognized him as a changeling, or recognized his host body, he could be in real trouble. He was well outside his assigned area. The ARC had threatened to stick him in a trailer out by Forks, far away from anything resembling civilization, good food, or fashion, if he were caught violating the PAX rules again.

Alynon casually pulled his black T-shirt from the back pocket of his leather pants, and eyed the path to the exit.

"If you leave now," the woman said, "you'll miss a great band. And an even better offer." Her hand reached out and grabbed his crotch.

Alynon jumped, both at the unexpected action, and at his human body's reaction to it, and said, "La! . . . oss is mine, I guess." He winced at the clumsy recovery. Maybe he shouldn't have had the absinthe after all. He needed all his wits about him now. "But sadly I must leave."

"That's a shame," she said, "I have a proposal I think you would most enjoy, changeling."

"Changeling?" Alynon said, stepping back so that her hand fell away, and he was able to slide on his shirt. Double pox!

"You are Alynon Infedriel, former First Knight of the Silver Court. And I am Jehnna te'Loki, ambassador of the Shores of Chaos. And should you help me, I can get a message from you to Velorain te'Uriel."

Alynon froze, hope welling in his chest. But he did his best to not let that hope show on his face. "I know not what you've heard, but I will betray neither my Demesne nor my family for Chaos."

A recording of Black Sabbath's "War Pigs" began playing over the speakers as the Fastbacks removed their equipment from the stage.

"Who said anything about betrayal?" Jehnna said, and

slid up close again. "All I wish is for you to sleep with me."

"What?" Alynon was certain he'd misheard over the music. "Why?"

She laughed. "Because it feels good? At least, the toys do, and I'm optimistic about the actual deed."

Alynon's eyes narrowed. "It is too great a risk just for good feelings. What other reasons?"

"What better reason to take risks than good feelings?" she asked. "But in truth, I had a thought. Know you the way that necromancers seek to ensure their child is born with the Talker gift?"

"No," Alynon said.

"They have the woman possessed by a spirit during conception. And I thought, well, here we are, both in the bodies of necromancers, and technically both bodies are possessed by spirits. What might *we* create?"

Alynon stared at her a second, then said, "You wish to branch—I mean conceive—an arcana child? The ARC would never allow it!"

"The ARC would never learn of it. Should you accept my offer, I shall have a public and untimely death soon after, at least where the ARC is concerned."

"Your Demesne would have to pay a significant fine," Alynon said, surprised. "And would not be allowed new changelings for quite a while. Arcana do not take the death of hosts lightly."

"We feel it an acceptable . . . investment." She stepped closer, and Alynon could smell the scent of apples. "But that is our concern." She traced a finger down his chest, to his stomach, and continued in a tone most often murmured in late-night promises, "For you, it will be no burden at all. That, I can promise."

Alynon grabbed her hand before she could go any lower, but shivered slightly at the feelings of pleasure that rippled out from her touch. "Why not do this with another Chaos changeling, then?" he asked, and cleared his throat, embarrassed at how husky his own voice had become.

"None are currently in the bodies of necromancers but me," she replied with a bit of a pout. "Plus the nature of our branching in Chaos raises concerns that any offspring might be . . . unstable. You, however, were branched in similar fashion to a child of Chaos, a true spirit like ours, yet not of Chaos. If any two might breed a child of human flesh and True Aalbright spirit, not some brightblood half-breed, it is us two."

"To what end?" Alynon asked.

She raised her hand in his, and placed one of his fingers in her mouth, while she grabbed his other hand and placed it very low on her back. "Mmm," she said as he slid his finger free. "Whatever end you like."

Alynon's leather pants felt entirely too tight just then.

He pulled back both his hands, and said, "I mean what is your goal? How would you use such a child?"

"We have no plans to use the child in any way that would harm you or the Silver, if that is your concern. Though I am surprised if it is, given the nature of your exile here. Betrayed by your own family . . ." She gave a sad shake of her head.

"I was not betrayed by my family. It was a . . . misunderstanding, and they acted only to protect our Demesne."

"And yet your brother took your love from you," Jehnna said.

"He acted only out of his nature, and he would not be with Velorain but for the actions of others." Alynon spoke as much to try and focus his thoughts as to answer her question. "I do not blame him. Not any longer, at least."

Jehnna shrugged, the lacy dress shifting to offer new hints of what lay beneath. "Well then, what I offer is a chance to help them, not harm them."

Alynon gave her a dubious side look. "How exactly will conceiving a child of Chaos help my Demesne?"

"La, consider, if we might have true children in the mortal realm, what need to take possession of arcana bodies? What need to invade this realm in yet another war that would divide our Realm, and cost countless Bright spirits? Why, Alynon Infedriel, you could very well save the world by fucking me."

Alynon laughed. "That *is* the best offer I've had in a while," he said at last. And Anansi *had* wished him to find new ways of advancing the Silver's cause in the mortal realm. "But I still fear it to be unwise."

"Then do not forget my offered payment. I shall get a message from you to Velorain."

Alynon stopped smiling. "How? She is surely long wed to my brother by now, and after what happened, I should think neither she nor my family would allow a Chaos agent anywhere near her."

"I give you my word, we may get a message to Velorain te'Uriel. I would not have offered else."

The next band introduced themselves, and launched into a growling, grinding tune as the lead singer shook his head side to side, his dreadlocks whipping around in a halo under the stage lights. The mosh pit started up again, pushing some people back into Alynon and Jehnna, but he barely noticed as he struggled with his choice.

He had asked several times to be allowed a message to Velorain, or at least for news of her and of his brother, but had been refused every time. He yearned to know if she still believed he had betrayed her. He wanted to tell her the truth at least, even if he had agreed not to deny the charges against him openly.

He ached to tell her that he loved her still, that even the gulf of time and worlds had not dulled that flame in his heart.

And in truth, the restrictions against changelings having sex seemed, well, just cruel. To stick them in these bodies flooded with hormones and hot blood, bombarded with constant images and promises of sexual pleasure, but not allowing them to act as their bodily nature demanded? May as well forbid them to eat, or sleep, or drink wine coolers! He could sleep with Jehnna and screw over the ARC at the same time, and that appealed to the rebel in him.

Yet should such an act be discovered, such a collusion with Chaos, he might lose all chance of returning with any honor to his home some day, of proving himself innocent of any former collusion.

"What say you?" Jehnna prompted. "Would you speak with your beloved?"

A final blur, and the memory projection faded.

I blinked, looking around the Counsel chamber at Dawn and the Silver Fey, feeling off balance from more than the memory projection, or the weird sensation of actually being someone else.

Alynon, did you sleep with her? I asked, the very thought that I might have a child out there—at least, a child of my body—more a shock than anything else I'd experienced in the Other Realm.

Of course not, Alynon replied.

I felt relief and, oddly, a touch of regret. But my eyes narrowed.

You hesitated before answering, I thought back. A pause no longer than the space of a heartbeat, but it had been there.

Finn, I have just relived many painful memories. What would you have of me?

I'm sorry. I just—sorry.

"I call a vote," Blobby said. "Do Alynon's memories satisfy Proof that he did not hold on to sufficient cause of Revenge, Selfishness, or Jealousy to kill his brother?"

Justitia said, "Three causes were charged, and three proofs given, what say the Counsel?"

Ecne said, "Proven without cause."

Lao-Tzu said, "Proven without cause."

And the rest echoed the response, until the queen said last, "While it fails to prove that they had no hand in the prince's murder, I do not believe they would have done so willingly, not for any motive we have ascribed them. Alynon is innocent of the causes laid against him by this Counsel."

Justitia gave a bow of her head. "Heard, and witnessed. The crime of murder against Prince Apollo may not be pressed again upon Phinaeus Gramaraye nor Alynon Infedriel lest some new and convincing cause or evidence is presented."

"So . . . I'm free to go?" I asked, hope rising in me despite being certain of the answer.

Marduk's lips pressed thin, then he said, "You are proven

innocent of the motive for murder of the prince. But you still have come here in physical form against the rules of the PAX, bearing a forbidden weapon, and having fled murder in the Forest of Shadows. You are not free."

"Indeed," the queen said. "We must call for the Shadows Proxenos now, that we may—"

The entrance archway flashed, and through it appeared a hallway with a knight literally flying down it. When he reached the chamber, his feet hit the marble floor and skidded to a halt.

"My lords and ladies," he said. "The Shadows Proxenos is dead."

"Oh come on!" I said.

26

THINGS THAT MAKE YOU GO HMMM . . .

Queen Ma'at stood as the other Silver Fey lords and ladies muttered around the half-circle table. "Murdered?" she asked. It did not escape my notice that several eyes looked to me when she said that, despite the fact that I'd been standing in front of them this entire time so couldn't possibly have done the act.

"No, majesty," the knight replied. "It appears to be suicide."

The queen sat, a look of horror on her face, and placed a hand on her chest, over her fan-like gorgerine.

"What did he do?" Dawn whispered to me. "Sing himself to death?"

"I— You know what?" I said. "I don't know."

How would *a Fey commit suicide?*

Not easily. And not prettily, Alynon replied, his own tone disturbed.

"Why?" Frigg said. "He was eager to address us but a moment ago."

The queen frowned. "Perhaps he feared what we would learn from our questioning of the arcana and Alynon."

"Gramaraye *was* found with the Shadows dagger," Shamash said.

Once again, suspicious looks were tossed my way like side glances in a suddenly smelly elevator.

"Or," I said, "the person really behind the attack is covering her tracks. Where is Lerajie te'Uriel?"

Zarlîk gave a dismissive wave of her hand. "That is your claim? The Chaos Proxenos departed during brightfall, before even the prince's murder."

Crap. *Could Lerajie have somehow controlled all of this without even being here?*

Doubtful. There are too many protections and barriers against willing any but the simplest of changes within the Silver Court, especially from outside the walls. It took the cooperation and combination of all those here just to change the nature of this room to enforce truth telling.

Then someone else in the Silver Court is in league with my grandfather's allies?

I am loathe to believe it, Alynon replied.

"Noble Aalbrights," Blobby-Wan Kenobi said. "If we have no reason to charge these two with the murder of the prince, and none present who may lay further charges against them, might we not be rid of them entirely? I propose we send them back to their ARC to face whatever punishment the arcana wish to mete."

"Yes, please!" Dawn said. "Or, I mean, please, no, anything but that!"

Frigg pursed her lips to the side. "The fact that the Shadows Proxenos is dead does not mean the Shadows charges against these two are dead. And offering them to the Shadows may dim somewhat their coming suspicion at their Proxenos's death. Perhaps we should consider it is time to place our relationship with our fellow Aalbrights in the

Shadows above our relationship with the arcana."

A couple of heads nodded, and Ecne said, " 'Tis true, we have some small favor of the Colloquy in this time, and the advantage over the Shadows. 'Tis better to reach out and foster ties from a place of strength and advantage, when our actions will appear most noble rather than done out of fear or weakness."

Lao-Tzu pursed his lips, then said, "And we might also send the exiles tithed us from the Shadows back to them, claiming it as compense for the death of their Proxenos. If Gramaraye speaks true, and these exiles are some form of weapon, then the Shadows may well refuse them, thus proving Gramaraye's claims in this matter at least."

Great. Not exactly the way I'd hoped my warning would be used.

Blobby hid his hands within the voluminous sleeves of his Jedi robes, and said, "Let us not forget why we now enjoy this position of advantage. It was Gramaraye and Alynon who brought word of the Shadows' prior plots to the Colloquy. Is it little wonder then that the Shadows should lay charges against them? Since when do we trust the Demesne of deception over our proven allies? Since when do we reward a warning of danger by sending the one who warned us into that very danger?"

That caused the gathered Fey to sit back and ponder for a second at least.

"Finally," Dawn said, leaning close and speaking quietly. "A Fey who doesn't have his head up his, well—do Fey have actual asses? I mean, do they need to poo at all?"

"You don't want to know," I replied out of the corner of my mouth.

"Why not?"

I sighed. "Well, you know how fish swim around in water filled with their own poop?"

"Yeah, why? Are you saying—" she trailed off, and looked up and around us. "Oh. No. I don't want to know."

Mandanu stood up. "Well, is it known that Gramaraye uncovered the Shadows plot. But it is also well known that the life of Gramaraye's own brother was in danger from that plot, and the very same brother received a great reward in exchange for his help. Gramaraye did not help the Silver out of any altruism or love of our Demesne."

The queen's form wavered, like vibrations on water, but she did not reply.

"Damn it!" Dawn said, and not at all quietly. "We just want to go home. We don't care about your politics, or rewards, or whatever."

Lao-Tzu said, "Your remarks are out of order."

Blobby cocked one eyebrow. "Patience, te'Lao-Tzu. Given that it is their fates on the line, I don't believe it unexpected they hold some small opinion on the matter."

Justitia nodded once in agreement, and said, "Indeed. Gramaraye, is there anything you wish to say that may influence the Quorum's decision?"

I squeezed Dawn's hand, and said, "Whatever the Counsel decides, please allow Dawn to go free. She is a mundane, and has no part in this. As for me, well, I think you're giving me too much credit. Most of what I've done, I haven't felt like I had much choice. I just did what I had to, what felt right at the time."

Ecne said, "Right for you does not equal right for us, however."

I shrugged. "Look. It's true, a lot of what I've done was to help my family. But it all seems to have worked out pretty good for you, too. I didn't want Petey to end up fighting in another Fey-Arcana war, but I don't think you want that, either. I'm here now because my sister's girlfriend was one of the exiles sent to you by the Shadows, but I also really do believe that the Arcanites plan to use those exiled spirits as some kind of weapon against you. And just like you're worried about your Demesne's future, I'm worried about my family falling apart. My brother Mort might not be dead like Alynon's, but we have a great wound between us, and I can't do anything about it from here. And my father is unstable, too, much like your king, despite everything we've done." I looked at Queen Ma'at. "Surely you can understand why I don't want to miss any time I have left with him."

Frigg gave a slight bow of her head, and said, "Your loyalty to your family is not in question, and it is valorous that you would fight for them. That does not, however, lead naturally to the conclusion that you have the Silver's best interest at heart, nor that your actions—"

Justitia raised her hands palms up, and said, "I judge that we have come to a point where arguments are but repeated, which indicates that it is time for decision. What is the will of the Counsel. Shall Gramaraye and Alynon Infedriel be delivered to the Shadows to strengthen our ties with that Demesne? Or shall we consider their claims of service and of the danger our exiles present, and return them to their own world to face the Arcana Ruling Council's justice, along with those exiles sent to us by the Shadows?"

Frak. Of course. The Silver wouldn't simply set us free. They would return us to the ARC, following PAX rules, and the ARC would charge us with the crime of crossing illegally and physically into the Other Realm. Assuming the

Arcanites didn't simply have people waiting to kill or capture us on our return.

Still, it would be easier to deal with the ARC than the Shadows again.

There was a tense few heartbeats before the votes began to be voiced.

"The Shadows," Ecne said.

"The ARC," Lao-Tzu said.

"The Shadows," Frigg said.

It continued down the line, until all but the queen had voted, with the vote tied between the Shadows and the ARC.

Gods, if Ma'at was somehow involved with the death of the prince, or wanted to frame the Shadows for his death, then what choice would prove the least risky for her? Or if she simply held any lingering blame toward me for the prince's death—

Queen Ma'at looked at me for a long moment as if trying to peer inside me and weigh my heart, fingering her tall ostrich feather. Finally, she said, "Let them be returned to the ARC."

I swooned with relief. A totally manly swoon, of course.

"Then this trial is concluded," Justitia said. "Let Gramaraye and the mundane be freed, and returned to the human realm along with those exiles whom we did receive from the Shadows."

"Come," Marduk said softly. "It is time for you to return to your world."

PART III

27

SHE TALKS TO ANGELS

As we marched down the path to the trilithon, Alynon remained silent. I glanced back at the shimmering castle of the Silver Court behind us, and the green fields of Avalon.

Someday, I thought at Alynon. *You'll have a real homecoming.*

No response.

I mean, it's fun to barely escape with our lives and all, but personally, I'm beginning to find it all a bit Demesning.

Alynon moaned, and said in a halfhearted manner, *Make another joke like that, and I shall make you slap yourself so hard that both ears end up on the same side of your head.*

I smiled. *Try it, and I'll play nothing but "Achy Breaky Heart" for the next week.*

Alynon didn't respond, but his presence felt a little less . . . heavy.

Blobby stood waiting for us in front of the stone trilithon in his Jedi robes and well-groomed beard, along with several Silver Guards, and a small crowd of formless Fey bodies like oversized transparent Slimers.

I looked at the formless Fey. "Fatima?" I asked as we

approached. One of the Fey raised a blob-like hand. *Here,* her voice echoed in my head.

"Thank all the gods," I said, feeling suddenly fifty pounds lighter. "I can at least cross Sammy off of the list of folks likely to kill me." I frowned at the small gathering behind her. "But only seven exiles?"

The Silver Guard holding Dawn's guitar said, "Only these could we confirm that their changelings are present beyond the portal for exchange."

I felt a chill as I realized what Fatima being here actually meant. This was either a bad thing, or a very bad thing. Since the Silver Court planned to open this portal to the Arcana Ruling Council's facility, it was bad if that meant the Arcanites had held on to Fatima's changeling and held her prisoner now at the ARC, or else very bad if Reggie had escaped with Fatima, Sammy, and the rest, but had then been captured themselves and were all being held by the ARC.

"So, Marduk, now that I've helped stop another plot against your kingdom and all, I don't suppose you'd just quietly send Dawn and me someplace other than the ARC?"

"No," Marduk replied. "The Silver will not compound your crimes by committing our own."

Great. "Out of the frying pan and into the fire," I muttered.

More like out of the frying pan, then out of the fire, and now into an ant lion's nest.

Stay positive, I thought. *We managed to gain our freedom twice today. Third time's the charm, right?*

Blobby-Wan Kenobi cleared his throat. "Before you depart," he said, "I feel I should share some final words."

My Finn senses tingled. "Why am I suddenly worried?" Or at least, more worried.

Blobby motioned for me to step aside with him, his brown robes swishing. I followed, and he said quietly, "First, I should tell you that I was asked to aid you in your defense, though in truth I would have done so regardless."

"By who?" I asked.

"One who is good at collecting favors. Velorain te'Uriel."

"What?" I asked surprised. "I thought she left the Silver Court?"

"La, yet did she reach out to me. She knew of our past experience, you and I. But, there is more."

Uh oh, here we go. "Like?"

Blobby glanced down at the ground. "I do not wish to speak ill of her, for clearly she has some genuine care for Alynon. But, I suspect that Velorain was involved in the murder of the prince."

"What?" I said again. "Why? How?"

" 'Twas through Lerajie that she did contact me, and I believe Lerajie and she share the same goals."

"Wait, are you saying Velorain is with the Chaos Demesne now?"

Of course. Alynon sighed. *Oh, Velorain.*

"I believe that, having earned the disfavor of both the Shadows and the Silver—and perhaps inspired by Alynon's suggestion of growing beyond her born nature—she went to Chaos, yes."

If she is indeed a true agent of Chaos now, then her future is bound to the goals of that Demesne, Alynon thought.

"Just because Velorain went to the Shores of Chaos doesn't

mean she's involved in what's been going on," I said. "Beyond helping us, I mean."

Blobby gave a grudging nod of acknowledgment. "Perhaps. Yet I agree with your suspicion that Lerajie was involved with the prince's death, and something in the words she spoke to me make me suspect she did act under the orders of someone who knew well the tensions between Alynon and his brother, and sought to exploit those very tensions."

"That could be anyone," I said. "I don't think Alynon's disfavor was much of a secret."

"La, 'tis true. Yet also I believe Velorain's original mission to our court long past was to sow the seeds of that very dissension between Alynon and his brother, to create division and disruption within the Silver Court by attacking its weakest link."

Gee, thanks, Alynon said.

"How was Alynon the weakest link?" I asked.

"Not Alynon. His brother."

Ah, Alynon said.

Blobby shrugged, and continued, "Apollo could ever be counted on to act according to his nature. And Velorain played on that nature expertly. But . . . I think she truly did fall in love with Alynon."

I no longer believe that true, Alynon said, but there was uncertainty in his tone.

"Why do you believe that?" I asked Blobby.

"She would have gained more opportunity to work mischief had she but stayed and bonded with Apollo. And had she wished it, I believe she could have caused you to be killed in the act of killing Apollo. But instead she seemed to have wanted Alynon's memories to be viewed by all."

"To clear Alynon's name," I said.

"And perhaps to have certain proof of whether he loved her in return," Blobby said.

"Then why is she hiding from Alynon? And for Merlin's sake, why kill his brother if she had any hope of being together?"

Blobby's expression became sympathetic. "I fear that such happiness was never her hope."

Dawn called over, "I don't mean to interrupt, but maybe you guys can exchange letters or Fey-mail or something later? I'd really like to leave before someone changes their mind, or a dragon attacks, or *something* goes wrong."

Blobby put a hand on my shoulder. "I am sorry, Alynon. I believe she may yet love you, and I have no doubt you love her still. But she is committed now to the course of Chaos, and if they truly are the ones manipulating the Shadows and Silver toward war, then I see no future with her except through betrayal of the Silver."

I waved at Dawn to signal I'd heard her and we were coming. "Maybe she joined Chaos because she had no choice," I said. "Or out of hurt over what happened with Alynon. Maybe she's trapped there, and is doing what she can to help anyway."

Blobby gave a sad smile. "Maybe. But the weight of evidence lends itself to a different belief."

"Come!" Marduk called. "This delay only makes us vulnerable."

Dawn threw up her hands. "See what I mean?"

I sighed. *I'm sorry, Aly. Maybe we can come back when this is done, or—*

Let us just be gone from here, he said. *There is nothing more to say.*

We moved back before the trilithon.

"We're ready," I said to Marduk.

Dawn snorted. "Oh, we are way past ready." She looked at Marduk. "Do I get my guitar back now?"

"I shall send it after you," he replied.

"You'd better. Or else I'll come back with bagpipes. If you think Cotten's a weapon—"

Marduk held up his hand before the trilithon, and said some liquid-sounding words. The space within the trilithon misted over and then solidified into a view of a bright ARC facility room beyond. But rather than the official ARC Portal Room, this room was cluttered with objects and devices ranging from a Simon Says and a Mr. Microphone to something that looked like that chair Bill Bixby strapped himself into to become the Hulk.

Verna's laboratory. I had traveled from it to the Other Realm before, using one of Verna's thaumaturgy inventions to hijack the connection between the Portal Room and the Other Realm. It looked like Verna had managed to do something similar again.

Gathered on the other side of the portal were Fatima's body and what I assumed were the other changeling hosts, with Reggie in his FBI-looking enforcer suit appearing to stand guard over them.

"Gramaraye," Marduk said. "You and the mundane must step through first. I must adjust for your physical passage before sending the others. And do not resist, for loathe am I to repay your service to our Demesne with a swift death."

"Yeah," I said. "That would suck for you."

I took Dawn's hand, and said, "Here we go."

Together, we stepped through.

A moment of dizziness, a feeling of vertigo, and then I stood in Verna's lab with Dawn, facing Fatima and the other changelings.

"Welcome home," a voice sounded behind me. I turned to find Verna, Father, and Sammy standing behind a ring of stone and steel in which the watery portal had formed.

Father looked like Doc Brown as played by Leonard Nimoy, with his frizzy white hair and outdated Sears suit. Verna was a good match for him, her own silver hair up in a wild bun held together with pencils and possibly some kind of antigravity spell, the ink stains on her lab coat pocket matched by the ones on her fingers and nose.

Sammy looked exhausted, but focused, now wearing the Captain Planet T-shirt and gray hoodie borrowed from Dawn, but the same red jeans from yesterday. No, the day before. Or . . . I glanced at my Casio. 10:09 P.M. So we'd been gone just over a day in the Other Realm. Gods, it felt like a lifetime since the Furies attacked at Bumbershoot.

The presence of everyone's spirits hummed on my necromantic senses, like the sudden return of birdsong in the woods after a long period of silence. Yet I did not feel as strong a hunger to touch that energy, to use it. Perhaps the near-complete absence of spiritual energy in the Other Realm had helped, or something about traveling physically into the Other Realm.

Or . . . I realized that it had never been just the spiritual energy, but something within me that responded to it, fueled the need for it. Anger? Guilt? Desire? Whatever that was, my experience in the Other Realm—in facing Mort and allowing him to win, in nearly losing Dawn forever, in experiencing Alynon's trials—had blunted that need within me that called out to the energy. I still felt it, certainly, that craving for the power and ecstasy of consuming the spiritual energy, but the craving was more a light thirst now than a consuming desire.

"Fatima's spirit?" Sammy asked, pulling me out of my internal exploration.

"Coming," I said, and she slumped in visible relief.

Dawn's guitar passed slowly out of the portal. She grabbed it gently as though it were an infant being handed off.

Then the portal gave off a slight hum, and the pitch increased slightly. The changelings started to swoon one by one, and blink as if waking.

The portal closed with a whoosh.

Fatima looked around the room, and spotted Sammy. She burst into tears.

"Oh stop," Sammy said in her usual sardonic tone as she crossed to Fatima, but her own eyes were watery, and her voice quavered just slightly as she continued. "It's not like I was going to let them keep you."

Fatima laughed with a slightly snot-filled snort, and said, "You're such a brat."

"And you're such a softie."

They fell into each other's arms. When they finally stepped apart, Sammy looked at me, and said, "Thank you."

My heart swelled. After all of the bad of the past few days, it felt amazing to have a family member view me not as a source of anger or hurt, but of something good. Before the tears started to flow, I said, "How did you all escape Stonehenge? And with so many exiles?"

"My friends came through," Sammy said. "They have experience getting people out of bad situations. Though usually it's rescuing mundies from abusive unicorns. I owe them big time."

"Merlin? J?" I asked.

"Safe and resting," Reggie said, stepping toward the lab's door. "Which is more than I can say for us. We need to get out of here, fast. Or your freedom is going to be very short-lived."

28

ALWAYS ON THE RUN

I looked at Verna's portal ring, and sighed. "I figured it was too much to hope the ARC allowed this. Were they expecting us?"

"No," Verna said. "But someone in the Silver Court somehow got news to us via the gnomes of your presence there. So I was able to divert the portal's exit point from the Portal Room to here for any portals opened from that Demesne. It's quite fascinating, actually, how I figured out the space-time jiggling of—"

"They didn't know you were coming," Reggie said, "but they'll still know a portal was opened within the facility, and trace it here."

"Oh, uh, yes, that is true," Verna said, pushing up her glasses.

Reggie added, "And the ARC is as likely to stone us as talk to us right now."

Father giggled. "New stones, blue stones, as natural as silicone."

"Interesting," Verna said, looking at Father. "Is this a vision?"

Father had a touch of prophecy, one of the gifts of sorcery. Of the five branches of arcana magic—wizardry, sorcery, thaumaturgy, alchemy, and necromancy—our family had a little of everything but alchemy in our bloodline. Father's dominant branch was thaumaturgy, the crafting of magical artifacts and the use of sympathetic magic, but his prophecy gift seemed to have been enhanced by his madness, and had helped me a few times since my return from exile.

The left side of Father's face twitched and he didn't speak, but he smiled, and his right hand tapped his thigh once. Once for yes, a response Verna had managed to condition Father to give, a way to get past his inability to speak. At first it had brought to mind the beeping of Christopher Pike's space wheelchair on Star Trek, and I felt conflicted about it. Father was not one of Verna's animals to be trained. But she genuinely cared for him, and he for her, and it *had* helped them communicate more.

"Hmmm, let's see," Verna continued. "New stones, blue stones—"

"Seriously, people," Reggie interrupted. "Remember the whole fleeing for our lives part?"

"Oh, yes," Verna said. "Quite. So sorry." She pushed her glasses up again. "The old passage?"

Reggie nodded. "The old passage."

I moaned.

"What?" Dawn asked.

I shrugged. "The old passage is the secret entrance behind the waterfall."

"Wait, Snoqualmie Falls?" Dawn said. "They'll crush us!"

"No no no," Verna said. "We'll be fine. But we'll get wet. Oooh." She began wandering along the shelves lining the far wall, rubbing at one ear. "I have this wonderful water repellant made from Mogwai oil that I've been meaning to try . . ."

"Verna!" Reggie snapped impatiently.

"At least, I'm pretty sure it will repel water," Verna said, oblivious to Reggie. "Or it may just make you irresistible to frogs. I haven't quite worked out—oh my, who left this turned on? I hope it wasn't me." She stopped beside a globe with what looked like a fireworks show going off inside.

Father took her arm, and said, "Come, dear. We must flee."

She blinked up at him. "Arlyn?" She glanced at her watch. "Oh, wonderful. I'd say we're seeing at least twice the baseline rate of lucidity—"

"We're leaving now, dear," Father said, and gently pulled her in our direction.

"What? Oh, yes, quite." Verna lifted a Nerf bazooka off of the nearby table. "Ready."

Reggie nodded, and said, "Okay folks, stay close."

We exited the room into a very industrial-looking hallway, entirely made of smooth concrete, with pipes and an air duct running along the ceiling, and colored stripes on the floor to help guide visitors to the various key departments. Reggie led the way, Sammy and the exiles following him, then Father and Verna. I brought up the rear with Dawn. We passed the Department of Mana Management and the Department of Interdepartmental Cooperation before the first stairwell came into sight.

"Hey!" A voice called behind us. "Verna? What's going on?"

I turned to find an enforcer had stepped out of one of the doorways we'd just passed.

"Oh poop," Verna said, then there was a *fwoomp!* sound as she fired the plastic bazooka past my head.

A yellow Nerf ball flew at the enforcer. He shouted the beginning of a spell in a startled and slightly squeaky voice but had no time to complete it before the ball splatted against him.

There was a *thwump* of displaced air as the enforcer disappeared.

No, not disappeared. He'd become a baby, sitting amidst the collapsed pile of an enforcer suit.

"Oh!" Verna said, frowning down at the bazooka. "I thought I soaked these in the MLSD."

"MLSD?" I asked before I thought to stop myself.

"Yes, magical LSD," she said distractedly. "I was going to call them Tripping Balls, but—oh yes, then I had the idea for the Baby Boomer, and . . . huh, I wonder where I put the MLSD? Oh dear."

"Come on!" Reggie whispered harshly from the front of the line. "Keep moving!"

"Right," Verna said. "Yes. Good idea." We started moving again.

Then I thought better of it and ran back. I snagged up the suit, and felt the silver-coated steel baton in one pants pocket as I rolled the clothes into a bundle. "Sorry," I said to the baby as I picked him up and moved him back into the room from where he'd emerged. I closed the door and hurried after the others again. When I caught up to Verna, I said, "He's going to be okay, isn't he?"

"Who?" Verna asked, her tone still distracted.

"The enforcer you turned into a baby?"

"What? Oh. Yes. He'll be fine. He should return to normal in twenty minutes or so. Or possibly into a man-sized baby for a bit, then himself."

Dawn snorted. "Finn does that all the time."

"Gee, thanks!" I said.

"Ssshhh!" Reggie said from the front.

We ascended into the old passageways, where the smooth concrete gave way to more roughened, natural tunnels that smelled like mildewed spices. Our footsteps were now soft susurrations on the sandy soil, and the dull roar of the waterfall grew steadily less dull and more roary.

We rounded a final curve, and mist rolled over us as we faced the backside of the falls, at least twenty feet above where they crashed into the river valley. A path cut into the side of the cliff, leading up to the top and Snoqualmie Forest—or rather, the oversized park that was what remained of Snoqualmie Forest. The path had been created with an uneven edge, cleverly following the natural contours of the cliff wall so that it remained invisible to viewers of the falls.

"We go single file," Reggie called back. "Be careful, the path will be slippery."

"Can I have that jacket?" Dawn asked, pointing at the bundle tucked under my arm.

"Uh, sure?" I unrolled the bundle and handed her the jacket. She wrapped it over her guitar.

"Here we go," Reggie said.

We stepped one by one out into the night. The path was a slippery climb at first, the gray and brown stone in layers like broken and discarded tiles, with the occasional weed growing from a crack. But the wall curved out above the path creating enough cover that no water fell directly on us, and once we had climbed past the edge of the waterfall, the path became less slippery and more a steep climb.

I realized that there were thirteen of us climbing up the cliff side, and I imagined myself Bilbo Baggins climbing the

Misty Mountains with the dwarves for a moment.

My legs burned by the time we reached the top. Reggie and Sammy were the first to step up off the path onto the cliff edge, and then they stood to either side of the path and helped up the string of men and women returned from exile.

"Stop in the name of the ARC!" a voice shouted from somewhere above.

"Keep climbing!" Reggie shouted down, then moved along the cliff edge back in the direction of the falls and the ARC facility.

The night lit up with the flash of lightning.

I fumbled out the steel baton taken from the babyfied enforcer, and grabbed Dawn's arm. "Put that on," I told her, nodding at the enforcer jacket. It would lend her protection, especially against anything fired at her back. I prayed to the fates that she'd have no reason to be charging *at* an enforcer.

The last few exiles on the path ahead of me began to back up, shying away from the danger above.

"Keep going!" I shouted up at them. "If they catch us on the path, they could just blast us off the edge!"

That seemed to register with the exiles, because they resumed climbing at double speed. I followed close behind, trying not to shout at them in my fear and impatience to know what was happening, to know if Reggie and Sammy and Fatima were okay.

My head crested the edge of the cliff, and I saw Reggie engaged in battle with two other enforcers. Thank the gods it was only two. I didn't know whether they'd been sent to look for us, or were just a routine patrol, but had there been many more we would have been screwed.

Reggie held his own for now, but was pressed to fight

them both. One of the enforcers had a nasty-looking cut on his forehead that leaked blood down the left side of his face, and the other swung his baton a bit awkwardly with his left arm, his right cradled to his chest. Reggie kept them both busy enough that they didn't have time or space to cast any more spells. But they were good enough to keep him from delivering a finishing blow, and it was only a matter of time before he made a mistake or ran out of steam.

Sammy ferried the exiles toward the nearby tree line rather than engaging the enforcers.

I looked back at Dawn, Father, and Verna, who all just stood at the top of the cliff with me, along with a couple of the exiles. "Run! Head toward town."

"I don't see *you* moving," Dawn replied.

La, perhaps take your own advice? Alynon said.

"Dawn, please help Father get to safety." I wrapped the enforcer pants around my left arm like a shield, and whipped the baton to full extension. "Reggie needs my help."

One of the enemy enforcers managed to maneuver behind Reggie long enough to kick him in the back. Reggie's jacket flashed a bright blue, as did the enforcer's boot, and Reggie stumbled forward, off balance.

"Reggie!"

The second enforcer swung his baton down at Reggie's head. Reggie managed to throw up his own baton to block, but the strike got through his block and gave Reggie a glancing blow on the shoulder that sent him stumbling further.

A fireball whooshed past my head in a bright streak toward the enforcer behind Reggie. Granted, it was a fireball the size of a walnut, but it was a fireball. I glanced behind me in surprise at the young woman who'd launched it, one of the exiles and apparently a wizard. I turned back in time to see the fireball strike the enforcer in the ear. It didn't so much explode as expand, forming a globe around his head.

The enforcer swatted at it, but didn't seem to be actually burning, the fire only blinded him and cut off his air.

As this happened, Dawn began leading Father toward the forest. But Verna strode in the direction of the enforcers, and raised the Baby Boomer to her shoulder.

I ran up to escort her, just in case.

Firehead fell to his knees, and a second later, to his face. The fireball dissipated as he fell, leaving negative-color imagery floating in my vision.

Reggie had turned his stumble into a tumble, and rolled up to his feet facing back toward the remaining enforcer. But he swayed a bit as he stood.

The enforcer advanced.

Verna fired her Nerf bazooka, but a breeze snatched the foam ball and sent it in a sideways curve over the edge of the cliff.

Reggie pulled out a silver pistol and fired twice at the other enforcer's legs. Two bright blue flashes as the bullets ricocheted off of the enforcer's pants, but the enforcer stumbled—right into a combination of blows from Reggie that crumpled him to the ground.

"Run," Reggie shouted at us, waving toward the forest with his baton.

"Come on," I said to Verna, and headed after Dawn and Father and the rest. Lady Fireball remained standing, staring in the direction of the fallen enforcers. I skidded to a stop and said, "Hey, you okay?"

"I just attacked someone," she said in a dazed tone. "I

mean, I knew it could be used like that, and I didn't want him to hurt Captain Reginald, but—" she trailed off.

"It's okay!" I said. "He'll live. You did the right thing. But we need to run, now."

She blinked at me, then nodded, and we ran together after the others.

The forest was a respectably thick stand of evergreens with enough space between them to see maybe fifteen feet in decent light. But to the right, a wide trail, or narrow dirt road, cut a swath through them. We angled for the path, and Reggie caught up with us.

"The ARC's going . . . to descend on us . . . any minute," he said in bursts between heavy breathing.

I understood. Even if that had just been a random patrol and not a pair sent specifically to find us, the gunshots and magic so close to an ARC facility would trigger a swift and overwhelming response.

"What are we going to do?" I panted.

"No damn idea," Reggie said.

I realized that the others had stopped running ahead of us, clustering on the path.

And then I saw why. Two imposing, shadowed figures blocked our escape.

"Bat's breath."

29

HUNGER STRIKE

My heart clenched, and I glanced to either side of the trail, looking for options among the trees and darkness. Then one of the shadow shapes fully registered.

"Pete?" I called out.

"Finn!" He called back. The shadow next to him resolved into the form of Vee.

Two more shadows detached themselves from the forest, and moved out onto the path, a willowy form gliding gracefully, and a huge form lumbering grace(half)fully. Silene, and Sal. In addition to her normal green dress made of leaves and moss and other growing things, Silene wore a belt with a dozen small pouches on it.

I made my way past the clustered exiles to where Dawn, Sammy, and Fatima stood facing the Elwha group.

My relief at seeing my brother evaporated as I remembered the circumstances of our last parting—banishment for destroying Dunngo's spirit. And they hadn't seemed too keen on seeing me again. Which meant if they were here, it meant nothing good.

Had Dunngo's sister demanded justice? Had Grandfather

incited them further against me?

"Greetings, Gramaraye," Silene said.

"If you've, uh, come after me for some reason . . . ?" I said.

"Not in the way you may think," she replied. "The Silver Archon must be stopped, and your brother felt you should be allowed to help." Her tone said she was not entirely convinced on the matter.

I looked at Pete, then glanced behind me, half expecting to see enforcers rushing at us. "I know the Archon's been a real pain, but I don't think right now—"

Pete said in a growl, "He has Mattie."

My head snapped around. "What?"

Sammy stomped up beside me. "Oh you've got to be kidding me!"

Vee placed a hand on Pete's lower back, and said, "Mort took her there. She's okay, for now."

"Why would—" I began, but Reggie interrupted.

"We need to save ourselves before we can save anyone else," he said. "The ARC's about to come down on our heads."

"We can help with that," Silene said.

Sal grunted. "Follow Iself into the woods."

He stalked off the side of the road toward the trees, great hairy arms swinging, head and shoulders taller than anyone else present, even Petey.

"Follow him!" I said to the exiles. "It's okay."

We all hurried off of the main road along a narrow break in the trees that barely qualified as a path, with me, Pete, Vee, and Silene bringing up the rear. Sal led us quick and confident through the shadowed forest, never seeming to run into snags or hit his head on the low branches despite his size and speed. Behind us, Silene walked with her hands splayed out at her sides as if feeling for heat rising off of the ground, her brown-and-green hair and the green living dress causing her to blend into the forest even without a glamour. The trees creaked as they leaned in a little closer together when she passed, ferns and shrubs grew to fill in the space behind us, and the underbrush rustled and snapped and shifted like a stirring beast.

I heard shouts in the uncomfortably close distance, men and women calling to one another.

Reggie dropped back to us. He didn't look great. Sweat caused his bald head to reflect what moonlight filtered through the treetops, and he looked less like Louis Gossett Jr. just then and more like Death's older brother Dearth. He said, "The dryad's magic will slow them down, but they'll still be able to track us. I'll buy you some time."

"Reggie—" I began.

He shook his head. "This is happening, Gramaraye. You need to go and get Mattie, and get Vee and the rest somewhere safe."

A series of little lights like fireflies appeared in the distance, spreading out through the forest and weaving between the trees.

"Shit. Go!" Reggie said.

"Be careful," I replied, and immediately winced. There are just some dumb things I wished I could stop saying. Like when a checkout person says "Thanks for shopping," and I say "You too!" Or, you know, when someone I care about is about to run straight at a pack of charged up enforcers in a suicidal attempt to save me, and I say "Be careful!"

But Reggie just said in a distracted tone, "Get going." Then he ran off perpendicular to the path, pulling something out of the inside of his jacket pocket.

I turned and found Silene waiting for me. I joined her and hurried after the others, relying on Silene to guide me along the hidden path ahead while it became tangled and covered behind.

Several of the little wispy lights appeared to be zigzagging in our direction, like photon torpedoes hunting for a cloaked Klingon Bird-of-Prey, glowing a bright blue-white.

"Someone let slip the bloodhounds of war," I said to Silene. "Anything you can do?"

"No," she said as we continued to sprint. Ferns and huckleberry branches whipped against my legs and hands. "The more I use my magic, the faster they will find us."

Two more wisps zoomed in from either side.

I think things are about to get nasty, Alynon said.

A sudden flash of purple light somewhere far to our rear cast long, menacing tree shadows that seemed to swoop in on us. A second later, a loud *BOOM* echoed through the forest.

The wisps froze, then all zoomed in the direction of the explosion.

Reggie. He must have set off some kind of magical grenade and created enough energy static in the area to draw in all the wisps, masking our escape.

I just hoped he had escaped as well. Yet again.

We regrouped in a clearing near the far side of the forest, on the outskirts of a residential neighborhood. The cool night air caused the sweat and remaining damp from the waterfall to feel chilly on my skin, and I shivered, despite feeling hot from sprinting so long. I wanted nothing more than to put on some worn flannel pajamas and crawl beneath a heating blanket with Dawn right then.

Dawn pushed through the crowd as if summoned by my thought of her, and I gave her a tight hug. As we parted, she said, "I saw the explosion, and—" she shook her head, her hair dancing in front of her face, the usual springy coils having fallen apart into frizzy knots. She frowned and dug her ever-present scrunchie out of her pocket, then pulled her damp hair up into a ball. "This whole running for our lives thing was fun for a bit, but I'm kind of done with it at this point."

Pete and Vee joined us and looked past me. "Reggie?" Vee asked.

Her brother, Zeke, had been Reggie's partner once, both personally and professionally. With Zeke dead, Reggie was the closest thing to family she had left besides Petey.

"Created a diversion so we could escape," I said.

Vee pushed her platinum blond hair behind her ears as she stared back into the dark forest. Pete put an arm around her and said, "He'll be okay."

She nodded.

Sal joined our circle, his wooly head blocking out the moon, and stood protectively behind Silene.

Silene looked up and back with a quick reassuring smile, then said, "We must make our plans, and quickly."

"First, tell us what the heck is going on," I said.

Sal grunted. "The Silver Archon ordered ourself's Elwha steading to attack Bainbridge Shadows steading."

"What? That's crazy!" I said. "That's not only going to escalate things with the Shadows, but the Department of Feyblood Management might just round you all up!"

Pete said in a gloomy voice, "Mort is with the Archon. He says the ARC won't punish us."

Mort, playing ambassador. "This is Grandfather's doing,"

I muttered, and said louder, "The Arcanites don't just want to wipe out the Fey, they want the brightbloods to decimate each other at the same time."

Sal rested his giant hands over Silene's shoulders, and she touched them as she said, "It matters little who is behind the Archon's orders. When no attack is made on the Shadows steading by midnight, the Archon will know we have defied them, defied him. He will be forced to move against us."

I shook my head. "I just don't understand it. Why would the Silver Archon work with the Arcanites? He knows they and their allies were trying to trick him and the Shadows into fighting, right?"

"Yes," Silene said. "But your brother must have played to his vanity and greed, and those trump reason where he is concerned."

My brother certainly understood vanity and greed. I sighed.

Sammy crossed her arms. "Um, isn't the Archon a sphinx? I thought they were all about the wisdom?"

"Knowledge is not wisdom," Silene said. "He gained his position through knowledge. Knowing what to say, knowing that which would most impress or influence, knowing how to let others do the work and what to say to take credit without appearing to lie. Yet for all that, he does not understand the needs of those he governs, does not understand the true purpose of his position."

"Uhn," Sal grunted in agreement. "Hisself does much to play leader, yet does not lead anywhere."

Dawn snorted. "So, your basic middle manager then."

"I feel your pain," Sammy said. "I've had to work for more unqualified idiots than a congressional intern. But maybe we should be focused on stopping whatever

Grandfather and his Tea Party of Doom have planned first? Stopping the Archon won't do much good if all the Fey are dead, I'm thinking."

"Do you know where they are or what they plan, then?" Silene asked.

An expression of frustration passed across Sammy's face. "No. Not exactly. But I found them once. If I can get online, I can find them again."

"If you *can* find them, Sammy, that would be awesome," I said. "I'm just worried they might have learned their lesson and won't leave you any clues this time."

"You did nearly get your brain fried last time," Dawn said. "And they weren't expecting you then."

"You what?" Fatima said.

Sammy gave a dismissive wave. "It wasn't that big a deal. And this time *I* know what to expect as well."

Pete, who'd been standing there looking miserable the whole time, said, "What about Mattie?"

I felt a near-instinctive urge to rush to Mattie's aid, but said, "Mort made it clear he didn't want us around. And if she's with him, then I'm sure he won't let anything happen to her. Hell, right now, he seems to be a lot safer than we are."

Sammy gave a bitter laugh. "Yeah. He always was good at covering his own ass."

Pete only looked sadder. "Mort is family. We should be helping him, too. They both need our help, even if Mort doesn't know it."

"Forget Mort, Petey," Sammy said. "I hope that sphinx eats him."

Pete got red faced. "Don't say that! He's our brother!"

"He's a jerk," Sammy replied. "I know you care about

him, Petey, though for the life of me I've never understood why. But the only person Mort cares about is himself."

"Mother said—"

"Don't!" Sammy snapped. "Don't bring Mother into this. She's been gone a long time, ghost or not. And Mort's done nothing but tease you, use you. Why would you risk your life to help him get out of a mess he made for himself?"

Fatima put a hand on Sammy's back and said, "You've helped a lot of people who got into trouble, people whose families had abandoned them."

Sammy gave Fatima a look of mixed hurt and irritation. "They had reasons for what they did. Their families were terrors, or they had abusive partners, or just fucking bad luck. And they got mixed up with bad feybloods seeking love. But I grew up with Mort and I'm telling you he has no excuse for being such a dickhead, except that he loves nobody but himself."

I flashed on memories of Mort being constantly put down or treated like a lesser child when it became clear he didn't have the Talker ability. To have been so dismissed by Grandfather in favor of me, and then to end up having to hold the family business together when I got sent into exile—

"He had some reasons," I said grudgingly.

"Jesus, you too?" Sammy said. "What is this, make Sammy feel like a jerk day?"

"No," I said. "He didn't have to do the things he did, obviously. He made choices. I'm just saying, he didn't exactly have a life free of suck. What I don't get is why he's helping Grandfather at all, when it was Grandfather who *made* it suck."

He cannot help but wish for the approval that was so long withheld from him, Alynon said.

Silene cleared her throat. "Whatever your brother's reasons, the results are that we are ordered to attack the Shadows. If we are to stop the Arcanite plot, and save my clan, then it seems our causes are joined, and the solution to both problems is the same."

I sighed. "We have to confront Mort and the Archon, and get Mort to tell us what he knows."

"Great," Sammy said. "Why the hell did he have to take Mattie there?"

Pete replied in a sad voice, "I offered to watch her, but he said . . . he said—" he choked to a stop.

Vee held him close, and said, "Mort said he didn't trust Pete not to bite her."

My hands balled into fists. That assrat!

"And you're still defending him?" Sammy demanded.

"He *is* her father," Pete said in a small voice. "And I *am* dangerous now."

"Oh, Petey—" I said.

Sammy snorted. "Fuck that. You've raised Mattie as much as he has, and you've done more to control your wolf than he did his lust for his pet succubus. Don't ever let Mort make you doubt yourself again, Pete, or I'll . . . I'll make you eat an entire bucket of lentils."

Pete's eyes widened in horror. I might dislike lentils, but Pete viewed them practically like tiny monsters determined to destroy his mouth.

Father walked forward and put a hand on Pete's chest. In a quavering voice, he said, "Mort is not *your* father. *Your* father is proud of you."

Pete's eyes filled with tears to match my own. Then Father blinked, and studied the hand he had placed on Pete's chest, holding it cupped with his fingers spread and curled upwards as though a claw grasping an invisible ball. Then he waggled them and said, "Funny little finger stones, dancing in the danger zone." He bounced his hand around and bobbed his head to a beat only he could hear.

I sighed as Verna gently took his shoulders and pulled him back.

Then I rubbed at my eyes, and said to Silene and Sal, "Looks like we're off to see the Archon. So what's the plan?"

The Silver Court Archon lived in a small complex on Whidbey Island, set back into a small patch of woods that butted up against one of the few remaining drive-in movie theaters in Washington. The theater had been around since the 1950s, built after the last Fey-Arcana War as part of the cover for the Archon's property, just one of the many ways in which the ARC rewarded the Silver for their alliance in that war. Much of the forest surrounding the Archon's property had since been cut back, and turned into fields and housing tracts. But the theater remained, and apparently had even expanded to include a small arcade and go-kart track. And there still remained enough forest for the Archon and his resident brightbloods to stretch their legs without too much fear of being seen.

We had to drive up and over Deception Pass to reach the island, as the ferries did not run so late. Pete drove the family hearse, with Vee and Dawn in the passenger seat. Me, Sammy, and Fatima sat in the backseat, while Father and Verna insisted on lying down in the far back. Silene, Sal, and the rest of the brightbloods were taking the fairy paths to

Whidbey, much faster than this agonizingly long two-hour drive. Unfortunately, while much faster than driving, the fairy paths were bad for human health in much the same way shotgunning a bottle of vodka found in the ruins of Chernobyl while walking a tightrope over an industrial taffy stretcher was dangerous. Well, dangerous for anyone not possessed of a Fey spirit, that was.

The fairy roads, or "Fey Ways," were remnants of a time when the Other Realm and our world were all snuggly. Whether some part of the Other Realm had merged with our world, or the fabric of our space-time had been warped in an attempt to reconcile with the chaos of the Other Realm, nobody knew. Only the results were known. No magic had been found that could protect human travelers from the paths' warping effects; but the brightbloods, being of both worlds like the Ways themselves, were able to travel them safely. Usually.

With Alynon sharing my body, I'd managed to travel a fairy path once. But it had nearly mutated me, and in the end had strengthened the bond between Alynon's spirit and my body, making it even less likely I'd ever be rid of him. Or so I had thought.

Pete and Vee could have traveled the paths as well, but insisted on driving us to make sure we arrived safely. I suspected Pete really just wanted to be around family for comfort. I couldn't blame him.

So we all raced south from the pass now down the island, hoping to arrive at the Archon's compound before Mort or the Archon did anything further to bring about a brightblood war.

I glanced for the hundredth time at my Casio. 2:19 A.M. If the Arcanites were planning to do anything today, it would likely be at dawn. Magic, particularly spells across the two worlds, were most powerful at the transition times between day and night, and dawn favored magic flowing from our world to the Other Realm.

That gave us, what, maybe four hours to figure out what the Arcanites were up to, and a way to stop them?

"So," I said as I watched the streetlights zip past, trying to distract myself. "Are we going to circle around and sneak up through the woods?"

"No," Pete said. "Silene says Vee and me—or, uh, Vee and I—we can just walk right up and demand an audience."

"He's not going to be happy to see you," I said.

Pete shrugged, looking miserable. "I'm not happy to be seen."

We arrived at the drive-in theater, and pulled into the lot. It was closed down for the weekdays, the movie lot empty, the colorful go-karts silent, the buildings locked and dark. Convenient, but also dangerous. If there'd been a lot of mundies in the area then at least the Archon wouldn't make too big a noise about us showing up, not until we were through his front doors at least.

We got out of the car and stretched, my lower back spasming from the combination of exertion followed by sitting in the car for two hours.

Sal and Silene stepped out from behind the nearby building.

"Well met," Silene said.

I looked past her. "You didn't bring your army?"

"If the Shadows attacks our steading, we need our brightbloods there to defend. We few should be enough to confront the Archon."

She led us toward the low snack bar, a blue cinder-block

building painted with images of dancing popcorn and sodas. While Silene picked the lock with a wiggling root of some kind she pulled from one of her pouches, I took the opportunity to lift up a nearby gnome statue and scratch Priapus's sigil in the dirt beneath. I wasn't sure what was going to happen here with the Archon, but we were running out of time and options before the possible end of the Fey world, and that seemed as good a time as any to flash the Hat Sigil.

We entered the snack bar. All the lights were off, but moonlight through the windows cast the counter with its soda and popcorn machines in a pale glow. The floor, counter, and walls were all a stark black-and-white checkerboard pattern.

"This way," Silene said, waving us forward, and headed toward the far end of the counter.

We were halfway there when my feet stuck to the floor. And not in the normal spilled soda and gum kind of way, but in a solid, unable to move, something-not-good-is-about-to-happen kind of way.

"Hello," a voice said, coming out of overhead speakers. "If you wish to pass the gate, you must first answer a riddle."

Silene looked around, and called back, "We are of the Silver, come under authority of our patrons. You must see us."

"True," the voice replied. "But there are those with you not of the Silver, one in particular I have been warned against. I cannot know his intent, or if you are under his power, without first testing him."

"Fine," I said toward the ceiling. "The answer is forty-two. Can you come up with the correct question?"

"That is a nice try," the voice said. "But as I said, I have been told of you. And I shall give to you the same riddle I give to all: that question whose answer most eludes you."

The air filled suddenly with the smell of popcorn, so overwhelming and delicious that drool practically shot out of my mouth in a Pavlovian river. But there was something more to the smell, something that made my arcana senses tingle.

Sammy began to sneeze violently.

Everything around me began to warp, and spin. The checkerboard stretched, and seemed to expand to the horizon, and I stood staring off into that psychedelic distance.

"Finn!" a voice shouted behind me. I found that I could move now, and I turned to see a small group fanned out behind me, a slightly different group than before.

Pete, covered in blood, his innocent face now a mask of pain and horror. Mother, a wasted shadow of herself, her once beautiful cascade of straight black hair now brittle clumps drifting off in the breeze. Alynon, looking like Ziggy Stardust's prettier brother, bound in silver chains. Zeke, Vee's brother, looking like Hulk Hogan with a Mr. T mohawk and Miami Vice outfit, except his skin peeled away burnt and blistered. Sal, his huge sasquatch body shaking as he wept, holding a knotted cord of hair in his hand whose color matched that of his dead sister. Felicity, our family's au pair in my youth, her mouth working in a silent scream, her tongue removed, her eyes haunted. And Dunngo. Dunngo, who could not be here. Dunngo, whose spirit I had utterly destroyed beyond all hope of an afterlife.

"No." Panic rose in me like the swelling soundtrack of a tragedy. "No!"

I fled.

30

JERRY WAS A RACE CAR DRIVER

The snack bar's checkerboard landscape sped by as I ran, but when I looked back, the ghosts of all those I had hurt or who had been killed around me were standing there, as if floating on a fixed platform behind me.

"What do you want?" I shouted at them.

"Why?" Pete asked.

"*WHY*?" they all echoed.

"Why what?" I shouted back.

Pete clawed at his chest, and ripped it open, pulling out his heart. "Why did you destroy me? Why did you let me be turned into a monster?"

Mother wept tears of blood. "Why didn't you come to see me when I was dying, *mijo*? Why did you not look after your sister and brothers like I asked?"

Alynon strained against his bonds, and said, "Why have you not freed me? Why would you torture me with watching your love knowing I am denied my own?"

Zeke spat, and said, "Why'd you let me die, fool? Why didn't you protect Vee better like you promised?"

Sal held the knotted hair close to his chest. "Why youself kill sistermine?"

Felicity, her Austrian features the pale gray-white of death, her eyes shadowed with pain, said, "Why were you so oblivious to your grandfather's plots, to your father's actions, lost in your silly world of games and daydreams? Why did you not stop me? Why did you not save me?"

Dunngo regarded me with his gleaming obsidian eyes, and said in a voice filled with gravel, "Why you destroy me? You kill Dunngo so not have to give own life?" His voice grew louder, sharper, with each question as he continued. "Why want so bad do it again? Why not admit you have grandfather's darkness inside. *Why you not kill self before darkness make you big bad like grandfather!*"

"*WHY?*" they all asked again.

"No!" I said. "I am nothing like my grandfather! I . . . I didn't mean to do any of that! I was just trying—I didn't have—" I turned and ran again.

I didn't look behind me. If I didn't look, they wouldn't be there.

"WHY?" they asked again, causing my shoulders to hunch as if I might be struck in the back.

I needed to get away. I needed to take control.

It was hard to concentrate on any thought, to build up a plan, each idea slipping away before I could stack the next on top. But this was not so different from the wildlands of the Other Realm, or the chaos of the fairy paths. I just had to assert my will, banish this nightmare, banish these ghosts—

I was Finn Gramaraye. I was in a snack bar. I needed to get out of here. I needed to get away.

I tried to hold the memory of the drive-in theater in my

mind, the large screen, the rows of raised earth for the cars to park along, the go-kart track—

Go-karts! If I could get to one, I could get away! I could drive into small places and hide from the ghosts. Go-karts were fun, a game, and gods I wanted to go back to life being fun, to playing games without feeling like I was stealing time away from Dawn, from my responsibilities in the necrotorium and the work of building a real life for myself, from helping free Alynon, from helping Pete and Vee and Mattie and Father and—

"WHY?"

I ran, and the go-kart track appeared ahead of me, with the miniature racing cars waiting.

It was working! I could escape!

I jumped into the first one, a Formula One–style red and blue car, and zoomed away, laughing.

A red turtle shell went zinging past me, and bounced off of the track wall ahead.

Startled, I looked behind me. All of the ghosts were now in cars, chasing me.

Dunngo hunched over in the first car, making him look like a stone turtle, gravel from the track flying up to form a shell on his back. Even as I watched, the shell flew off of him and for my head. I ducked, and swerved, then looked behind me again.

Pete drove the next car, dressed now in green overalls and matching cap, both covered in blood.

Mother wore a rotting pink princess dress, the wind blowing away her hair to expose bald spots as she sped along.

Alynon's skin had gone a scaly dinosaur green, and his spiky hair had gone red to match his car.

Zeke, already an intimidating figure, had swollen to even greater size, wearing what looked like a giant Viking shield on his back and studded leather armbands, his eyes filled with berserker fury as he sat squeezed into his car.

Sal hunched over in the next car, looking more apish than ever as the fringes of his red-brown fur flapped in the wind.

Felicity, a witch who'd had some special skill with plants, now wore what looked like a poisonous mushroom cap as a hat, the poison running down and leaving angry red welts across her face.

This was insane. I knew it was insane, and ridiculous, and couldn't possibly be real.

Yet the crawling sense of terror that filled me was certainly real. And it propelled me forward, screaming for me to get away from this mob.

A glowing cube appeared ahead of me like a portal. A way to escape? Or a trap?

I heard Zeke shout something, and from the words I realized he prepared to summon wizard lightning down on me.

I swerved into the glowing box.

Time slowed to a crawl, and I heard a sound like one of those electronic prize wheels spinning past choices, slowing down with each beep.

Images appeared in the sky, one replacing the other, quickly at first then slowing down in time with the electronic beeps:

Sal holding his sister in his arms, howling in heartbreak.

Felicity laying dead on the floor of Alynon's trailer, staring at me, dead, her face frozen in a scream of horror.

Pete hurling a cologne bottle at Mort's television as I revealed that we had lied to him about being a waerwolf most of his life.

The image of mother laying in her bed, wasted and frail—this last image rushed up to swallow me.

I held Mother's hand. It felt too light, too fragile, too thin. Like the rest of her, it had withered away in the final days of the cancer. She lay with her eyes closed now, her breath rattling in her throat.

I hadn't come to see her for a week, unable to face what had become of her, as if my memories of her smiling and healthy would be forever lost, and with them the last remaining hope that she might somehow really, miraculously, be healthy and smiling again someday.

Bottles of medicines from both mundy and arcana healers covered the bedside table. But there were some things even magic couldn't fix. Healing potions sped up the body's natural healing processes, but couldn't heal something that the body itself could not. And if anything, magic had led to Mother's death, her body weakened by a Talking session gone wrong, allowing the cancer to take hold.

I wiped the tears and snot from my face with my free hand, and focused. I refused to believe there was nothing I could do. In the histories, necromancers had restored the dead to true life, bound living spirits to skulls and artifacts, had even made decapitated heads live on for days. Maybe Grandfather and the other necromancers were afraid to break rules or risk their own health, but I wasn't, not when Mother was about to die.

I summoned up my magic, and fed a trickle of my own life energy to my mother's body.

I felt a weak resistance from Mother, a barrier of will that felt more like tissue than steel. She squeezed my hand with what little strength she had. "Don't," she whispered.

I opened my eyes to find hers looking at me, golden brown and glazed over with pain and exhaustion, but I knew she was fully aware of who I was and what I was doing.

"But I can help—"

"You can't do anything for me," Mother said. "And that's okay, *mijo*."

Tears started to stream from my eyes. "I can't—" I choked up.

Mother squeezed my hand again. "Oh sweetie. *Mira*, I need you to look after your brothers and sister when I'm gone."

"You're not going anywhere," I said emphatically.

"Of course I am," Mother said, patting my wrist. "We are necromancers. We can't be afraid of death. And when I am gone, you will need to help your siblings. Especially Mort."

"Mort?" I said. "He's older than me, and—" I stopped. I didn't want to say bossy, or anything else bad, not now. "And Petey and Sammy are younger."

Mother gave a weak smile. "Samantha has my fire within her. And you all look after her as the youngest anyway." A tear leaked from the corner of her eye. "Petey, he is so sweet, he draws love to him. But your brother Mort, I worry for him, *mijo*. He is so angry, so worried about all the wrong things. Don't let him push you away. He—" Mother winced, her breathing grew quick for a second and her body tensed. When she relaxed again, her breath hissed out in a long, slow exhale before she continued to breathe in that weak rattle once more.

I cleared my throat, which had grown tight. "Do you need water, or—"

"I'm okay," she said, her voice weaker now.

Understanding fell on me like a collapsing building then. This was it. This really was it, the last time I would get to spend with her. I had lost precious days with her, and I couldn't get them back no matter what I did, no matter how powerful a necromancer I became. I wanted to beat myself bloody, scream at myself for being so stupid, such a coward.

Mother coughed, then said, "Just promise me, sweetie, that you'll remember what I've taught you." Her hand rose trembling to press against my chest. "You have such a gentle heart. Follow it, trust it, not just with your family and friends, but with everyone, every being, and you'll be okay. You'll be happy. And you'll do great things. I know it."

"I will," I managed to choke out.

"And you'll take care of your brothers and sister?"

"Yes," I declared emphatically, as though to convince the entire universe. "I'll take care of them, I promise." I would not let my fear or stupidity make me lose time with anyone else, ever again.

"Good. You each hold a little piece of me within you. As long as you have each other, you'll always have me around, too."

I began to sob. "Yes, Mother."

"I love you, Finn. Now please, go and get your father."

The memory began to flash brightly at the end, then suddenly evaporated like a movie projected onto a wall of smoke as I broke through it.

My head whipped back as the go-kart propelled at double speed around the track. Within seconds I had nearly lapped the others, coming up on the rear of the horde.

At least now they could not hit me with their shells or lightning. Not without hitting each other, or—

Felicity's car began to drop bananas, brown-spotted and swarming with flies, and as they hit the ground the gravel hissed and steamed as though struck with acid.

I swerved to avoid the acid bananas, and despite my best effort was forced into another glowing cube.

Again, the roulette of images:

Zeke charging to his death as Heather's son Orion blasted him with lightning.

Alynon's expression as I escaped Chauvelin's grasp in the Other Realm, after Alynon had betrayed his own Demesne just for the chance of keeping me there.

The image of the light fading from Dunngo's obsidian eyes as the last of his body and his life washed away into the river.

The image of mother holding open the changing room door at the Salvation Army thrift store. Again, this last image rushed toward me, swept over me, transported me . . .

I stepped into the changing room and Mother closed the door behind me with a click. I wore my school gym outfit, because it was loose enough to fit. I had grown several inches taller while sleeping away the week: my first experience of being rapidly aged from using my "gift" of Talking to the dead.

And my first experience with someone I knew dying.

I had been raised around death in the family's necrotorium, helped prepare bodies, learned the theory if not the practice of summoning and capturing spirits, dissipating spiritual energy safely, capturing the lingering magical energy from the dead, and the dangers of trying to animate the dead. But

I had never seen someone actually die, not until Johnny swerved his bike into the path of that speeding truck.

I winced, suddenly back in that moment, and the memory of holding his head in my lap, Talking to his spirit until the police and ambulance arrived—

"You okay in there, *Flaco*?" Mother asked in a gently teasing tone.

"Yeah," I lied, and began hanging up the items I'd brought in with me, the metal hangers clicking softly on the wall hook. Two pairs of loose pants, several shirts including T-shirts with *Thundarr the Barbarian* and *Star Trek: The Motion Picture* on them, a mustard tweed sports coat, and a vintage military-looking wool jacket.

Mother sighed. "Ah, *mijo*, it isn't easy, I know. Death of your friend, and the loss of your own life, and you had to deal with both at the same time."

"I'm fine," I lied again. "I just don't know why these changing rooms always have to smell like BO."

I pulled off my gym clothes and slid the pair of brown cargo pants off the hanger. As I did, I could see in the mirror all of the changes that had happened while I slept.

"Mother, I don't think I want to be a Talker," I said as I slid on the pants.

"Why not?"

"I don't want to be an old man at twenty."

"You won't be," Mother said. "You won't be asked to use your gift unless absolutely needed, and never as much as you did this time."

"Well, all the kids are going to look at me weird if I have a full beard by the time I'm a sophomore."

Mother laughed. "*Mira*, interesting fact," she said.

"Sleeping Beauty was an alchemist who actually put *herself* into a magical sleep. Do you know why?"

Despite myself, I said, "No, why?" I pulled the sports coat down.

"Well, she was betrothed to a neighboring prince, and could find no way out of it. Even though he was just a year younger than her, she was only fourteen. And Beauty knew enough to know that many young men, well, let us say their love is but a fleeting thing when young, in more ways than one. So, if she was to be forced into marriage with this boy, she decided she would rather wait until his apples were ripe, as it were."

"Mother!"

"I'm just saying, don't complain too much about aging a few months, not at your age."

I blushed, and said, "It's still lost time."

"I'm surprised you would even notice. You spend too much time in your room with that computer, it isn't healthy. And the Krowleys' daughter is back from that fancy private school for the summer. I seem to remember you following her around like a love-struck unicorn last summer—"

"MOM!"

I thanked all the gods that we were alone in the store except for the employees, and that they must be well out of earshot if Mother was talking about magic.

Mother laughed, and said, "All right, all right. Come out, let me see how it looks."

I sighed, and opened the door.

"Oh, look at you," she said, and held my cheeks for a second, then tugged at my lapels. "You look so like your grandfather at your age. Though your looks are all you got from him, thankfully."

I blinked, my head shifting back to look at her more fully. "What do you mean?"

"Ah, pea soup, nothing. I shouldn't have said that. I just have too much on my mind these days."

"Would me being like Grandfather be bad?" I pushed. For some reason, I had begun to become uncomfortable sometimes in his lessons, but couldn't put my finger on why.

"Of course not," Mother said. "But being like your father is better, for you." She smiled fondly, and touched my cheek again. "Your head is in the clouds too much, I think, just like your father, but if you ever learn to pay attention to the people around you, to get your head and your heart lined up, you will do amazing things."

I didn't tell her my plan was to create a computer game empire. Actually, it had been to build that empire with Johnny. But now he was dead. Forever, he was gone. He wouldn't play a single other game, wouldn't ever see our game ideas made real.

My eyes started to burn for the tenth time that day. Damn it!

Mother saw my expression, and pulled me into a hug.

Gods, now I *really* hoped none of my friends walked into the store.

"It's okay, *mijo*. It is not your fault," she said softly.

"If only I'd paid attention," I said suddenly, the words coming out as if spoken by someone else. "I should have watched out for him when he went to cross the street. If I'd just looked back over my shoulder to check on him, or stopped and waited for him—"

"No, no, no," Mother said, and released me. "I meant what I said, you will grow up to do amazing things, but not if you keep taking too much on yourself, and also not if you are too afraid of mistakes. There are too many people already who do nothing with their lives because they are too afraid of making the wrong choice."

"But Johnny died!" I said.

"Did the thought that he could die come to you before you crossed that street?"

"No."

"Because we are not gods, Finnito. Not even seers know everything that will happen, what every choice will bring. We must just trust in this," she touched my chest, over my heart. "And if something bad happens, be kind to yourself, but be honest, too. Learn, and try to make better choices next time. That is all we can do."

I smiled weakly. "You sound like a *Brady Bunch* episode."

She raised her eyebrows. "You watch too much television."

"Probably," I said, then grew serious again. "My heart still tells me I should have stopped to make sure Johnny was safe."

"No, your guilt tells you that," Mother said. "Guilt is like a Jekyll and Hyde creature, of two natures. Sometimes it shines a light upon those things we need to admit to ourselves, so that we can do better. But sometimes it speaks from our fears and doubts, because hiding in their shadows is easier than risking another choice."

"I feel like we should have had, like, the *Chariots of Fire* theme playing just then," I said. "That was totally inspirational. Really."

Mother slapped my arm. "Your sense of humor is what will really get you in trouble some day, young man."

"No, really," I said. "You should go on a tour with Mr. T talking to school kids about making good choices and drinking their milk."

"You're going to keep making fun of your mother?" she asked. "And I was going to take you for pizza when we were done here."

"What? Really?" I didn't wait for her response, jumping back inside the changing room and closing the door as I said, "You are the best mother ever! I mean it."

"I know you do, *mijo*."

The memory flashed, and again dissipated.

No burst of speed followed this time. Instead, the memory had released something inside of me, something that had been growing and pushing against the constraints of my guilt and doubts for the past several days as I confronted my grandfather at the diner; as I confronted Mort in the Other Realm; as I fought beside Dawn, and Sammy, and Pete, fought for my family, fought for the brightbloods, fought for a life not dictated by the poisonous hatred and greed of people like my grandfather, or by the daunting barrier of years lost and experience ungained.

I'd been running away from these ghosts long enough. I was a necromancer, for cheese's sake. I was Finn the Gramarayean, Brother of Pete and Sammy, Uncle of Mattie, Son of Arlyn, Lover of Dawn, Fighter of Evil Assholes, and Protector of the Unjerky. And as much as I regretted the lives lost since my return, as much as I would go back and save them all if I could, every single one had made their own choices, had given or forfeited their lives so that the people I loved would live.

I had made mistakes, but I was not going to make even more because of guilt over those past mistakes.

Fuck these ghosts. I'd been running from them long enough.

"Bangarang!" I shouted. It was time to shove my toe pick up the arse of these phantoms.

At that thought, lightning began to dance around me.

I slammed my foot down on the accelerator, and the motor revved in all its 50cc glory, jerking the car forward again.

"Felicity!" I called as I came up on her first. She turned her mushroom-capped head to look at me as I shouted, "It was your choice to help my grandfather, and to keep silent all the years I was in exile."

She spat words like venom back at me, "If not for you, I'd still be alive! I want to live!"

"I didn't kill you," I replied. "But I forgive you."

Lightning leaped from me to strike her. She flashed bright like a Star Trek phaser victim, appearing briefly as she had in my youth, happy and beautiful, before fading away.

Sal glanced back at me, then hunched forward even further, speeding up. Banana cream pies began to drop from the back of his kart, exploding after a second to send sizzling whipped cream flying. I swerved madly around them.

"Youself killed sister-mine!" Sal shouted back at me. "Always youself are death-giving."

"It was the Krol witches who killed her," I called out, "because she killed one of them."

"But youself *sent* the badbright witches."

"I sent them against my grandfather. It was your sister's choice to defend him. I won't accept blame for her death either!"

Another lightning strike, and Sal faded from view.

Zeke with his shell-like shield and massive bulk slowed down to drive beside me, and tried to knock me off of the track.

"I pity the fool who trusts you!" he said.

"Your death wasn't my fault!" I shouted. "And neither is Vee's danger!" I swerved hard into him, my lightning leaping out to envelope him. He crashed into the guardrail, and faded away.

Then I reached Alynon, and my confidence wavered. His spiky red hair flapped in the wind as he pulled parallel to me, matched me move for move, and spat insults at me, his tongue his only real weapon, as always. "You are a joke," he said. "A criminal. A fraud. You complain about exile, yet it saved you. Saved you from abandoning your family to make pointless games for obsolete machines. Saved you from becoming your grandfather even sooner!"

"Screw you!" I shouted back. "Even if that is true, it has nothing to do with you."

"Does it not?" he asked, easily avoiding my attempt to sideswipe him, his kart dropping around behind me then racing up on my other side, his engine buzzing loudly. He continued shouting, "Do you not associate me in some way with your being exiled, do you not seek to punish me on behalf of those who held you, fed upon you? Since your return, cruelly have you held me trapped here, away from my own family, away from my own love."

"That wasn't my choice!" I said. "It just happened."

"So you tell yourself. Yet you refuse to return in spirit to my Realm where we may fairly inhabit separate bodies. You instead use the excuse of your family's need and your heart's desires to stay here. But tell me, who places your family in danger? Who placed Dawn in danger? You create the need to protect them, then hold me captive for it. And you have treated your promise to separate us somehow as a thing only to be brought out and toyed with when convenient!"

"I—" I felt myself shrinking along with the car, growing slower, more vulnerable. The lightning flickering around me dimmed, the arcs growing smaller and weaker. The problem was, Alynon—ghost Alynon—was right. Or at least, he wasn't entirely wrong. And I knew it. His words hurt too much not to hold some truth.

"I didn't create the problems that have kept you here. But you're right. I haven't done everything I could to send you home. I know I have promised before, but I swear now, not to you, but to myself, that I will do what it takes to send you home just as soon as I stop my grandfather's plot. You will be home by tomorrow."

And I meant it. I felt the shift inside of me, a decision I had been avoiding for some time in the hopes that a better option would present itself, made at last. I'd figured out a way to separate us. It was just not going to be pleasant, for me at least. But I would do it. It was time. It was fair.

The lightning flickered brighter once more.

"Forgive me," I said.

Lightning leaped from me at Alynon, and he faded away. I grew back to my normal size, the kart lurching forward as it grew in bounds, spitting gravel out from beneath its tires.

Mother looked back at me, her head entirely bald now, her rotting pink princess dress too loose on her shrunken limbs. I pulled up behind her, and said quietly, "I'm sorry I didn't come to see you more. But I know you forgive me. I know you understand. If you were here, you'd tell me some crazy story about Cinderella and her real mother and forgiveness or something. But I just have to forgive myself, and make you proud of the choices I make now."

Mother lit bright for a second, wreathed in my lightning, her long beautiful hair flowing once more behind her like a cape, her loving smile radiant, then she, too, faded away.

Pete rode in the next car, looking ridiculous in the green overalls and too-small cap despite the blood covering them. He looked back at me, and his eyes went from dark brown to wolf blue. "You—"

"No," I said, simply. Lightning struck, and Pete spun away, fading.

And then it was just me and Dunngo racing around the track.

Dunngo's stone turtle head rotated like an owl's so that he stared at me over the shell of stone and gravel on his back.

"You destroyed me," he said.

"Yes. You told me to."

"You said no choice."

"*I* had no choice," I replied. "Petey would have died. Sal and Silene would have died."

"You no do it for them. You do it for you."

"I didn't know the effect using dark necromancy would have on me. If I had—"

"Not effect. You don't want pain of losing brother or friends. Not for them. They go to spirit place when die. You the one who suffer if they die. But instead you destroy me forever. I never go to spirit place now."

As with Alynon, there was truth in what Dunngo said.

"It was unforgivable," I said. "I should have tried something, anything, else. Even if it meant we all died."

And having said it, I accepted it. Not on the theoretical level, not on the philosophical level, where I had been told since childhood that dark necromancy is bad. I knew it as a certainty, I had certain proof of it, a personal understanding of it. Dark necromancy had destroyed everything that was Dunngo forever. I had created a void in the universe, and there was no way to fix it, no hope that things would be balanced in some future life or land beyond the veil of death.

I'd fucked up. Big time.

"I'm sorry," I said, and felt it, like a willingness to leap into a volcano to prove my sincerity, like a readiness to let Edward Scissorhands give me a full body massage if only Dunngo would accept that I truly meant it.

"Sorry no good enough. You live for two now," Dunngo said. "You, and me. You understand."

The dust of the track was replaced with a warm breeze that carried the smell of popcorn, and my kart spun out of control, the world whirling by, making me dizzy—

Dawn caught me before I hit the checkerboard floor of the snack bar.

"Finn!" she said. "Are you okay?"

I blinked up at her.

And then I began to cry.

I was only vaguely aware of the Silver Archon's voice tinged with surprise and perhaps fear coming softly out of the speakers. "You . . . may enter."

31

HEY JEALOUSY

A door clicked open behind the snack bar, and we filed through it. Stairs descended into a concrete tunnel that led us to a steel door. The door swung open as we approached it. One of the Archon's loyal henchfauns greeted us, and led us through the Silver Archon's underground compound beyond as I regained my composure and wiped at my face.

The compound was plush, though behind and beneath the modern fixtures could be seen the original 1958 design. The brick wall, the pink and sea-foam green tiles, the mural on one wall of forest, it all had a faded, Polaroid feel to it. It had the cool damp feel of a basement that never gets warm, and smelled like clothes that had been in the closet far too long.

We soon reached an ornate wooden door, and the faun opened it but did not pass through, waving us on instead.

Beyond was a library that was, for all intents and purposes, also a throne room. Rich cherry wood bookshelves lined the walls, stuffed with books and scrolls. Above them a balcony ran around the entire room. Six pillars held up the domed ceiling with its mural depicting a great celebration of brightbloods, all illumined by the giant chandelier that hung from the dome's center. And the heat in this room had been cranked up to the point where it felt nearly like a sauna.

The Archon sat upon a dais at the far end of the room on a wide cushion of red velvet. He appeared much as I'd expected—the body of a winged lion, the head of a man with sharp, hawkish features, his hair and beard shimmering in black ringlets beneath the glow of a smaller globe chandelier. And he wore headphones.

Mort stood on the middle of the dais's three steps, to the left of the Archon, dressed sharply in one of his black bespoke suits that still hung a bit loose on him after the weight he'd lost. And he looked ready to throw a tantrum. I got the sense he wasn't completely surprised to see us, but that he had not truly believed that he would, or at least had seriously hoped he would not. And I couldn't blame him. Sammy alone was likely to beat him senseless at this point.

The Archon stood, and his lion body morphed into a human's with white robes, though the wings still rose from his shoulders, and a lion's tail swished behind him.

"I am surprised to see you," the Archon said to Silene, removing the headphones and tossing them back down to the cushion. "Should you not be with your clan attacking the Shadows' compound?"

Silene said, "My clan is at Elwha, where they belong."

The Archon's nostrils flared. "You would defy the orders of your Archon?"

"I would," Silene replied. "If they are dangerous and foolish."

The Archon's entire face went red, and he said, "Ware, dryad. I can have you exiled from the Silver for such insult and disloyalty."

Silene stood straighter. "Where is *your* loyalty, Archon, to the brightbloods you were chosen to protect?"

"I protect you in many ways," the Archon said. "Including by not concerning you with the terrible knowledge of all the ways the Shadows threaten your clan. You would not sleep well knowing what I know."

"Such as?" Silene asked.

The Archon blinked, then cleared his throat, and said, "I feel no need or desire to bring such an unreliable and rebellious vassal into my confidence. Suffice to say, that with the help of the ARC," he motioned to Mort, "the Silver Court shall have the greatest peace and prosperity in this region since the PAX was first established."

I stepped up beside Silene. "That guy there is playing you for a fool, Archon. He's part of a group seeking to destroy your patrons."

"You see?" Mort said to the Archon, and gave a pitiful imitation of a laugh. "Exactly like I said." He turned back to me. "You're wanted for arrest by both the ARC and the Colloquy. You've been busy making yourself popular, as usual. And yet you storm in here with a bunch of rebellious feybloods and expect anyone to believe your lies?"

"Lies?" I demanded. "You want to talk about lies? How about—"

Pete shouted, "Stop it!"

I turned in surprise to see him red faced and panting, his eyes gone wolf blue. "Pete?"

"Stop fighting! Mort, come down here. Make this stop. Please. I don't like it when you guys fight."

I blinked, then looked up at Mort. This felt so far removed from the old fights we'd have over who got control of the

ColecoVision, or got to ride shotgun, or got to hold the mana vial as Grandfather or Mother funneled magical energy into it.

That realization made me sad.

Damn it.

Mort actually looked embarrassed as he glanced from Pete to Father to the Archon and back. "Pete, don't let Finn get you in trouble again. Don't forget who took care of you and Father while Finn was gone. Don't forget all the bad things that have happened since he's been back."

"No," Pete said. "Finn tried to help. You were sick, and he tried to help. Now come home and we can be a family again."

"Home to what?" Mort snapped, appearing to forget the Archon for the moment as he took a step down toward Pete and gave an angry wave of his hand. "You're never there, and you can't help with the necromancy if you were. Father, I love you, but you can't help, you *need* help. And Finn"—he didn't look at me—"if he's not trying to get one of us killed, he's playing his stupid games. I'm tired of working my ass off just to wake up the next day wondering if we'll be able to stay in business another week, or what disaster Finn's going to bring down on our heads next. So excuse the hell out of me for being just like the rest of you and doing something for me and mine."

Sammy snorted. "Cut the crap, Mort. You've never done anything that wasn't for yourself. You liked playing king of the castle. And you always had enough money to blow on your asinine outfits and expensive toys."

"You have to look successful to be successful," Mort said. "Not that you'd understand anything about the business, Samantha, since you ran away the first chance you got. That didn't stop you coming around guilting me for money though whenever, surprise surprise, your job 'saving the world' didn't pay the rent."

"Once!" Sammy said. "I asked for money once! Okay, maybe twice. And how often did I save your ass by sending clients your way?"

"*Okay*," I said. "Obviously, we could all use some family therapy. But Mort, I can't believe you'd hurt all of these people just to protect the business, or your position. Mother raised us better than that. You're better than that. Pete's right. Come on, man, just . . . stop this. Please. We'll find a better way, together."

Mort crossed his arms, and looked petulant, but I sensed him wavering. Or perhaps I just wanted to believe he was.

"Very entertaining," the Archon said. "But I am not amused by rebellion." He raised his hand, and brightbloods poured into the room from the door behind us, and the door behind the Archon's dais—at least a dozen serious-looking fauns, a centaur, and a couple of human-looking brightbloods who might have been waers or sirens or a hundred other possibilities, many holding crossbows or swords.

Sal's fur fluffed up, and he growled slightly before saying, "What youself doing?"

The Archon's wings spread, and he said, "If you do not follow my orders and attack the Shadows encampment, then you will be stripped of your bond to the Silver, and transplanted to the Turnbull Refuge."

Silene put a hand in one of the pouches on her belt, and said, "Either would be a death sentence for many of us."

"The Shadows will never see an attack coming," the Archon said. "This will not be some raid or blood vengeance, this will be a full-scale assault. Overwhelming."

"It is beyond reason," Silene said.

"We will get rid of the threat in our region once and for all. And when we do, the ARC will grant us their lands. What better reason?"

I stared unbelieving at the Archon. "You're going to start a war!"

"No," Mort said. "The ARC is prepared to share intelligence with the Colloquy showing that the Shadows were plotting a massive attack against the Silver. This will be self-defense."

"Right," Sammy said. "Because the whole preemptive strike thing always works out great."

"Why?" Silene asked. "Why risk this without the blessing of the Bright Lords and Ladies?"

"*Because* of them!" the Archon shouted, his voice suddenly like a lion's roar, and he jabbed a finger toward Pete and Vee. "Do you know how many times I have asked to be transferred to the Topanga compound, to take over the California Region? Begged even? A hundred. A thousand. But do they grant my request? No. All I ever heard was what an amazing job the Archon there was doing, and that rewards come to the deserving when the time is right. And then, they bring these two in. The message is pretty damn clear to me: do something impressive, do something deserving, or lose my position altogether!"

Pete and Vee exchanged looks, and Vee said, "We didn't ask for any power, Archon. And we've tried to stay out—"

"So you say! But that doesn't keep the other Archons from laughing about it behind my back. There haven't been Vice-Archons in generations, so why now, why do *I* need them?"

"Wait," Sammy said. "You are going to start a war because of job insecurity and promotion bullshit? Can't you just implement a trendy new buzzword or do a reorganization thingy like any other executive?"

"Not helping," I muttered at Sammy, then louder, "I'm the one who asked Oshun for a way to help my brother and Vee. Making them Vice-Archons was just an honorary title, it had nothing to do with you, I promise."

Except now we know it likely did.

When a guy has his finger on the nuclear button, it's not the time to tell him that people don't trust him.

Silene raised a hand signaling for a pause, and said in a calming tone, "Why don't you tell us why you want to go to California. I'm sure there's a better way to get there than war."

"I am sick of the rain!" he shouted. "I am sick of the moss growing on everything, creeping across everything. I am a sphinx, for Bright's sake! I want the desert!"

"There's eastern Washington," I suggested.

"Fa! It isn't the same," the Archon said. "No Archon can rule this region from there."

"So you don't just want to be in the desert, you want to rule the region?" I clarified.

Dawn leaned close and whispered, "He thinks he *is* the Kwisatz Haderach."

"It is what I deserve!" the Archon said.

"Oh gods." Sammy sighed.

"What?" I asked.

"Topanga is near Universal City and all the game shows," Sammy said to the Archon. "Right?"

Ah. Of course. Dry heat *and* shows filled with riddles. Where else would a sphinx want to be?

"Where's Mattie?" Sammy asked suddenly. "Mort, where the hell is Mattie?"

"What?" Mort looked at her.

"I said, where's Mattie?"

He stood a little straighter, defiant, and said, "She is safe, far from here."

"She's not with you?" Sammy snapped. "You ass. She needs to be with family right now."

"She is," Mort said.

It took me a second, and then I said, "Gods, no. Not Grandfather. Mort, he'll *kill* her!"

"He gave me his word he would protect her," Mort said.

"He freakin' *kidnapped* her before, have you forgotten?"

"No, he took her to keep her safe." He glanced sideways at the Archon, and said in a careful tone, "It's the safest place she could be."

Sammy stepped toward Mort, her hands in fists, shaking. "And of course it didn't hurt that he gave you a shiny promotion and the pat on the head you've been chasing all your life."

Four of the brightbloods stepped down off of the dais to form a line between Sammy and the Archon.

"Mort," I said, putting as much conviction in my voice as possible, "Grandfather will either use her as a hostage, or steal her body. I swear I'm not lying about this."

"Where is he?" Sammy said.

Mort pursed his lips and shook his head, then said, "Did it ever occur to you that if you had just helped Grandfather instead of fighting him, maybe all of the bad stuff you've been complaining about would never have happened?"

"Dude," I said. "You do remember he's the one who sent me into exile? He's the one who killed Felicity, and drove Father mad?"

"Nice try, Finn, but he told me why he sent you into exile."

"So he could get at the raw magic through me?" I said.

"No, because Father saw that you were going to become a dark necromancer!" Mort practically spat.

"What?" I said. "That's crazy! That's not what—"

"Crazy?" Mort said. "So you didn't use dark necromancy within months of being home?"

Shit.

"I was not going to turn into a dark necromancer," I replied, as much to convince myself as him. "Grandfather admitted everything to me. He killed Felicity. He used Mother's ghost to—"

"Merlin's balls! Just stop with the lies, Finn!" Mort said. "Seeing visions of you killing with dark necromancy is what drove Father mad. That's why Father, Grandfather, and Felicity all worked together to send you into exile before you could hurt anyone and destroy our family, destroy our business, destroy everything."

"Oh come on," Sammy said. "You're going to believe that?"

"Just ask Father," I said. I looked over to where Father stood with Verna, watching the argument as if watching a tennis match. "Father, please. Focus. Tell Mort that Grandfather is lying. Tell him what really happened."

Father looked from me to Mort, and the left side of his face began to spasm. After a second, he blurted out, "Ring around the rosies. Poison's in the posies."

"You see?" Mort said. "And you're the poison, Finn."

"B-bright flows right," Father said, his face seriously spasming now. "Death flows left."

"Bright" was the Fey term for magic, among other things.

Father was speaking of Grandfather's ritual, I felt certain.

We were running out of time.

I looked back at Mort, and opened my mouth to speak, but Dawn grabbed my arm.

"Don't bother with your brother," she said. "The levels of cognitive dissonance in that man's head could shield him from Death Star strength blasts of the truth. Nothing you say is going to get through."

I sighed, but she was right. "Archon," I said. "The Arcanites are going to poison the Other Realm. If we don't stop them, now, your patrons are all going to die."

"And I should believe a criminal dark necromancer, why?" the Archon said.

"Well, uh—" I said.

Why does your tongue only work when you are being a smart ass?

"Because," Silene said. "You clearly will not get our help fighting the Shadows. And this entire mess will not look good to our patrons." She waved around her. "I have met Oshun, do not forget, I have her ear, and she did not grant these two the role of Vice-Archon lightly. Do you truly believe exiling or killing us all will earn you the reward you seek?"

"Right!" I said. "Yeah! But just imagine if I'm telling the truth, and you help stop a plot that would have killed all of the Bright Lords and Ladies? I'd say they'd pretty much give you whatever reward you asked for, right?"

The Archon visibly pondered this for a minute, stroking the wavy ringlets of his beard. Then he said, "Upon careful consideration, I have decided that the best thing to do is to let you all go in the custody of this ARC representative." He motioned to Mort. "Guards."

Two of the fauns flanked Mort, while the other brightbloods formed a kind of corridor from Mort, to us, to the exit.

"Wait!" Mort said to the Archon. "You can't make me leave with them! They're going to hurt me, torture me, or worse!"

"I'm so sorry," the Archon said. "I cannot hear you." He sat back down, and replaced his headphones.

Mort reached us, goaded by the fauns, and we all left the light and heat of the library for the chill, faded hallway. Our guide and two guards escorted us along a different route than we'd come, and we climbed up and out into the basement of the Archon's house and property in the woods. We were led up concrete steps to a back door, and out into the wooded property.

Cool night air and the chirping of crickets greeted us, the bright moon overhead illuminating the park-like forest around us.

As soon as the fauns had retreated back into the house, Sal grabbed Mort by the collars of his nice suit and lifted him from the ground.

"Youself try to kill us all!"

ONE

Mort tore and beat at Sal's hands and arms as his toes dangled and kicked above the ground. I knew from experience that trying to tear at a sasquatch's arms was like tearing at stone covered in steel wool. Mort fumbled at his jacket pocket, and pulled out the family's revolver.

Sal slapped the gun away with his free hand. Sammy grabbed it up from the dirt, and blew off the dust.

Mort shouted, "Let go, sasquatch, or you *will* regret it!"

I could see Pete anguishing over whether to help. He knew what Mort had done, knew we were all in danger. But Mort was family, and Pete might actually fight Sal to help his brother.

I was more worried about Mort's threat to Sal, however. Mort may not have been able to Talk to spirits like I could, but he was still a necromancer with far more years of experience and training than I had. He might just be able to rip Sal's spirit out of his body.

"Sal!" I said. "Please put him down."

Sal gave me a dubious look, but grunted, and opened his hands, dropping Mort to the ground.

Mort hit the dirt and fell back onto his butt.

"Now," I said to Mort, "tell us where Grandfather is, so we can save Mattie and prevent a war. Pretty please."

He shook his head. "This is what you do. You just keep coasting along like an evil Ferris Bueller, somehow making everyone your friend, making everyone do what you want, getting your way, and then next thing you know we're all going to be dead because of you and you're going to just order a pizza and play your stupid video games on our graves."

I raised my eyebrows, and stared at him a second. "Wow. Okay. Putting aside the fact that it would be completely ridiculous to set up a game system in a graveyard, I am very sorry you feel like Ferris Bueller's sister. First, you aren't nearly as cute as Jennifer Grey, and second, you don't know what you're talking about. Now." I looked around at the others, then back to Mort. "I promise, you tell us where Grandfather is, and we'll let you go. Once we save Mattie, she's still going to need her father after all."

Mort looked past me, then into my eyes. "You really think Mattie is in danger?"

"Yes."

He bit his lip, then said, "Fine. There's nothing you can do to stop Grandfather anyway. He's at the library."

I didn't need to ask which one.

The main branch of the Seattle Public Library sat on top of a natural portal to the Shores of Chaos Demesne. Libraries were often built on chaos sites, since knowledge was one of the strongest weapons against chaos. But because this was a particularly strong and volatile site, the library had been built as a kind of geometric wonder of alchemically treated glass supported by a latticework of iron and steel in order to handle any leakage of chaos or magic.

If Grandfather really had formed some kind of Faustian bargain with the Chaos Demesne, then it made sense that he would be there.

The problem was, it was about a two-hour drive away. And the nearest fairy path exit that I knew of was in Discovery Park, which would still put us too far to get there by foot in decent time.

"Shit," I said. "We have to leave now, and hope we're not too late."

"Fates?" Sammy said. "You okay?"

I looked over. Fatima swayed beneath an evergreen tree, sketching with a stick in the needle-covered dirt.

Dawn and I walked over to her while Pete helped Mort to his feet.

Fatima had drawn what looked like a dolmen: a simple, square tomb structure made of upright stones for walls, and a flat capstone for a roof. When made with the proper materials and rituals, they greatly eased a necromancer's ability to reach spirits beyond the Veil, and reduced the drain on the lifeforce of Talkers when speaking to the spirit of anyone entombed inside.

In the sketch, someone appeared to be trapped inside the dolmen, hands stretched out between the stones as if reaching for help.

Next to the dolmen loomed a set of standing stones. Much simpler than Stonehenge, the thirteen tall fingers of stone had an oval drawn at their center—a portal, I guessed—and Fatima had drawn a skull and crossbones within the oval.

"What—?" I asked.

I recognized the structures, or close enough, because they were only a short ferry ride north from Port Townsend—on this same island, in fact.

"That's the Earth Sanctuary, isn't it?" I asked.

Fatima swayed, and fell back into Sammy's arms. "I'm sorry," she said, her voice heavy with exhaustion and slightly slurred. "I was just thinking of Mattie, trying to remember what I'd drawn at Bumbershoot, and"— she waved the stick at her drawing— "I think she's there, now. And she—" Fatima passed out, and a small trickle of blood dribbled from her nose.

"Oh my god!" Dawn said, helping Sammy lower Fatima to the ground. "Is she okay?"

Sammy's hand trembled as she used the sleeve of her hoodie to gently wipe away the blood from Fatima's nose, then she jerked off the hoodie and rolled it into a pillow.

I put a hand on Dawn's shoulder. "The closer to the present a seer tries to see, the harder it is on them," I explained gently.

Silene joined us. "I can help soothe whatever ill was done," she said, and knelt beside Fatima, placing one hand on Fatima's forehead, and the other on the roots of the nearby tree.

Fatima moaned softly, then sucked in a sharp breath, and opened her eyes. They took a second to focus on us.

"Fates?" Sammy asked. "You okay, honey?"

"Yeah," Fatima said. "A bit of a headache, but I'm okay."

Sammy let out a long exhalation of relief, then stood and stalked back to Mort, wielding the family revolver.

"You fucking asshole. You lied to us!"

"Wait—" Mort said, raising his hands.

Sammy knocked his left arm aside and in the same motion whacked him across the face with the gun handle.

Mort tumbled back as Sammy advanced on him, falling again to his butt.

Pete grabbed Sammy's arms from behind, practically lifting her off of the ground. "Sammy, stop!"

Mort held the side of his face, and waggled his chin. "I think you broke my jaw!"

"Don't be an idiot," Dawn said. "You couldn't talk like that with a broken jaw."

Sammy tried to kick Mort, but Pete pulled her back just far enough that it missed. "Come here and I'll break something for sure, you lousy excuse for a human being!"

"Sammy!" I said, running up to her. "Save something for the real fight."

Sammy stopped fighting against Pete, but continued to glare at Mort. "This bastard was going to send us running all around Seattle while Grandfather sacrificed his daughter! He doesn't deserve to fucking take another breath!"

"This has to be some kind of trick," Mort said, whether to us or himself I couldn't tell. He stared at Fatima. "You planned this to trick me."

"You're the mistake!" Sammy said. She shook her arms. "Damn it, Petey, let me go. I'm done with Mort. For good."

Pete hesitated a second, but let her go, and stepped back flinching as if she might hit him, too.

Sammy rotated her shoulders, gave Mort a disgusted look, then strode back to Fatima.

Vee joined Petey, taking his hand.

I looked from Vee to Mort. Gods, I wished Vee still had access to her sorcery gift. I could just have her share with Mort my memories of what Grandfather had done to me, to us. But the ARC had blocked Pete and Vee's arcana gifts and even the memories of how to use them once they were officially declared brightbloods.

"Mort," I said. "I know we haven't had the easiest relationship."

Mort barked a laugh.

I took a deep breath and continued, "Please believe me, I am not your enemy. I just want to save Mattie, and Petey, and everyone else from what will happen if Grandfather succeeds."

"You're a dark necromancer," he said, the words coming as if by rote. "You brought a witch curse and waerwolves down on Petey. You got Dawn almost killed. You—" his voice broke as he said, "You sent Brianne to the Other Realm, to who knows what fate."

"Mort, I will help you get Brianne back. I swear it. Once we've stopped Grandfather."

He stared at me for a minute. "You're just saying that because you want me to betray him."

"No. I want you to believe me, so we can save Mattie together."

"And who's going to get hurt this time?" he asked. "Which of us is going to suffer because you're determined to play hero yet again?"

"Mort, come on, man. Is it really worth risking Mattie's life if you're wrong?"

Sammy called over to me, "Come on! Why are you still talking to him? We need to go!"

I looked over my shoulder at her. "Because Mattie is his daughter, and he won't be able to forgive himself if anything does happen to her."

"Who cares? Let him stew in his fucking guilt," Sammy said.

I looked back to Mort. "Dude," I said. "Help us, please. I'm sorry, okay?"

"Like that solves everything."

I sighed. "Come on. I love you, man. You're my brother."

Mort stared at me a second, then began to cry. I blinked in surprise, and stood there uncertain of what to say.

After a minute, Mort said, "I worked hard, you know. I worked hard, and all I wanted was to finally get some reward for it all. I wanted Mattie to respect me. But it was like my whole family was against me, and—"

I heard Sammy make an exasperated noise of disgust. I had to hold my own reaction back, and just said, "Mort, I understand, man. You had to deal with a lot. But right now, we need you to help us. Please."

Mort nodded. "Okay. Okay, fine. How?"

"I need to know anything you can tell us that will help. How many Arcanites there are, what they have planned."

"I don't know, and I don't know," he said. "Grandfather didn't tell me. He just said that if you did show up to send you to the library, he had a surprise."

"Wow, Finn," Sammy said. "So glad you made us wait to get that golden turdnugget of info."

"Hey," Dawn said. "Ease off, Sam. We all want to help Mattie."

"Whatever." Sammy pulled her hoodie back on, then stuffed the revolver into a pocket. "I'm heading for the car. Anyone want a ride, be there in five or get left behind."

Dawn watched her leave, then said to me, "She's not wrong, you know."

I sighed, then said to Mort, "You should go with Sammy."

Mort scrambled to his feet, and wiped at his face. "Screw that. She wants to kill me."

"You joining her to save Mattie will go a long way to fix that, I think." I hoped.

"What about you?" Mort asked.

I looked at Pete and Vee, Sal and Silene. "If we take the fairy paths, we can get there much faster than driving."

"Wait," Dawn said, grabbing my arm. "I thought you said the fairy paths drove people mad."

"Unless the person's bonded with a Fey spirit," I said. "I was able to walk them before, with Alynon."

"About that—" Mort said.

"I know," I replied. "That's the other reason I'm taking the path."

"Know what?" Dawn asked, suspicious.

"The last time I took the fairy path, it bonded Alynon and me more tightly. But, well, I thought I was mutating, but I think maybe that was Alynon separating and I willed him back into me. If I do the opposite, if I will the separation to happen, I think it might actually succeed."

What?! Alynon practically shouted. *I—wait. Where would I go?*

Most Fey spirits could not last very long in our world without being anchored to something physical.

If I'm right, then Grandfather will be opening a portal to the Silver Court at dawn. You will hopefully be able to reach it and go home.

"Hold your horse d'oeuvres," Dawn said, her eyes narrowing. "If you separate from Alynon in the fairy path, and Alynon is what's keeping you from going mad—"

"I'm hoping to time it so we separate at the end of the journey, right before I exit," I said.

"Maybe you can take the car instead?" Dawn said. "And do this whole separation thing after you've had a little more time to work it out?"

I shook my head. "Whatever Grandfather has planned for

Mattie, it involves necromancy. And I have a feeling we're going to be outnumbered as is. They need me. She needs me, as soon as possible."

"God damn you," Dawn said, her eyes growing watery. "I love you, but I'm not sure I can handle this constant risk of losing you without taking up some seriously unhealthy drinking."

"After this, hopefully I won't have to risk my life anymore," I said. "If we stop Grandfather, and Alynon is gone, it's going to just be boring old me trying to figure out my life."

"Fine. Then maybe I'll start drinking unhealthily out of boredom. But at least I'll have you around to pick me up off the bathroom floor."

"You and your rock star life," I said.

"Get used to it, baby," she replied.

I took her hand, and stepped close, looking into her eyes. "I'd really like to."

Mort groaned. Pete punched his arm.

I kissed Dawn. Except it was less a kiss, and more an exchange of promises through the touch of our lips, the give and take of gentle pressure and warm breath, and then the touching of our foreheads.

The honking of the hearse's horn broke the moment.

I looked in the direction of the car. "I don't suppose I can talk you into just heading home?" I asked.

Dawn arched one pierced eyebrow at me. "So, if you do have some control over the whole fairy path Monster Maker thing, rather than an extra limb maybe you can go for a third nipple, or, like, apple flavored genitalia?"

I coughed, and choked on my own spit as my face felt on fire and Pete and Vee made a show of looking anywhere but at me. When I could speak again, I said, "I'll see what I can do."

"Good," Dawn said. "Just don't screw up, you dork."

"And don't you make everyone look too bad by comparison."

"Hey, I have no control over the awesome," Dawn said. Then she grabbed Mort's jacket sleeve and said, "Come on. Let's go not get killed some more."

I sighed as I watched her go.

"Finn," Pete said. "Sammy's not going to hurt Mort, is she?"

"No," I said with as much confidence as I could. "Now come on, we have a Fey apocalypse to stop, Mattie to save, and an annoying spirit to be rid of."

Hey!

I was talking about Grandfather. Mostly.

La. Be that as it may, Finn, thank you. And I should say—and I mean this most sincerely—it is about damn time.

"Silene, Sal," I said. "Can you guide us to the Earth Sanctuary?"

"Yes," Silene said. Gratefully she, at least, didn't have any commentary to share on my decisions.

"Not without us, you ain't," a familiar voice said behind me. I turned to find Priapus and his small gang of loyal gnome captains marching up to join us. As promised, he had responded to his sigil placed under the gnome statue.

"Priapus!" I said. "I won't lie, we can use all the help we can get. But, well—I think the Chaos Demesne is involved in this whole mess."

"So?" Priapus said.

"So, we might be saving their butts from a double cross here, or this whole mess may be what they wanted all along.

I don't know which, and have no idea how they'd look at you helping us."

"You think I give two humps of a hippogriff at this point?" Priapus asked. "Forget about it. Them Arcanite jergoffs are gonna bring the apocalypse, yeah?"

"Pretty much," I said.

"Bada-boom. We're gonna stop them. And when we do, you'll owe us. These here Silverbrights will owe us. Hell, the whole friggin' Bright Realm will owe us. And I figure that will come in real handy when it comes time to start taking back what's mine, got it?"

"Got it," I said.

"Gnome," Silene said. "Can you send word to my clan of where we go and why?"

Priapus frowned, but looked behind him, and said, "Yeah, I think that can be arranged. For, say, three quarters normal rate?"

"Are we not allies in this?" Silene asked.

"Sure, but allies don't mean you get somethin' for nothin', honeytree."

Sal growled. "Youself best to speak more carefully."

"All right, all right," Priapus said. "Don't get all in a fluff there, Fist of Furry. Like the lady says, we're allies and all. I'll go ahead and do this one for half-rate, because I like you all. Joey the Hoey, get up here."

The youngest-looking of the gnomes came up, carrying a long-handled hoe like a spear. "Yeah, boss?"

"Message for the Elwha Silvers camp. Lady there'll give ya the words."

While Silene gave Joey the message, I filled Priapus in on what we knew. Then Silene said, "This way." She motioned for us to follow, and led us into the woods surrounding the Archon's house. This was not the old and tangled growth of the Olympic National Forest, but a lighter kind of forest, the trees well spaced, the underbrush a low carpeting of ferns and moss. Crickets cricked and gnats gnatted at our passing, and a light breeze rustled the leaves and fronds, carrying the rich pine scent down to us.

A moment of peace, the calm before yet another storm. I took deep breaths, and worked through the mental exercises meant to calm my mind and focus my will. I prepared to turn that will against the man who had taught me to use it.

I suppose I should not have been surprised that Grandfather would use the Earth Sanctuary as the launch point of his attack.

The sanctuary was the work of one of the guys who'd been behind officially mapping the ley lines in Seattle. He'd arranged for hundreds of acres of property to be designated as a nature preserve, with a five-hundred-year plan to restore it to old growth habitat. And as part of that, he'd consulted with experts in spiritual energies and sacred spaces to install a number of symbolic and ritualistic structures, like the dolmen, and the standing stones. He wasn't an arcana, or even Gedai, but the ARC had made sure to guide his work given the sensitivity of the area, and now took care to secretly patrol the area against Fey invasion or dark magical practices.

It was a place intended to help people connect with the spiritual side of nature and themselves. So of course my grandfather would use it as a weapon.

"Here," Silene said as we approached two trees whose trunks grew together and merged, forming a low arch.

I felt a strong mental resistance as we approached it, like

trying to press two opposing magnets together, or trying to win a political argument, or thinking of your parents having sex, compelling me to turn away, to forget its existence. But I focused on it with my arcana senses, and the resistance was replaced with a sense of nausea, like seasickness, as if space-time were gently rocking on waves of distortion.

Petey stood behind me, with Vee before me, and put a hand on each of my shoulders. "Hold on to Vee," he said. "We won't let you get lost."

"Bangarang." I took a deep breath. "I'll need you to signal me just before we exit."

"I'll pat you," Pete said, and slapped my shoulder twice.

I nodded, and we walked forward into that tree arch in a single line.

The forest vanished, and suddenly I was squeezed through a tube of warped rainbow color and underwater sound. The world spun around me, and I didn't so much walk along a path as move from one unexpected state of being to the next, all sense of up or down lost.

And as before, my body began to stretch and warp and change like the reality around us. A second head began to grow out of my chest like Kuato come to prophesize blue skies on Mars. The head developed Alynon's features.

Rather than fight it as before, I tried to sense the boundaries between that which was me, and that which was Alynon, and to slow but not stop the separation of the two.

Then two pulses echoed from my shoulder.

Pete. The signal.

I focused, and . . . pushed. I gave birth to Alynon from my chest. And as I did, I began to lose the sense of myself. Did Pete grip my shoulder, or the edge of a cliff overlooking a rainbow ocean, or perhaps he held the end of a mountain chain where my head rose as a giant volcano at its center?

Reality began to unfold around me, revealing its true nature, like a million origami flowers blooming in geometric neon beauty, taking me deeper and deeper into their secrets, into dimensions and levels of perception beyond—

We emerged. Or at least, the wondrous beauty of the universe's hidden code abruptly vanished, and my mind scrambled to readjust, to shrink back down to limited human perception and understanding. But none of the colors or sounds or sensations that blasted into my awareness made sense to me. It was like trying to experience the world through a kaleidoscope.

Was I convulsing, or was that the spin of the Earth jostling me around?

A bright light pierced my mind, then diffused and gently resolved itself into the yellow-green glow of sunlight through leaves. It faded, and I realized I lay on the ground, my eyes closed, someone holding my head.

I opened my eyes and saw that we were in a forest again, in a small clearing with the night sky and bright stars overhead.

Pete held my head in his lap, and Silene stood over me, one finger pressed to my forehead.

"Finn?" Pete asked anxiously.

"I—I'm okay," I said, and sat up. I could see the shimmer of a pond ahead of me, a little ways downhill from us, and frog song filled the night air.

Aly, you there?

No response. And no sense that he was holding back one, either. It was . . . strange, after all this time.

Then I spotted him, floating around the edge of the

clearing, where the gnomes had fanned out to guard the perimeter. Alynon looked like his Ziggy Prince self, but made of dry ice, semi-transparent with misty wisps evaporating off of him as he slowly lost the energy holding him together.

He put his hands together and gave me a regal nod of his head in thanks. Somehow, he made even that gesture feel sarcastic.

I sighed, then gave a courtly flourish of my hand and nod of my head in response.

Pete frowned from me to where I was looking, and said, "I think maybe you need more healing."

I realized then that the others couldn't see Alynon. Not surprising if he were a human spirit, but surprising since he was a Fey spirit. "I'm fine," I said. "Alynon is free, and floating over there." I waved in his direction.

While the others tried to spot Alynon, I eased myself to my feet. "Where are we?" I asked.

"Earth Sanctuary," Silene said. "Sal is scouting our enemy."

Sal stepped out of the tree line as if summoned, his red-brown fur resolving itself out of the mottled colors of the forest. "Dolmen is yon direction," he said. "Path leads from it to where badbright mages are gathered. Iself could not tell if a portal is opened."

I felt for magical resonance in the direction Sal pointed, and could just sense something like a buzzing on the edge of hearing.

"I think it is, or they're in the process of forcing one open."

Alynon waved farewell, then flew in the direction of the portal.

"Let's go get Mattie," I said.

We moved quietly through the woods in the direction of the dolmen. Or at least, everyone else moved quietly, while I snapped branches and made "Oof!" sounds with each sudden hole or dip discovered in the uneven ground of thick grass and bracken.

Then we reached the tree line, and I saw the dolmen on a slight rise, a cube of stone slabs about the size of a low-roofed closet. And staring out from a window-like gap in the stones was Mattie, her expression terrified, her green-and-blue hair a wild mess.

I reached out with my arcana senses, and could feel the tingling of magic between my eyes. "I'm guessing it's trapped," I whispered.

But Pete already strode toward the dolmen.

"Pete, wait!" I ran to catch up with him. "Didn't you hear me?"

"Help me, please!" Mattie said, her voice trembling with fear.

"I'm not leaving her in there!" Pete said. "I can heal fast."

"Not from death," I said. "Mattie, just hang on. We'll get you out of there."

"Hurry, please!" Mattie said. "This place, it hurts!"

"I help," a gravelly voice said behind us. I turned in surprise to find Borghild, Dunngo's sister, rolling on a mound of dirt across the path toward us, her obsidian eyes fixed on me.

"Where'd you come from?" I asked.

"Steading," she said, her voice echoing out of the opening that formed in her stone face. "Gnome bring word."

"Borghild," Silene said. "You should not have come. What if the Shadows attack our home?"

"I come make sure badbright mage no destroy other brightspirit."

I knew she meant me, not Grandfather.

Borghild rode her wave of dirt up to the edge of the dolmen hill, and studied it for a second, then appeared to shrink.

No, not shrink, but sink. She disappeared into the ground, leaving a tunnel sloping into the earth. After a minute, Mattie exclaimed, and looked down. A second later, she dropped from sight. I heard noise in the tunnel, and countless anxious heartbeats later Borghild came rushing out.

"Is trap!" the dwarf shouted, just before the earth behind her exploded outwards pelting us with bits of dirt and grass and chunks of Borghild, her still-living head spinning off into the forest trailing an angry shout. As earth elementals, Dwarves were notoriously hard to kill as long as any large chunk of them remained intact to hold their spirit. But any concern for Borghild I might have had was quickly pushed aside.

Mattie appeared. Except where her legs should be, something else burrowed up out of the earth, some dark machinelike form on top of which Mattie waggled like a hand puppet.

"That was very clever," the Mattie puppet said, and straightened to look at us. "You avoided all the traps the Master set on the dolmen. All except one."

And then Mattie disintegrated, revealing the horror beneath.

RUSTY CAGE

“Oh shi—” I said, then scrambled back as Mattie’s skin cracked and flaked away, and what was beneath impossibly unfolded itself like Wilt Chamberlain climbing out of an airplane seat in coach. It rose up, a massive armored body of rusted iron and tarnished brass, seven feet tall at least, like a four-armed ogre sculpted by a mad welder as the stage prop for a death metal band.

An autozombaton. Oh gods.

“Gnomes!” Priapus shouted. “Form up!”

I chose to Run Away, the excellent advice of Python’s King Arthur, and any martial arts instructor worth their salt when retreat is an option. I turned and ran past the gnomes as they formed into a wedge shape behind Priapus. It would have been suicide for me to stand toe-to-toe with that creature.

I stopped when I reached Pete and the others, now hopefully out of easy striking range, and turned to face our enemy just as Priapus raised his deadly little sickle and shouted something in gnomish. Vines twisted up around the creature, and its plodding march toward us halted.

I knew that would not last.

"Fate protect us," I whispered.

These horrific automatons had been banned since the Fey-Arcana War of the Civil War era that spawned them, for much the same reason civilized countries tried banning chemical weapons, human cloning, or tabloid journalism—the cost to our humanity was just too great.

How they came to exist in the first place had been a series of desperate solutions to problems that should have been dropped into a dark hole and forgotten to begin with.

First, you have to understand that zombies tend to move slower than a frozen slug past a traffic cop, and are dumber than a Biff Tannen book report. Part of that is that their brains and bodies are rotting away of course, and part of it is that they lack a real spirit to give them true will. Zombies are just meat puppets animated with life force stolen from other living beings. Which is why, even in the most desperate times of war when the ban on dark necromancy and zombies had been given a blind eye, there were no zombie armies, and certainly no zombie apocalypse. All you had to do to escape a zombie was be able to move. At all. And failing that, just hit them hard—rotting corpses tended to fall apart pretty easily.

Then it was discovered that, for some weird reason, the slowness problem goes away when you re-animate a hardcore bigot.

Before banning experimentation on arcana prisoners, researchers learned that some people were severely lacking in will, the force that not only helps us get up in the morning but allows us to make the difficult choices and changes. These people were instead partly animated by a kind of small nuclear power source in their lizard brain, as if a small bit of their spirit had been mutated by the primitive, unreasoning emotional energy there: a kind of spiritual cancer. Nobody truly understood how or why it happened, but on further research it was found that all of these people were serious, scary bigots in some way.

Anyway, the point being, even after death the bigot had a brain capable of driving action. And after death their hatred and self-loathing could be manipulated by necromancers like spiritual energy, in much the same way they had been easily manipulated by the worst politicians and religious leaders in life.

But there remained the problem of a rotting body. A rage zombie was still a stiff, disintegrating-sack-of-decay zombie.

And that's where the thaumaturges came in.

The thaumaturges had created automatons as weapons, but with similar problems to the zombies. While thaumaturges could animate the machines and enspell basic instructions into them—as they had with the Dalek prop and other animated traps I'd faced in the sci-fi museum a few months ago—the automatons were useless for doing complex tasks or fighting wars. And simply sticking someone inside to operate the suit had proven too difficult, especially before the age of microprocessors and modern composite materials—the sheer bulk and convolution of controls and gears needed to manually operate such a beast and all its weapons proved too great, and the complexity and mass of the machines when you added manual controls reduced its speed down to that of a zombie.

But animate a ragey hate brain with necromancy, and transplant it into a mobile suit Gundoom, and you got an autozombaton. Or as they were later called, robigots.

Yet even then, there remained a problem. Using a robigot

as a weapon was a bit like unleashing a pack of rabid lions in your studio apartment to deal with a mouse problem. It wasn't likely to end well for anyone, especially yourself.

That is, until they figured out that if you also stuck someone basically decent and sane inside the contraption, not as an operator but more as a battery of magical and spiritual energies, it balanced out the ragebrain and made the robigot somewhat controllable and versatile. Somewhat.

Of course, that eventually drained and killed the fuel source. In the war that spawned the robigots, they started by using volunteers, people who were dying anyway, or condemned prisoners looking to redeem their family name or earn a small reward to leave their survivors. Problem was, they only lasted weeks, and then needed to be replaced like any dead battery, and the thaumaturges quickly ran out of volunteers. The stories of what the experience did to the minds and bodies of those inside the machines before they died was still the stuff of campfire horror tales among arcana youth.

In short (too late), robigots were fine examples of that old maxim, "Don't just ask if you *can* do something with magic, ask yourself if you *should*." They had been banned for good reason.

Facing the four-armed mechanical terror before us, I felt my stomach drop out at the sudden certainty that Grandfather had trapped Mattie inside the thing. I just prayed to all the gods she had not been inside long enough to suffer any damage that couldn't be undone.

And I prayed I got the chance to make Grandfather pay for this.

"We can't destroy it!" I shouted. "We have to capture it! Mattie's inside."

Sal, Silene, Pete, Vee, and I all formed a line facing the robigot, with the forest at our back.

The robigot strained against the gnomes' vines, and they began to snap.

Silene tossed something from one of her pouches at the ground around the robigot then raised her hand, and more vines rose up, these thicker than the first. The robigot disappeared inside a writhing green cocoon.

"What is that thing?" Vee asked.

"A robigot," I said.

"A row begot?"

"Yeah," I said, "and I don't think we—"

The sound of quickly spinning metal keened in the air as circular saw blades the size of compact discs emerged from the robigot's chest, its forearms, its shins, cutting easily through the fibrous green vines. With a flex of its four arms, the robigot sent the severed vines flying. And then, the saw blades shot out of the robigot at us.

I dropped, and tracked the flight of the blades as they zipped over the heads of the gnomes and barely missed me. One grazed Vee's arm as she shoved Pete out of its path, and one ricocheted off of Sal's fur with a burst of sparks as Silene ducked behind him. The rest thunked and pinged into the forest behind us.

At the sight of Vee's bleeding arm, Pete began to wolf out, his eyes going blue, his nails elongating, his hair growing out.

"Pete!" I said before he was too far gone to understand. "Go stop Grandfather! This is not a good fight for you." Among the other things robigots were famous for, they had slaughtered entire armies of waercreatures. Pete was strong, but his teeth and claws were useless against this metal beast, or its silver-coated armaments.

And if anything happened to Mattie because he'd lost control, Pete would never forgive himself.

Pete looked from me to the robigot to Vee, and gave a frustrated bark, then grabbed Vee's hand and together they ran into the woods.

At the same time, Sal roared and charged at the robigot.

Priapus shouted, "Retreat!" The gnomes broke in formation for the woods, following Pete and Vee in the direction of the standing stones and, presumably, my Grandfather. I couldn't blame them. This wasn't the fight they'd come for.

"Sal!" I shouted, and scrambled to my feet, feeling useless. "Sal, be careful of Mattie inside!"

The robigot raised one of its four arms, lifting its hand as if also motioning Sal to stop. Except a hole opened in its palm. There was a clicking and whooshing sound, and then flame roared out of the hole to envelop Sal.

Sal threw one arm over his face, and roared in pain. Not much could cut through his fur, but the flesh beneath could still be crushed or burned or frozen. He crashed into the robigot, grasping half-blind for the arm, and the breeze carried the smell of burning flesh and fur to me.

Sal yanked the arm with one hand, and punched at the shoulder joint with the other. The arm bent, and the flames trickled to a stop. Sal punched again, and again, as the robigot began to pound at Sal with its own free fists.

"Don't hit the body!" I shouted.

The flamethrower arm broke free, and with a roar Sal pitched back, then swung it hard at the robigot's knees. The creature wobbled, but remained standing, and then it landed an uppercut that sent Sal staggering backward several steps before he toppled onto his back like a falling tree, shaking the ground. Sal's eyes fluttered closed.

"Saljchuh!" Silene shouted, and ran to him.

I stood there, my mind racing for a solution. Retreat seemed the only good option, but that would leave Mattie to be destroyed in the heart of that abomination. And Grandfather would destroy who knew how many other lives using this monster.

The ground under the robigot suddenly gave way, and the creature sank into a pit up to its shoulders. Then the earth collapsed in on it.

Borghild's head rose up out of the ground behind it on a newly formed body of dirt and pine needles.

The robigot began working its way free.

I stared a second in surprise, then lurched into motion. I ran around behind the robigot, and placed my hands on its head.

Please, oh please, let my magic work.

I sensed for Mattie first. She was there, as I'd feared, in the body of the automaton. But her spirit felt strong, and bright. If being trapped in the robigot had damaged her, I couldn't sense it at this level.

The ragey bigot brain, housed in the beast's head, required no effort to sense. It screamed for attention.

I was happy to give it some.

I summoned up magic from the locus of my being, focused my will, and said, "Spirit, I banish you to the beyond."

My power responded, thank the gods, rising up in me, reaching out, and—

I hit a wall. Not the kind I had before, not one built of my own guilt and self-doubt. This wall was made of layered protections: necromantic spiritual barriers, thaumaturgic shielding lining the brain's container, and—

I withdrew just in time to avoid a nasty and possibly deadly shock from a wizard trap.

The robigot shook its head back and forth now, and started to rise out of the dirt.

"I will crush!" Borghild said.

"No!" I said. "Wait! There's someone inside!"

I didn't have time to try and reach the brain past all of those protections. But there was another option.

I reached out with my magic and sent a surge of life energy into Mattie.

I sensed her energy levels rise to a state of wakefulness. If we failed to save her, maybe she could find a way to save herself.

Then the robigot's top arms broke free of the earth with twin sprays of dirt. I flew back into the mounded earth behind it, and immediately second-guessed my decision as I scrambled through the loose dirt to get away from the living weapon. Perhaps it would have been better to let Mattie die in her sleep, even in terrible dreams, rather than awake in the horror of her reality.

The robigot lifted one arm and pointed it at Silene. A rifle shot echoed through the forest, and Silene went flying back to the earth amid an explosion of blood from her shoulder.

"NOOO!" Borghild shouted, and the earth began to tremble as she sank down into it.

The robigot swung its other arm around, and a shotgun blast exploded Borghild into a thousand fragments before she was half-submerged.

The robigot's head rotated to look at me, and it rose up out of the dirt.

Oh, shazrobot.

34

EVEN FLOW

I jumped back onto the robigot, grasped at its head. Maybe I could create enough spiritual feedback before the thing killed me, just fry the damn thing's brain, protections or not. I summoned up my magic, and—

A vice-like hand clamped around my head, and began to squeeze.

Blinding pain disrupted any ability to think, to summon, to fight.

I screamed, and expected death to come blasting in through the fractures surely forming in my skull.

The pressure stopped.

The robigot slumped down in the dirt, and stopped moving.

I pulled the metal hand off of my head with some difficulty, feeling the rough fingers and sharp edges taking away skin and hair. A banging noise began, and it took a second with my nearly-split-head ache to realize what it was. Mattie pounded on the inside of the robigot.

I skidded down into the crater that had formed around the mechanical monster, my feet clanging against its back, and found two small wheel locks on either side of a brass handle between its shoulders. I twisted open the locks, and pulled on the handle. A large hatch popped open and thumped down into the dirt. Mattie sat inside the machine, her arms in iron bands at her side, and more bands around her neck and waist, holding her in place.

"Mattie!" I said. "Are you okay?" I lay across the open hatch and studied the iron bands.

"I think so," she said after a second.

"What did you do?" I asked. I thought perhaps she had sabotaged the mechanics, but she obviously couldn't move. I yanked the skeleton key from around my neck and began opening her iron bands as fast as I could.

"I learned some of Papa G's thaumaturgy while helping him with his experiments," she said. "I figured out how to trick this thing into turning off for maintenance."

"I didn't realize you'd inherited the thaumaturgy gift."

"Me either," she said, and laughed. And the laugh turned into crying.

"Hey," I said. "It's okay. It's over. Here we go." I got the last band open, and reached under her armpits to lift her out. She climbed up and back, flopping out onto the hatch with me, and together we scrambled out of the crater.

Mattie threw her arms around me, and sobbed into my chest.

I held her tight, and said, "I know, sweetie. It's over."

She pushed back, and wiped at her eyes with one arm. "Did you stop Grandpa G?"

"No," I said. "I don't think so. I haven't faced him yet."

"Then it's not over," she said in that same practical tone she used when explaining what needed to be done around the house to us less organized adults.

When I'd seen how she dealt with the news that her mother had been possessed by a ghostly spirit during her conception, I'd realized that her amazing self-reliance and positive attitude were a coping mechanism much as my own constant use of humor. Now, it downright scared me. She was only sixteen. She should not be talking about fighting to stop her grandfather from destroying worlds like it was just another thing to be done: take out the trash, file the mana taxes, defeat your arch-villain grandfather.

"Mattie—"

Silene's sudden groan of pain reminded me that there were others who needed urgent help.

"Come on," I said, and worked my way around the edge of the robigot's crater. Sal stirred on the ground, and Silene sat up, her face pale and covered in a sheen of sweat. She shouted in pain as she held one hand cupped under the hole in her right shoulder, her other hand digging into the grass beside her. From the pink scars and puckered flesh around the hole's edges, I guessed it had been considerably healed already. A round slug of metal squeezed out of the closing wound, and plopped into Silene's hand. The wound finished closing. As it did, the grass around Silene went brown, and the leaves of a nearby tree shifted rapidly from green to orange.

Then Silene slumped forward, her green-streaked brown hair falling over her face and shifting in time with her heavy breaths.

I knelt beside Sal, placed a hand on his chest and probed with my necromantic senses. His spirit was strong, but its hold to the physical body was fluttery, tenuous. He was on the verge of death. My guess was he only remained alive because of whatever healing Silene had managed before being shot herself.

"Silene," I said. "Sal still needs your help."

She raised her head, her hair falling back to reveal eyes sunken and bruised-looking, her normally deep tan skin slightly gray. But her eyes fixed on Sal, and she crawled across the needle-strewn dirt to him.

"Saljchuh," she said. "Come back to me, my heart." She placed a hand on his chest, and shuddered. "I—I have no more magic. Do you have mana?"

"Frak. No." I looked around me. As if a mana vial might be lying around. Idiot.

"Please," Silene begged. "Might you gift me some of your own?"

"I can't," I said. "Necromancers can only transfer magic from a dead body." I looked behind me. The robigot. It wasn't a body, exactly, but it had been designed to take magic and spiritual energy from Mattie and use that to power the living brain inside. "Mattie?" I said.

"Yeah?"

"Do you think you could find a way to extract the magic left in that thing as mana for Silene?"

Mattie looked at it. "Maybe," she said in a reluctant tone. "I mean, Dad taught me how to extract magic from bodies. And Papa G showed me how to channel and store magic in artifacts using thaumaturgy. But—" her voice broke, and she shook herself and balled her hands into fists for a second, then said in a more even tone, "I don't want to go back in that thing."

"Please," Silene said. "Do not let Sal die."

I pulled Mattie a little ways aside, and said softly, "It's okay. You don't have to. I understand why you don't want to do this. But maybe taking back what this thing took from you, and making sure it can't hurt anybody else, maybe that will help you sleep a little better tonight."

Mattie looked from Sal to the robigot, her jaw shivering a bit, then she gave a sharp nod. "I'll rip this thing's heart out."

She marched back toward the machine.

In the distance, a wolf howled in pain.

Petey!

I looked at Silene. "If anyone else comes, I expect you to get Mattie into the woods and hide her. Please."

"I will," Silene said. "I promise."

I nodded, then shouted, "Mattie! Petey needs me. Silene will keep you safe."

"Go!" Mattie said. "I've got this." But the quiver in her voice belied her bravado.

Gods, I wish I'd had half her heart at her age. She really was amazing, like she'd inherited the best bits of everyone in this messed-up family. I had no idea how Mort of all people had managed to father her. But I knew that even if I died here this morning, even if we failed to stop Grandfather, just the fact that Mattie was safe, that she would carry on the Gramaraye name, it made such possibilities somehow more bearable.

I took off running down the dirt path that cut between a wetlands on my left, and the rising slope of the woods on my right. The path curved around and down, until I could see two stacks of stones ahead like gateposts, and a clearing beyond. Over a wall of shrubs and tangled blackberry vines to the right of the gateway, the tops of eight or nine gray standing stones about the width of gravestones but tall as small trees became visible.

The sounds of battle grew clear—grunts and shouts and

metal striking metal—and I could feel the tingle of an open portal clearly now. I halted my mad dash and moved to the side of the path to hide myself. Running with no weapons and no plan into the middle of a battle between powerful arcana and brightbloods would probably get me killed faster than being Annie Wilkes's second-favorite author.

Do you think the Silver Court can shut down the portal on their side? I asked, then remembered Alynon wasn't in my head anymore.

Weird how talking to yourself and *not* hearing voices could come to feel unusual.

I looked around, and stuffed a few rocks into my pockets, then picked up a sturdy-looking stick that might serve as a club. Captain Caveman to the rescue, when what they needed was Captain Marvel. Or even Captain Kirk. He'd at least managed to turn a stick and some rocks into a canon when fighting the Gorn.

I eased toward the stone gate markers, and saw a dead gnome next to one, his little red gnome hat riddled with burn holes. The gate stones must have had some kind of trap spell to guard this approach, and the gnome had died disarming it.

I tentatively eased a toe forward, and winced, but when no doomy fireworks went off I continued creeping forward.

The battle came into full view.

A dozen standing stones maybe nine feet tall formed a ring, with three more stones at the ring's center. Twelve stones in the outer ring, and bound to either side of each stone, arms intertwined, were prisoners. Three more were bound to the shorter inner stone. I sucked at arcane arithmetic, but I felt pretty sure that three times nine sacrifices tied to thirteen stones added up to some serious ritualistic mojo. Glowing lines of twined spiritual and magical energy ran from the prisoners toward the center of the circle.

I recognized a couple of the bound men and women immediately, important and powerful members of the ARC leadership. The relatives of all those exiles that Grandfather had framed, I realized, no doubt the ARC members most opposed to the Arcanite agenda. Grandfather was killing two birds with one stone by using the sacrifice of his ARC rivals to fuel his grand spell to kill the Fey. Or, I guess, killing lots of birds with thirteen stones.

Circling the outer ring of stones, at least fifteen arcana stood ready to defend Grandfather and protect his spell. Not all were wizards. I saw alchemists with potion grenades and squirt guns; thaumaturges holding bizarre contraptions that I could only guess the purpose of, or with large balls of stone in front of them ready to crush their opponents; wizards with their tattoos and wands at the ready; and others that might be sorcerers or necromancers, but until they threw an illusion or ripped out someone's spirit I couldn't tell which.

Inside the ring of stones blazed a fire in a small fire pit, its flames blue and green and sending sparks flitting up to join the stars. And between the two taller stones floated a shimmering doorway into the Other Realm, revealing the green hillsides of Avalon outside the Silver Court castle.

A bright flash from the portal as Alynon's faint spirit attempted to pass through it, and bounced back. He didn't look good, much of his mass lost now, the wisps of dissipating energy fainter than before. I could only imagine his frustration, to be so close to home and unable to reach it. I should have realized that of course Grandfather would put a shield over the portal to make sure no Fey could pass through.

Grandfather. He stood at the center of the ring beside the fire. The lines of energy flowing from the bound prisoners converged beneath his hands, to some object sitting on top of a short stone pillar—

Frak. So that was what happened to the Kin Finder 2000.

The microwave-sized contraption normally located one living spirit using resonance with a second spirit, either through family bond or true love. Grandfather had found some way to pervert it, using it to link the bound arcana here to their exiled relatives in the Other Realm, cutting through whatever protections the Fey had created against spiritual attacks after Verona's spirit bomb. Links that he used now to poison the Other Realm.

Grandfather turned to study the portal, his face fully illumined. He looked much younger than the last time I'd seen him, and for a second I wondered if this entire ritual was really just his bid to achieve true immortality at last. Then I noticed the upside-down heart birthmark had changed sides on his face, and realized Grandfather must have claimed the second twin's body after using up the first. He seemed blissfully unaware of the fighting and noise outside the stone ring.

Both the fire and the portal cast flickering azure light and long shadows over the battle being waged. Or more accurately, the battle being lost.

The gnomes had done some obvious damage on the far side of the ring. There were several arcana bodies that looked to have been smothered in vines, or severed at the kneecaps, writhing or twitching on the ground. But there were also a scattering of charred, smoking lumps that I assumed were gnome remains. Priapus had rallied his last four gnomes in a small wedge behind him, and they retreated before a pair of wizards who fired lightning and fireballs at them. Priapus was able to focus the combined magic of his little squad of gnomes into a shield so that the blasts peeled off to either side of the wedge as if sliced in half. But even as I watched, each blast got closer and closer to Priapus before splitting, and I could see the gnomes' beards fluttering and smoking in the searing drafts of heat and electricity that blew past them.

Pete and Vee fared little better. Pete had gone full wolf, transformed into a creature the size of a small bear, his coat shifting between grays and light browns as he danced and dodged his way amidst three arcana who surrounded him. Two other arcana were already fallen with enough blood covering them to mask exactly where Pete had taken a chunk out of them. But Pete limped on his front left leg, had lost most of his right ear, and had been scored by fire along his side.

Vee stood in her half-squirrel state, still largely human but with squirrel ears and a giant fluffy tail waving up behind her like something a Ziegfeld Follies girl might wear. She seemed entirely occupied with running back and forth distracting several men who had wands or fingers pointed at Pete. She would dodge in front of them, and make a weird chittering noise while vibrating her tail, and the wand or finger would sink as the man's face went slack. But before she could take advantage of his distracted state, another man started to recover and raise his hand again, and she would run to distract him.

Why didn't more arcana join the fight and simply overwhelm Pete and Vee? They—

A bloated-looking fellow with a goatee started to leave his position near my end of the ring and raise a silver pistol toward Pete. Damn it.

While there were arcana who used guns, like Reggie, the purist types who might join an arcana supremacist group like the Arcanites tended to view using guns in much the same way a famous movie actress might view flying coach—sure, you could do it, by why lower yourself to the level of a mundane?

The man edged even further out of line, and the woman next to him snapped, "Don't break the circle! They could be a diversion."

And then a couple of the enemy arcana not being distracted by Vee laughed at her display, the kind of mean laughs I remembered well from my less popular days in middle school.

Oh frak. They were just toying with Pete and Vee at this point. Whatever damage the pair had done must have been done in the first minutes of the attack with the element of surprise, or momentum. Now, the Arcanites were back in control.

Someone called out, "Stop playing with the beastbloods and finish them."

Damn it. I had to put an end to this.

I dropped the stick, raised my hands, and walked out into sight of the Arcanites. "Wait!" I shouted. "Let them go, and I will—"

A gunshot. I looked to Pete and Vee, but they were okay. I felt suddenly lightheaded, and my knees went wobbly. I looked down, and noticed blood spreading from a hole to the right of my belly button.

Huh. That was strange.

"Don't shoot," I muttered in a daze. "I'm with the science team."

35

STEP BY STEP

Suddenly, the hole in my stomach hurt. A lot.

"Ahhhg! Son of a—" I pressed my hand against the wound, and sank to my butt on the cool dry earth.

This sucked worse than a *Highlander* sequel. And it hurt even more.

The world took on a slightly watery edge. I heard Patrick Swayze saying in my head, "If you project weakness, you draw aggression. That's how people get hurt."

I should have listened to the Swayz. Such a wise man.

"No more shooting!" Grandfather shouted.

The small part of my brain not fuzzy with pain and shock noted that Grandfather didn't move from his position to actually make sure his followers stopped shooting. Whatever he was doing, he was locked into it, committed. He probably couldn't even stop to defend himself from an attack. That was good, right? All I had to do was somehow fight my way through a small army of Arcanites to get to him, and game over.

"Bangarang," I muttered. Yet I remained sitting there, feeling dazed.

Grandfather shouted again, "Bring me Finn alive. Kill the others."

Sammy's voice rang through the clearing, "Like hell, you sick bastard!" The booming gunshots of the family revolver sang out, causing me to startle and look over at the battle. The two wizards attacking the gnomes jerked and fell to the ground.

A distant soft *foomp!* sounded between the gunshots, and a Nerf ball struck one of the arcana hemming in Pete. With a soft implosion of air he disappeared, replaced by a baby wallowing in a pile of clothing. Verna shouted, "Down with the man!"

Pete took advantage of the distraction to leap on a second enforcer, knocking her to the ground.

Sammy changed her aim to the enforcers facing Vee, but her first shot ricocheted off of the enforcer's damned suit.

Meanwhile, the four black-suited enforcers from the near side of the ring began marching toward me like the Reservoir Dogs, their faces promising I would be joining them as Mr. Black-and-Blue.

Dawn ran around the near edge of the clearing, past the fighting, racing the enforcers to me. One of them fired a wand at her. A venomous green magic missile streaked across the night and struck Dawn in the side—and shattered into sparks against her own borrowed and beautiful enforcer jacket.

I wanted to shout at her to go back, to get away, but sucking in the breath to do so caused a pain in my gut like swallowing a whole ghost pepper with a cup of boiling ouch-this-really-hurt!

The gnomes, slightly singed, rallied behind Priapus and began marching back toward the fight. Priapus shouted something, and vines sprang up around an enforcer about to unleash something unpleasant at Pete's back. Pete scrambled off of the writhing body of his downed opponent.

Several of the arcana to either side of Vee began to march toward Sammy and the gnomes. Apparently, they were done with playtime and concerns of trickery. The Arcanites were responding full force.

Sammy and Verna had bought us a few minutes of life, but we were still on the losing end of this fight.

Dawn reached me shortly before the Wizervoir Dogs did, and stood between me and them. She wielded the tire iron from the hearse in her right hand.

"Back off!" she shouted at the enforcers. "Or I'll unleash my power."

This actually made the enforcers stop, and blink at her, confusion clear on their faces. Here was a woman with wild purple hair in an ill-fitting enforcer jacket, wielding a tire iron, known to be a mundane.

"You have no power," Mr. Red Head said, coming to the obvious conclusion. Yet they didn't come any closer.

"Dawn," I whispered. "Run."

One of the enforcers began to raise his hand.

Dawn raised the tire iron and shouted, "Shazam!"

The enforcers backed up, surprise and uncertainty flashing across their faces.

I, too, was surprised, that they'd fall for such a bluff.

Then over the sounds of battle, I registered the growing *clunk clunk clunk* of metallic feet thudding on the dirt.

I turned, wincing at the pain, and went cold. The robigot marched at us. Was it running free now, rage brain unleashed from any constraints?

Then it raised an arm, and fired a saw blade at one of the enforcers.

The blade ripped right through the man's suit, knocking him back onto the ground.

The other three Wizervoir Dogs fled back toward the protection of the standing stones and their fellow Arcanites.

The robigot stomped past me and Dawn, and I watched it advance on the line of Arcanites who formed up to defend Grandfather's ritual.

Dawn turned to me. "What in Gort's name—?"

"Long story," I replied. "And the short version is I have no idea."

Pete and Vee had retreated to join with Verna and Sammy in the shielded space behind the gnome wedge, and were squared off against a knot of Arcanites. From behind the gnome's protection, Sammy and Verna fired their guns, and Pete and Vee struck out to either side against any Arcanites trying to flank them.

One of the thaumaturges moved a golf ball–sized stone across the palm of one hand, and the knee-high boulder at his feet responded to the sympathetic magic and sped across the ground. It bounced toward the triangle of gnomes like an oversized bowling ball.

A bank of earth rose up in front of the gnomes, angled past them. The stone hit the bank and deflected, rolling harmlessly off to the side, and then suddenly dropped into a sinkhole.

Borghild's head rose out of the ground beside Petey.

The arcanite wizards unleashed a full-on barrage of lightning and fireballs at the gnomes' invisible wedge-shaped shield, colorful flashes lighting up the area like a disco.

Closer by, a similar wave of energy blasts rolled over the robigot.

The strikes had little effect on the magically shielded robigot.

More of the arcana went down as punches from the death machine sent them flying. Two, three, four arcanites down. None of the fallen were enforcers, though, the real fighters.

One of the enforcers shouted something, and he sank into the dirt as if a hammer had pounded him on top of the head—a density spell.

Then a thaumaturge sent his stone ball crashing into the robigot's legs.

The robigot kicked at the ball, the collision ringing with a hellish *gong!* through the night air. The stone stopped, the hulking machine wobbled, but managed to stay on its feet. Still, its momentum was blunted. The dense enforcer stomped forward and began pounding at the robigot, and the robigot stumbled back, barely holding its own against the aggressive heavy hitter.

"Uncle Finn!" Mattie cried behind us, rushing down the path with Mort.

"Thank the gods!" I said. Dawn grabbed Mattie, and used her momentum to swing her over behind the gateway stones. "I worried you were inside that thing again!"

Mort pulled up short, as if worried we'd attack him.

"It's Papa G!" Mattie said.

"What?" I looked back to the robigot. Father?

I stared, fully smacked in the gob.

I suppose if anyone could have gotten that thing working again, it would be Father. Gods damn it. Had he even really understood what he was doing, or did he think this was all a fun game? My eyes filled with tears of frustration as I watched the dense enforcer land a blow against the robigot's head containing the ragebrain, denting it in. He was not attacking Father directly yet, but it was only a matter of time before the robigot went down.

I clenched my jaw, and lurched forward, one hand pressed hard against the wound in my gut.

Mort grabbed my arm. "Don't!" he said. "You can't help him."

"It's Father!" I said.

"I fucking know who it is!" Mort replied. "Don't you think I'd help him if I could?"

"Would you?" I snapped back.

Mort looked like he wanted to Carrie me to death with his mind. "You saved Mattie after I fucked up. I have to make that right. But you don't get to question *my* love for Father!"

Dawn gripped my other arm, as much to hold me up as stop me. "Do you have any magic that could help?"

"No," I said reluctantly, watching the robigot exchanging blows with the density enforcer. Father retreated a step with each blow. Pete, Vee, Sammy, Verna, all being overwhelmed. And I could do nothing.

I shivered. It seemed to be getting colder, despite the growing light in the predawn sky. But at least the wound felt less painy and more numb.

Silene stumbled down the path to join us, looking ready to collapse on the spot. She was alone.

"Sal?" I asked, afraid to hear the answer.

"He will live," she said. I felt a surge of relief, even as I wondered if Sal was the only one who *would* survive.

"We need to save my father." I pointed to the robigot still retreating before the enforcer's blows. "Is there anything you can do?"

"Wait," Dawn said. She moved between me and Silene. "Finn's shot. Can you heal him?"

Silene studied me, then the chaotic scene, and closed her eyes as if she'd just been asked to build a life-size Mall of America out of toothpicks. "I can stop one, maybe two of the weaker fighters, and stop your bleeding, but I cannot do more."

"Do neither!" Mort said. "Damn it Finn, we need to stop Grandfather! Or else we're all dead anyway. Mattie included."

I looked at the enforcers now surrounding the robigot, and then at Grandfather, still focused on the Kin Finder. Stopping either seemed an entirely and equally unfeasible task.

But I knew which was the unfeasible task I had to fease. Mort was right, damn it.

"Get me to my grandfather," I said to Silene. "And then help my father if you still can."

"Finn!" Dawn said. "You can't stop anyone if you're dead!"

"I love you, too," I said, ignoring her argument. I waved my hand once in front of her face, and intoned, "You want to go home and rest up for your record tour."

"Nice try," she said, slapping my hand down. "But I'm not letting you kill yourself charging into that!" She jabbed a finger at the battle, and the standing stones with their bound prisoners and arcing lines of bright magic.

"I'm not afraid to die," I said, which was true. Not because I was all heroic and brave, but because as a necromancer I knew perfectly well that my spirit would continue on just fine afterward. "But I hope not to. And I couldn't live if you and everyone I love were destroyed by Grandfather."

"Finn—" Dawn began again, but then just shook her head. She knew I had no choice.

I nodded to Silene.

Silene reached into one of her pouches, and pulled out two

small twigs. She tossed them in the direction of the standing stones, then knelt. She nearly fell over, but caught her balance, and dug her hands into the grass at the edge of the clearing.

Two thorny, tangled walls rose up and shot forward, punching through and past any Arcanites in their path, shoving them aside to create a corridor from us to my grandfather. The bastard remained transfixed over the Kin Finder, rocking slightly as he mouthed something.

I charged forward.

For one whole step. Then I fell to one knee and almost did a face plant in the mossy grass.

"Oh for pizza's sake," Dawn said, frustration clear in her tone. But she grabbed me under one arm, lifted me up, and helped me move forward.

"No!" I said, and pushed away from her. "I'm not dragging you in with me."

"Oh, shut up," Dawn said. "Since when are you the only one who gets to save the world?"

As we spoke, Silene flung a handful of small dark blobs at the dense enforcer attacking Father. She closed her eyes, and within seconds burr bushes began to grow sideways out of him. The roots of the insanely tenacious plants dug down into his dense flesh. The enforcer screamed, and tried to pull at the bushes despite the pain of touching those prickly branches and burr blossoms, but could not rip them free. I looked away as he fell to the ground.

The robigot was severely damaged now, between Sal's attack and the enforcer's, but managed to limp forward and swing one arm at the next enforcer.

Father stood a fighting chance of surviving now, at least.

Mort joined us in the entrance to the leafy corridor, and

placed a hand on my back. "You're such a martyr," he said. I felt a sudden jolt, like a surge of adrenaline mixed with winter sunlight. Mort had given me some of his life energy.

"Thank you," I said to him, then turned to Dawn. "Please, help get Mattie to safety."

"Oh, that's not fair," Dawn said.

"I'm sorry," I replied. "For everything."

I turned, and with the new surge of energy from Mort, I sprinted forward into the leafy corridor of interwoven blackberry vines. A stone ball crashed into the thorn wall on my right, punching partially through and nearly catching my shin, but the tangled vines halted it.

The wall on my left smoldered and smoked, and bursts of flame began to punch through, like some dungeon trap on a video game except I couldn't carefully time the flame bursts here, or roll against my dexterity to deactivate traps. One blast hit me squarely on the side. The vines caught the brunt of it, but my clothes were singed and my left hand burned. I shouted in pain and began to slow, the initial effects of Mort's life boost wearing off.

"Damn it, don't kill Phinaeus!" I heard someone outside the wall shout. "We want him alive!"

Deputy Dolph, Grandfather's pet He-Man enforcer, beat down a section of the thorn wall to glare in at me, and continued tearing a passage through it. Not great for me, but at least that meant he wasn't attacking Father or the others.

My eyelids drooped. Gods, did a nap sound like a really wonderful thing right about then.

Someone grabbed my arm, and I startled, but it was Dawn. Mort grabbed the other, and together they carried me forward in an awkward sprint along the corridor toward

Grandfather. We passed within the ring of standing stones, their blue-gray tops peeking over the vine walls.

"You . . . are in . . . serious trouble," I said, every bounce sending waves of pain up from my abdomen.

Dawn squeezed my arm. "You can spank me later."

"Really you two?" Mort said. "We're about to die."

"Then I hope there's spanking in the afterlife," Dawn replied.

"Jesus," Mort groaned. "I just hope death means I don't have to be tortured like this anymore."

Deputy Dolph broke through the thorn wall behind us, and charged. Mort and Dawn sped up, dragging me along. If we could just keep running, we might reach Grandfather before the enforcer reached us.

An alarm went off in my head then, mostly because Grandfather didn't seem to be paying any attention to us. Was he that lost in his spell, or—

"Wait!" I said. "Stop, I think—"

We slammed into an invisible wall, and fell back onto our butts in the dirt. Dust rose from our fall, spreading out in a light cloud only to break like a wave against an unseen cubicle around us.

"—it's a twap," I moaned.

36

U CAN'T TOUCH THIS

Grandfather glanced over, and frowned down at my stomach. "Don't die," he said. "I'll need you when I'm done, especially if you freed Matilda." Then he went back to his work.

Goosebumps sprang up all over my body.

The thudding steps of Deputy Dolph halted behind us. Gravel displaced by his feet hit my back and bounced off of the inside of the trap's curved invisible wall, able to enter but not to leave. I glanced up behind me. The hulking blond enforcer stood just outside the barrier, glaring at us, standing guard against any move we might make against Grandfather despite the trap.

Mort and Dawn scrambled to their feet, and helped me up. Which was a shame, because lying in the dirt had felt like a wonderful idea.

"What now?" Mort asked.

"I have no idea," I murmured, struggling to not just close my eyes.

"Damn it," Mort muttered, and grabbed my hand. Another surge of life energy flowed into me, and I perked back up.

An annoyingly arrogant expression spread across Dolph's face, and he said, "Now you'll all suffer the fate of traitors."

Dawn snorted, "As long as we don't have to suffer your dumb threats."

The enforcer's face went from haughty to red haught.

I had an idea.

"Hey, Mort," I said loudly, "didn't you say Grandfather was only bringing his expendable followers here, the real suckers, so it wouldn't be a big deal if they all died?"

If I could just provoke Dolph into attacking—

"What?" Mort said, in his typically slow manner.

Maybe this wasn't such a great idea. At least, not relying on Mort's acting skills. If he'd been in *Troll 2*, he would have made the other actors seem Oscar worthy. If he was the last man on Earth and auditioned for an amateur Pizza Boy porno, they would politely turn him away without even trying to explain why improvising "mushrooms and pineapple" was not an acceptable substitute for sausage in this particular case.

Dawn was a natural performer, of course, but I didn't want to put her in the line of fire. And Dolph wouldn't attack *me*, not with Grandfather's orders. But luckily, what Mort lacked in acting ability, he made up for in his ability to annoy the crap out of people.

"So that makes this guy the big dumb muscle, right?" I continued. "But he can't hit us because of the barrier. So I guess that just leaves big and dumb then?"

"I'm not the one stuck in a trap," Deputy Dolph said.

"Oh, wow," I replied. "Mort, I think we have a genius here. Why don't you explain to him where wizard powers come from?"

"Come from?" Mort asked.

"Yeah, you know, explain about their tattoos, and how the first arcana were created," I said.

Mort frowned at me, obviously still confused as to where I was going with it all, especially since nobody really knew how the first arcana got their powers. But since he clearly had no better ideas he slowly began to take a stab at playing along. "Well, the ink comes from alchemists working with wizards, and—"

"Remember," I said, "this is a *true* arcana we're talking to here, not some filthy feyblood lover. Don't hold back the truth."

"Oookay. I— Oh! Right. Well, alchemists make the wizard ink from various feyblood creatures like waersquid or sasquatchtupi mixed with whatever the spell requires, and thaumaturges form the needles out of manticore or chupacabra quills or similar materials. In fact, even wands come from feyblood parts. I think wizards would basically be powerless if they didn't steal from the feybloods."

The enforcer's face got even redder, and he said to me in a low angry tone, "You know I can't hurt *you*, but I'd tell your brother to shut up or I'll show him exactly how powerless I'm not."

Dawn squeezed my arm. "Finn?" she asked, clearly not convinced I knew what I was doing. Probably because she knew me.

I patted her hand, and said, "Mort, weren't you going to explain where wizards came from in the first place?"

Mort emphasized each word as he said through a clenched smile, "Are you sure that's a good idea?"

"No. But it's an idea."

Mort looked extremely annoyed, but took a deep breath

and said, "Well, in the way back, some humans found their way into the Other Realm, and were, uh, possessed by Fey spirits. When they returned, they had children, and those children were the first arcana. Then—"

"You goddamned Fey lover," the enforcer said. "You'd love to screw a Fey, I'm sure."

"Well," Mort said, "if your dad was an arcana, and arcana are descended from Fey spirits, then I guess technically your *mom* actually screwed a F—"

The enforcer shouted an invocation, and a fireball burst from his outstretched hand through the wards at Mort.

I'd been ready for it, but even so I barely managed to jump in front of the damn thing.

My butt cheeks twitched, and the giant, ghostly Pac-Man with its tribal-style tattoo appeared in front of me and swallowed the fireball. I felt the energy coursing through me, being transformed by the magic of the tattoo, and I flung my own hand out to point back at the enforcer, channeling the energy along it.

The enforcer's eyes widened as a stream of dark crackling energy like liquid black light shot out from my hand, ate right through the ward barrier like acid, and splashed out onto the enforcer.

I turned away as a large and messy hole appeared where his chest had been, and he began to topple backward. I heard the thud of him hitting the ground, and winced.

Well, *that* would be haunting my dreams for a while.

"What the hell was that?" Mort asked. I'd never seen fit to reveal Alynon's tattoo to him, and now didn't seem like the best time for explanations.

So all I said was, "Lucky." I turned back, and avoided

looking at the fallen enforcer as I picked up some of the dry dirt and flung it in front of me. It spread like dust, and struck the barrier with a thousand small yellow sparks. So I hadn't broken the wards entirely. But some of the dirt passed through what appeared to be a head-sized hole eaten away by the energy blast.

"Well done, but pointless," Grandfather said. I turned around, but he had already returned to his ritual.

"He's right," I said. "None of us are getting out through that hole."

Mort grabbed my arm, and leaned close. "But we can extend our magic outside the barrier now."

"And that helps, how?" I asked.

"You can Talk to that dead asshole, and figure out what Grandfather is doing? Maybe there's a way we can stop it."

I looked back at dead Deputy Dolph. Great.

I went to the edge of the barrier, and summoned up my magic, then reached out with my will toward the dead body. "Spirit, I summon you, and compel you to speak the truth."

The magic responded, and I felt a sudden tug and then slow trickle of my life energy and magic draining away, being drawn into the summoning.

I had only a second to be elated at my magic actually working before the enforcer's voice echoed out of his body, "What the hell just happened?"

I was the only one able to hear the voice—Talking to the dead was a rare gift even among necromancers—and I didn't feel like expending the extra effort or energy to make the voice heard by the others.

The drain on my life energy wasn't nearly as bad as it could have been, since there remained enough residual energy in the enforcer's corpse to help pay the cost of the summoning, but I was already on borrowed energy as it was. I had none to spare, and no time to waste.

"What is Grandfather doing?"

I could feel the spirit resisting the compulsion to answer, but I pushed with my will, and he said in a rush, "Poisoning the well!"

"What does that mean?"

"Death to all Fey."

"Yeah, but how?" I asked.

"I don't know," the enforcer's spirit replied smugly. Pride in ignorance, what a shocker.

"What did he say?" Mort asked.

"That Grandpa Poobah back there didn't tell his evil water buffaloes anything useful."

I focused on the spirit again. "How can we stop it?"

"You cannot. Only the Supreme Arcanite may stop it."

"Or we stop him," I said.

"You cannot," the enforcer replied, definitely smug now.

"Why not?" I asked, and could sense the smugness falter as the spirit realized it had given me important information freely. Once again he resisted answering, and I had to push to get the answer.

"It . . . is an act of sacrifice, the ultimate choice, and once begun it can only be stopped by choice."

"Frak me," I muttered.

"What?" Mort asked.

Dizziness washed over me, and I swayed. Dawn caught me, steadied me.

"Spirit," I said, "I release you. May you find what you deserve beyond the Veil." It was bad luck to curse or threaten a spirit, but one could always hope that there was some justice in the afterlife.

The drain on my own life force and magic cut off, and the spirit dissipated.

"You okay?" Dawn asked, putting a hand to my cheek.

"As okay as I can be," I said, finding it suddenly hard to dredge up the energy even to talk.

"So what did he say?" Mort asked.

"He said Grandfather has to choose to stop," I murmured.

"So we're basically screwed then," Mort said.

Another flash from the portal as Alynon attempted yet again to break through. He appeared on the verge of disappearing now. If Fey were made of memory, was he losing his memories as he faded, or just the life energy that they gave shape to?

Despite my better judgment, I considered allowing him to rejoin with me to at least prevent him from dying. Well, at least until I died shortly thereafter, or Grandfather took over my—

"Wait," I said. I thought about it a second, then said, "I have an idea."

Mort groaned. "Whenever you say those words, it never works out well for me."

"Buck up, little camper," I said. "You get to be the hero. But I need another boost."

"Of course." Mort sighed, and placed a hand on my head, sending another surge of life energy through me.

Revitalized, I called to Alynon, projecting my will toward him, hoping he could still hear me.

His spirit flew down from the portal, and stopped just outside the barrier.

Well, this worked out well, he projected into my mind. It felt different from having him actually in my head, like hearing a voice coming from down a long tunnel.

"Already, I miss your positive attitude," I responded. "I have an idea. But I'm not sure you're going to like it."

"I already said I wouldn't," Mort said.

Fine, I'll rejoin with you, Alynon said. *It's better to Finn out than to fade away.*

Mort looked from me to the space above us where I stared. "Wait, what are you doing?" he asked.

"Talking to Alynon. Hang on." *Actually,* I projected back with an effort of will, *I need you to join with my grandfather.*

I'd ask if you are joking, but you're not this funny.

Mort and I will perform the joining ritual and get you past Grandfather's defenses.

I need to remind you that a changeling cannot inhabit a body inhabited by a human spirit.

We've already proven there are exceptions. And I think you especially can do this. Whether because of the way Alynon had been created, or his illegal experiences as a changeling, or his time bonded with me, or all of the above, Alynon's spirit now felt like something between a human spirit and a true Fey spirit. And Grandfather's own spirit was an invader in the body he now possessed, which might give Alynon the opening he needed. *Your entire world needs you to do this.*

La, is that all? Lines of distortion rolled across Alynon, his form wavering.

Remember, I said, *fear causes hesitation, and hesitation will cause your worst fears to come true.*

Bright, what an excellent Point, Alynon said, then continued in a defeated tone, *It seems I am doomed whether

I will or won't, so I will just have to shall.*

Get ready then. When I raise my hand, merge with Grandfather.

And then what? Have the body commit suicide?

No. We are going to make Grandfather see the madness of his choice. I hope. And if nothing else, being stuck in a body that Alynon controlled would be fitting punishment.

"Okay," I said to Mort, "now we—" the world spun, and I fell.

"Finn!" Dawn said.

I blinked up at her. "I've fallen and I can't get up." At least, I think I said that. It came out rather slurred.

"He's dying," Mort said, leaning down next to my head. "The Talking was too much a shock to his system."

"Well, help him!" Dawn snapped. Her voice sounded oddly distant. "Do that thing you do again."

"He basically needs an energy IV," Mort replied. "A steady stream of life energy, not short bursts. And if my will is focused on keeping him alive, I can't stop Grandfather at the same time."

"I need to help you with Grandfather," I said. "We need to use Alynon—" The effort to speak suddenly felt like trying to lift words made of freight trains in Conjunction Junction.

"What about me?" Dawn asked Mort. "Can't you give Finn some of my energy or whatever?"

"I could," Mort said hesitantly. "But I'd still have to maintain the link, and have less chance against Grandfather. My will would still be split."

"But if we revive Finn, then he'd be able to help you fight your grandfather," Dawn said. "You'd still have more will than alone, right?"

"So . . . I help you help Finn so he can help me with his will?"

"It takes a willage, dude," Dawn replied.

Mort sighed, and said, "Since I don't know what Finn has planned anyway, not sure I have a lot of choice."

"There's that brotherly love I was looking for," Dawn said, slapping Mort on the arm.

"Don't get me started," Mort replied as he sat down next to me, unbuttoning his fitted suit jacket with one hand. Dawn sat on my other side. Mort placed one hand on my head, and I felt him shift as he reached across me to take Dawn's hand.

After a few seconds, I felt a slow but steady stream of life energy flowing into me, waking up my mind, warming my muscles.

I took a deep breath. "Thank you," I said to them both.

Dawn grinned. "Now I can really say I shared the best years of my life with you."

"And I can honestly say you make me feel alive."

Mort gave a martyred sigh. "Seriously, you two. So, brother, what's your brilliant idea exactly?"

I explained the idea to Mort, keeping my voice low so that Grandfather couldn't hear, and projecting the conversation to Alynon.

After their expected accusations of insanity and bleak predictions of failure, we began.

Mort reached out through the breach in the barrier with his necromantic senses, and I piggybacked on his effort, working in tandem with him like in the old days when we were being trained. Guided by the strong resonance between my spirit and Grandfather's, we located his spirit within his stolen body.

"What—" Grandfather said.

Together, Mort and I threw our will against Grandfather's.

By our powers combined!

37

IT'S SO HARD TO SAY GOOD-BYE TO YESTERDAY

Even with Mort and I combining our will, we probably would have lost a direct confrontation with Grandfather on an average day. Especially with Mort's will divided keeping me alive, and me being on life support, we should have had about as good of odds as a sloppy drunk Aeon Flux assaulting the Death Star trench.

But Grandfather's own will thankfully remained largely consumed by his ritual. Our will hit his like a rhinoceros ramming into another rhinoceros, except if we rammed the other rhinoceros from the rear.

Only, uh, less messy.

Our will met resistance, but it was like squeezing a balloon. The tension increased, and then suddenly gave away as we broke through.

The ease of it shocked me. Then, as my awareness settled into the mind and body that Grandfather also possessed, I realized the truth. Grandfather had turned this body into little more than a living conduit. The twined magical and spiritual energy flowed through him, and was transformed through him, transmuted from the energy of life into the energy of death, poisonous and infectious and terrible, before flowing on through the portal in a dozen smaller streams. I wasn't even sure killing Grandfather would end the flow, because the life energy and magic flowing into him would keep this body essentially alive as far as the needs of the spell were concerned, even if you chopped off his head and cut out his heart. Deputy Dolph had been right.

And it was also obvious that Grandfather would need a handy body to jump into once he'd used this one up.

Grandfather whispered, his words reflected in his host's mind, "You waste your time. You cannot stop this."

No, I projected back at him. *But* you *can. Please, Grandfather. You must realize you'll be seen as the next Hitler, or Mordred, or Vlad.*

"I will have as great an impact as them, perhaps," he replied. "But history will view me as the savior of our world."

Holy Ozymandias. He really had drunk his own Kill-Aid. Despite his constant rants, I'd always had some doubt, some certainty that he couldn't be this far gone, that his holy crusade was really all just a mask for a power grab, something to pull in a bunch of zealous and expendable followers he could exploit, like most ambitious ideologues or corrupt religious leaders. But there was nothing more dangerous than when the leader of a crusade *actually* believed that he was on some holy mission.

Mort's voice rose up, *Grandfather! You bastard. You would have killed Mattie. You used* me. *You've destroyed the Gramaraye name forever!*

"And you were never going to be anything more than a tool at best, a disappointment at worst," Grandfather said in a bored tone. "Forgive me if your opinion holds little weight here, boy."

I directed my thoughts to Mort, so that only he could hear, *Don't let him get to you. We need to open the way for Alynon to possess him, now.*

Whatever you say, Mort replied. *The tool is happy to help. Wouldn't want to disappoint.*

I sighed. I understood why Grandfather got under his skin so easily, I just wished it didn't always seem to come back on me.

You're the one with the real skill here, I said.

Grandfather probed at us with his will, tried to push us away, but we easily resisted.

"Are we pouting now?" Grandfather asked. "Done whining?"

Thankfully, Mort didn't take the bait. I felt him opening a kind of spiritual tunnel, like the eye of a tornado into the brain of Grandfather's freejacked body, holding at bay Grandfather's own spirit.

I diverted a small portion of will to raise my physical hand. Then I felt for Alynon's spiritual resonance, and summoned him into Grandfather's body. It was a little more difficult than usual, and not just because of my state, but because I had to work through the filter of Mort, like operating robot hands to do a delicate job rather than using my own, which was especially hard to do on a job like this that relied so much on feeling your way along.

Alynon's spirit responded, however, and with my guidance settled in to Grandfather's borrowed body. I felt a shift in the body's spiritual energy as Alynon took possession.

We waited until Alynon had formed his own mental and

spiritual fortifications around himself before releasing our protective funnel. Grandfather's spirit crashed in instantly and tried to exorcise Alynon.

Neither Mort nor I were sorcerers, or at least had never attempted to manifest any small ability we might have in our blood from sorcerer ancestors, so we lacked the ability to manipulate Grandfather's mind directly. But Alynon was a creature of memory, raised to feed on spiritual memory, to pick and choose and shape it, to understand it the way a master chef understands food. So Mort and I ran interference on Grandfather's attempts at exorcism as Alynon went to work, digging, seeking the heart of Grandfather's hatred for the Fey.

I've found something, memories locked deep within, beneath a lot of pain and anger.

Can you access them?

I'm trying. I—there. I think I can manifest them with a little bit of—

Grandfather's memories rose up, and enveloped us all.

Gavriel Gramaraye followed his older brother into the library where their father entertained several men from Seattle. The house still had decorations up from the Winter Solstice and turning of the year. Their mother said that since it was such an important year—the start of a whole new decade, one hopefully free of the wars and the difficulties the world and arcana had seen in the last ten years—that the arrival of 1920 deserved to be appreciated for a while.

Their father sat in his throne-like armchair, and the three visitors sat across from him in less ornate armchairs, the table between them holding Father's special collection of decanters and potion samplers on a silver tray, the contents all illegal in one way or another.

This was not a meeting with necrotorium clients. Father met with clients in the entry parlor, where the bodies were shown. This was another one of his "special" meetings. Which meant Gavriel had to be on his best behavior.

One of the men said, "Those radicals shut down Seattle for nearly five days with that strike, Don." He made a wild motion, causing the yellow liquid in his glass to slosh over his hand. "Ah, damn it." He set the glass down on the silver tray, and grabbed out his handkerchief. "My point is, this is not a friendly place for business anymore. Seattle will be a ghost town in ten years, take my word on it."

"Bah," Gavriel's father gave a dismissive wave of his hand. "That Palmer fellow is cutting the knees out from under those radicals, and Hoover's working on deporting the rest of the damned Russians and Italians."

One of the other men raised his glass in a toast, and said, "And they're talking about finally creating real immigration laws."

"Here here," Father said, raising his own glass, and taking a sip. "We can't let a few socialists scare us, gentlemen. More importantly, Port Townsend isn't Seattle, which is exactly my point. If you bring your businesses here—" Father glanced over, and spotted Gavriel and his brother. "Ah, Geoffrey, Gavriel, come here."

Gavriel followed his brother's lead. Gavriel always followed his older brother's lead. If they both did something wrong, then at least if Geoff did it first he would get the worst of the beating. Even if that usually meant Geoff would later turn around and beat Gavriel the first excuse that came up.

"Boys, how many arcana friends do you have around your age?"

"Lots," Geoff said.

Father frowned. "I didn't ask for useless terms. Give us a number. And remember your respect!"

"Sorry, sir," Geoff said. "At least twelve, sir."

"And how many mundanes. Gavriel?"

"None, sir," Gavriel said. Not that there weren't plenty of mundies also around ten years old, just that Father forbade them from playing with any.

And then just in case that wasn't good enough, Gavriel said, "I mean zero, sir."

"You see?" Father said, turning back. "And half of those arcana are girls. You want your children growing up to marry mundanes? Then move to some big city. Or you can move your business here, and your families can be among true people, among other arcana."

Gavriel's mother entered wearing her entertaining dress, carrying a tray of fresh-baked cookies.

"This is 1920, Don," the mustachioed man in the center said. "It is an age for enterprise, and opportunity. Have you seen these new radios? The mundanes are creating their own kind of magic now. It is, frankly, time to leave the old ways behind and embrace the new."

Mother set the tray down on the table, and said, "Well, I don't feel—"

"Nobody wishes to hear your *feelings*, dear," Father said in a joking tone tinged with reprimand. "Clean that up, will you?" He waved at the glass the visitor had spilled drink out of.

Mother did as instructed, and left the room.

Once she'd left, Father said, "With all this talk of giving

women the right to vote, they suddenly think we want their opinion."

The other men chuckled. Father glanced back at Geoff and Gavriel still standing there. "You're dismissed, boys. Go do your chores."

"Yes, Father," both boys responded, and left.

As they stepped outside, the boys found their mother there, finishing off the liquid from the glass with a shaking hand, and Gavriel thought he saw tears on her face before she quickly turned away and wiped at her eyes. "Oh, boys, why don't you go into the kitchen. I left a cookie for each of you." Softly, she added, "Don't let your father know."

A blur . . .

Gavriel shifted uncomfortably in the heavy robes. Nervous sweat trickled down his arms despite the cool night air as he stood with his father in the center of a ring of men, all wearing their own robes. Torchlight flickered across the thick, mossy trees surrounding the clearing, and downhill from them Lake Quinault glittered beneath the full moon.

Gavriel felt less nervous about this ritual than what came after: the not-so-secret rite of passage most arcana boys enjoyed when they turned fifteen.

Father continued speaking in his ritualistic tone, "And do you, Gavriel Gramaraye, swear to uphold the sacred duty of an Arcanite, to protect the purity and honor of arcana blood, to stand watch against the Fey and their corruption of our world?"

"I so swear," Gavriel replied.

Father raised his hands over his head. "And thus are you named an Arcanite, with access to all the secrets and privileges thereof."

The ring of men all intoned, "So it is witnessed, by blood and by magic, by moonlight and arcana sight."

Father lowered his hands, and a mischievous smile spread across his face. "Congratulations, son. You are a man now. Well, almost." He motioned to one of the men, the alchemist Mr. Flowers, and Flowers strode off into the forest along a barely visible trail.

The remaining circle of men shifted to form a line from Gavriel to the trailhead.

Father slapped him on the shoulder, and turned to guide him along the line. Calls of "Congratulations," and "It's your lucky night, boy," and "Welcome to the order," followed him as Father lead him down the line. When they reached the end, Father stood with one hand remaining on his shoulder. It was a strange feeling, a good feeling. Father had never been one for affection, certainly not for hugs or other womanly shows of emotion.

"Did you hear, Don," the nearest man in line, Mr. Mills, said. "The Klan marched forty thousand strong on Washington. Imagine if we could organize those numbers, what we could do."

"I heard," Father replied. "They overplayed their hand. The country is not ready to rally behind their cause openly, not yet."

Mr. Davis leaned forward to see us from down the line, and said, "It is a foolish war to wage regardless, this concern with dividing humans by race and country. They bicker over which flavor of pie is best while a bear is breaking into the pie shop."

"It's not like they know about the Fey, Reginald," someone further down the line said.

"Don't dismiss their concerns entirely," Father said. "We cannot deny that certain countries seem to have bred dangerously radical and criminal breeds of mundanes."

"I think that is more a question of mundy ideology than race," Mr. Crawford said.

Mr. Davis replied from further down, "I imagine all this race nonsense the Klan is focused on will go away soon enough, anyway. The mundies are finally seeing past their old myths. Did you hear about the Scopes trial?"

Mr. Mills said, "If they are so undone at the thought of being descended from monkeys, imagine how they'd feel if they ever met a centaur and worked out *its* origins."

That brought some laughs.

"I think this new move toward science is dangerous," Father replied. "If the mundies aren't fighting amongst themselves, or dismissing magic as miracles, they might begin to recognize and fear *us* as the outsiders."

"But forty thousand! Just imagine if we could get those numbers," Mills repeated.

Mr. Davis leaned forward again and said, "The Klan has preachers and the radio helping them out, and can talk openly about their concerns. We need to find some way of spreading our message like that, without exposing ourselves to the mundies."

"I like the Catholic way," the man beside Mills said. "Breed ourselves an army of followers."

"You would," Mr. Crawford said. "You've got that young new bride."

Father slapped Gavriel on the shoulder. "Well, my son will

soon enough have a more informed opinion on the matter."

That brought chuckles from the men down the line, as movement in the forest drew Gavriel's attention.

Mr. Flowers returned, and following him glided the most beautiful woman Gavriel had ever seen. She looked maybe twenty years old, with deeply tanned skin and hair traced with green and orange streaks.

And she walked fully naked.

Gavriel blushed, his heart now racing.

Father turned to face Gavriel, and handed him a potion bottle as Mr. Flowers and the nymph approached. "A love potion," he explained in a voice pitched low for Gavriel's hearing alone. "She will follow her nymph's calling without it, but I've found that love can make them even more . . . passionate about their work, willing to behave more fitting with their animal natures. And control is a powerful feeling, one I would have you appreciate. There's a reason we don't just take you to a common lady of the night. You can learn much here besides how to simply christen your manhood, if you have the fortitude to take advantage of this opportunity."

Gavriel took the potion. "Yes, Father."

Father nodded in approval, and said, "Just don't ruin her for the rest of us. That would be bad form."

Father handed the nymph a small mana vial.

"So little," she said, looking down at it as if she were a starving woman handed moldy bread, wrestling between refusing it or giving in to her hunger.

"I am sure you would love if I gave you enough magic to attack us, or to leave your tree," Father said, holding out his hand as if to take the vial back. "But if you don't want this much—"

"No! No, I— Thank you, masters. I am pleased to serve." She held the vial against her breast with one hand, and took Gavriel's arm with the other, then led him back into the forest.

"Have fun!" his brother called after him.

The nymph led Gavriel down winding and hidden paths until they reached a tree with a broad canopy of leaves over a bed of thick moss.

"How shall I please you, master?" the nymph asked in a voice devoid of any emotion except a hint of fear.

Gavriel looked down at the potion in his hand, feeling suddenly awkward, uncertain. There were the theories, the hints, shared between boys in class or while up in Greg's tree house looking at pinup girls. But that had not given him an exact map to follow, a certainty of what to do first, or how, or even where exactly.

"Uh, what is your name?" he asked.

"I am called Sylia."

Gavriel didn't know what to say next. What if he couldn't do this? What if he failed? Father would know somehow. They'd all know. Gavriel would never live it down. Father might even punish him.

One piece of advice rose up sudden and strong above all others. Mother, looking at him with sad eyes, and saying, "Promise me something, Gavriel. Promise me you will only be with a woman for love. You will both be happier if it is for love."

Gavriel raised the bottle, considered its contents.

"Do you wish me to drink that?" the nymph asked.

"No," Gavriel said. He uncorked the bottle, and drank the potion.

And then Gavriel realized Father didn't matter, his fears didn't matter. All that mattered was that he had found his true happiness at last. Sylia was perfect in every way. As long as Gavriel had her, he didn't need Father's approval, or to prove himself as an arcana or necromancer, as a student or son.

"I love you," Gavriel said.

A smile spread across the nymph's face, a genuine smile.

"I can sense it. It has been . . . a long time. Do you offer yourself to me, and my tree?"

"Yes," Gavriel said. "Whatever you want, it is yours."

The nymph removed Gavriel's robes. Hands that felt like sunlight and silk stroked his skin and lowered him to the ground. Sylia's lips touched him everywhere, music made into kisses, and wherever they touched became the entire universe to him; the rest of his body seemed nothing more than mist. Then, Sylia lay on top of him, stared into his eyes, still smiling that knowing, promising smile. And warmth enveloped him.

She moved on top of Gavriel, her body rolling along his like a wave, over and over. His tongue eagerly sought out Sylia's, trying to lap up more of whatever magic was in her kiss. Gavriel felt something pouring, or perhaps sliding, back down his throat, into his chest. He began to panic, to gag; but Sylia held him tight, and soft reassurance touched his mind, washed away any fears.

Gavriel felt the magical energy being drawn from his locus into Sylia. Payment. No, an offering. Then, euphoria: transcendent, soul-shattering pleasure. It pulsed through him stronger and deeper than the greatest physical sensation, causing his legs to shake convulsively, his stomach to spasm rhythmically, his mind to lose consciousness yet remain aware, over and over. And it did not end. Gavriel wanted to scream his pleasure, to laugh and cry, to tear himself open and pull Sylia wholly inside himself.

Their two bodies joined by Sylia's kiss, it felt as though their spirits swirled together like liquid sunshine stirred into warm honey.

Gavriel became one with Sylia.

Gavriel was eternal.

Eternal thirst, eternal yearning toward warmth, eternal need.

Long were the ages since he'd felt the presence of another tree spirit, his sapling planted here by the arcana to serve their purposes. Long and lonely were the seasons without the touch of a human soul. Gavriel marked time as a tree marks time, in languid seasons, in years of plentiful rain and years of dryness, in years heavy with the fear of lightning fires, or free of the bitterness of ice. Gavriel slept, and waited, and yearned for another spirit to come and join his.

Suddenly, terribly, the ecstasy ended. The kiss broke, the joining dissolved, whatever had entered him pulled out at the same time as Sylia slid off of him. Then they lay together, entangled, and Gavriel fell asleep, his body trembling with exhaustion and the afterglow of the experience.

Somebody shook him awake.

Father, his face like a stone mask. Geoffrey stood beside him, smirking, and the rest of the men stood on the trail behind them.

"What happened?" Father demanded. "Where is she?"

Gavriel bolted upright, panic rising in his chest. "She's gone? Where? Why? I need her! I love her!"

A brief moment of silence, then several men burst out laughing. "He drank your potion, Don. The fool's in love with the nymph."

Someone else said, "She's taken what she needs to start a new sapling and fled."

"We could go to the nymph up in the Moss Cathedral," Mills suggested.

"That sounds exhausting," Crawford said. "I'm heading back to the lodge."

Mr. Flowers slapped Father on the back. "I'll whip up a cure for the boy, Don. But I have to say, this initiation will certainly be one that is remembered."

More chuckles as the other men left.

Father's face turned bright red, a vein pulsing visibly on his temple. Even through Gavriel's concern for Sylia, he felt a deeper fear.

Geoffrey said, "Don't worry, Father. I'll bring that tree bitch back here. If she's taken some of Gavriel's energy, she'll be easy to sense."

"Do that," Father said. "And bring her back alive. Mills, go with him."

Mr. Mills looked annoyed, but nodded, and he and Geoffrey marched off into the night. The rest of the men headed back in the direction of the clearing, and the lodge.

"You have embarrassed me, boy," Father said. "And shamed the Gramaraye name. You let a beastblood make a fool of you, to use you. I will teach you the cost of that. And when your brother returns with that creature, you will take back everything she took from you, and more."

The tingle of magic being worked, and then Gavriel's entire spirit exploded in pain every bit equal to the pleasure that Sylia had given him. His nervous system burned.

The pain felt like it lasted an eternity before Gavriel became aware of someone shouting, "Don! Damn it, you need to listen!"

The pain stopped, and Gavriel flopped on the ground, drenched in sweat, his muscles on fire from clenching so tightly.

"What!" Father demanded.

"It's Geoffrey," Mr. Mills said. "He cornered the nymph, and she . . . she fought back. You need to come quick."

"What are you talking about?" Father demanded.

"Your son, he's been impaled. There's nothing I could do for him. You need—"

Father ran off into the night.

Gavriel lay on the moss, sobbing, afraid of what Father would do to his beloved, his Sylia. And Gavriel felt betrayed by her. She had abandoned him, and mortally injured his brother. She must have good reason, Gavriel knew, but he could still feel that sense of betrayal settling deep into his bones. Betrayal, and the horrible feeling that Gavriel had not been worthy of her love.

And somewhere, beneath the haze of his concern for Sylia, Gavriel howled for the loss of his brother, and trembled at the thought of the punishments to come.

38

KILLING IN THE NAME OF

Finn, Alynon's voice interrupted the flow of memory.

What? Are you okay? Our barriers continued to hold off Grandfather's attempts at exorcising Alynon, and if anything the attempts were getting weaker.

La. But these memories, they are becoming part of me. And I truly do not wish them a part of me.

I'm sorry, Aly. But if there's any chance these can help us stop him, help us save your Realm, we have to try.

Silence. Then, *I had better get a damned ballad for this.*

The memories swept over us once more.

I—Gavriel, my mind adjusted—came down the stairs to find his wife Gwendolyn stepping back inside from the front porch, dressed as if to leave the house, with hat and shawl.

Irritation flared, and Gavriel said, "If this is your way of pressuring me to go to the dance tonight at Foster's, I don't appreciate it." Gavriel continued past her, heading for the hallway. In the five years since Father had died, it had been a constant challenge to keep the necromancy business successful, leaving little time for pointless dances with mundies where there would be few if any arcana customers.

"You appreciate very little, Gavriel, least of all me."

Gavriel stopped at her tone, and turned back.

"Excuse me?" he asked.

"You heard me."

"I did nothing but brag about you last night at bridge."

"Because it makes you look good to have a wife who won a Good Gardens award," she said. "And it gave you an excuse to mention the damn business again."

"This damn business is what paid for your garden, dear. And that lovely outfit you are wearing."

She laughed. "Pennies compared to the four hundred and fifty dollars you paid for that fancy car of yours, and it just sits there collecting dust. We never *go* anywhere."

"Four hundred and thirty-five, and that car was an investment. You have to look successful to be successful. Half this nation is out of work, the other half starving. Would you rather we were living in one of those so-called Hoovervilles?"

"I would rather be happy," Gwendolyn said. "Which is why I am leaving you. This is good-bye." She took a half step back and flinched slightly as if Gavriel might strike at her, though she did her best to hide it.

That irritated him even more.

"And where will you go?" Gavriel asked in as dismissive a tone as he could muster.

"I—I have fallen in love with someone else."

Gavriel stared at her, as the sound of rushing blood filled his ears. "Who?" His mind raced over the possibilities, but he could think of no arcana in town who he would believe her attracted to, or at least none that would so betray him.

"She's a euterpe." At least she had the decency to show a modicum of embarrassment as she said it. Or was that simply anticipation of his reaction?

Gavriel stared, heat flushing up his neck now. His brain locked up in a battle for which of those words to be more upset about. "She?" he exploded finally, taking the offenses in order.

Gwendolyn sighed. "For someone who complains about mundies, you have always been quick to take on their prejudices."

Gavriel dismissed that with a wave. "A muse? Merlin's balls, Gwen, a gods damned *feyblood*?"

"She makes me happy, Gavriel. We are going to Olympia, to take advantage of the Arts grants being offered."

"Do you realize what this will look like?" Gavriel shouted. "The damage this will do?"

Gwendolyn shook her head, and gave a sigh. "Thank you for making this easier."

"I—I won't let you go."

"Do you really think you can stop me?" Gwendolyn said, standing a little straighter.

Gavriel opened his mouth to laugh, then stopped. Gwendolyn was a strong necromancer. That was one of the main reasons he had married her, to strengthen the business and bear children guaranteed to continue the family traditions. She had been a complete disappointment on the children front. But Gavriel had never really considered what would happen in a fight between them. Not in a clash of powers.

"Bah, go," he said. "But when your beastblood bitch turns on you, don't come running back here."

"Oh, I won't." She turned to go, but stopped in the doorway, and looked back. "By the way, you may need to hire a new 'assistant.' I'm afraid you've gotten Camila pregnant." Then she left.

* * *

Gavriel sat in the library in the throne-like armchair once favored by his father, facing a row of three men and one woman.

Katherine Verona stood, setting her ever-present knitting back into her handbag. "I've heard enough. I appreciate your ambition, and your concerns, Gavriel, but you are headed down a dangerous path, and I wish no part of it."

Gavriel stood, as did the other men. Out of proper decorum, not from any intent to try and stop her. He would not have been surprised if she could overpower all four of them if it came to that.

"Katherine," he said. "You yourself have already proposed formalizing a new kind of ruling council. Surely this is not so different."

"It is very different," Verona replied. "And you should think on why that is. When you have the answer, maybe you'll understand the folly of this crusade of yours."

"I trust I have your discretion on this matter, at least?" Gavriel asked.

Verona stood silent a minute, then said, "I won't destroy your reputation based on parlor talk, Gav. But I urge you to reconsider. Should your plans come to threaten the peace we are trying to build, I fear for the outcome."

"Thank you," he replied.

Verona shook her head and gave an exasperated sigh, then left.

Gavriel and the other men retook their seats.

"If we are committed then," he said to them, "we must recruit. We current Arcanites shall remain the leadership, but we need an army of true arcana followers. Many of the arcana here in town will join us, I feel certain. But we should start only with the pure arcana to form the core of our movement."

"Not all arcana are as pure as others," the portly man in the center muttered over his drink. The other two looked uncomfortable at the statement.

Gavriel slowly steepled his fingers. "And what might you mean by that?"

"It is one thing to get your 'assistant' in an unfortunate way, understandable even when your wife has proven to be . . . lacking, but to marry her, a Mexican Sorceress? Do you know the kinds of rituals—"

"Chadwick," Gavriel said, making his voice as cold as the corpses in his necrotorium downstairs. "I advise you to pick your next words with care, and RESPECT!" He slapped the arm of his chair.

Chadwick raised an eyebrow, but said, "Of course. Apologies, Gavriel. Clearly it is more than a matter of convenience or decorum for you, my mistake."

Gavriel leaned back. "Apology accepted. And you were not mistaken. Marrying Camila was, in fact, a matter of convenience and decorum. But to be concerned about the, shall we say, quality of any pure arcana based on gender or even race is the last thing we should be doing in such a critical time, when we have arcana breeding with mundanes, or worse, gods-be-damned feybloods."

The other men murmured agreement.

"Good," Gavriel said. "I think we know what must be done. I suggest we each form proposals for realizing our mission, and we will discuss them at the next lodge meeting."

The men understood a dismissal when they heard one, and made their good-byes, then left.

As Gavriel stepped out into the hallway, he found Camila there, crying. She tried to hide it, turned quickly away and rubbed at her face.

Gavriel sighed, feeling annoyed as he foresaw the long minutes he would now have to spend soothing her feelings, when he had so much work to do, and when he had already explained to her why he had to say such things about marrying her. Reputation and respect were everything.

"I love you," he said. She started to cry again. Gavriel threw up his hands and turned to march away, but stopped.

Her crying hurt him, damn it.

He turned back, and pulled her into a hug. "I'm sorry. I really do love you, sweet Camila. If you forgive me, I promise not to say such things again."

The battle at Fort Worden was not going well. Gavriel could tell. Everyone could tell. The Fey were winning, chasing the arcana down, wiping them out. Gavriel stumbled across the rain-damp grass to the edge of the woods, where one of the Knights Arcana rallied survivors for another attempt to contain the Fey here, and not let them spread into town.

"Come on, Katherine, damn it," Gavriel muttered. Whatever her grand plan was to close the breaches between worlds and stop the Fey, it had better be damned good, and come damn soon.

Maybe if she had listened to him in the library—gods, what was it, almost ten years already? If she had listened about the need to eliminate the Fey and feyblood threat, maybe they wouldn't be in this mess today.

As he reached the group, his heart clenched.

"Camila!" he shouted, striding over to her. "What are you doing here? The children need—"

"Our children are at the post office with the others," she said in her still-thick Mexican accent. "I was needed here."

"I don't want you—"

Someone at the other end of the group shouted in alarm, and suddenly a wave of enemy feybloods crashed out of the woods and into the arcana. The screams of the dying filled the night.

"Camila, run!" Gavriel shouted, then rushed around the back of the group toward the nearest fallen. If they were alive, he could give them a boost of life energy to get them back into the fight. And if they were dead, he needed to extract any magical energy left in them before the Fey reclaimed it. Wizards, thaumaturges, and sorcerers could do little good if they ran out of magic.

Before he reached the dead body, a faint shimmering form lifted off of one of the berserking minotaurs and flew down into it.

The body twitched, then rose to its feet in front of Gavriel. Chadwick, one of his most trustworthy Arcanite partners and friends. Even from here, Gavriel could smell the stench of released bowels.

A Fey had taken possession in that brief window between when the human soul had departed, and the body shut down beyond reviving.

Chadwick turned toward him, and smiled, pupils slightly hazy like trying to see the night sky through the halo of a streetlamp.

Gavriel extended his arcana senses, tried to find something within Chadwick's body to grab on to, something he could use to incapacitate the body long enough to strike this changeling down somehow. But Chadwick's human spirit had departed, and necromancy did not work on Fey spirits—because the bastards weren't spirits, they were abominations.

Gavriel would need to touch him, try to work directly with the body's nervous system. And somehow do so without getting beaten down in the process by a man already twice his weight and now possessed with the strength and speed of a Fey spirit.

Easy as stealing the Maltese Falcon from the Invisible Man.

A scream behind him froze his blood. Gavriel whipped around, and saw the Knight Arcana stab his long sword through Camila's heart.

"NOoo!" he shouted, the sound tearing at his throat.

The knight looked toward him with eyes that had the same hazy glow as Chadwick's.

"Camila!" Gavriel ran toward her as the knight slid his sword free. Camila slumped to the ground.

Gavriel had no better way to stop this Fey than the last, and this one held a sword. But he charged toward the changeling knight screaming in fury regardless.

A sudden flash lit up the night sky. The two Fey-possessed bodies fell to their knees, clutching at their heads. Gavriel's momentum carried him to the knight. He blinked against the spots in his vision, and managed to wrestle the sword free from the distracted changeling.

With a shout, Gavriel chopped at the Fey bastard's neck like at a log of firewood.

The sword cut deep, but not completely through, and as the knight twisted away and fell, the sword wrenched out of Gavriel's hand.

Gavriel fell to his knees beside Camila, pressed a hand to her wound, felt for her spirit.

She was gone.

Her beautiful brown eyes stared up at him, seeing nothing.

His blood-soaked hands clenched into fists.

"You'll be avenged," he promised. "I won't stop—I won't *die*—until you are!"

The flood of my grandfather's memories ended.

There are more, but none so painful, Alynon's voice said.

My mind reeled a bit as it readjusted to being me me, not Grandfather me, and some distant part of my awareness realized tears ran down my face.

I was not going to be able to convince Grandfather to stop from poisoning the Other Realm.

I was not going to be able to stop him from killing every Fey there.

39

COUNTDOWN TO EXTINCTION

I *'m pulling us out,* Mort projected at me. *I need to regroup.*

Wait! I thought, but Mort had already disengaged from Grandfather, and my full awareness suddenly dropped back into my own body.

Frak. I hoped Alynon would be able to hold his own against Grandfather's attempts to exorcise him. He should, with Grandfather so committed to the ritual, but I didn't like the feeling that we'd abandoned him.

I gave Dawn a quick reassuring smile that I didn't really feel, letting her know I was back, then looked around us. I could see nothing of the battle, couldn't tell if anyone still lived on either side. But half of the prisoners bound to the standing stones looked dead, or passed out and on the verge of death, and the rest looked like they were more than ready to join that first half.

"Jesus," Mort whispered. "Jesus." He wiped at his own face, and looked at me. "I—I'm sorry, Finn. I thought I understood him, you, us, but—" He shook his head. "What do we do now?"

"I don't know," I said.

Dawn said, "Can you reverse the polarity?"

"What?" I frowned at her, confused.

"Or rotate the harmonics. I don't know. One of those is always the solution on television."

"Well, that is basically what we have to do, actually," I said. "Reverse the flow, withdraw the poison. I just don't know how to get Grandfather to do it."

"Well, if Alynon's in there, can't he do it?" Dawn asked. "He was able to grab my ass when he controlled you."

"Not the same," I said. "We'd been bonded by several different—" I stopped.

The magic flowed through Grandfather's physical host body, being transformed without his conscious will at this point. The spell would only respond to Grandfather still, but Alynon had just absorbed some of the memories that were at the core of Grandfather's desire to destroy the Fey to begin with. And Grandfather's spirit no more belonged to Jared's body than Alynon did. It might be enough to trick the spell.

But Alynon would need to bond fully with the body, to become its actual, inhabiting spirit.

To allow that, we would have to exorcise Grandfather. Yet if we banished his spirit now, with the spell still connecting him to the Other Realm, I feared he would simply be pulled there as Brianne's spirit had been rather than traveling beyond the Veil, and the spell might remain locked to him.

My stomach suddenly turned to acid, and fear flashed through me like a fever chill.

I closed my eyes. Gods, anything else.

But I could think of nothing else. And around me, the screams of the prisoners continued.

"Mort," I said. "We have to go back in. I've got a plan B."

"I think we're easily on plan K by now," Mort said. "But as long as it works—" he closed his eyes.

I turned to Dawn, and gave her a hard kiss, as if I could press all of my love into her in this one act, as if I could escape into her, and live forever in this single moment.

But the kiss ended as I felt Mort's summoning begin. "Dawn, I—" I couldn't think of what to say.

Dawn said, "I know. You love me. Now go kick ass, and don't get killed."

I closed my eyes again before she could see the truth in them.

Then together, Mort and I punched our way through Grandfather's spiritual barriers once more.

Alynon, I projected directly to him. *You need to fully take control of the body, bond with it. Mort and I will get rid of Grandfather. Then you can hopefully reverse the flow of this spell, draw the poison back out of your realm.*

Wait, Mort said. *Where will the poison go?*

Into me, I projected at him. *I am going to summon Grandfather's spirit into my body. Then I will become a focus for the spell, making it easier for Alynon to reverse the flow into me.*

A moment of silence, then Alynon said, *Fa, if you still feel you must atone for Dunngo or some other crime—*

No, I said. *I mean, I do need to make that right, but I'm not being a martyr here. This just has to be done. I can't just let Grandfather wipe out an entire world.*

Mort projected to me privately. *Look man, I'm really not trying to be a dick here,* he said, a sure sign he was about to be a dick. *But maybe we just escape, and rally the troops or whatever. I mean, it's terrible about the Fey and all, but to die for them?*

I sighed. *Mort, it isn't just the Fey. If Grandfather takes control of the Other Realm, he'll control magic itself. He'll have the power to rule the world, and use us like puppets. And he's not going to be too happy with me, you, Mattie—*

Shit, Mort said. *Shit. Gods damn it! So you're literally going to save the world? Like* that *won't come up at every damn Thanksgiving and Solstice dinner.*

I do not know what concerns you have, Alynon said, *but if we are to do this, then it must be now!*

Release the Kirken! I thought back.

Shit, Mort said again. Then, *Fine. Fine. Okay, let's do this.*

I returned my attention to the spiritual world within Grandfather's host, the tumultuous hurricane of Grandfather's spirit still beating at the fortifications around Alynon's presence, and the stream of destructive energies that flowed from the prisoners, through this body and into the Other Realm.

I summoned Grandfather's spirit.

There was a painful jolt and his spirit yanked free of my summoning, as if I'd tried to grab hold of a passing train car.

Shazbutt!

I focused my will again, and this time imagined my summoning not as a pulling but as a wedge that I sheared into the flow of spirit, severing it and diverting it into myself.

Grandfather resisted, his will pushed back against mine.

Give it up, boy! he projected. *You have lost. Your energies would be better spent seeking my forgiveness.*

I know, I replied. *That's why I'm giving you what you wanted. Come on in, Finn Hotel is open for occupancy.*

Grandfather was silent for several heartbeats, then replied, *I think not. I'm sure you have some fine trap laid for me, and while I would love to teach you a final lesson in humility, I think I shall wait and punish you properly once my plans are fulfilled.*

The wedge that I had tried to force into the flow of spirit began to erode, like a wall of sand in a high wind.

Mort, a little help here? I projected.

I felt Mort join in the summoning. It was not the smooth joining that I had experienced in my youth with Grandfather or Mother as they had guided me in learning necromancy. Mort might be helping me, but his spirit and will were clearly not in agreement with the decision, nor in synch with my own. It was a forced joining, like being paired up with someone in school that you barely knew and didn't particularly like. But I accepted his reluctant spiritual handshake and felt his strength join mine.

The erosion stopped, the wedge of our joined will grew solid and strong enough to cut through Grandfather's resistance. The hold of Grandfather's spirit on its stolen body was severed, and it began to flow toward me, through the link of Mort's power.

Mort threw me out of the link, and I slammed back into my own body with the force of an elephant falling off of the Space Needle.

The disorientation faded and I had a full sense of my body. "What the—"

Dawn, who had been holding my hand the entire time, lifted it and said, "Finn? Are you okay?" The flow of life energy that Mort had been maintaining from her to me ended abruptly.

"Yeah," I said. "But I think Mort just betrayed us. Again."

"No," Mort said, his voice strained. His eyes opened, and

he blinked at us. "I have Grandfather's spirit. Damn he's strong. It's a good thing I'll be dead soon, otherwise I'd be dead soon." He winced, and his hands clenched into white-knuckled fists. "Damn he's strong," he said again.

"Mort, what the hell are you doing?" I said.

Mort looked down to where Dawn held my hand against her chest. "Jesus, look at you. You've been back six months and you're practically married. I've had twenty-five years and all I managed to do is nearly lose my soul to a succubus."

"Hey," Dawn said. "Love is hard, man. The music industry would collapse if it weren't."

"Mort, it's not too late," I said. "Give Grandfather's spirit to me. You've got Mattie—"

"Wait," Dawn said. "What's going on here?"

"If Mattie is to ever believe I loved her, to not . . . not hate me—and if there's going to be any honor left to the Gramaraye name—I need to do this."

"Show Mattie you love her by being a good father," I replied.

"Don't ruin this for me," Mort replied. "I helped Grandfather do all this. If you stop him, you'll be a dead hero and I'll end up in exile anyway, and there will be *nobody* to help Mattie. Nobody also willing to stay in Port Townsend and help her save the business anyway. Believe me, this isn't my first choice, but it has to be this way. Now tell Alynon to do his part, before I come to my senses and stop being so incredibly heroic."

My throat grew tight, and I had a hard time saying, "You always have to outdo me."

"It's not that hard, really," Mort replied.

"Douche."

"Dork."

"I-I love you, brother."

"Who can blame you?" Mort twitched, and closed his eyes. "Shut up, you old bastard," he said. "It's long past time you showed *me* some gods damned respect!" He waved at me. "Finn, hurry!"

I closed my eyes, and felt for Alynon's presence. I could feel myself fading, the darkness beginning to close in around the edges now that Mort's energy IV had ended, but I found Alynon's spirit, and managed to connect with him long enough to project *NOW*!

A second later, Mort slammed backward to the ground and began spasming. A terrible scream ripped from his throat and cut across my ears like the claws of a thousand tortured cats.

Mort's body began to smoke, and blacken, and crack, and from the cracks a sickly green light shone out. The smoke billowed up, pressing at first against the confines of the ward trap, then blowing into the trees as the trap collapsed.

"Oh my god," Dawn said, and turned away.

It seemed to last for hours, though it was surely only a handful of minutes. The silence that followed was like the peace of the cold and black ocean depths, crushing and merciless.

Then Sammy and Pete and Vee surrounded me, while Silene and Sal marched with grim purpose toward cousin Jared's body, slumped now against the pillar holding the Kin Finder.

"Wait," I called, my voice sounding weak even to me. "Wait!" I called louder, the effort causing the blackness on the edges of my vision to pulse and then creep inwards further. "That's Alynon now!" I looked up at Sammy and Pete. "Grandfather's gone. Father—?"

"Bruised, but okay," Sammy said.

"Is it over?" Mattie asked, running into the circle of standing stones, and then she screamed. "Father!"

Oh no. "Mattie," I called. "Don't look."

But of course she'd already seen, and she ran to his body, falling to her knees beside him. "No. No. Why? Father, why?"

I felt the tingle of a spiritual summoning, and Mort's voice echoed out of the crumbling remains of his corpse, "Because I love you, Mat-cat. And now you have a hero for a father, instead of a fool."

Mattie was Talking. She was a Talker, like me, just as her father had wanted.

Gods. Poor Mat. Her life had just changed in more ways than I could even guess at. Again.

"Dad, don't talk like that," she said. "I love you. I don't care—"

"Yes you do. And you should care," Mort's spirit responded. "Don't ever *not* care how you are treated, sweetie, please. Finn, if you're listening, I want the business to go to Mattie. I expect you to help her, not run off and join some gamer commune or get her caught up in your problems."

A dozen different responses clashed in my head—that he'd almost been decent for a second there before dying, that it was a shame death hadn't cured his chronic dick-itis, that I was sorry for everything that had happened in his life that left him so scarred even in death—but in the end I simply joined Mattie's summoning so that Mort could hear my response, and said, "Of course. I'll watch after her. We all will."

"Thank you. Now Mattie, let me go. I don't want you losing any more life energy Talking to me."

"But Dad—"

"Mat-cat, please. I love you. Good-bye."

Mattie began sobbing, and I gently guided her toward ending the summoning. As I did, Mort said, "Shit! Finn, I have just one more thing. Just for you, not Mat."

I ended Mattie's summoning, but held on to my own connection to Mort's spirit.

"Look," I said. "I know you're worried, but I promise, I'll treat Mattie like my own daughter."

"Great, thanks for making me regret my decision," Mort said. "But that's not what I wanted."

"What is it, then?" I asked, and prepared myself for some new revelation about Mort, or our family, or the business. Were we in debt to the gnomes again? Had he slept with Dawn at some point? Gods, no, not that. I shuddered.

Or maybe he just wanted to go beyond the Veil with true peace between us.

"Only you can hear this, right?" Mort asked, increasing my level of concern.

"Yes."

"Look, dude," Mort said. "There's some DVDs in the back of the bottom drawer of my dresser. And some files on my laptop, in a folder labeled "Boring Tax Info." If you could maybe just get rid of those before Mattie sees them?"

I stared for a minute as my brain processed his request. "Wait. You're wasting my life energy and possibly your last words to be heard in this world asking me to get rid of your porn?"

"Hey, I died a hero!" Mort said. "You should be kissing my ass, not giving me a guilt trip!"

I shook my head. "Sure. And I'll make sure to make up some better final words from you to put on the plaque beneath the giant statue we're going to build to your honor."

"Good," Mort replied. "Make me sound gods damned eloquent. Good-bye, Finn Fancy Necromancy Pants."

"Good-bye, Mort."

I released the summoning.

And blackness swallowed me.

EPILOGUE

A young faun guided Dawn, Mattie, Sammy, Fatima, Father, Verna, and me along the hidden paths through the forests above the Elwha River.

It was a beautiful day for a wedding.

The sun slanted down through the trees in beams of white and gold, shifting as the trees swayed and whispered to each other, shimmering across motes of pollen, intricate spiderwebs, and dancing clouds of gnats. The warm air rising off of the baked riverbanks and open patches of clover smelled of green living things growing out of earthy decay, and the light summer breeze carried the piney scent of sun-warmed fir fronds.

I wished I had thought to wear hiking clothes rather than the gray suit borrowed from Father, as sweat dewed my back, and the heels of my dress shoes caught on tree roots.

A week since the battle with the Arcanites, and I still didn't feel quite myself. I felt . . . bruised, in more than just body. I would suddenly burst into tears at random times, or imagine I could feel spirits around me when there were none, even as I felt the absence of Alynon, and Mort. But I was doing my best to put on a good show for Mattie's sake, and to keep Dawn from worrying too much. I had already ruined what could have been some of the best days of her life, the chance to celebrate the release of her first single on the radio. I was determined to devote myself to them both going forward, to doing all I could to support their happiness.

"I can't wait to see Vee!" Mattie said as she practically skipped along the trail. "I bet she looks amazing! A white dress with her practically white hair? Oh my god! Do you think they will shapeshift at all? Can you imagine if Vee has her train *and* a tail? That would be so amazing!"

She was doing her happy-bouncy thing. I had an increasingly hard time telling when it was genuine, and when it was her just masking pain.

"You know what would be amazing?" Sammy said, waving furiously at every insect that came near her. "Air-conditioning."

"Her dress won't be white," I reminded Mattie. "Brightbloods dress in red and blue—"

"Oh yeah yeah yeah, to represent mortal spirit and bright spirit together. I knew that, I just forgot. That's going to be even better! With her white hair, and blue eyes? *So* amazing I bet!"

Fatima, watching two birds dancing through a break in the trees, said in her dreamy voice, "I can't believe they're still going—" Then her eyes fell on Mattie, and she blushed, looking around her. "Uh, can't believe how beautiful today is."

"I know!" Mattie said, clapping her hands. "It is *perfect*!"

I understood what Fatima had meant to say. It was both strange and wonderful that Pete and Vee were still getting married today. The two had actually tried several times to postpone the date out of consideration for Mattie's grief, not to mention the chaos that had ensued following the attempted genocide of the Fey, the complete overturning of the regional Arcana Ruling Council, the uncertainty of the Silver Archon's status, and the recovery from a probing attack on the Elwha steading by some Shadows brightbloods.

But Mattie's own enthusiasm about the wedding had overridden their fears, and the general consensus seemed to be that a joyous celebration of love and the joining of two futures together was exactly what everyone needed right now.

"By the way," I said to the faun, "you look familiar, but I'm sorry, I didn't catch your name."

"Hermes," he said. Then after a beat, added, "But everyone calls me Crockett."

"Why's that? You a *Miami Vice* fan or something?" I joked.

He gave a martyred sigh. "Because I'm Don Faun's son."

"Oh. Uh, well—" We emerged from the forest into the clearing of the Elwha steading.

The hidden lodge and spa at Elwha had been restored to something of its original glory for Pete and Vee's wedding. White flowers covered everything, grown with the help of Silene and the other plant-friendly brightbloods no doubt, and fairies were zipping about with colored streamers like Olympic hummingbirds. The fauns, centaurs, and other brightbloods had ribbons tied in their hair, or wore necklaces and bracelets of woven flowers. And a large number wore knit ties or bonnets, no doubt courtesy of Sal and his growing circle of brightblood knitting enthusiasts.

Sal strode up with his long swinging strides, his fringe of red-brown hair gleaming in the sunlight. "Welcome!" he said. "Youselfs all go inside quickfast! Pete and Vee are very nervous."

His tone made me worried.

"Is everything okay? They're not having cold feet or anything?"

"I am not thinking so," Sal said, frowning. "Iself knit them many warm socks. But Pete started to, erm, mark areas. And Vee keeps trying to run off with the food to hide in her favorite tree."

"It's just nerves," Fatima said, looking back at me. "It will be okay. We've got this."

"Yeah," Sammy said, sounding much less convinced.

"I'll deal with Petey," Dawn said and marched off toward the lodge, with Fatima and Sammy falling in beside her.

"Wait!" Mattie said. "I'm coming, too! I want to see Vee!" She ran to catch up with the other women, leaving me with Father and Verna, who were distracted by all the color.

I looked past Sal at the brightbloods moving about. "So, uh, you sure it's okay I'm here? After the whole exile over Dunngo, I mean?"

"For the bonding, youself invited," Sal said, then blushed slightly. "Well and true, youself still not most popular magebright with someselves. But Borghild no longer speaks against youself. And there are sure-true many magebrights that are liked less."

"Well, I guess that's something."

Sal slapped a giant hand on my shoulder, nearly knocking me to the ground. "Do not Chihuahua. Even big-bad wounds can heal."

"Chihuahua?"

"Yes." He lifted his hands up close to his chest, shivered, and made a whimpering sound. "Be all full of fretting and worry and shiver-shakes. Chihuahua. They say this is why there are no waer-Chihuahuas, because theyselves all scared themselves to death."

"Right. Okay. Thanks, Sal. Where is Silene?"

Sal stood up straighter, his chest puffing out, and said in a voice with a hint of purring, "Silene is being named new Silver Archon."

"What?" I said. "That's great!"

Sal nodded. "Herself is very nervous, but also very excited, already talking about many changes."

I remembered then how I'd first met Silene, and why she'd run into trouble with the ARC, agitating for brightblood rights and speaking of one day having brightbloods on the Arcana Ruling Council itself.

We were in for interesting times.

"She'll be a great Archon," I said, leaving it at that.

Sal led me toward the lodge. I noticed that a number of those who wandered the grounds held crossbows, staffs, or swords.

"Worried about another Shadows attack?" I asked.

"Not big-worried," Sal said. "The Archon Assembly gave the Shadows Archon much bad-words for the attack."

"That's it? Just another warning?"

Sal shrugged. "The Shadows Archon said heself did not know of it, it was the action of 'rogue' selves and heself would investigate and give great punishments."

I rolled my eyes. It was no coincidence that the attack had coincided with our battle against the Arcanites. The Shadows Archon knew of the battle, and so likely had the Shadows Fey. "That guy is slippier than a naked cat dipped in oil," I said.

Reggie stepped out of the lodge as we approached, wearing his old *Miami Vice*–style enforcer outfit of white jacket and pants and azure T-shirt, the jacket clearly stretched a bit over his modest belly, though not terribly so. Merlin followed him, flowing brown robes covering the Samoan druid's considerable girth, and a polished metal helm gleaming in the sun.

"Looking good," I said as we reached them.

Reggie tugged at his jacket. "I wanted Vee to feel Zeke's presence, at least a little," he replied, looking down. "Though it is kind of depressing how hard it was to fit into these pants again." I patted my own stomach. "I don't know. Now that Alynon isn't complaining about how I let all his hard work go to waste, I'm looking forward to letting some things, well, go to my waist."

Merlin laughed. "That is why I wear robes. That, and the breeze."

"Uh," I said. I turned to Reggie, and asked in a quieter voice, "So how's the cleanup at the ARC going?"

"It's a mess," Reggie said. "There's no easy way to tell which of those who remained in power were Arcanites, or just deemed harmless by the Arcanites. And there are a lot of important positions unoccupied. They're even bringing George—or, uh, Merlin here—in from the cold."

Merlin garumphed. "Didn't say I'd go. Lots of work still to do in the world. And J needs someone to keep him out of trouble."

"How is he?" I asked.

"Recovering," Merlin said. "He'll be fine. The ARC's already wiped his memories of the fight and healed his wounds."

Reggie grunted. "Except now he plans to sue HBO, and we have to go back in and undo that as well."

"What?" I said. "Why?"

"Apparently the infomancers gave him a memory of binge-watching *Game of Thrones* to explain the time-loss, and now he's convinced the show was purposefully created with an addictive subliminal signal to distract anyone who might be inclined to seek out true magic, or some such nonsense."

I slapped Merlin on the arm. "Sounds like we still need our ambassador to the lunatic fringe."

"Funny you should say that," Reggie said. "I happen to know the ARC is going to offer *you* an actual ambassador position."

"What?" I said. "Me? Why?"

"Well, you've already gone into the Other Realm twice to basically do an ambassador's job. I guess they figure if you're going to go over there anyway and represent arcana, you might as well do it officially."

"In other words, they want more control over what I say and do over there."

"Pretty much."

"Well, I don't plan to go back. Ever. So if they do ask, I'll politely decline."

"Uh huh. And when you got back from exile, exactly how many times did you think you'd be going back over there?" Reggie asked.

"But we've stopped the Arcanites," I argued. "And it's just a matter of time before the conspirators in the Other Realm are exposed."

"Right. And the Chaos Fey are going to confess to everything and promise to stop whatever grand plans they had."

"Not my problem anymore," I said, as much to convince myself as him. "I mean, the ARC and the Colloquy can't deny at this point the need to get involved and take care of things themselves. They don't need me anymore. Dawn and Mattie, they're my only concern now."

Father giggled. "Odd to see, all on TV, Phinaeus Fancius gods at sea."

I pretended not to hear him. I could drive myself mad

trying to figure out if there was some meaning in his words, and what that meaning might be. And I didn't want to understand, not right now, especially not if gods were involved.

Reggie glanced sideways at Father, then said, "Hey, look, if you can really step away from all of this, including Alynon, then I'm happy for you."

I winced. "Anyone found him yet?"

"Alynon? No. You sure you don't have a way to find him? Or a guess about what his plans might be?"

"Nope. No idea," I lied.

"Uh huh," Reggie replied, fully able to detect my lie. "How about we just pretend for today that everything is great then, and enjoy the moment?"

"Here here," Merlin said. "Let us find the beer."

"Enjoy," I said. "I'll see you at the ceremony."

"See you there." Reggie gave a nod to Father and Verna before marching off with Merlin in tow.

I led Father and Verna into the lodge, and nearly ran into Garl and Heather as they strode across the lobby area. Garl remained in his normal attire of baggy jeans, no shirt, and no shoes, his waerbear winter weight clearly evident. Heather wore a red dress that ended at the knees, her bare shoulders deeply tanned for the first time since I'd known her, her straw-blond hair up in some kind of weave with flowers in it.

"Finn," she said, thrusting a blue-collared shirt in the direction of Garl. "Will you explain to him that nobody wants to see his giant belly at a bonding ceremony."

Garl patted his belly. "I am proud of this belly. And shirts itch and scratch and choke."

"Well—" I said, and with that, I was swept up in the frenzy of last-minute preparations.

* * *

I escorted Pete up one sloped side of the grassy "stage," as Reggie escorted Vee up the opposite side, until we met at the peak where Silene stood waiting behind a pedestal holding an ornate two-handled chalice.

Vee looked like an American Valkyrie, or perhaps a superhero with her red and blue dress and Nordic features. She wore a crown of flowers that bloomed and shed their petals, then bloomed again, creating a colorful snowfall around her. And a veil of spider silk hung over her face, the shimmering strands strengthened against breaking, and bejeweled with morning dew that could not be shaken off.

Pete had been outfitted by a waer-Elvis he once battled, the remorseful rocker now clean of the mana drug used to manipulate him and seeking to make amends. Pete was also dressed in red and blue, his high-collared jacket bedecked with rhinestones, and his pants flared out at the bottom. He looked like a disco nobleman.

Silene stood between them in a dress made entirely of white roses in full bloom, presumably without the thorns.

Vee and Pete joined hands, and Reggie and I both grinned while we placed our hands on top and bottom of theirs as a sign of blessing and approval.

Then I descended the hill to join Dawn in the front row with the rest of our family and friends, and Reggie did the same. The crowd of brightbloods spread out beside and behind us in a fan shape, occasionally adding a snuffle or soft bleat or sniffle to the background noise of chirping birds.

Silene raised her hands. "Cousins, and guests," she said. "We gather in the light of the sun and the grace of the Aal to bond these two brightsouls together. For as our own nature teaches us, when two spirits are bonded, it creates something greater than just the sum of those two souls, it creates a new life filled with possibility and promise.

"Paeterus Gramaraye and Violet Wodenson were not born brightbloods, but they have chosen to serve the Silver, and this clan. And so I now have the honor and blessing to bond them in their love."

The ceremony continued, as Silene spoke to each of their bond and their responsibilities to the other, and then had them seal the bond by both picking up the Quaich, the large ornate chalice, off of the pedestal and taking turns sipping from it.

Silene smiled as they set the Quaich down.

"Now you shall be the shelter for one another, protecting each from rain and snow. Now you shall be root to one another, providing a strong foundation for growth, nourishing each other in mind, body, and spirit. Now you shall be trunk to one another, supporting and helping each not to fall. Like two trees entwined, you are separate yet joined, with one shared fate before you, one shared life. May that life be filled with beauty and happiness."

"Paeterus wolf-bright and Violet squirrel-bright, you are now bonded in love."

Applause burst from the gathered crowd, causing a flight of starlings to erupt from the tree line and flutter into the blue sky.

I watched them lift free of the earth, swirling in a choreographed cloud, their shifting patterns mesmerizing. They each had the greatest form of freedom, the ability to go anywhere in the world they wanted, anywhere their wings could carry them at least, and anywhere where they could find food and a bit of water. And yet, they flew together, wheeling through the air like a single body.

And I realized, looking around me, that this is what I now wanted, too.

Before my exile, I had wanted to escape the life of necromancy, of Talking, of dealing every day with death and facing the possible request to drain my own life energy to meet my "duty" as a Talker. I wanted to avoid my mother's fate. I'd wanted to create games instead, without any real idea of how to make that dream come true.

When I returned from exile, I'd intended to pick up where I left off, to take advantage of my absence to start a new life away from the family business, away from necromancy. It was almost a reflexive, conditioned drive at that point.

And yet I'd felt unmoored, without direction or purpose, in this world of smartphones and dumb television, where video games had evolved from the simple pixelated programs of my youth to become multimillion-dollar cinematic epics, and the people I'd known best were now virtual strangers.

But I realized that bit by bit, person by person, I'd somehow fallen into a new life while I was running around trying to figure out what life to live.

I looked down the line of smiling faces, and remembered the hardships brought on so many of them by Grandfather, or his conspirators. Sometimes because Grandfather had acted against me, sometimes because I got myself involved in his conspiracies.

I did not blame myself though. It felt like a great weight being lifted off of my shoulders just to think that. I wished I could have spared everyone gathered here any pain I had been involved with, of course. I wished more than anything I could bring Mort, Zeke, and Dunngo back, and undo Father's madness and Petey's waer curse. But I could not.

I turned my thoughts instead to the good.

Father had found Verna. And in trying to help him remember himself, I had also learned so much about him, and grown closer to him.

I'd got to see Sammy happy with Fatima and a job that she took pride in. Or at least as happy as she had ever been.

I helped Petey find true love with Vee, and helped in his transition to a new life.

Mattie struggled with all that had happened, but it all seemed to have also propelled her growth, the transition from childhood to adult, of figuring out who she was beyond all the old fears and disappointments. And I could already tell the person she would grow into would be amazing, possibly a true leader of the arcana.

And then there was Dawn.

Dawn, always happy to put me in my place, but also to support any dream I chose to pursue. Dawn who continued to show me what love really was.

I leaned over to her. "Can I talk to you a minute?" I nodded my head toward the forest.

"You can talk to me for two. After that, I have to charge you."

"Uh huh." I led her away from the crowd a little bit.

"What's up?" Dawn asked as we reached the shade of the trees. "You look weird."

"Dawn," I said. "Will you marry me?"

Damn it. I hadn't meant to just blurt it out, I'd meant to make a nice romantic speech.

She looked at me a long, silent moment, then said, "No."

It took a second for my brain to process that. "What? Why not?"

"Finn, I wanted to wait until after the wedding, but I'll just tell you now, I don't want you to come with me on my album tour. I think it will be good for us to have that time apart."

"But—you were just gone for a month. We've been through so much, I just—"

"I love you, Finn. I really do. But, frankly, I just need to step back and make sure you're good for me. I kind of have a history of getting mixed up with guys who aren't good for me. I thought you were different—"

"I am! Or at least, I hope I am," I said. "I know there's been a lot of craziness, and you've gotten hurt, but—"

"Damn it, Finn, you were going to sacrifice yourself! Without even telling me, without even saying good-bye. I mean, I understand why, and it makes me question if I'm really just a selfish person, but I *am* angry that you were going to do that after I just risked my life and put my dream on hold for you. And, I don't know, I'm trying to think of when you've done the same for me, sacrificed for me, put your world on hold for me. Not that I wish you had to, but . . . I just need to make sure I'm not being stupid for love, here."

"But—" I tried to think of something I had done for her, just for her, and came up short. I had gone with her to the massage therapy sessions for her shoulder, where they worked to loosen up the damage done by the jorõgumo attack, but she wouldn't have even been attacked if not for me, and that had hardly been a sacrifice. "Was there something I should have helped with, something I could have done that I didn't?"

"I don't know. That's part of the problem: I don't know

what the problem is. It's more like it feels like there should be a problem, and I need to make sure the fact that I don't see what the problem is, well, that that's not a problem."

"Are you leaving me?" I asked, confused.

"No. I'm leaving on tour. And you need to focus on helping Mattie. We're just going to be doing our own things for a bit, which we need to do anyway. It isn't that big a deal. Don't freak out and let your imagination run crazy the way you do. I love you, Finn. I really do. All this means is, I just can't say I'm going to marry you, not right now."

I couldn't think of what to say.

"Ouch, that had to hurt," a voice said from the tree line.

I turned and felt a split second of panic as cousin Jared peered around a tree at me, before I remembered that this was not Grandfather but Alynon. My remembrance was helped by his outfit as he stepped fully into view, and apparently stepped out of an Adam Ant music video with that green military band jacket and high-collared white shirt.

"Nobody asked for your opinion," I said, blushing hotly. "What are you even doing here?"

"I wanted to see the bonding," Alynon said, and shrugged. "I have grown somewhat fond of Pete and Vee. As vassals, of course."

"Of course," I said.

"Dawn," he said, and bowed his head at her.

"Alynon," she replied, her tone somewhat dubious. "Looking good."

"Well, since it sounds like you and Phinaeus are on a break, if you wanted to—"

"Watch it!" I snapped. "Or I'll call Reggie over and have you arrested."

Dawn put a hand on my back. "It's not a break, Aly. Just some self-evaluation. You should try it sometime."

"La," he said. "I've had way too much self-time as is." He looked at me. "In fact, that is why I have truly come here. I need your help to steal Velorain away from the Shores of Chaos."

I shook my head. "No way. I just told Reggie, and I'll tell you, I have no plans to ever go back to the Other Realm."

"You owe me, Gramaraye," Alynon said. "And Velorain."

Bat's breath. I opened my mouth to say I'd do what I could, then stopped.

I shook my head. "I owe Mattie, Dawn, and myself more. I'm staying out of trouble for a while." I glanced sideways at Dawn. I had to prove to her that I was safe for her to love. "Maybe we can—"

"There you are!" Mattie called, bouncing up.

I looked from her back to the trees. Alynon had disappeared.

"Wasn't it amazing?" Mattie said. "Come on, they're moving inside for the food. Are you going to give a toast?"

"Yes," I said, feeling a little dazed.

"Awesome! Come on," Mattie said.

Dawn took my hand, and said, "Everything will be okay."

"Yeah," Mattie said. "You're going to do awesome, I'm sure." Then she led Dawn and me toward the flow of bodies filing into the lodge.

I looked back up at the wheeling birds and tried to tell myself everything really would be okay.

At least the worst of the craziness was behind me now, and I could truly focus on building a new life for myself.

Hopefully with Dawn.

"Release the Kirken," I said quietly, then turned to join my family and face the future, together.

ACKNOWLEDGMENTS

Holy macatrinity, how time flies.

First and foremost, a shout-out to all the booksellers and librarians who shared the Finn Fancy love with your readers. In addition to being incredibly wise persons with great taste in literature, you are fine human beings, and I thank you, truly and sincerely.

And of course thank you to all the awesome individuals and book clubs who read *Finn Fancy Necromancy* and *Bigfootloose*. I am really excited for you to read book three and complete this arc with Finn and me.

I wrote this book over the latter half of 2015. Good news is, the world agreed on fighting Global Climate Change. But then we had the Syrian refugee crisis, Greek economic troubles, ISIS attacks, and U.S. gun violence epidemic (among other tragedies). And while this book itself was written before the true craziness of the 2016 U.S. election cycle (or the emotional tumult of Brexit for that matter), I am writing these acknowledgments at the end of August 2016, aware of these events but as yet uncertain of the true fallout from them.

So whether that means you have dug this book up in a cave near the half-buried Statue of Liberty far from the Ape Capital, or smuggled a copy out of the Ministry of Truth, this book was written in parallel with the events of 2015 but not because of them. Still, upon rereading it, I realize that some scenes may appear to be a reaction to the darker forces and events of 2015–2016, and I also realize that my words will always be interpreted through the context of whatever future you are in. So I look forward to seeing what readers say. Writing is a weird kind of time travel in that sense.

Oh, and there is also the fact that I saved you all from termination by robot overlords, which was literally due to time travel. But don't let that influence your decision to buy my books at all. Really.

Of course, I did not wage such epic battles alone.

Thank you to Christy Varonfakis Henderson, for helping me to be and to do more than I could manage alone.

To my parents, Frank, Mary, and Elaine; my brother, Dave Henderson; and the rest of my family: I'll say thank you for your support, even though that sounds like the closing of a political ad. I will also note here for the record that Finn's family is clearly not modeled on mine. Except for the bits that were.

To the children of my heart, Lucas and Kylie, and true friend Shelly, who made the '90s and beyond a fun adventure together, I hope you find much laughter in this book, and in life.

To everyone who provided feedback on the early drafts of this book, thank you. To name a few (alphabetically): Isis D'Shaun, Christy Henderson, Andrew Romine, DeeAnn Sole, and Caroline Yoachim.

To Finn Fancy champion Beth Meacham, without whom, again, Finn Fancy would not exist, thank you for being a frank and supportive editor, friend, and guide through this experience. And thank you to the entire Tor team, including Amy Stapp and Jen Gunnels for shepherding the book through the process; to my publicist, Desirae Friesen, and publicity rock star Patty Garcia, for continuing to help spread the Finn Fancy love; the copyediting skills of Debbie Friedman; and everyone else at Tor who helped Finn look Fancy—thank you, truly.

To Peter Lutjen, and the rest of the Tor art and design department, thank you for yet another amazing cover.

To the folks at Titan Books (U.K.), including Natalie Laverick, Philippa Ward, and Cat Camacho, who provided a world of readers across the sea, not to mention the cool 8-bit alternate covers and much support: Cheers!

Thank you to my agent, Cameron McClure, for faith and encouragement as we continue the writing and publishing journey forward; as well as to Katie Shea Boutillier and everyone else at Donald Maass Literary Agency.

Thank you to actor Todd Haberkorn, and the team at Brilliance Audio, for lending voice to Finn's stories for folks like myself who like to read while cooking, exercising, and driving without causing major accidents or burns in awkward places.

To those who through the years have served as best of friends and suffered with good humor through my terrible early writings, including but certainly not limited to Reginald Jackson, Jonathon Thompson, Jeffrey Waddell, and Benjamin VanWinkle, I thank you.

To my writer families from HM Seattle, Cascade Writers, Clarion West, and WotF for continuing to inspire and encourage me, though some might ask you to encourage me less.

To Gerry Pitter and Pamela May, Glenn Cotter, Carmen Hall, and Nina Novikova, bosses who encouraged growth and supported opportunities both within and outside of the Day Job.

And finally, to David Bowie, rock god and speculative fiction avatar, for years of entertainment and inspiration: You left our capsule and stepped through the final door, I hope your spaceship takes you someplace amazing.

And now, on to the next adventure.

ABOUT THE AUTHOR

Randy was born in the States of wonder, awe, and Washington. He quickly learned the joy of escaping to fantasy worlds, from Middle Earth to Earthsea, from Amber to Pern, from Valdemar to Midkemia.

After toying with such impressive creative pursuits as Latch Hook and recording really clever answering machine messages, Randy realized that what he wanted most was to write that which had brought him much joy. It was not as easy as it looked.

Many years of dabbling followed, during which Randy studied social sciences and worked a variety of jobs such as weight-loss counselor, Alaska factory-boat worker, and writing tax sob stories for CPA clients (his first paid fiction), before finally settling in IT. Randy decided to get serious about his writing, and attended the Clarion West writing workshop where he learned things, dark, mystical things about the art of writing, things best left unspoken. Ask him, and he'll gladly speak of them.

Randy then wrote new stories, faster stories, stronger stories, and was published in wondrous places like Realms of Fantasy and Escape Pod before winning Writers of the Future. His first novel, *Finn Fancy Necromancy*, was published in 2015.

www.randy-henderson.com

ALSO AVAILABLE FROM TITAN BOOKS

FINN FANCY NECROMANCY

Found guilty of a crime he didn't commit in 1986, 15-year-old Finn Gramaraye was exiled to the Other Realm for 25 years. But now he's back in the mortal world and is disappointed to discover that he's middle-aged, DeLoreans can't fly, and he's been framed for dark necromancy, again. He has three days to clear his name, but his father has gone mad, his mother's a ghost, and his brother is most unhappy to see him - who can he trust to help him?

WWW.TITANBOOKS.COM

ALSO AVAILABLE FROM TITAN BOOKS

BIGFOOTLOOSE AND FINN FANCY FREE

Finn Gramaraye is settling back into the family necrotorium business after his long exile in the Fey otherworld. But Finn has a business idea of his own: he's figured out how to use his half-mad father's Kinfinder invention to find True Love and wants to set up a magical dating service. When he agrees to help his Bigfoot friend Sal, they walk right into a Feyblood rebellion fomented by unknown forces and fueled by the drug created by Finn's own grandfather.

WWW.TITANBOOKS.COM

For more fantastic fiction, author events, exclusive excerpts, competitions, limited editions and more

VISIT OUR WEBSITE
titanbooks.com

LIKE US ON FACEBOOK
facebook.com/titanbooks

FOLLOW US ON TWITTER
@TitanBooks

EMAIL US
readerfeedback@titanemail.com